*For Barbara Graebe, who made me try again.*

# The Never Ending Summer

## EMMA KENNEDY

arrow books

1 3 5 7 9 10 8 6 4 2

Arrow Books
20 Vauxhall Bridge Road
London SW1V 2SA

Arrow Books is part of the Penguin Random House group
of companies whose addresses can be found at
global.penguinrandomhouse.com.

Penguin
Random House
UK

First published in Great Britain by Arrow Books in 2021

www.penguin.co.uk

A CIP catalogue record for this book is available from
the British Library.

ISBN 9781787463295

Typeset in 10.32/13.35 pt Palatino LT Std
by Integra Software Services Pvt. Ltd, Pondicherry

Printed and bound in Great Britain by Clays Ltd, Elcograf S.p.A.

The authorised representative in the EEA is Penguin Random House
Ireland, Morrison Chambers, 32 Nassau Street, Dublin D02 YH68.

MIX
Paper from
responsible sources
FSC® C018179

Penguin Random House is committed to a
sustainable future for our business, our readers
and our planet. This book is made from Forest
Stewardship Council® certified paper.

# WEEK ONE

# MONDAY

# 1

Between two low, fat beech trees, off in the distance, a figure was moving at full pelt.

It was a young woman, gangly, running with the lopsided effort of a just-born foal. She was wearing thick spectacles, a powder-blue cardigan done up to the neck and a pair of navy nylon trousers that any normal person would accept they'd grown out of. On her feet brown sandals, above which screamed a pair of bright red socks.

Bea was coming and everything was about to change.

Agnes stood watching and felt the same surge of relief she always felt when her friend appeared. She was looking out across Christ Church Meadow. She was between two rivers: behind her ran the Isis, ahead of her the Cherwell. In her hand a Sherbet Fountain, the end of the liquorice moist.

In front of the galloping Bea, a rowing eight – all long legs and wellingtons – were strolling back from the boathouses. There was a gracefulness to them, like gazelles slowly crossing a savannah. A few of them stopped to chat to a young woman. Her hair was up, in her arms a pile of books. They were laughing easily.

Agnes watched, sucking on the end of her liquorice. She and Bea were not a part of this world. They were the girls dumped by their parents into a secretarial college neither of them wanted to be at. Their lives were to be played out within boundaries: there were to be no adventures, no surprises. They were expected to be compliant and unremarkable.

Fine. Except Agnes wanted to be *that* girl, the one with the books who was being talked to lightly, enthusiastically, seriously. It would have been different if Agnes's parents had sent her to a run-down, concrete-clad, anonymous secretarial in Reading or Basingstoke or Slough, where she could have blended in to the background and forgotten about everything that might have been. But they hadn't. They'd sent her to Oxford, the place she could have come to, properly, if it hadn't all gone wrong. It was hard not to think it cruel.

Bea came to a halt. Her face was bright red and she was panting.

'Well?' said Agnes, as her friend stopped in front of her. She could feel herself trembling. She knew what they had come to discuss.

Bea held out a finger, slumped down to the grass and put her head in her hands. 'Hang on,' she mumbled. 'I feel a bit sick.'

Agnes sucked on the end of her liquorice again and cast a look back towards the rowers. They were heading towards Merton. She wondered what they were all studying and felt the usual pang of jealousy. No, it wasn't jealousy; it was worse than that. It was regret.

She glanced downwards. Bea abhorred all physical exercise. She must have run at least half a mile. No wonder she felt ill.

'OK,' Bea said, exhaling heavily, and pushed herself back up. 'Have you finished it?'

Agnes reached into the blue canvas bag slung across her chest and pulled out a battered-looking book. It was *The Female Eunuch*.

'I have.' She handed it to Bea.

'What did you think?'

'It's the filthiest book I've ever read.'

Bea's face lit up.

She was an odd-looking girl: one eye that veered in towards her nose, teeth that seemed as if they'd been thrown into her mouth and a ruddy complexion that left her wind-blasted. She would have been perfect on a farm in the middle of nowhere but here, on Christ Church Meadow, among the willowy rowers and the beech trees, she was out of place, a mongrel among the thoroughbreds.

'Filthier than Chatterley?' Bea narrowed her eyes.

Agnes nodded. 'So much filthier than Chatterley.'

Agnes stared down at the cover, the naked female torso hanging from a hook. Bea's hand was hovering over it, as if it might be a crystal ball. Her eyes were wide and staring. She looked delighted and astonished.

'It's definitely the filthiest book I have ever read. Absolutely definitely. And the most daring. And the most startling. And the most powerful. Did you like the bit about courage and independence?'

Agnes nodded.

'And the bit about security being the denial of life?'

Agnes tilted her head. 'I wasn't quite sure what that meant?'

Bea gripped Agnes by the shoulders. 'It's about your mother. It's about my mother. It's about us. We have to throw it all off, Agnes. We have to wave goodbye to safety. We have to take the bull by the horns.'

'After our exams ...'

Bea's hands fell from Agnes's shoulders. She gave a shrug. 'Yes, after our exams.'

They both stood for a moment, minds racing at different speeds.

'I liked the bit about personal responsibility.' Agnes didn't want Bea to think she wasn't embracing these new ideas but, in truth, it scared her a little. It's hard to break away from the only things you've ever known.

Bea gave a small nod but didn't seem overly impressed.

Agnes tried again. 'I think it's entirely dangerous. How do you feel about that?'

Bea winked. 'Thrilled.'

'Me too.' Agnes smiled. She wasn't sure she meant it. Still, Bea would be happy.

Everything was so easy with Bea. They had known each other forever, both from the same small village, the comfortable intimacy of a lifetime of scuffed knees and jokes only they understood. You have to love your family, Agnes knew this only too well, but you choose who you like.

'I think I might be a bit in love with Germaine Greer. What do you think about that?' Bea's face shone with excitement.

'Why wouldn't you be?'

'We need to become second-wave feminists immediately. They seem to be able to do whatever they want. I can't quite get over it.' She shook her head.

'Shall I give a copy to my mother?' Agnes sounded playful, as if the thought was outrageous.

Bea stopped, her mouth slightly open. 'I'm not sure she's ready for it. Are you? Women putting themselves first?'

Agnes laughed. 'Her brain would explode.' She paused. 'Maybe she needs her brain to explode.'

'Maybe everyone needs their brains to explode?'

Agnes looked back towards the rowers.

'After we've finished our exams.'

'Yes,' nodded Bea. 'After we've finished our exams. Agnes,' she said, gripping her friend's arm, 'there's a revolution going on, right now, out there ...' She turned and pointed off towards the distance. 'And we need to be a part of it.'

'Yes, we do.'

'I have given this some thought,' said Bea, her face settling into seriousness, 'and I think the first thing we need to do, after we've finished our exams, is lose our virginity. I can think of nothing more important. We cannot be full-blown second-wave feminists until we have had sex.'

It was a subject Agnes felt uncomfortable about. Kissing, after all, had ruined her life back then when everything had still seemed possible: one kiss in a village disco and that was that. She was done for. It had been a friend's seventeenth birthday party, a village hall decked with faded bunting. There had been sausage rolls and someone had brought vodka and there had been dancing in the dark and he had grabbed her and slid his hands around her waist. She had felt, for the nineteen minutes they had been together, special, desired, liked. His breath smelled of cigarettes and ethanol. She'd never been kissed, properly, by someone who made her feel wanted. He had made her dizzy. And then he had made her very, very ill. It had been heartbreaking, not least because Agnes had found it so impossible to escape its after-effects.

She frowned, unsure of how to respond. Bea was different from her: enthusiastic, confident, irrepressible. She was a whirlwind of ideas and possibilities. She was everything Agnes was not.

Bea gripped her forearm tighter.

'We need to seize the day, Agnes Ledbury. We need to knuckle down or be left behind. I mean it. The minute we have finished our exams we must have sexual intercourse as soon as is humanly possible. The rest of our lives is waiting for us!' She thrust her hand out. 'Are you with me?'

There was so much to be nervous of. Agnes glanced back again, towards the rowers who were now far dots on the horizon. They were not, like her, passive participants in a life carved out by others. They were forging their own destiny. Agnes didn't have a brave bone in her body, but Bea did. It was impossible not to hang on to her.

Agnes dropped her liquorice into the tube of sherbet and took Bea's hand. She shook it firmly. 'I am with you, Beatrice Morgan.'

'Then the pact is made. You've got sherbet all down your front.' Bea gestured towards Agnes's blouse. She eyed the sugary tube. 'Have you got another one?'

Agnes licked her finger and dabbed up the wayward sherbet. 'No. Do you want the dry end?' She pulled out her liquorice stick and offered it up. 'We can share the rest. There's always too much anyway.'

'Yes, all right,' said Bea, taking it. She licked the end and dipped it into the tube in Agnes's hand. 'Do you know anyone you could have sex with?'

'Not a single person.' Agnes wasn't entirely sure she minded.

'Me neither,' said Bea. 'But that needs to change, doesn't it?' She gave a broad smile and sucked the end of her stick.

Agnes mustered a smile in return but her mind was tumbling. It wasn't so much the prospect of having to lose her virginity that terrified her, it was the idea that she might do whatever she liked.

It was an impossible thought.

# 2

Florence sat, her hands on the steering wheel, knuckles white from tension. She could have done without this.

Glancing up towards the front door beyond the driveway, she saw her eldest daughter, Eleanor. She was standing, leaning against the open doorway into the house, exactly as she used to when she was child. It startled her momentarily, the flashback to what once was. But Eleanor wasn't a child any more and she no longer lived here. She looked relaxed, untroubled, the opposite of how Florence felt.

What was she doing here?

She gave a casual wave down towards her and Florence, force of habit, gave a tight wave back.

She hadn't rung to say she was coming. The inconvenience fluttered through her.

She glanced up at herself in the rear-view mirror and ran a fingertip under her bottom eyelid, gathered her things from the well of the passenger seat and got out.

'You look in a frightful mood,' said Eleanor, as Florence walked towards her. She strode with purpose, businesslike, as if she had been sent to deliver grave news. 'Has something terrible happened?'

Florence shook her head as if the suggestion was an affront. 'No. I thought I was having lunch with Marjory but she didn't turn up. I must have got the wrong day.'

She walked up the steps, stopped as if remembering there was something expected of her, leaned towards Eleanor and kissed her on the cheek before moving past her into the hallway.

'You? Get the wrong day?' said Eleanor, kissing her back. 'The tides are more likely to forget to come in.'

'Well, I must have been stood up then. I must be easily forgotten.' The words drifted away.

She needed to tether herself, reacquaint herself with the familiar. She hung her coat up, smoothed down her blouse and placed her handbag on the top of the sideboard. Her car keys were placed carefully onto a flat silver tray next to some unopened envelopes ready for her husband when he returned home. She glanced down at them and quickly fingered them into a neater pile.

'What are you doing here?' she said, as if it were an afterthought. 'Are you staying for supper? Is Charlie with you?'

She was in bustling mode, wanting to shake off the humiliation. She didn't look at Eleanor as she spoke.

'No and no,' said Eleanor, shutting the door behind her. 'I wanted to chat to you about Saturday.'

'I should call her. Perhaps I should call her?' Florence's mind was still lingering. 'Perhaps something's wrong?'

'You don't need to go begging, Mother.'

Florence ignored the slight and walked to the kitchen, Eleanor just behind her.

'Do you want tea?' She frowned and fingered the top of her forehead, trying to soothe away her own thoughts.

'No, thanks.' Eleanor pulled a glass down from a cupboard to the left of the sink and placed it under the tap.

Florence watched her. She didn't like it. Eleanor didn't live here any more. She was a guest. She went to reach for a plastic cup to replace the one in her daughter's hand but, as she held it out, Eleanor was already drinking. She swallowed and eyed her mother.

'Did you want me to fill that for you?' She glanced towards the childlike beaker in her mother's hand.

Florence stared down at it and put it quietly down on the counter behind her.

'Your father will be home in an hour. I need to get changed.' She shot a quick look towards the large clock on the wall above the sink.

Eleanor gave a small laugh. 'You don't still do that, do you?'

'Do what?' There were things she needed to do. Eleanor was preventing her.

Florence walked towards the fridge and opened it. She pulled out a chicken pie she'd made earlier and shut the door with her elbow.

'Get spruced up for Daddy coming home?' Eleanor took another gulp from her glass.

Florence ignored the provocation and slid the pie into the oven. She picked up a plastic egg timer, shaped like a fat hen, moved it to forty-five minutes and placed it neatly down.

'Eleanor, I'm really not in the mood for this. Agnes will be home soon. You can make yourself useful. Go and pick some green beans from the garden.'

'But I want to talk to you about Saturday.' She swirled her water and stared down into it as if it might be far more interesting than the conversation she was trying to have.

'Not now,' said Florence, walking away. 'Later. Go and pick the beans.'

She trotted briskly towards the stairs. She could feel Eleanor's eyes boring into her, the silent judgements being made. She didn't need to be told. She knew her faults all too well. She'd never change. She was a woman for whom every moment of every day was rigid and defined. If she didn't keep moving, Florence knew, she'd feel every inch of the sadness of her life.

She glanced back towards Eleanor in the kitchen. She was draining the last of the water from her glass and Florence watched as she slowly looked around the room. Nothing was out of place, everything was immaculate: the chairs were all tucked to attention under the table; the white linen cloth on top of it was crisp, ironed and gleaming; a pot of fresh flowers cut from the garden stood proud at its centre; the work surfaces were clear of all clutter; the floor was spotless. It was as if nobody lived here, a home for show only. She could see it in Eleanor's face: she didn't know how her mother did it. Or why. It was a space for living that nobody was allowed to live in.

'The bowl is in the cupboard to your right.' Florence stopped on the stairs, her hand gripping the banister. She knew full well Eleanor was aware of where it was.

Eleanor went to the cupboard and pulled out a dark blue Tupperware bowl.

'Are you still doing your plastic parties?' she called up, turning it in her hands. 'For the Tupperware.' She rolled the word in the mouth. She was making fun of her.

'Yes,' Florence replied.

Eleanor gave a small nod and walked off towards the long sitting room that looked out over the garden. Florence watched her, waiting for what, exactly? The murmurs of appreciation? Like the kitchen, it was immaculate: the chintz sofa, the matching armchairs, the coffee table with the porcelain geese, the tassled lampshades, the framed photographs of her grandparents, a picture of her father in his war uniform; it was all sitting, waiting to be approved and instantly ignored.

It was a waste of a room, really. They never used it. If Eleanor ever came back to live here, it would be perfect for a studio: all the light that poured in, begging to be noticed. Eleanor's own studio, a converted hut at the bottom of her garden, wasn't quite

14

fit for purpose now she was being taken seriously. Florence had never expected Eleanor to be successful. It seemed to have happened by accident. It hadn't, of course, but the right gallery owner had come to the right end-of-year show and there had been no looking back. Now her paintings commanded vast sums. She was in demand. She needed somewhere bigger. Florence quietly totted up in her mind when Eleanor might be able to move in but dismissed the idea. It felt ghoulish.

Florence continued up the stairs. There was a heaviness to her. She had been stood up, dropped for something better. Marjory was her most glamorous friend, an old chum from schooldays who had done rather well for herself. Married money, all that. She even had a cook.

She drifted along the corridor into her bedroom and sat on the end of the bed. She'd been looking forward to today. All for nothing. Her days out were few and far between. Instead, she'd sat staring into a bowl of soup, embarrassed and alone. She should call Marjory, she really should, tell her off. It wasn't the first time. It wasn't on. All that time, effort, hope. She let her fingers tangle themselves together on her knees. She knew she'd say nothing.

She slipped out of her shoes and stood to unzip her skirt.

Florence glanced down from her bedroom window.

She was not a natural gardener: she had a few containable rose bushes and a row of lavender for the bees but, other than that, it was all vegetables, a hangover from coming through the war and the clarion call of self-sufficiency. The garden was for function, not pleasure. Everything had to have a purpose, to be useful, to do its bit.

She watched as Eleanor stepped down onto the lawn, walked towards the rows of beans and slipped between the sticks of willow. She was doing as asked. It made Florence visibly relax.

Routine. That would settle her.

She changed quickly into a floral dress, belted at the waist, short sleeves, round collar, and put on her string of evening pearls. She touched up her day make-up to add a bit of night-time glamour and applied a thick coat of blood-red lipstick.

Better. She felt better.

She stepped back and looked at herself in the full-length swing mirror that stood to the right of the window. She let her hands drift to her stomach, stroking the flatness of a belly that had been swollen not once but twice. She turned sideways to admire herself. She was still slight and would, if she weren't married, think herself attractive to other men.

Eleanor had her looks. She was naturally beautiful, all big blue eyes and golden curls. She could be even more beautiful if she made more of an effort but Florence had long given up nagging. Girls these days didn't seem to be interested in making the best of themselves. As for Agnes, well. She would always be something of the pit pony.

She touched lightly at the back of her hair, a convoluted bun in the style of Grace Kelly. She looked neat, in control, unflappable.

Satisfied she passed muster, Florence reached for a pair of heels tucked to the left of her vanity table. She dipped her feet into the shapely black teardrop pumps and fastened the buckle at the side. Her attitude was brisk and efficient.

This was the same thing she did every day at precisely the same time. She wasn't going back out. She would be spending the evening at home serving her husband his supper, washing up and sitting in near silence until he decided he wanted to go to bed.

This was her life. It was all she knew. There was nothing else.

# 3

A voice drifted up from the garden. Agnes was back.

'She's got you at it already?' Agnes pushed open the garden gate and walked halfway up the path. She stopped and watched her elder sister dropping beans into the blue bowl. She was always pleased to see her but was careful not to show it.

'Yes,' said Eleanor, casting a glance towards her. 'She's in a frightful mood. Stood up by Marjory. I think I know why too.'

'Why?'

'I'll tell you later. For maximum effect.' She raised her eyebrows. She was looking forward to it.

There was something unobtainable about Eleanor; she always felt out of reach. Her life was too interesting, too unique for Agnes to be able to catch hold of any of it. Now, she only told people she had a famous sister if she had to. She'd gone through a phase of telling anyone who cared to listen but she was showing off, asking people to like her because of someone else, someone they would never meet. A few people were jealous. The glamour of it! A famous artist for a sister! Agnes had seen Eleanor being sick into a shoe. She'd seen her cry until snot came out of her nose. She'd seen her naked in the bath, ill with flu; she'd seen her get ready on her wedding day. All the same, it was intoxicating: the glitzy parties, the requests for interviews in glossy magazines. Eleanor was sought after. They were hungry for her in a way Agnes couldn't fathom, so she had mentioned her sister at every opportunity; but it was no good, not really. Agnes wanted people to like *her*. Not her sister. There should be nothing left to know about her elder sister, but Agnes didn't really feel she knew her at all.

She stood, bag slung over the back of her shoulder, and wondered if she should pursue the Marjory thing. No point. Eleanor clearly wanted to make a grand announcement.

'Are you staying for supper? Is Charlie here?' Agnes glanced towards the house.

'No and no. We need to work out what we're doing on Saturday. My exhibition. Daddy's birthday.'

'And Charlie's birthday.' Agnes reached for a bag of boiled sweets in her pocket. She held them out. 'Do you want one?'

'No. Come and help me.' Eleanor waved the Tupperware bowl in Agnes's direction. 'Did you have exams today?'

'Yes. Last one in two days. Shorthand.' She pulled a face.

Stepping between two lavender bushes, Agnes dumped her bag on the lawn and wandered over towards the vegetable beds. Summer still felt as if it needed to get going but today was warm and woozy, a day for lying on your back in the buttercups.

'How are they going? Think you've passed? Here,' Eleanor added, passing her sister the Tupperware bowl, 'you have that. I can use the bottom of my smock.'

Agnes noted her sister's outfit: a loose cheesecloth top with a daisy motif around the wrists. She was wearing a pair of bright red shorts with large pockets at the front, on her feet a pair of Jesus creepers. Her legs looked amazing.

She stared down at her own legs: shapeless with thick ankles and a slightly unattractive fuzz of hair tufting across her shins. Her hair was unstyled and dirty, the overgrown remains of an ill-thought-out pixie cut done six months ago that didn't suit her then and didn't suit her now. She had the pale, greasy look of someone who needed a week in the sun. Her clothes were a decade out of date and she had the aura of someone who would always be running but never catching up. There was something about Agnes that was intensely sad. She seemed incapable of doing anything about it.

It had taken its toll, that year of being so unwell. It wasn't just the exams that crumbled to nothing; it was the anxiety it had left her with, the self-confidence withered to the ground, the fear of falling back to how she had been, how she had felt.

'I don't think it's possible not to pass secretarial exams, is it?' said Agnes, taking the bowl. 'They may as well point at a type-writer and a telephone and ask, "What are those?" and then, for a distinction, ask you to refill a stapler. I can't quite believe I've spent the last year preparing for this.'

Agnes was painfully aware of how embarrassed she was. Her path was already limited, her choices closing down. It was only now, at the end of this dull, dull year, that she was starting to fully appreciate how limited her options were. This was it for her. Nobody was coming to save her. She was trapped into a life that would never make her happy.

'You should have gone to university, Ag,' said Eleanor, picking a bean and dropping it into her upturned top. 'You're going to be wasted on secretarial.'

'I couldn't go, remember?' Her voice fell away to a mumble. 'I mucked it up.' She shot her sister a small sideways glance.

'No,' said Eleanor, pinching a bean away from its stalk, 'you gave up.' She reached sideways into a row of peas and snapped off a shell.

Agnes said nothing. She was so used to feeling despondent, it was impossible to feel cross at the slight. Besides, her sister was right. She had given up.

'Anyway. Do you want to know about Saturday?'

Eleanor ran her thumbnail along the seam of the casing and pushed the row of bright fresh peas into her mouth.

'Yes, all right.'

'I thought we could roll everything into one,' she said. 'There'll be booze and nibbles and whatnots. If we sort out two cakes for Daddy and Charlie then we don't have to bother with anything else.'

She turned and smiled.

Agnes watched her carefully. It was hard not to feel her own inadequacies. Her sister was beautiful, successful, lived life on her own terms. She had everything Agnes did not. She always had. Agnes loved her, looked up to her, admired her, but she wasn't sure she liked her. No, it wasn't that she didn't like her. It was that Eleanor reminded Agnes of how little she liked herself.

A flash of stubbornness kicked in. She didn't know if she was in the mood to quietly acquiesce. Eleanor always got her own way.

'Birthdays are supposed to be about the people whose birthday it is, though, Eleanor. Not you.'

'It will be about them.'

'No, it won't; it's your exhibition. It'll be all about you.'

Eleanor glanced towards the house. Their mother was striding towards them.

'She's coming,' she said and turned back to picking the beans.

'How many have you got?' Florence called out as she walked towards them. 'Don't go mad. We only need enough for three.'

Agnes held out the Tupperware bowl to show her hoard. 'How's that?'

'Plenty. Are you sure you don't want to stay for supper, Eleanor? Your father would be so pleased to see you.' She creased her face into a polite smile.

'Really?' Eleanor emptied the contents of her smock into the bowl. 'Are you sure that's true?'

A moment of something brittle flittered across Florence's face but she composed herself immediately.

'Of course it's true. What a strange thing to suggest.'

She took the bowl from Agnes's hands and turned to walk back to the house.

'Are you going to ask me how my exam went?' Agnes called after her.

But her mother didn't reply.

Agnes's face fell. Ignored, again.

'What are you going to do with your summer?' Eleanor asked, stepping out from the peas. 'When you've finished your exams? One last hoorah and all that?'

'I don't know. I need to talk to Bea.' Agnes raised a hand to her forehead and looked out towards the long horizon beyond the garden. 'It really is very hot, isn't it?'

'Yes. I suppose it is. Come on,' Eleanor said, touching her sister's arm. 'I've got something to show you.'

'What is it?'

'You'll see . . .'

Eleanor wandered up the garden, following their mother back to the kitchen. Agnes stood for a moment, the usual deadened sense of her current predicament enveloping her. There was no point in feeling upset. Even she wasn't interested in how her exams were going. She picked up her bag and brought up the rear.

'Shut your eyes.'

Agnes dropped her bag to the floor of the kitchen and joined her mother. There was a soft sound of something being placed on the table.

'OK. You can look.'

Agnes and Florence opened their eyes and stared down at the odd, rough-skinned green thing that sat in front of them. Agnes touched it gently with her finger.

'What is it?'

'It's an avocado pear.'

They all tilted their heads.

'Is it really?' said Florence, peering. 'I've heard about these. What do you do with it? Put it in a fruit salad?'

Eleanor smiled. 'No, it's savoury. Do you want to try it?'

Florence glanced back towards the clock. 'You have it, Agnes.' She turned away back to the stove and the beans.

'Pass me a knife, Ag,' said Eleanor, taking a plate from a cupboard behind her. 'By the way, I think I might know why Marjory didn't turn up. Did I tell you I bumped into her?'

Florence stared at her. 'No. Why didn't you mention it earlier?'

'Forgot.'

Eleanor was clearly lying.

'Well. I have quite the news. She's getting a divorce.'

Agnes glanced towards her mother. She was visibly shaken. 'What? That can't be true!'

Agnes watched Eleanor's face. There was the fizz of something excited behind her eyes, a sharp little enjoyment. She wished she had the capacity to shock their mother like that.

'It is. From the horse's mouth.' Eleanor took the knife from Agnes and gripped the avocado in one hand. 'She's getting one of those new ones where nobody's to blame. Irreconcilable differences, she said. She applied for one as soon as it was made legal. You have to be separated for two years. Five years if your husband won't agree.' She slid the knife into the skin.

'I don't know what to say.' Florence backed herself up against the work surface, shoving herself as far away from this news as possible.

'She looked absolutely delighted. I don't think I've ever seen her more happy. There.' Eleanor pulled the avocado open. 'Look at that. You have to take the stone out. And you don't eat the skin. Put a bit of salt and pepper on it. Give it a go.'

Florence was still floundering. 'But why? Did she tell you why?' She wrapped her arms around her torso, protecting herself from this dangerous information.

Eleanor shook her head. 'Not really. I think she'd just had enough. She's young. What is she? Same age as you? Forty-five?

Forty-six? She's got ages to have fun. She looked fabulous too. New hair-do. Lovely togs. Very with it.'

Agnes's eyes flitted between them. Eleanor was standing tall while her mother had folded in on herself. She dug a teaspoon into the avocado and lifted it to her nose. 'Doesn't really smell of anything,' she muttered but nobody was paying her any attention.

'I don't understand why it's happened.' Florence's voice drifted off, her eyes filled with confusion.

'Perhaps she read *The Female Eunuch*,' said Agnes, trying to insert herself back into the conversation.

Florence blinked. 'What do you mean, "read *The Female Eunuch*"?'

'You must know,' said Agnes. 'It's that new book. Everyone's banging on about it. It's all about female empowerment and how women must leave their husbands and have loads of sex and orgasms.' She put the spoon into her mouth, frowned and then widened her eyes. 'Oh! It's lovely!'

Eleanor beamed. 'It *is*, isn't it?'

'Have you read it, Eleanor?' Agnes dug her spoon back into the avocado.

'*The Female Eunuch*? Of course I have. It's all anyone's talking about.'

'You're not going to leave Charlie, though, are you?' Agnes took another mouthful.

'No, I'm not going to leave Charlie.' Eleanor leaned forward, her hands resting palms down on the top of the kitchen table.

'See,' said Agnes, waggling the spoon in her direction. 'I expect that's because Charlie gives you loads of orgasms.'

'Agnes!' said Florence, sharply. 'That's not the sort of conversation that's going to get you anywhere.'

Agnes turned and looked at her mother who was now angrily tossing new potatoes into a pan of water. 'Nothing is going to get *me* anywhere, Mother.' She paused. 'Have you ever had an orgasm?'

Florence shot a glare in her direction, wiped her hands again on the faded tea towel of the Queen and left the room, her daughters watching her as she went.

'That's a no then,' said Eleanor. She looked back at the plate. 'Hey, leave some for me.'

# TUESDAY

# 4

Florence stood in the hallway, her ears straining to hear William's car door shutting. She was motionless, poised like a cat, terrified of moving a muscle until she knew it was safe to do so.

She had thought of little else since finding out. She was up to no good and she knew it.

The familiar deep thud sounded from the driveway and, as if a starter gun had rung out, Florence turned and paced towards the telephone in the small sitting room. It was an old black Bakelite: a telephone engineer had tried to sell her a more modern turquoise model back in 1967 but Florence was having none of it. She liked the weight of the receiver in her hand and the handy pull-out tray for numbers.

Florence flicked it out and ran her index finger down the line. 'Marjory,' she mumbled and dialled.

She cradled the receiver tight to her chin, consumed with a need to be furtive. Her shoulders were rounded, her eyes wide and staring. She was aware of holding her breath. The news had shocked her and she had thought of little else since being told. As to whether she would bring it up over the phone, that was a different matter. No, it didn't seem right. Besides, she had a plan.

'Chelsea 4967!'

Florence breathed out. 'Marjory! It's Florence!'

'Oh darling! I was just thinking about you! I bumped into Eleanor. Did she tell you?' Her voice was light and untroubled.

'No.' Florence hesitated as she lied. 'Mind you, my girls tell me nothing these days. You know how it is.' She stared down at her shoes, comfortable tan slingbacks. Lying did not come easy to her. She was worried it made her sound nervous.

'She looked terribly well. She's got your looks all right! Charlie's a lucky fellow. She invited me to her exhibition. Is that why you're calling? Oh wait, was I supposed to see you for lunch? When was it?'

Florence hesitated. It made no sense to make a meal of it.

'Why I was calling you, actually; I wasn't sure myself.'

'Phew, thought I'd forgotten it.'

'I was wondering if you're free tomorrow? For lunch?'

'In Brill?' She said it as if it were a ridiculous thought.

'No, in town. I'm coming up to get a few things. It's William's birthday on Saturday. And Charlie's. All go. As per.'

'You never stop, Florence.'

'No, and I suddenly thought of you and how I haven't seen you in an age ...' Her voice trailed off.

'But I will be seeing you on Saturday ...' Marjory let the thought hang. She clearly wasn't keen to do lunch but Florence had to persist.

'Yes, but you know how it'll be.' Florence grappled to control the situation. 'Those things are hopeless for catching up. You spend the first half saying hello and the second half saying goodbye.'

She stopped and waited. If Marjory pushed back again there would be no undoing it. Florence understood how these things worked.

'You're right. Well,' said Marjory, 'I've got a game of tennis at ten but that won't last long. Barbara Grimbles. Have you seen her lately? Size of a house! I'll be surprised if she lasts a set. So yes. Why not? What time shall we say? Midday? At the Savoy Grill?'

Florence felt herself relax. 'Yes. That would be lovely.'

'Forgot the crossword.' A voice sounded behind her. Florence span round.

William was walking towards her. He leaned towards an occasional table to her left and picked up a navy-blue fountain pen and the folded newspaper underneath it. Florence felt a surge of panic.

'I'm just on the phone to Marjory!' she said, smiling and pointing towards the receiver.

'Hello, William!' shouted Marjory.

Florence mustered an awkward laugh. 'Marjory says hello!'

William glanced towards her but nothing registered in his face. Tucking the pen into his jacket pocket and the paper under his arm, he turned and walked back towards the hallway.

'He's waving hello,' Florence lied. She was gripping the receiver so hard she could feel the blood pumping through her fingers. Her voice was little more than a whisper, as if her words were retreating in terror.

'So sweet. Well,' said Marjory. 'I shall see you tomorrow! Heaps to tell you. Heaps.'

'Yes. Bye-bye, then. Savoy at midday. Bye-bye.'

Florence put the receiver down and stood for a moment, her heart beating. She thought about running out to William. Did he suspect anything? Did he disapprove? She paced briskly across the sitting room, out into the hallway and down towards the front door. Pulling it open, she waved towards William as he reversed the car out from the driveway.

'I'm going up to town tomorrow!' she shouted, brightly. 'To have lunch with Marjory!' She attempted a smile.

William glanced sideways, gave a cursory nod and put his foot down on the accelerator.

Florence stood watching, not quite knowing what to do. She felt grimly electrified; embarrassed, yes, but she had clawed back a little sanity for herself.

Now she wouldn't have to lie and that, she decided, was worth the small moment of shame.

# WEDNESDAY

# 5

Agnes lifted her face up towards the sky and closed her eyes. That was it. Last exam finished. She never had to go back to that stuffy room that smelled of boiled cabbage or use the ancient typewriter with the Q that always stuck. She never had to take dictation, to stare down at the spider scrawls of her shorthand that withheld all sense. She no longer had to sit, staring out the window at the doorways into St John's or Balliol, and wonder if her life might be different had it taken the turn it was supposed to.

She should be feeling unencumbered, relieved, raring to go, but she wasn't. Instead, all she felt was gnawing dread at the thought that a conveyor belt was laid out before her. She had taken her exams and she would pass and she would spend the rest of her life sitting behind a typewriter tapping out other people's careers.

It's a terrible thing, to feel trapped. Eleanor was right. She was wasted on secretarial. She should be sitting in the Bodleian Library, hunched up against a stack of books that smelled of a hundred years, a Victorian novel pressed open in front of her, pen in hand, ink on her forefinger, dreaming of who she might become and where knowledge might take her.

'I feel magnificent,' said Bea, hands on hips. She was standing legs apart, as if she might be considering getting on a horse. 'I've always hated exams. Revision is simply awful, sitting them's even worse, and then suddenly they're all over and you feel like a gambolling lamb. Or a kite. Or a bicycle. Maybe not a bicycle.'

Agnes wished she felt that way.

Bea shoved her specs up her nose and gave a fulsome nod. 'So it's sort of worth it. Anyway. I feel super. Shall we go to the Bird?' She nudged her nose in the direction of the Eagle and Child.

'Is everyone else going there?' Agnes glanced over Bea's shoulder to the other secretarial students. They were petite and well turned out, all of them chomping at the bit to marry the first boss that would have them. She and Bea had absolutely nothing in common with those girls but were well used to it: they were forever the outsiders. It had been the same at school and was the same now.

'Probably. We can tuck ourselves away in the Rabbit Room. Come on.' Bea gave Agnes's upper arm a punch. 'I'm gasping for a half of apple cider. We could go mad and order a cheese sandwich.'

Agnes's eyes widened. 'To share?'

'Obviously.'

The Rabbit Room was a snug of sorts: wood-panelled walls covered with memorabilia of the infamous Inklings Club. Once upon a time, J. R. R. Tolkien and C. S. Lewis and all manner of literary brainboxes had sat there to discuss matters of great import. Now it was a little less snug, having been opened out in a recent renovation, and was being used to discuss different matters of great importance: namely, how to get laid.

'I have drawn up a list,' said Bea, taking a small sip of her cloudy apple cider. She reached into the pocket of her trousers and pulled out a scrap of folded-up paper. 'We need to take a scientific approach to our quest for sexual equality and I always find lists are a very good place to start.'

She opened it out and flattened it down on the table with the palm of her hand.

Agnes peered at the list. There was one name on it.

'Mr Hannity? The baker in Brill?' Agnes looked up, astonished. 'Bea! He's about fifty! What on earth are you thinking?'

'He's also a widow,' Bea said, holding up a finger to pause any further criticism. 'So he'll have done it before and will be grateful that anything is on offer.'

'He's got false teeth. Is that it? Is that the only person you've got?' Agnes picked up the piece of paper and turned it over to look at the other side. 'Oh Bea,' she said, on seeing that really was the only name on her friend's list, 'I think you can do better than that.'

'Oh, it's not for me. That was my suggestion for you.' Bea took another sip of her drink.

Agnes stared at her.

'He's only a hundred yards from your house,' Bea added, with an encouraging smile.

'No. Thank you. I do not want to journey into the brave new world of the sexual revolution by having sex with a man who has no front teeth and smells of yeast. I mean, really, Bea. Come on.'

'He's got a van.'

'Stop it. No.' Agnes took the cheese sandwich on the plate between them and bit into it: chunky white bread with a decent crust, the Cheddar good and strong with just the right amount of pickle. 'I mean, there might be free buns.'

'Exactly.'

'But still. No. I couldn't. I don't remotely fancy him. This Cheddar's excellent.' She waved her half-sandwich towards Bea.

'Are we factoring in actually being sexually attracted to someone?' Bea asked, picking up her own half. 'Because that rather narrows the field.' She took a bite. 'Ooh. It is good.'

'Why wouldn't we?' said Agnes, swallowing. 'The point is we're supposed to have fun ... I know there's the temptation to get it over with but it would be preferable if we actually enjoyed it.'

'Yes,' nodded Bea. 'That would be preferable. Who's on your list?'

'I haven't really got one. There's nobody from college.'

'Well, they're all women.' Bea shook her head, dismissing the thought.

'I know. And as for Brill ...' Agnes shrugged her shoulders.

Bea wiped a few crumbs delicately from the corner of her mouth. 'I wasn't going to suggest this. But let's throw caution to the wind. I have a rather daring proposal.' She leaned forward.

Agnes eyed her suspiciously. 'Oh yes?'

'You know Daphne and Brenda and Lois?' Bea lowered her voice to a conspiratorial hush.

'The Terrible Trio? From the course?' Agnes curled her lip. They were the rotten cabal, the top of the food chain, the ones to whom all deferred.

'The Terrible Trio. They're off to Europe for a month.'

'Right.'

'And I wondered ...'

Agnes held her hand up. 'There is absolutely no way I am going anywhere with them. A very small potato is more use than Brenda Williams. I couldn't care less if she's got tits that could take your eye out. *She's useless*. Besides, they *hate* us.'

Bea tightened her lips. 'No, that's not the daring proposal. The daring proposal is that we *pretend* we're going to Europe with them. Our parents are far more likely to agree to a cultural sojourn. But we don't. We don't go to Europe with them *at all*.' She sat back and grinned.

Agnes paused. 'Nobody, and I mean *nobody*, is going to believe the Terrible Trio invited us anywhere. They *loathe* us.'

'Doesn't matter. Our parents have no idea who or what they are. Our parents will totally believe us.'

'But what's the point?'

'Because, Agnes, we can go somewhere else. Like *London.*'
Bea said the word as if it were a fictional wonderland. 'What do
you think of that?'

'Can't we just go to London?'

'Will your parents let you go to London?'

'I doubt it.'

'Precisely. They'll be gung-ho about a cultural trip to Europe;
London – forget it. My brother's got a friend.'

'*Your* brother's got a friend?' Agnes made a small scoffing
noise. '*Really?*'

'Honestly. He has. They play in a chess club or something.
Anyway, he's got a friend whose sister's a model. And she lives
in London. And she's said I can go and stay.'

'Stop it.'

'It's true. We can go and stay with an actual model in actual
London. Think about it! She'll know loads of chaps. They'll be
like bees to the honey.' Bea looked very pleased with herself.

Agnes chewed her lip. 'What if we're found out? What if we
bump into someone we know? Someone our parents know?
How are we convincing our parents we're where we say we
are?'

Bea held up her finger. 'I have already thought this through.
We both write letters home to our mothers. One for each week
we're supposed to be away. And we pretend we're in the place
where Daphne and Brenda and Lois are. And then Daphne or
Brenda or Lois will take the letters with them and post them
from the European city we're supposed to be in. As for the rest,
don't worry about it. If we're found out, we're found out. What's
the worst that can happen?'

'The Terrible Trio aren't going to take letters for us and post
them. They hate us, Bea. Daphne calls me Quasimodo.'

Bea looked over her shoulder to check no one was listening
and reduced her voice to a whisper. 'You know the long typing
exercise we had to hand in?'

'Yes.'

'I did it for Lois. She owes me.'

There was something different about Bea, Agnes thought. She was emboldened.

'And then, when we've joined the sexual revolution,' Bea added, 'we shall start the real business of taking complete and utter control of our lives.'

Bea was brimming with enthusiasm. It filled Agnes with a flush of hope.

'All right. Let's do it. I'm mildly terrified, but let's do it.'

'Thank you.'

'But let's not give the letters to Brenda. She is *useless*.'

'Agreed. Then let us shake on it, Agnes Ledbury.'

'Yes, let's, Beatrice Morgan. I'm in.' Agnes withdrew her hand and leaned back into her chair.

Bea took another bite of her sandwich. 'Did I tell you about Joanna Peel?'

'No.' Agnes shook her head and also took a bite.

'Gave a postman a blow job. They were all talking about it. I haven't done one. I imagine it's like blowing a trumpet.'

She made a fist and blew into the top of it. 'Bit like that.'

Agnes watched her friend carefully. There was something so adorable about her. 'I'm feeling thrilled with this plan, Bea. Shall we have another sandwich?'

'Yes,' said Bea, with a grin. 'Let's.'

# 6

'Here you are!' Marjory stood up from the table and, with a touch to Florence's forearm, kissed sideways off into the air. 'This is fun, isn't it?' She grinned and sat back down. 'I expect you're thrilled to be up in town. Makes a change from sleepy old Brill.'

'Yes,' said Florence, lightly. She could have screamed it from the rooftops, she was so relieved to be there. She was also relieved Marjory had deigned to turn up but she'd keep that to herself.

The immaculately dressed maître d' who had escorted Florence to the table gently pulled out the chair opposite Marjory and waited for Florence to sit.

'Can I take your coat?' he asked, casting a glance at her tweed jacket.

'Oh. Yes. Thank you.' Florence slipped it off and handed it to him.

'Tweed? On a day like this?' Marjory nodded towards the window. 'Aren't you boiling?'

'I was, rather. But you know me. Never go anywhere without a jacket.'

Florence mustered a smile. She sat back and looked at Marjory, properly, for the first time. Eleanor was right. She looked entirely different. Her hair, once done up into a military knot, was now cascading down, loose curls bouncing just above her shoulders. A rich chestnut wash gave her a lustrous, expensive look and her make-up – gone were the prim bow lips and grey eyeshadow – was now an explosion of brash colour. Her bright blue eyes popped out from dark smoky pools, her cheekbones highlighted with a bold blusher and her lips glossed with a provocative red. She looked glamorous, confident, sexual.

Florence felt jealous.

'How are you, darling? In rude health, as always. You always look so wholesome, Florence. All that clean Brill air. Shall we have wine? White?' Marjory was taking charge, as she often did, and, before Florence could reply, she had already summoned a waiter. 'Bottle of the Chablis, please. On ice. Thank you.'

She dispatched the waiter with a dazzling smile and then turned her attentions back to Florence.

'So, I have news,' she said. 'I have left Derek.'

Florence, prepared for this moment, widened her eyes and tried to look shocked.

'Oh Marjory,' she said, her fingers locking together in her lap, 'I'm so sorry.'

She tried to form more words but her mouth seemed to dry to nothing. Her mind plunged away from her. She didn't know what else to say.

'Don't be. Best thing I've ever done. I feel like a new woman. Technically, I haven't left him. I've thrown him out. Changed the locks. The lot.'

Florence sat, trying to pay sharp attention to what was being said but instead feeling consumed with a cold terror.

Marjory was staring at her, waiting for a response. 'What do you think of that?' she asked. Her voice was coquettish, almost as if she were flirting. She was pleased with herself. Florence hadn't expected that.

'Isn't that a little extreme? Changing the locks? Really?'

Marjory leapt in, waving her hand to dismiss the idea. 'Absolutely necessary, darling. If I want that divorce we have to be separated. If I don't change the locks he can argue he's still coming and going. Bread?' She held out the round wicker basket in front of her.

'No, thank you.' Florence looked down at the rolls staring up at her and then to Marjory. She's not remotely embarrassed, she thought. She's not frightened or ashamed.

Marjory plucked a plump white roll and ripped it open with her thumbs. 'I haven't been entirely awful. He's staying at the cottage in Henley. I've agreed not to go there at all. Two years. That's all we have to manage. And then I'm free. Could you pass the butter?'

Florence pushed the small silver butter boat across the table. She needed to dig down, pick at the edges, see where the unravelling had begun. 'The last time I saw the pair of you everything seemed fine.'

Marjory dipped her knife into the ridged swirl of butter and smeared it thickly onto her roll. 'All for show, darling. But you'll know that.' She shot Florence a knowing wink.

'I'm not sure I do.' Florence felt herself bristle.

'Oh, come on,' said Marjory, brightly, 'we're all friends here. No need to be coy. All those years stuck in a loveless marriage, toeing the line, playing the dutiful wife. Well. No more. Times are changing. I can have a life of my own. One I enjoy. And I intend', she said, taking a hearty bite of her roll, 'to enjoy it to the full.'

'Would you like to taste the wine?'

The waiter had reappeared. Marjory glanced up towards him.

'No need. You can pour, thank you.' She turned her attention back to Florence. 'Have you looked at the menu? I gave it a thorough read before you got here.'

'No, I ...' She reached for her handbag and opened it. 'Good-ness,' she said, rummaging through, 'I seem to have left my reading glasses. Silly. I can't quite ...'

She never forgot her reading glasses.

'Shall I tell you what you can have or order for you?' Marjory was smearing the other half of her roll with butter. 'I don't nor-mally have the bread. But I seem to be ravenous.'

'I could have sworn I ...' Florence was still peering into the dark corners of her bag.

'Never mind,' said Marjory, wanting to move things along, 'we've all done it. Shall I do the ordering?'

'It's fine,' said Florence, putting her handbag back down to the floor. 'I'll have whatever you're having.'

'Super. Two lemon sole please, waiter. You do eat fish, yes?' Florence nodded. 'And there we are. That was easy.' Marjory smiled again at the waiter, a young, handsome man with large brown eyes, and handed him her menu. She watched him as he walked away. 'Honestly,' she said, her eyes sparkling, 'I've gone sex mad. You have no idea how many younger men want to sleep with women old enough to be their mothers.'

'Marjory!' Florence glanced quickly at the adjacent tables, not wanting anyone to hear their conversation.

Marjory's lips slid into a curl of satisfaction. 'You're such a prude. There's a world beyond the four walls of King and Cas-tle, you know. I haven't a single regret. And stop looking so worried. I'm having a fabulous time. You'd love it too. Nothing wrong with a little adventure in your life, Florence.'

Florence sat, rigid. She couldn't recall ever feeling less relaxed. She felt as if she were being told dangerous things, things that might threaten the fabric of her being. It terrified her. She shook her head. 'But I don't understand, Marjory. What went wrong?'

'Nothing went wrong, darling!' Marjory's hands were rest-ing on the edge of the table. 'Everything went right. I woke up one morning and thought, Is this it? Is this all there is? Boiling his egg. Waving him off. Plumping cushions. Staring at the walls. There's a world out there, Florence. I want to be a part of it. I like myself and I'm getting a divorce and I've never been happier.'

Florence didn't know quite how to respond. She wanted to ask her when she knew, what had been the final straw; she wanted to know whether there had been ultimatums, tears. She wanted to know how she had done it.

Marjory tilted her head. 'Do you like yourself, Florence?'

Florence blinked. 'Of course I do.'

But Florence knew she was lying.

# THURSDAY

# 7

Agnes stood, her arms hanging by her sides. It was the same routine every evening. She would be summoned to the kitchen and would wait until her mother pointed at something to carry out to the dining room. She glanced around the room. Nothing had changed in her lifetime: not the chairs, not the ornaments on the shelves, not the pictures on the wall. Nothing. Everything was expected to stay exactly the same forever. Perhaps her mother would change, Agnes thought, when she finally left home? Perhaps it would kick-start a reawakening?

'That please,' said Florence, pointing to a porcelain bowl.

Agnes picked it up and carried it with both hands. The smell of carrots boiled to oblivion wafted upwards. Ahead of her, Florence's heels clipped along the wooden floor, in her hands a thin, marble carving slab hosting a rather unimpressive gammon.

'Did you bring the parsley sauce?' Florence spoke as she walked.

She was in Meal Mode: pan to plate with as much brisk efficiency as she could muster.

'Yes,' said Agnes, following her mother into the dining room where her father, William, already sat at the top of the table, his face hidden behind a book.

Florence presented the gammon and gently edged a carving knife towards it, took her seat to her husband's right, picked up a rolled napkin and smoothed it over the top of her skirt.

Agnes, behind her, placed the carrots within reaching distance and pulled out the chair to her father's left. She sat down, unravelled the perfectly ironed linen napkin from a wooden ring at the side of her plate and let it collapse into her lap.

They sat, both looking at the cover of the book William was reading, and waited.

Agnes's mind was whirring. She knew she couldn't blurt out her plans willy-nilly. She had to be stealthlike, strategic, sow the seeds and wait for thoughts to germinate.

Her father, William, was a difficult man. She barely knew him, to be honest, not in the real sense. He was ex-army, had fought in the Second World War, been taken prisoner and marched off to a POW camp. He was emotionally distant; a family man, but isolated. He was affable but no fun at all. He was the figure of authority to whom all things deferred but there wasn't the slightest indication that he was interested in any of them.

Her mother, on the other hand, was a different matter. She was a fusser, a stickler for rules, obedient. In many ways, she was the trickier customer.

Agnes wasn't even sure if her parents could be called friends. It was a business arrangement, a contractual marriage. Everything about them left her cold.

She gripped her hands together in her lap.

'It's lovely not to have any more revision to do,' she said, clearing her throat.

Florence shot a look towards her and gave a soft smile. 'I can imagine.' She turned her face back towards the upheld book.

'I don't get my results for at least four weeks,' Agnes persisted. 'I imagine I won't be able to apply for positions until I do.'

'No.' Florence was still staring towards her husband. She darted a quick, anxious glance towards the ever-cooling carrots. 'William,' she said encouragingly, 'would you like to carve?'

Agnes watched her father. She knew how this played out. It would never cross her mother's mind to tell him to hurry up and do something, that everyone was waiting, that it might be considered rude to sit reading your book at the dinner table. Instead, she would offer up the manly chore of carving as if it were some fantastic treat.

William gave an indiscriminate mumble, folded over the corner of a page and laid the book down to one side. 'What is it?' he asked, picking up the carving knife.

'Gammon. I know it's Thursday but the butcher didn't have any decent chops.'

William pushed back his chair, took a fork in his left hand and stood. Plunging it into the joint, he carved mean, ungenerous slices. 'Agnes,' he said quietly, and she held up her plate to allow him to layer two thin pieces onto it.

'Help yourself to carrots,' said her mother. 'And parsley sauce.'

Agnes dug a spoon into the soft, collapsed carrots and heaped them next to the meat on her plate. As she poured parsley sauce over them, Florence eyed her.

'Not too much, Agnes, it's rather rich.'

Agnes knew what that was code for so she slid the jug back towards the middle of the table and let her hands rest in her lap again. The usual flush of shame burned through her. Her mother was tiny, slim. Eleanor was beautiful and cool. She was none of these things. She was lumpy Agnes who wasn't allowed any more parsley sauce. She watched as Florence poured the slightest dribble over her gammon. She ate like a bird, always had.

'I suppose I should give some thought as to what I'm going to do with myself,' Agnes began. Underneath the table, she twisted her napkin between her fingers.

'What do you mean?' asked Florence, pushing the sauce boat towards William. 'When you get your results? I've heard there's some very good positions going at the Pru.' She pursed her lips together and turned her attention back to her husband.

'The insurance company?' Agnes's voice betrayed her dismay. The thought of working in that deadly dry atmosphere was beyond the pale.

'Don't turn your nose up,' said Florence. 'They're a very good company. Steady work. That's a job for life if you play it right. And they're always in need of young women. You can stay there till you get married. You never know, you might meet a nice chap.'

Agnes stared at her mother. Florence may as well be telling her she was off to prison. London, she knew, was her only chance of escape. She had to make it happen.

'No, I mean for the next four weeks. Before I get my results.' She twisted the napkin tighter.

'Oh,' said her mother, watching as William finished with the sauce. She picked up her cutlery, ready. 'Well, I'll be very happy to have you round the house. You can help with the vegetables. Or paint the front fence. That could do with a freshen-up.'

William picked up his knife and fork and cut into his gammon.

'Or I was wondering,' began Agnes, her knuckles whitened around the napkin, 'whether I should organise some sort of holiday?' She released her grip and looked down at her plate. 'Seems a shame to have this time – before I start work, I mean – and not make the most of it.'

She took up her cutlery, her eyes fixed on the soft carrots and the thin gammon and the small pool of accusatory sauce.

'Then, who knows? I can come back so refreshed I end up going to work at the Foreign Office!' She shot a smile towards her father. He wasn't looking at her.

'Foreign Office,' scoffed Florence, pushing her carrots about her plate. 'Girls like you don't get to work in the Foreign Office, Agnes. Remember who you are. There's no point expecting anything because you won't get it.'

Agnes felt appalled. She balked slightly, visibly so. Her mother wanted to bleed her of all ambition. Know your place, get used to it, this is the sum total of what you can hope for. Her walls were crowding in.

She cut a small corner of meat and lifted it to her mouth. She sat, silently chewing, not looking at either of her parents for fear of giving herself away. She was trying, desperately, not to cry.

'I think a holiday is a good idea,' said William, unexpectedly. 'Better than hanging round the house doing nothing for a month.' He scooped some parsley sauce onto the back of his fork. 'You should encourage it, Florence. Or she'll be under your feet all summer.'

Florence glanced towards him then back down at her plate. Agnes watched her, the way she instantly deferred. There was an opportunity here. Agnes seized the moment.

'There is a plan, actually,' she said, looking towards her father. 'A trip to Europe. Bea and Lois and Daphne and Brenda. You know, from college. They're all going.'

She let the idea hang.

Florence trimmed a tiny slither of fat from her gammon and pushed it to the side of her plate. 'Well, your father will have to think about it.'

William was chewing his gammon with an air of vague suspicion. 'A trip to Europe seems a little extravagant, Agnes.' He sounded measured. 'Maybe you should think closer to home? Trip to Devon. Or the Norfolk Broads.'

'Yes,' nodded Florence, fast on his heels, 'that would be much better. You could go for a week. That would be plenty.'

'But Bea's going to Europe. And I'm not a child any more ...' Agnes's voice trailed off. It wouldn't do to press any harder and she didn't want to sound as despairing as she felt.

In any event, the comment was ignored.

'What's for pudding?' asked William, eating the last of his gammon.

'Spotted dick,' said Florence. 'I thought I'd make up for the lack of chops.' She smiled towards her husband, waiting for a gratefulness that would never come.

She's so desperate for his approval, thought Agnes, watching her. It was sad, really. How had she allowed this to happen to herself? When did it happen? She must have been fun once. When did the shift from vibrant young woman to unpaid slave occur? Did it creep up, unnoticed, dragging her into a state of grateful drudgery?

Agnes would never become her mother, she decided. She must swear it to herself, make a blood promise if necessary. She would have a life of her own choosing. She would somehow get to university or have a career that was her own. She would be independent, be her own woman, just like Eleanor. She would make her own future and, most importantly, she would never be dependent on a sense of worth from anyone other than herself.

Her chest sunk in on itself. There would be none of that, she realised, if she didn't manage to escape the path she was already on. Who was she trying to fool? She'd never made a success of anything. The illness had put paid to that. Before it she'd been a confident young woman, funny and lively and full of hope, but all that was gone. What on earth made her think she could start now? If she was to change her story, she was going to have to convince her mother that other doors were open to her. It felt impossible.

'Do you want some?' Florence turned and asked her.

'Pudding? I don't think I do,' said Agnes.

Florence shot her a withered smile. 'Probably for the best.'

# FRIDAY

# 8

'You're baking your own birthday cake?' Florence stood, coat done up to the top, handbag hooked over her wrist, and stared in horror at her son-in-law.

'Not quite. Practising. Nothing wrong with that,' Charlie said, smiling. 'At least I get the flavour I like. Coffee and walnut. Delicious.'

Florence put her bag down on the hallway table and methodically undid the buttons on her coat.

'I don't think I've ever seen a man in a pinny, Charlie. I'm not sure it's entirely becoming.'

Charlie stared down at his flour-covered apron, his expression a mixture of sweet bemusement and mild astonishment. 'Never, Florence? Really? Has William never had a go at making a cake?'

'Don't be ridiculous!' Florence hung her coat on the hook by the front door. 'Men doing chores? No thank you.'

'Where do you want all this stuff?' Agnes bundled in behind her mother, hands full with plastic bags near to bursting.

'Kitchen please, Agnes,' said Charlie, rushing to help. 'Here, let me take that.'

Agnes had come with her mother to her sister's house in Barnes. It was a small, pretty cottage with a garden that drifted down to the water's edge. Eleanor and Charlie had moved there after Eleanor's last exhibition.

'Eleanor's in her shed,' said Charlie, as he walked away down the hallway. 'Do you want to go and get her, Agnes? I'll put the kettle on. Make you some tea, Florence.'

Florence gave a small grunt and followed briskly after him. 'Let me do that, Charlie. Honestly.'

Agnes turned right into the sitting room and walked towards the door beyond into the garden. It was a bright room with a stunning view of the river. She pushed the doors open.

Two banks of French lavender served as a corridor down to the water's edge. A thick heady scent filled the air. Fat, happy bees, their low hum underpinning the call of a lone song thrush sitting in a lilac tree to the left, filled the purple flower heads with activity. It was warm, again, but there was always something about coming here that made Agnes sad. Or was it envy? Perhaps they were one and the same? Perhaps not. It was impatience tinged with the sour taste of resentment. Eleanor had escaped. Agnes had not.

Eleanor's shed was at the bottom of the garden, a long, wooden rectangle with a glass roof at one end.

'Hello,' Agnes said, opening the studio door. 'We really need to do something about Mum.'

Eleanor turned round. She was wearing a loose light-blue top covered in speckles of paint and was standing, palette in hand, in front of a canvas that was almost finished. She looked entirely unburdened.

'What's she done now?'

'What she's always done,' said Agnes, throwing herself into a battered leather armchair at the back of the studio. 'That's the problem. She's never done anything different. And now she wants me to be the same.' She spread her fingers out across the armrests. Eleanor wasn't responding. 'Look at what she's like at home. Monday – laundry. Tuesday – clean out the bedrooms. Wednesday – do the stairs. Thursday – bathroom, toilet, oven. Friday – living rooms and bake. Saturday ...'

'Weekly shop,' said Eleanor, putting down her palette.

'And wash the linen.'

'And the towels.'

'She never changes. Same thing week in, week out. Every day the same. It's like she's in the army.' Agnes picked idly at a weathered hole in the armrest.

'She gave that book to me, you know,' said Eleanor, wiping her hands on a small towel. 'After I got married. *The Housewife's Pocket Book*. I took one look at it and chucked it in the bin.'

'Charlie's baking a cake. She nearly fainted on the spot.'

'I don't know why she's still surprised. I don't do any of the cooking. He likes it. I don't. And he's better at it. Where's the problem?'

'Exactly. She'll be in there now, wrestling the teapot from him and insisting he sit down and smoke a pipe in his slippers.'

'And not talk to her.'

Agnes laughed. 'Yes, sit over there and ignore me, please. That's what I like. Honestly. It's tragic.' She smiled. It felt validating to have her sister agree with her. It felt important.

'She's never going to change, Ag,' said Eleanor, slipping the light-blue top over her head. She was wearing a thin white T-shirt underneath.

'No, I know,' replied Agnes. She rested her cheek into her hand.

Eleanor leaned back, her shoulder against the wall, and looked at her little sister. Agnes was wearing a green polo-neck jumper, knitted, and a pair of rather heavy brown corduroy trousers.

'Aren't you enormously hot?'

'Yes, as a matter of fact, I am,' said Agnes, staring down at herself. 'But Mother wouldn't let me out of the house unless I was dressed for rain. There isn't a cloud in the sky!'

'Agnes, you're twenty. You don't need to still be told what to wear by your mother.' Eleanor's voice was soft but certain.

'Tell her that!'

'No. *You* tell her that.' Eleanor pointed a finger firmly in Agnes's direction. 'Come on. You're not a child any more.'

Agnes knew it was true, but forever being the baby of the family was so ingrained, it felt impossible to shift anyone's thinking. She still lived at home, she still slept in her childhood bed, she still had to sit up at the dining table and not lean on her elbows. Her mother still washed her laundry and folded it away. Her meals were cooked for her. She had no responsibilities. She made no decisions. She simply did what she was told. Life and circumstance had squeezed the ambition from her. Her year of being fragile and unwell had done nothing to help her break free: it had left her dependent, forced to be looked after by her mother. It had prolonged the maternal grip. Florence, Agnes was all too aware, was reluctant to let Agnes out of her sight.

'I'm not sure I'm brave enough. Can't you do it for me, Eleanor? She listens to you.'

'No, she doesn't.'

'She does. You're ... successful. She admires it.'

'Not really. Besides, she'll change the subject and it'll lead to the When You're a Mother speeches which will segue nicely into why Charlie and I haven't had children yet. No thanks.'

'I'm rather looking forward to you and Charlie making me an aunt. I think I'll be brilliant at it.'

'Do you?' said Eleanor, smiling. 'What do you think you'll be good at?'

'Moaning about their grandmother, for a start. Anyway, get on with it. I need someone younger than me in this family. It will help enormously.'

'We're trying,' said Eleanor, moving towards the door. 'I've come off the pill. Don't tell Mum.' She swung round and stabbed a finger in Agnes's direction. 'Promise?'

'Promise,' said Agnes, pushing herself up. 'That's exciting. Are you having loads of sex and orgasms?'

'Loads.' Eleanor walked out into the garden. Agnes followed.

'Bea and I are planning on doing it.' Agnes trotted to catch up.

'Doing what?'

'Having sex.'

Eleanor stopped and looked at her. 'With each other?'

'Don't be stupid,' Agnes recoiled. 'Neither of us are remotely dangerous enough to be lesbians. We're planning on losing our virginity so we can become second wave feminists. This summer.'

Eleanor shook her head and laughed. 'Don't take this the wrong way, Ag, but I think you might be the squarest person I've ever known. I do love you for it, though.' She threw an arm about Agnes and gave her a squeeze.

'Don't tell Mummy, though. That's very important.' Agnes folded herself in to her sister's shoulder.

'You don't tell her about me trying to get pregnant and I won't tell her about you trying not to get pregnant. Deal?' Eleanor offered up her hand.

Agnes shook it. 'Deal. Actually, that's a good point. I don't want to get pregnant. Can I have your pill?'

'No, you can't.' They walked together slowly between the lavender.

'But you're not using it!'

'Girls!' A tinkling call came from the door of the sitting room. They both looked up.

Florence was standing, waving them in. 'Tea's ready!'

'Coming,' shouted Eleanor.

She extricated herself from the close embrace and poked Agnes in the chest. 'Go and get your own. You might as well get used to asking. You need to toughen up, Agnes. It's time to grow up.'

She turned and strode away.

Agnes stood and watched her sister march up towards the house. Everything about her oozed confidence and certainty and a sense of purpose. On top of all her own failings, Agnes knew she was a coward.

She glanced back towards the water. A duck and seven ducklings floated past.

No, she definitely didn't want to get pregnant.

# 9

'This cake's lovely, Charlie,' said Florence, licking the end of her fork. 'I'm very impressed. You've got the butter cream just right.'

They were all sitting at the kitchen table, a scarred and battered oak relic that Eleanor had rescued from a second-hand shop.

'I used icing sugar,' said Charlie, smiling. 'Watched you doing it last time I was at Brill. All the credit is yours.'

'Such a suck-up,' said Agnes, with a groan. 'No wonder she likes you more than she likes us.'

'That's not remotely true,' said Florence, raising an eyebrow, 'although it would be nice if one of my daughters showed the slightest interest in baking. How it's come to this I do not know. Still, I must say, I can't imagine William making a cake.'

She paused. Agnes watched as a shadow of something far away and sad flitted across her face.

'When did you meet him?' Charlie leaned over and let his hand rest on Florence's forearm. 'I'm not sure I've ever been told the story.'

Florence's face reignited. 'Really?'

Charlie shook his head. 'Tell me. I love all that stuff.'

'Twenty. Agnes's age. Introduced at a tea dance. Courted for a few weeks and he asked me to marry him.' She gave a soft smile. 'He was quite a bit older than me. Think he wanted to get on with things. You just did. That's how it was after the war. We barely knew each other, really. And to think I thought I was on the shelf.' She gave a soft tut. 'It's all different now. Nobody's in a hurry to do anything.'

'I'm never going to get married,' said Agnes, licking some cream from her finger. 'Germaine Greer says you shouldn't.'

Florence rolled her eyes. 'A married woman is a happy woman. Look at your sister,' she added, nodding towards Eleanor. 'Does she look miserable to you?'

Agnes shot a glance towards her sister who was leaning back in her chair, arms folded, looking bemused.

'She's not miserable because she's got a husband who cooks cake.' She paused. 'And a career.'

She pushed the end of her cake onto her fork with her finger. She was treading on eggshells, desperately wanting someone to ask her about what she might want, about whether she'd like to make something of herself. She needed a gap to open up so she could press it wide but it never did.

Florence stood and gathered up the rest of the plates. 'It's just dreams, Agnes,' she said. 'Your sister is a talent. You and I live in the real world. You'll get a job at the Pru and marry a nice man and have children. And that will be that.' She turned her back and walked to the sink.

Agnes, feeling a sudden fury, pushed her chair back from the table. She wanted to complain, to make a stand, raise her voice, articulate what she needed, but instead she muttered, 'I need the loo,' and walked towards the door. She was paralysed by her own inadequacies.

'Use the one upstairs, Ag,' Eleanor called after her. 'Downstairs chain needs fixing.'

Agnes trudged her way up the staircase. She was fuming. 'Bloody cheek,' she muttered. 'Bloody, bloody cheek.'

She pushed open the door to the bathroom and sat grumpily on the toilet. Eleanor was right. She needed to be more asser-tive. She needed to make her feelings known. She needed to stand up for herself, be her own person. She pulled at the toilet roll and tore a few strips off, stood and flushed.

She walked to the basin to wash her hands and looked at herself in the cabinet mirror. She wasn't pretty. She'd always accepted that. She looked like William. She had his prominent nose and chin and there was a squareness to her face that was almost masculine. Who was going to want to marry that? she thought. Nobody. Not that she wanted to get married. Be like her mother? No thanks.

She wiped her hands on the towel draped over the radiator to her left. She looked back towards the cabinet.

A thought presented itself.

Standing, for a moment, she listened to the idle waves of chatter seeping up from the kitchen. She walked carefully, her steps secret and gentle, and quietly opened the cabinet door. There was a bottle of Milk of Magnesia, some aspirin, a pot of Vaseline, a tube of cotton wool, some talcum powder and a jar of Oil of Ulay face cream. Next to it was a strip of pills.

Agnes picked them out and stared down. If all went to plan, she'd need these over the next weeks. 'Start in the green sec-tion,' it said at the top. Each pill had a day of the week above it. She knew what they were. Tucking the strip into her trouser pocket, she flattened down her jumper, turned and opened the door.

Eleanor was standing outside. Agnes looked at her and pushed past.

'What are you doing?' said Eleanor, as Agnes trotted down the stairs.

Growing up, thought Agnes.

# SATURDAY

## 10

Agnes picked up the receiver, dialled Bea's number and waited, twopence piece hovering over the pay slot.

'Brill 592!' It was Bea's mother. Agnes thrust her coin downwards.

'Hello, Mrs Morgan,' said Agnes, brightly. 'Is Bea there?'

'Bea!' called her mother. 'Agnes on the phone!'

Agnes stood, listening. She glanced out from the telephone box towards the pub. Thomas, the junior barman, was at the front, clearing up the discarded pint pots from the lunchtime opening. He saw her and she gave a wave.

'Hello?' It was Bea.

'Bea, I've written the letters to give the Terrible Trio and I have stolen contraceptives.' Agnes sounded very pleased with herself.

'How have you managed that?'

'They're Eleanor's. We're in the clear. We now cannot get pregnant. I've got twenty-eight pills. So we can either have sex fourteen times each or we can split each pill in two and really go for it.'

There was a pause. 'Are you sure that's how it works?'

'No.'

'When do we start taking them?'

'On any day we think we might have sex?'

'So they're like aspirin?'

'Yes. But for sex.'

'Oh, well done, Agnes Ledbury.'

'Thank you, Beatrice Morgan.'

'I've spoken to my parents.' Bea's voice became hushed. 'And they are totally on board for the Europe thing.'

'Hmm,' said Agnes, curling her finger into the thick telephone cord. 'The starter flag has not gone down here, Bea.'

'Agnes!' Bea took on a sharp urgency. 'If we're going, we're going tomorrow. It won't work otherwise. You need to get them to say yes. Today!'

Agnes screwed her mouth sideways. 'I might need your help. Can you come over later? Before Eleanor's exhibition.'

'No,' said Bea, her voice returning to normal, 'I can't come to that now.' Then, louder, *'Because we're going to Europe tomorrow.'* She wanted whoever was in listening distance to hear it.

'Disaster. Seriously, Bea, I need you to come over.' Loud pips sounded and Agnes pressed another twopence into the slot. 'This isn't going to happen unless we unleash all guns, Bea.'

'I'll ask.' Bea called out, *'Can I pop over to Agnes's this afternoon? Mum!'* There was a pause. 'Hang on, Agnes, I think she's gone into the garden.'

The sound of the receiver clattering onto a wooden surface fluttered down the line. It was ridiculous, really. Here they were, two twenty-year-old women tiptoeing around their parents as if they were both still twelve. The fact she wouldn't dream of having this conversation from the home phone spoke fathoms. It was like being held hostage.

Agnes pressed her forehead against the glass of the telephone box. Thomas was picking up abandoned crisp packets. She watched him as he meandered about, his long brown hair flapping around his ears. He was wearing jeans, flared at the ankle, some tatty white plimsolls and a blue T-shirt emblazoned with the name of some band she hadn't heard of. She'd known him since nursery.

Bea came back. 'Yes. I'll be there in half an hour.'

Agnes turned to the telephone. 'Super. See you then. Over and out.'

'Over and out.'

Agnes replaced the receiver and pushed the door of the telephone box open. It had a tendency to fight back and you had to jump out before it bit your arm off. There was a problem with the springs on the hinges, everyone said. Not that anyone ever did anything about it, but still. The door snapped shut behind her and Agnes wandered over to the front of the Pheasant.

Thomas, bin in hand, was emptying ashtrays into it.

'All right,' he said, looking up.

'All right,' said Agnes, scratching her neck.

'Up to anything nice?'

He reached for another ashtray and tipped it into the bin.

'Might be going away tomorrow,' said Agnes. 'If I play my cards right.'

'Somewhere good?'

He put the bin down and flicked at a lump of chewing gum stuck on the edge of a glass.

'Europe,' said Agnes, with a nod.

'Blimey,' said Thomas.

Agnes watched him as he picked up a packet of peanuts from the window ledge. He peered into it.

'There's still peanuts in here,' he said, his voice rising, as if he'd found gold. He held it out towards her. 'Do you want some?'

Agnes shook her head.

He emptied the contents of the packet into the palm of his hand and threw them into his mouth. 'Starving,' he said, mouth full. 'How long you away for?'

'Month. If I'm going.'

'Blimey.'

He stopped and looked at her. She was wearing a bottle-green tracksuit with two yellow stripes up the sides. He frowned. 'Isn't that your old school PE kit?'

Agnes looked him straight in the eye. 'Yes,' she replied. She ought to be feeling embarrassed right now, she thought, but she didn't. Still, it was only Thomas. He didn't count.

'Right, then. Well.' He cast an eye around. 'All done. See you about.'

'Yeah, see you about.'

He pushed open the door into the public bar with his shoulder. 'Have a nice time in Europe,' he said and with that he was gone.

Agnes turned, stuck her bottom lip out and stuffed her hands into the pockets of her tracksuit bottoms. She had half an hour to kill before Bea arrived. The village, post lunch, always went into a semi-coma and the likelihood of her bumping into anyone else she knew was slim. Probably for the best.

She kicked her leg out and looked down at herself. Other girls her age would be dressed to the nines, spending hours on their make-up, dainty toes peeping out from tiny heels, hair flicked and sprayed and smelling of whatever the latest perfume in vogue might be. Agnes looked like something out of a Soviet boot camp.

She wasn't sure how this had happened. Her mother and sister were constantly and effortlessly glamorous. Perhaps it was the age gap? Eleanor, five years older, had left home by the time Agnes started thinking about what she looked like. Agnes wasn't sure she cared. The life had been knocked out of her, back then, when it happened. It was the shame of everything that had flowed from it. Eleanor's words rang in her ears.

*No, you gave up.*

She could remember the moment, quite precisely: staring down at her A-level paper, pen in one hand, forehead in the other. She was so tired, the illness had given her that, but she could have chosen, in that moment, to fight it, to claw her future back, yet she hadn't. She had a hazy recollection of putting the lid back on her pen. It was so easy to lay her head into the crook of her arm and close her eyes. If she didn't look at it, it would all go away.

She'd have to make an effort for this evening. The thought felt like a dead weight.

Deflated, she wandered back to the house and, lifting the latch of the front gate, glanced across the garden to see her mother in a deckchair. She wasn't reading or knitting or drinking a cup of tea. She was sitting, staring off over the horizon, lost in a million and one thoughts that Agnes would never be privy to.

The anger she felt towards her still felt raw and, rather than go over and see if anything might be wrong, Agnes crept sideways towards the garage and let herself into the house. She could hear the television in the back sitting room gently rumbling. William would be watching *World of Sport*. For some inexplicable reason, he was inordinately fond of the wrestling. It was quite out of character.

Agnes paused as she passed the doorway. William had his back to her and she could see his large brown shoes, polished to within an inch of their lives. His elbow was resting on the arm of his chair, a pipe sitting in an ashtray on the table next to it.

She turned away and walked up the stairs to her bedroom, opened the door and threw herself, somewhat dramatically, onto her bed. She must never be like her parents. She had to change her life, she thought, and nothing would stop her doing it.

## 11

It was always best, when plotting, to do it just behind the tomato plants.

Bea was wearing a striped velour short-sleeved top with matching trousers that stopped mid-ankle. She was in her usual brown sandals. Her socks were also striped but they didn't match the outfit.

Agnes looked at her. Bea's boldness was astounding.

'If you were spinning round, Bea,' she said, 'you could hypnotise someone.'

'Don't,' said Bea, shaking her head. 'Birthday gift from my aunt.'

'Now listen. My mother went soft for a moment two days ago but there has been no movement since. My father is in there ...' Agnes pointed towards the house. 'He is watching the wrestling and you have to go into the sitting room and persuade him, once and for all, that I can come away with you. If you don't, Bea, then all is lost.'

'That's probably a bit overdramatic.' Bea put her hands on her hips.

Agnes gripped her friend by the shoulder. 'I cannot be abandoned. I cannot.'

She had to get away, she had to forge a new path. The idea of spending the rest of the summer without the only person with whom she felt entirely comfortable was unthinkable.

Bea nodded. 'All right,' she said. 'I shall spare nothing.' She jutted her chin out. 'Come on,' she said, pushing her way through the tomato plants. 'Let's get this done.'

Agnes trotted after her. 'What are you going to say?'

'I don't know yet.'

Agnes felt a surge of anxiety. Her parents were not happy-go-lucky relaxed people. They were uptight, suspicious, the exact opposite of spontaneous.

Agnes lacked the skills to kick-start her own life. Bea, on the other hand, despite all her oddities, was able to tap into a seam of bravery that was entirely unexpected. She would have to make it happen for her. Bea stomped her feet on the red clay tiles of the terrace and gestured with her finger for Agnes to do the same.

Florence was in the kitchen rolling puff pastry she had made the day before. She was making cheese swirls for Eleanor's exhibition. A row of Tupperware containers were spread out across the counter, some of them filled: mushroom vol-au-vents, coronation chicken and crackers, pigs in blankets and the ubiquitous party essential, cheese and pineapple with a little silverskin onion on cocktail sticks. As she heard the garden door open, she looked up to see Bea, a vision in heavy stripes, striding past.

Bea raised a hand as she walked by, 'What ho, Mrs L!' and disappeared off in the direction of the small sitting room.

Agnes lagged behind.

'Agnes,' said Florence, as her daughter caught her eye. 'In here, please.'

Agnes watched Bea vanish into the room ahead of her and slipped sideways into the kitchen. She stood and leaned, back against the wall, hands tucked behind her. She looked ill at ease, furtive.

'What are you up to?' Florence turned back to her pastry.

'Nothing,' Agnes said. She gave a small shrug. She was clearly lying.

'Really?' said Florence, placing her rolling pin to one side. She picked up a large lump of cheese and began to grate it across the length of the pastry

'Bea wanted to speak to Daddy,' said Agnes.

Florence let the moment hang. If she said nothing, more would come.

'About Europe.'

The cheese formed small mounds.

'Are you sure you want to go, Agnes?'

'Yes, I do.' Agnes's voice was quiet but certain.

Florence looked at her again. 'Isn't that your school PE kit?' She frowned.

Agnes tugged at the bottom of the tracksuit top. 'I thought it would be good for knocking about in. I was out in the vegetable patch. The tomatoes.' She had nothing further to add to that. She thumbed off beyond the walls.

'Did you bring some in?'

Agnes chewed at her lip. 'No. They didn't look ready.'

Florence scattered the grated cheese with her fingers. 'You're going to change before tonight, aren't you, Agnes?'

Agnes nodded. She thought about telling her mother she didn't particularly want to go. It would be another evening worshipping her perfect elder sister. She felt the usual pang of guilt. Eleanor's exhibition was a big deal; it would matter to her that they were all there. All the same, Agnes knew she would stand in a corner, legs crossed awkwardly. She'd hold a catalogue in both hands. Nobody would talk to her.

Florence smoothed out the mounds of cheese then rolled the pastry over on itself to the other side. She took a knife and cut circles from the end, laying each one flat on a baking tray.

'What are you making?'

'Cheesy swirls,' said Florence, not looking up.

'Did Eleanor ask you to?'

'No. But it's a nice thing to do, isn't it?'

Agnes watched Florence as she slipped her hands into a pair of floral oven gloves. It was such a familiar sight. She wasn't sure her mother would know what to do with herself if she wasn't playing out constant gestures of gratitude. Agnes felt a small flush of shame. She took her mother for granted but it was worse than that: she didn't take her seriously; but then, nobody took *her* seriously either. The thought was chilling.

Florence slid the baking tray into the already warmed oven.

'Agnes!' William called from the other room.

Agnes pushed herself away from the wall and walked out.

Bea was sitting on the sofa, next to him. She had her feet up on a leather footstool and they were both laughing. Agnes stood between them and instantly felt left out. Her relationship with her father was at arm's length. They rattled around the same house, never bothering to get to know each other, just like her mother.

'He's wearing a cape, Mr L! Look at him!' Bea was pointing towards the television.

A rather portly and serious man, in a dark leotard and tights, hand on hips, was swishing about the wrestling ring in a long black cape. He had a voluminous moustache and had the aura of a villain in a children's book. In the opposite corner was a rather weedy chap in a lighter leotard with oversized pants. They looked like the worst superheroes ever.

Agnes stared down at her father. He had tears in his eyes, he was laughing so hard. How did Bea do this? He never laughed.

'Look at him bouncing about!' Bea said, in hysterics. 'He's probably an accountant Monday to Friday. Do you think he wears it to the office?'

William gave another loud guffaw.

Bea glanced up towards Agnes. 'Oh hello,' she said, as casual as you please. 'I've squared it with your pa. Mr L thinks it's a super idea if you're my chaperone for the next four weeks.'

'Really?' Agnes's eyes widened and she turned to look at her father.

William drew a handkerchief from his pocket, removed his glasses and dabbed at his eyes. 'Oh dear,' he said, shaking his head. 'Oh dear, oh dear.' He cleared his throat. 'Now,' he said, pulling himself together, 'Bea's run me through the itinerary. Paris. Lausanne ...' He twirled a finger through the air and looked to Bea for help.

'Milan. Rome,' Bea said, still watching the television.

'Milan and Rome. Yes.'

'An odyssey of culture, Mr L,' Bea added, with some emphasis.

'What's going on?' Florence appeared behind them, drawn by the unfamiliar sound of enjoyment. She was wiping her hands on the bottom of her apron, her face frozen into an assimilation of fun.

Agnes knew how she felt. She didn't know how to join in either.

'I've agreed to Agnes going to Europe,' said William. He folded his legs and knitted his fingers together in his lap. He was looking at neither of them.

'But doesn't that mean she has to leave tomorrow?' Florence frowned. 'There's ironing, packing – have you even got a current passport?'

She shot a panicked look towards Agnes.

Agnes nodded. 'Yes.'

'It's fine, Mrs L,' said Bea, standing and putting a hand on Agnes's shoulder. 'We really won't need much. My brother has a couple of rucksacks. We'll be travelling super-light.' She shot Florence a toothy grin. 'Handful of T-shirts, shorts, something to swim in. We'll be fine.'

She waved her hand through the air as if nothing could be more breezy.

'Are you sure this is sensible, William?' Florence's voice was low and anxious.

William picked up his pipe and a matchbox. 'It'll be good for her,' he said, then struck a light.

Agnes watched her mother like a hawk. She could see a cold, unwelcome surge of something unpleasant running through her. She knew it for what it was: her younger daughter didn't need her any more. That's what she was worried about. Agnes was escaping. The sense of relief was overwhelming.

# 12

The back of the Morris Minor was rammed with Tupperware boxes. Agnes was squashed up against them under strict instructions to stop them sliding. Under no circumstances must the canapés be ruined. William had been dropped off at Eleanor's house in Barnes where he had been dispatched to the sitting room with a crossword. He would come on later with Charlie.

The gallery was in Fitzrovia, tucked down a side street next to a Greek restaurant, and as Florence parked, Agnes glanced in to see Eleanor, her back turned, pointing up towards a blank wall. Agnes had made something of an effort. She had found an old yellow minidress and a pair of white slingbacks. The dress wasn't quite the loose fit it had once been but if she stood ramrod tall and sucked her stomach in she could just about pull it off. Besides, she didn't have anything else that was smart enough. It would have to do.

Her mother had stared at her, with barely concealed horror, and said, 'Is that still in fashion?' which had rather withered Agnes's enthusiasm.

'Now then,' said Florence, turning off the ignition, 'pass the Tupperware up to me, you can bring the cake boxes in.' She got out of the car and did a little wave into the gallery.

Eleanor came to the door. 'What's all that?' she said. She didn't look entirely pleased.

Agnes handed two of the large Tupperware containers to her mother standing on the pavement.

'Canapés,' said Florence with brisk efficiency. 'Come on, Agnes,' she chivvied. 'Chop-chop.'

Agnes shuffled out from the car, her minidress riding up her thighs as she pressed herself across the leather seats. She needed to tug the bottom down but her hands were full. She stepped onto the kerb, painfully aware that her underwear was probably on show.

'The gallery has done the catering,' Eleanor said, bewildered. 'I wish you'd asked. I'm not sure there's going to be anywhere to put them.'

Florence ignored her. 'Agnes and I can walk round with them. I've brought platters.'

'But ... we don't need them.' Eleanor shot Agnes a look. 'What are you wearing?'

Florence glanced at the bottom of Agnes's dress. 'For good ness' sake, Agnes, if it's not for sale, don't put a ticket on it. Cover yourself up.'

Agnes felt her stomach plummeting. Her dress was clinging in all the wrong places. No amount of tugging was going to fix that Eleanor was wearing an ivory crêpe shirtdress with black banding and a pleated skirt. Florence was in a daisy-print silk dress with a white sectioned collar. Agnes wanted to disappear. Tomorrow, she could. She clung to the thought like it was the last lifeboat on the *Titanic*. 'One more night,' she mumbled and in she went.


'Do you think your mother is a bit drunk?' Charlie was standing with Agnes who had pressed herself into a far corner of the gallery. The place was packed.

William was staring up at a large painting of a hare on the far wall. He had a glass of wine in hand. Agnes hadn't seen him talk to anyone. He had an amazing capacity for getting through entire evenings without having a single conversation. Florence, bloody-minded as ever, was forcing vol-au-vents on anyone who came near.

The whole thing was making Agnes cringe.

'I wish she was,' she replied, pressing herself against the wall. 'Honestly. She's like something out of a Greek tragedy. One of those characters that won't listen and ends up suffering a fate worse than death. Hoisted by hubris. Or whatever it is.'

'I find it rather endearing,' said Charlie.

Agnes was disbelieving. 'You can't be serious, Charlie? She's like a machine and the problem with machines is they're entirely lacking in self-awareness.'

'You'll miss her when she's gone,' said Charlie, sipping at his glass of red wine.

Agnes looked out into the press of people gathered to admire her sister. Eleanor was off somewhere, howling with laughter and enjoying being surrounded by important people who thought her every kind of wonderful. Agnes couldn't even begin to imagine what that must feel like. Charlie was only talking to her because he had to.

Eleanor waved at Charlie across the room for him to come. 'That's me,' he said and hopped to it.

Agnes stood and tugged down again at the bottom of her dress. 'This will be over soon,' she said to herself, as she looked out across the crowd. 'And then I can start living.'

Eleanor was smiling and gesturing to two gallery staff who were holding birthday cakes. A small cheer went up and a rather languid version of 'Happy Birthday' began to be sung.

William was still standing, staring at the hare.

Florence carried a tinfoil platter of cocktail sausages through a tangle of strangers and waved towards Marjory, who had just arrived.

Her mother looked manic, Agnes thought. It was terrifying.

# SUNDAY

## 13

Florence stared down at the egg quietly frying in the knob of butter she'd added to the pan. The edges would brown just how William liked them. Beside it were two rashers of bacon, good smoked back with the rind still on.

She had cooked this breakfast more times than she could count but all the while the ground beneath her feet was shifting. Eleanor had left long ago; Agnes was about to disappear for a month. For the first time since the children came, Florence would be alone in the house with her husband and it filled her with dread.

William wandered into the kitchen and picked up the *Sunday Times* that was folded ready for him. He was wearing what he always wore on a Sunday: a pair of navy corduroy trousers, beige socks, suede brogues, a cream shirt with brown checks and a pale blue tank top. He had shaved and the faint smell of Imperial Leather soap wafted across the room. He was as precise and tidy as always.

He pulled out a chair, sat down, opened the paper and disappeared behind it. He hadn't said a word.

Florence slid the perfectly fried egg onto a plate with a blue rim. She forked the bacon next to it and pressed two slices of bread into the toaster. She pulled down a mug, a large green thing that had come from a county fair a lifetime ago, and poured tea into it from a pot that had sat stewing for precisely five minutes. She added a splash of milk and stirred it with a teaspoon.

Behind her, the toast popped upwards. She walked back, took out the slices and buttered them. Cutting the toast in half, on the diagonal, she stacked the slices to the side of the bacon. She carried the plate to William and slipped it in front of him without interfering with his reading of the paper. She walked to the chair opposite and sat down. She had no hot drink and no breakfast. William had still not said a word.

'Morning,' said Agnes, bustling into the kitchen.

Florence gestured towards the toaster. 'I've just cut some bread. Help yourself.'

'Do you want me to put one in for you?' Agnes glanced down towards Florence's empty plate.

'No,' said Florence, her voice flat and lifeless. 'I had some tea earlier. I'm not feeling that hungry.' Her eyes were boring into the back of William's newspaper. She blinked and looked up towards Agnes. 'What time do we need to leave?'

'Bea's mother's picking me up in half an hour.' Agnes dropped two slices of bread into the toaster.

Florence frowned. 'I thought I was taking you? To wave you off?'

'You can wave me off here,' said Agnes, back to her mother. 'No point in everyone coming to the station, is there?'

'But I wanted to drive you, Agnes. I'm not going to see you for a month.' Florence's wounded look went unseen by everyone in the room.

Agnes reached for a mug and began to pour herself a tea. 'It's fine. She's going into London anyway so it makes sense.' She splashed in some milk and took a gulp.

Florence sat, gripping her hands together in her lap.

'It's fine, Florence,' said William, folding his paper down onto the table. 'Don't fuss. She's got a lift. And she's right. There's no need for you to travel up to London when you don't need to.'

He picked up his fork and burst the skin on the top of his egg. The yolk ran sideways towards the bacon. Taking a piece of toast, he dipped it in.

Florence glanced towards him. He didn't have a care in the world. Nobody gave two hoots about what she thought or felt. She wanted to scream at him, she wanted to yell the house down, but she knew she would do neither of these things. She would say nothing and hold her pain in, like a woman being drowned.

She looked back to Agnes. 'Do you need help packing?' she said, her voice weighed down with defeat.

'No,' said Agnes, reaching for the toast, 'all done.'

Florence wandered over to the counter by the stove. She felt disorientated, like a flag that had come loose.

'Does anyone want anything?' The words fell from her mouth unformed, as if she was speaking in her sleep.

Nobody answered.

# 14

'I went to France for a week once.' Bea's mother was smiling up from the car, window down. 'I got frightful sunburn. And nothing ever seemed to be properly cooked. Most peculiar place.'

Florence was standing at the garden gate, arms folded. She was trying to muster interest but her mind was in turmoil. William was standing off to her left, casting a quiet eye over a row of hollyhocks threatening to bloom. A burst of raucous laughter sounded behind her and, shielding her eyes as she looked back into the sun, she could see Agnes with Bea, running out from the front door carrying a large rucksack between them.

'Here they are,' said Bea's mother. 'So lovely to have an adventure to look forward to, isn't it?'

Florence felt her innards tighten. She watched as her daughter bundled towards her, broad smile, happier than she had looked in as long as Florence could remember.

'Have you got everything?' It was impossible not to sound anxious.

'Yes,' said Agnes, pushing past her.

'Stick it in the boot,' said Bea's mother, with a smile. 'Plenty of room.'

'Here,' said Bea, taking the full weight of the rucksack, 'I'll do it.'

Agnes let the bag slip from her hands and watched Bea grapple it into the rear of the car. She couldn't believe this was actually happening.

'You'll write, won't you?' Florence reached her hand out towards Agnes's forearm but she couldn't quite reach.

Agnes nodded and tried not to smirk. The letters were already written. They were sitting inside the blue canvas bag slung across her chest. 'I'll send you one a week,' she said. 'If I can work out the letter boxes.'

Bea's mother gave a small hoot. 'Harder than you think,' she said, squinting into the sun. 'I once put a postcard in a bin. Had no idea.'

'All in,' said Bea, slamming down the boot door.

'Super,' said her mother, reaching for the ignition key. 'All aboard! Say your goodbyes, Agnes, and let's get you on your way.'

Agnes turned towards her mother, ready for the usual peck and off, but was surprised to find herself held in a deep grip. She could feel every contour of her mother's body: the slender back, the breasts held in a corset, the way her hips were far smaller than her own. She was aware of her own stomach, protruding into the top of her shorts, pressing doughy into the flatness of Florence's. Even with this last act of maternal concern, her mother was managing to make her self-conscious.

Agnes pulled herself away. 'I'll see you in a month,' she said, looking off. She tried not to sound too ecstatic.

'Please be careful,' said Florence but Agnes avoided her gaze.

Florence could feel it. The slipping away for good had begun. She felt guarded, bruised, desperate. Agnes was itching to get away. A dark pain grumbled in her chest. What was she, without her children? What would she do alone in the house with a man who barely noticed her?

Agnes looked over her shoulder towards her father. He was standing, one hand in his trouser pocket, the other drifting somewhere behind his back. She raised a hand in his direction. 'Bye then,' she said.

She considered whether she should walk to him and hug him but the idea felt so alien and peculiar she dismissed the thought instantly. He raised his hand and waved goodbye. It took a moment, but Agnes realised he was waving at Bea. She turned and got into the car. Bea was in the front, leaning across her mother and waving enthusiastically at Agnes's parents.

'Bye, Mr and Mrs L!' she was shouting.

They waved back at her.

'Don't be wearing any leotards while I'm gone, Mr L!'

Agnes looked up towards her father and watched as his face broke into an easy smile. 'I won't!' he called back.

Look at me, she thought. But he didn't.

'Right then. All set?' Bea's mother gave a short, functional nod. 'I'll phone you later,' she added, shouting up towards Florence. 'Let you know they got off all right.'

Florence said nothing. She was afraid she was going to cry.

'Goodbye!' Bea was still yelling. 'Goodbye!'

Agnes sat, her back pressed into her seat. She watched her father. He was already turning away. He would barely notice her gone. As they pulled off, Agnes glanced back towards her mother. She looked horrified.

Florence stood, watching until the car had entirely disappeared. Her arms hung by her side. She felt hollowed out and nervous. William had his back to her, inspecting a line of roses. He had already shifted seamlessly into the next phase. Did nothing bother him? Nothing at all?

And just like that, all purpose in Florence's life vanished in an instant.

## 15

They stood, hearts pounding, eyes wide, as the small blue Ford Anglia chugged away from them. As it stopped at the junction at the bottom of the road, Bea's hand floated towards Agnes's arm and gripped it. Agnes had stopped breathing. The car, indicating left, pulled out and disappeared.

A noise squealed out from Bea.

Agnes exhaled. 'Oh my God. We've done it. Beatrice Morgan. We've actually done it.'

'Not quite, Agnes Ledbury,' said Bea. 'We've got to hand over the goods to the Terrible Trio. *Then* we've done it. Come on. We're meeting them at the coffee stall on Platform 5.'

'And we're giving the letters to Lois?' Agnes picked up the pace and followed Bea into the station. 'Not Brenda.'

'Brenda gets nothing,' said Bea, striding away. 'And then, Agnes Ledbury, our summer begins. We shall find gentlemen callers, we shall have sexual intercourse often, or, at the very least, as many times as we have pills for. We shall become liberated and independent. But we absolutely must not get pregnant.'

'Yes, we really don't want to get pregnant.'

'We are on a collision course with destiny.' Bea held up a finger. 'Because you and I are going to sack off the lives our parents have handed to us. There is a shining future out there and we are going to march into it.'

'To hell with secretarial!' Agnes thrust her fist into the air.

'To hell with it!'

It felt amazing. Agnes felt unburdened for the first time since she'd fallen ill. Everything that followed was now down to her. She had her best friend, enough pants to get her through any given week, and a heart full of hope. Opportunities were here for the taking. She just needed to be brave enough to seize them. Agnes was free.

'We set sail for new oceans,' said Bea, picking up her rucksack. 'Anchors aweigh. Because if not now, when?'

It was the single best chance Agnes was ever going to have. Best not blow it.

# WEEK TWO

# MONDAY

# 16

Their home for the next four weeks was in Hampstead, tucked into a tight corner of a leafy cul-de-sac off Frognal. It was an odd, ramshackle affair, at odds with the impressive Georgian town houses that towered over it. It looked like an afterthought, tossed in at the last minute: vaguely unloved, not quite ugly. It felt perfect.

The house was owned by the parents of Bea's brother's friend. His name, it turned out, was Jacob and his sister, Sasha – a vision of limpid loveliness – had been entrusted with living in it for no other reason than to deter squatters.

Sasha had welcomed them in with an air of puzzled forgetfulness but she was easily persuaded and here they were. There was no doubting she was a model: porcelain skin and eyes the colour of forget-me-nots. She had an ethereal, untethered quality like a floating dandelion seed. She was beautiful but insubstantial, delicate, and had greeted them with a moment of initial shock: Agnes wasn't sure whether it was because they'd actually turned up or because of what they looked like. She suspected it was more the latter.

Agnes and Bea would be sharing a box room at the back of the house. The wallpaper, speckled with daisies, promised eternal spring but instead the room delivered something rather dank and damp. There was no proper furniture, for a start. Agnes was rather used to the standard bed and chest of drawers, a wardrobe if you're lucky. All that stared up at them was a dilapidated double mattress squashed into a corner on the floor.

It was 'all the rage', according to Sasha. 'Very Swedish,' she had told them. 'You know, another way of living.' She had said it as if this was patently obvious but Agnes had wondered how the mattress with no bed frame made her feel. Abandoned was one word that came to mind. In danger was another.

There were two other housemates: Kiki who worked as a bunny girl and Camilla who was glossed over quickly. Bea and Agnes weren't sure what she did but, as for the bunny girl, it had elicited audible gasps from the pair of them. Bunny girls were famous, weren't they? Or was it infamous? They were yet to meet them. Kiki worked late and crept back during the small hours. As for Camilla, she was nowhere to be found.

'She's probably being furious somewhere,' Sasha had muttered, but as to what Camilla might be being furious about, they were none the wiser.

Sasha had left them to it. She was travelling to Cambridge for a photo shoot and would be gone for a few days and, after handing them a key on a string, she had slipped away.

It had been odd, that first afternoon, on their own in the flat. For the first time in their lives, they didn't have to answer to anyone. All the same, they had been nervous, tiptoeing around the communal areas, whispering so as not to disturb the spiders and not daring to peer into the other bedrooms.

They had dumped their bags and walked into Hampstead and found a store that sold olives. It felt like another world. They bought a pot and a large slice of a French cheese that oozed onto their fingers. An off-licence provided a rather good bottle of red wine and they had sat, cross-legged, grinning at each other as they discussed how their life was about to change forever. They couldn't believe their luck.

Despite Agnes's reticence, it felt magical, grown up: a flat in London with women, only a little older than they were, who had jobs and income and purpose. There were no parents breathing down their necks, no norms, no strangled expectations, no chairs to tuck under the table, no overcooked vegetables to stare at, no sauce boats to avoid.

A noise was coming from the kitchen.

Agnes, forehead squashed up against the wall, opened one eye. She hadn't slept well. She was too excited, too rattled, too astonished to settle. Bea, on the other hand, had passed out the moment her head hit the pillow. Agnes pushed herself up onto one elbow and glanced over towards her friend – lying on her back, mouth agape, she looked like a sprung trap.

'Bea,' Agnes said softly.

Off in the kitchen, she could hear a kettle boiling and the gentle rattle of crockery.

'Bea,' she said again, giving her a poke in the shoulder.

'What?' Bea's eyes were closed, her voice a thick mumble.

'Someone's in the kitchen,' said Agnes.

'I was having an amazing dream,' said Bea, her eyes still shut. 'Who's in the kitchen?' She opened her eyes.

'I don't know.'

'I slept like a log,' said Bea, leaning upwards. She gave the mattress a pat. 'Well done the Swedes. We should go and say hello.'

Agnes put a hand against the wall and pushed herself up. She was wearing a pale blue nightie with a floral trim, like Doris Day in a romantic comedy. It had been a gift from her mother at Christmas. 'I didn't sleep a wink.'

'I think I could sleep anywhere,' said Bea, running a hand through her hair. 'I think I could sleep like cows. Standing up.'

'Should I get dressed?' Agnes asked, glancing over at her rucksack. 'Do people dress to go to the kitchen in London?'

'I don't think it's ...' Bea stopped to get the word right ' ... necessary?'

'I've brought an avocado,' Agnes added, reaching into the side pocket of her bag. 'Should I take that out, now? I thought it might help.'

Bea squinted. 'How might an avocado help?'

Agnes stared down at it but seemed to lose confidence.

'You're right. I'll leave it here for now. We can save it for an emergency.'

A small smile drifted across Bea's lips. 'If I didn't know you very well indeed, which I do, Agnes Ledbury,' she said, 'I'd think you were consumed with nerves.'

'I'm not, Beatrice Morgan,' said Agnes, pressing herself against the wall.

Bea said nothing.

'All right,' said Agnes, shifting, 'I am a bit. But if we go together, I won't be.'

There had been such a change in her these past few years. She had been such an ebullient child but now she was so wary, so wracked with shyness, she no longer trusted herself to adequately read new people.

'Come on then,' said Bea, throwing the blankets off herself and picking up her glasses. 'Let's go say hello.'

Bea pushed herself up. She was wearing a set of pale grey long johns and a matching thermal vest and looked as if she might be about to mount a pommel.

'Sasha's warned them we're here, yes? She will have done? Won't she?' Agnes sounded anxious.

'Of course. Hello!' Bea opened their door and called down the hall. 'Hello!'

Agnes followed her out, holding on to the back of Bea's long johns.

A puzzled face appeared from the kitchen doorway. A woman with tousled brown hair and piercing green eyes looked out at them. She was brandishing a knife. 'Who are you?' she asked. Her voice was steady but suspicious.

'I'm Beatrice Morgan,' said Bea, pointing into her own chest. 'My brother is a friend of Sasha's brother. We're staying here for a while.'

Agnes peered over Bea's shoulder. 'And I'm Agnes Ledbury.'

The woman lowered the knife and stepped into the hallway. She was in a pair of tiny red pants and a yellow T-shirt that ended just above her belly button. She was cool, sexy. She looked them up and down. 'Is it school holidays?'

Agnes felt her cheeks flush.

'We've just finished secretarial,' said Bea, ignoring the unintended slight.

'Oh.' She reached back into the kitchen and put the knife on the counter. 'I'm Kiki, I've got the kettle on. Do you want some tea? Coffee? I've got instant?'

'Coffee,' said Bea, eyes widening. 'Yes please. I've never had a cup of coffee.'

Kiki frowned. 'Are you being serious?'

'Entirely.'

Kiki looked towards Agnes. 'Have you had a cup of coffee?'

'Yes. My sister's an artist.'

Kiki let out a small, bemused laugh. 'You two are quite the pair.'

'Are you the bunny girl?' Bea sounded thrilled.

Kiki leaned against the doorframe and let her right leg sweep out to the side. 'I am, yes.'

'Gosh.'

'Where do you stand on all that?' Kiki watched them carefully.

'What do you mean?' asked Bea.

'You know,' said Kiki, folding her arms. 'What we wear, what we do. Some women get frightfully cross about it. Camilla, for starters.'

'Do they?' said Bea.

'Yes, they do.'

'I don't think I'm cross,' said Bea, with a shrug. She turned and looked at Agnes. 'Are you?'

Agnes shook her head.

'Good.' Kiki unfurled herself like a silk scarf. 'So do you want tea or coffee?'

'Coffee,' they both said, together.

Beyond them, at the end of the hallway, there was the sound of a key in the front door. Kiki glanced over her shoulder, pulled a face and disappeared into the kitchen.

Another young woman came in and threw a bag down onto the floor. She had messy blonde hair, shoulder-length. She was skinny and wore a tight white T-shirt. It had a blue clenched fist emblazoned across it and was tucked into faded denim bell-bottoms. A pair of blue and white plimsolls peeped out from under them. She stopped and looked at them.

'Who the fuck are you and what the fuck are you wearing?'

Bea and Agnes looked down at themselves.

'We're staying here for a bit. We're in there.' Bea pointed off towards the very spare room. 'We just got up.'

'They're friends of Sasha's brother,' shouted Kiki, from the kitchen.

'Actually, my brother is friends with Sasha's brother,' corrected Bea, pushing her glasses up her nose. 'We've come to London to embrace the modern age. But we're mostly here for sex.'

Camilla laughed. 'What an introduction.'

'And other things,' added Agnes. This was painful.

'Three cheers for the sexual revolution!' yelled Kiki. 'Freedom!'

'Freedom for who?' Camilla yelled back. 'Men can't believe their luck. Sex, yes; I'd rather have political power, thanks.'

'She's off,' said Kiki, walking out from the kitchen with two mugs. 'I don't need political power, thank you. I'm perfectly happy with a pair of tights that don't ladder, port and lemon, a ride home and that'll do. Here. Coffees. She's never had a cup of coffee, Camilla.' She nodded towards Bea as she handed her the mug.

Bea gave it a small sniff, then a tiny sip. She pulled a face. 'It's very bitter.'

'Add some sugar. There's a bag by the kettle.'

Agnes mustered a smile as Bea walked away but both Camilla and Kiki were staring at her.

'I've got an avocado.'

Neither of them said anything.

Bea was much better at this. She could slip into any situation, make her entrance and leave. Agnes, on the other hand, could not, not any more. Suddenly, Agnes was painfully aware of what she was wearing. 'I'll just go and put something on,' she mumbled, backing away.

She felt awkward, vulnerable, exposed. Leopards can't change their spots, can they?

# 17

'Is that for me? Are you sure?'

Florence watched as a brand-new washing machine was unloaded from the back of a van on the driveway.

'Yes,' said Eleanor, smiling. 'Freezer too. You'll need to tell them where you want them. Freezer can go in the garage.'

'A freezer as well. Goodness.' Florence's hand went to her chest as if protecting herself from a sudden onslaught of modernity.

'You'll love it. You can batch-cook things. Pop them in the freezer. Take a meal out when you fancy, slam it in the oven. Done. Easy.'

Florence tried to muster a smile. She was naturally wary of new things.

'Where do you want this?'

A man in a beige overall was standing, washing machine leaning against the back of a lifting trolley. He had a black cap on, stub of a pencil behind one ear, and had the air of someone who might make a fleeting appearance in a *Carry On* film.

'Do I want it in the pantry?' Florence looked momentarily confused.

'You need a water source, missus,' the man said. 'And a drain.'

'Right.'

'The pantry's perfect. Where else would you put it? In the kitchen?' Eleanor was trying to encourage her.

Florence cast quick glances between her daughter and the delivery man. They were both staring at her waiting for her to make a decision. She hesitated. 'How much did this all cost? I can't let you give me this ... it's too much ...' She instinctively turned towards the house. 'I should get my chequebook ...'

'No, Mum,' said Eleanor, pulling her back. 'It's fine. I wanted to get them for you. They'll make everything easier. Give you more free time.'

Florence turned and paused. 'Free time for what?' She frowned a little, unsure of what was being suggested.

Eleanor let out a small laugh. 'For fun, Mum. There's plenty more things you can be doing than hand-washing all the sheets. We're not in the Dark Ages any more. Machines can do the chores.'

'It's not whether machines can do the chores, Eleanor, it's whether they can do them properly.'

'Sheets come up lovely in this,' offered the delivery man. 'Done in a quarter of the time, too.'

Florence wasn't sure why she felt so anxious. These were amazing gifts. Anyone would be rightly glad of them. 'All right,' she said, remembering she needed to be gracious. She placed her hand on Eleanor's forearm. 'Thank you. It's outrageously kind. I'm not sure I deserve it.'

'My pleasure. Now, come on. You need to tell him where you want the washing machine.'

'Put it in the pantry.' Florence gave a decisive nod then gestured to the delivery man. 'Follow me, I'll show you the way.'

Eleanor stepped forward. 'It's all right,' she said, walking towards the open door. 'I'll do it. Will you manage to get it up the steps?' she called across to him.

'Not a problem, missus,' he said.

Florence stood, her shoes pressed down into the gravel beneath her. She looked back towards the squat white rectangle still sitting on the tail of the delivery van. She didn't trust it. Not one bit.

# 18

The egg sandwiches were particularly fine. Agnes had made them with just the right amount of salt and a pinch of white pepper. They had been wrapped in wax paper and everything about them was familiar and comforting.

The two of them were sitting on a checkered rug, legs crossed, looking out from a high edge of Hampstead Heath over some spectacular views of the city. The weather was changeable.

Sitting there, Agnes felt overwhelmed. This was a chance to change, to take a different path, but staring out at the vastness of the city, it presented such endless opportunities it felt impossible to imagine she might find something just for her.

'What do you want to do, Bea?' She leaned back onto her elbows. 'Not this afternoon, I mean. For the rest of your life?'

'I'd like to be one of those fiercely impressive women who appear on the news talking about obscure scientific discoveries whilst wearing wool jackets that are ever-so-slightly too tight. The sort of person my mother narrows her eyes at and quietly disdains.'

'With thick specs?'

'Tremendously thick.'

'I can see this. Totally. You with your arms folded in front of a Petri dish while a visiting dignitary peers into it.'

'Don't sniff that, Mr Mayor.'

Agnes laughed.

'What about you?'

Agnes picked at a small blade of grass. It was almost startling to be asked. 'I don't know. I'm not sure I'm good enough at anything.' She could feel herself crumbling.

'Then you must give yourself the chance to find out.'

'Yes, it would be a start, wouldn't it?'

'We should sign up with an agency. There's plenty of them about. Make best use of our time.'

'Yes.'

'Earn a bit of money. Keep us afloat.'

Agnes didn't reply.

'You're good at egg sandwiches.' Bea picked another half out from the waxed paper and bit into it.

'It's the white pepper. Makes all the difference.'

Agnes looked out and exhaled. 'Have we done the right thing, Bea? Coming here?' A small hum of anxiety nagged at her.

'Absolutely.'

'I'm feeling a little nervous. Do you mind?' She pressed the grass between her thumbs.

'No, I don't mind a bit.'

Agnes lifted her thumbs to her mouth and blew between them but nothing happened. She let the blade fall. 'I'll never be able to do that.'

They sat for a moment, Bea quietly eating the last of her sandwich.

'I think it's quite normal to feel nervous,' said Bea, elbows on knees. 'We're on the run, Agnes: fugitives from our dull lives. No, actually, we're more than that. We're foot soldiers. Centurions in the epic battle of the sexes.'

Agnes wanted to believe her but she wasn't there yet. She needed to feel less adrift.

'Where do you think we should start looking?' Bea turned to her. 'I'd rather hoped there would be a steady queue of gents at the front door. Knock. Knock. "Hello, is Sasha in?" No. She's not. But we're quite keen to have a go. My friend has an avocado.' She gestured politely in Agnes's direction.

Agnes smiled and looked off, across the skyline. Dark clouds were threatening to their right. 'Did we bring an umbrella? By which I mean did you bring an umbrella?'

'I did not, Agnes Ledbury.' Bea followed her gaze towards the metal-grey clouds. 'Do you think it's going to rain?'

'I think it's highly likely, Beatrice Morgan, yes.'

'Shall we find a pub? Men like pubs, don't they? They're always in them.'

'They are, yes.'

'Well, then. Seize the day and all that. Hop to it. A-hunting we shall go.'

They took up the blanket and folded it into a neat square.

'Shall we go that way?' said Agnes, tucking the blanket under one arm. She pointed off towards a path behind them.

'Why not. I expect that path will be as good as any. There'll be pubs everywhere. Rammed with men.'

'Yes,' nodded Agnes. 'But you're not planning on losing your virginity in a pub, are you?'

'Obviously we shouldn't lose our virginity at the pub.'

'No, that wouldn't be right.'

'But it would be good to have a mild browse. Always try before you buy, Agnes.'

They linked arms and walked off towards the edge of the line of trees.

'Into the wood we go,' said Bea.

'Into the wood we go.'

# 19

Florence stood in front of the washing machine and stared down. By her reckoning, the bed linen had taken forty-five minutes to wash. Now all she had to do was hang it up.

It was a job that would have taken up all her day: soaking, scrubbing on a washboard with carbolic soap and a hard brush, rinsing, wringing.

Now here she was, pulling perfectly white sheets from a round drum: done in no time and with no effort from her.

Part of her, understandably, couldn't fail to be impressed.

The sheets were pristine and, rather than the usual slightly antiseptic smell that came with the soap, the washing powder (one box provided free with purchase) had a sharp freshness that was undeniable.

But Florence was afraid. She could feel it, gnawing in her gut, and she knew, even if she wasn't quite ready to admit it, that a bare truth was staring her in the face: she was becoming obsolete.

Children gone, chores to be done by machines, Florence's day-to-day purpose was being chipped away. More free time?

Yes. The problem was, Florence was at a loss as to what to do with it.

She bundled the sheets into a wicker washing basket and carried it out to the garden. She would always make sure the linen was dried and off the line before William came home.

A machine couldn't do that, she thought, and reached for the pegs.

# TUESDAY

## 20

Florence was tidying a room that didn't need to be tidied.

She was doing it because it was Tuesday and it was what she had done every Tuesday since she got married. She was an automaton, clanking through life, delivering the same thing day in, day out.

How many other women are out there, she thought, right now, tidying bedrooms that have been fled, that require nothing and are ready for someone who isn't coming back?

She gave a short but deep sigh. Catching sight of herself in Agnes's dressing-table mirror, she stopped and looked. It wasn't a passing glance to check her blouse was in place or her lipstick wasn't smudged. She was looking properly at herself for what felt like the first time. Her hair, a dulled blonde, was in the same style she had had since 1955. Her clothes were old-fashioned. She looked ten years older than she was.

'You're forty-six, Florence,' she mumbled. 'Not sixty-six.'

She glanced around the room. The bed was made, the rug was hoovered, the ornaments on the dressing table dusted. Agnes wasn't coming home for four weeks. What was she doing this for?

She thought of Marjory, of how happy she seemed, how relaxed, how sensational. She thought about the way she had looked at the waiter, the confidence of her, the sense of command. Florence felt none of these things. She was the faded wallpaper in a room that had been forgotten. Florence thought about Marjory. She hadn't stopped thinking about Marjory.

An outrageous idea flitted through her. It took hold, like a hook in the mouth. She glanced down at her wristwatch.

Ten to eleven.

Could she? Did she really dare do it?

Why not? Before she changed her mind, she trotted out onto the landing and made her way downstairs to the small sitting room. Walking briskly to the telephone, she picked up the receiver. If she didn't do this now, she told herself, she never would. No need to look up this number; she knew it off by heart.

'May's Salon,' sounded a chirpy voice.

'It's Mrs Ledbury,' said Florence, seizing the brief moment of bravery. 'Would it be possible to pop in for a cut and colour?'

'Colour, Mrs Ledbury? Got something fancy?'

'Not particularly. Can you fit me in? Straight away, if possible.' Florence let the cord slide through her fingers.

'Half an hour? How's that?'

'Perfect. I'll leave now. See you shortly.'

Florence put the receiver back down and took a deep breath.

The first step was taken. The anticipation electric.

# 21

Mr Adler's Agency for Go Getting Ladies was on the third floor of a crumbling town house in Poland Street.

Bea had spotted the advertisement in the *Evening Standard*. *Have you got what it takes?* it yelled. *Vim, verve, a little bit of street smarts. If you want an adventure every day then come see Mr Adler.*

Agnes had taken some persuading but Bea was so keen it seemed mean to deny her. She wanted to give it a go and Agnes felt obliged to acquiesce.

Mr Adler was quite something. He had a black moptop, gold-rimmed frosted glasses, sideburns the size of lamb chops and was wearing a cream three-piece suit with a red satin shirt. It was as if he couldn't quite decide whether he wanted to be John Lennon or Elvis.

He was sitting behind a large mahogany table that was covered in phones.

'My secretary is off sick,' he said, fingering towards them.

Agnes looked around the room. There was only one desk. Mr Adler clearly did not have a secretary. She felt a little uneasy. Could they trust him? What would they be expected to do?

He reached for a small lacquered box, flipped it open and picked out a cigarette. 'Want one?' he offered.

'No, thank you,' they both said.

He narrowed his eyes and sucked his top lip. 'How old are you?'

'Twenty,' they both said.

He tapped the end of the cigarette on his desk before inserting it into a rather dainty cigarette holder. He was making an indiscriminate mumbling noise as if he was totting up numbers in his head.

'Can you type?'

Agnes glanced at Bea. They had discussed this. 'No,' they lied.

'Dictation?'

'No,' Agnes lied again.

'We're after the more challenging positions, Mr Adler,' said Bea.

'The adventures,' added Agnes, half-heartedly.

'We're entirely unsuitable for secretarial.'

Mr Adler picked up a large paperweight that seemed to double as a lighter and thumbed it into life. He sipped at his cigarette holder, leaned back and held it, rather ostentatiously, between his thumb and forefinger.

'Yeah. All right,' he said. 'But you need to get a bit more with it. You look like a pair of librarians out for a walk with an owl.'

He took another sip from his cigarette.

Agnes glanced down at herself.

'We have new housemates,' Bea interjected. 'This will not be a problem.'

'Good, good.' Mr Adler nodded sagely. 'Right then. This is how it works. You phone me every morning at nine. It'll probably be me answering the phone. The secretary doesn't come in till ...' he looked at his watch ' ... ten-ish. And I'll tell you where you need to go. Client pays me. I pay you. Got it?'

'Yes, Mr Adler,' they both said.

'Right then.' He reached into his waistcoat pocket and pulled out a small black card. 'That's the number. One at the bottom. Ignore the other two. You don't need them. Mistake at the printer's.' He held it out.

Agnes took it and stared down. 'There was no hyphen in Go Getting and 'For' was misspelled 'four'.

'Got any questions?' He drummed his fingers on the desk.

Agnes shook her head.

'We'll be doing lots of interesting things, yes?' asked Bea.

'Oh yeah,' said Mr Adler, leaning back again. 'It'll be interesting, all right.'

Agnes pressed the card down into her trouser pocket. Perhaps Bea was right. Perhaps this was precisely the start they needed.

# 22

Florence gazed into the mirror held behind her head. It was a startling difference. Gone was the military-style bun; in its place a soft golden bob that curled towards her jawline. It had taken years off her.

'How's that?' said the hairdresser, a young man with a tidy beard and far-too-tight trousers.

Florence, before today, might have dismissed him as flamboyant but his attention towards her had been precise and non-judgemental. There is nothing more thrilling to a hairdresser, she had discovered, than the words 'I want you to change my look.'

His eyes had lit up and she had been ushered into the chair like a queen about to be anointed. He had undone her bun delicately and let her long dull hair float through his fingertips. He had suggested some colour to 'brighten' her up and Florence had nodded and told him to do whatever he wanted.

'You might regret that,' he had told her.

But she hadn't.

She looked at herself in the mirror. She was younger, relevant. She didn't recognise herself.

'Now you need an outfit to match!' he said, smiling.

Florence thought of her solid brown wool skirt, the American tan stockings, the sensible beige shoes. He was right. It was time for a change. She always bought her clothes from the same boutiques, where everything was in hushed don't-look-at-me tones and grey-haired shop assistants wore glasses on chains.

Not today.

She strode purposefully down Oxford High Street, catching sight of her new haircut in every window she passed. She felt buoyant, light-headed. There was a new, rather interesting clothes shop in the covered market, just off the high street. She had noticed the bright mannequins in the window a few weeks before while buying lamb cutlets from the butcher, opposite. She had thought little of the lively colours and new styles then. Now she was desperate to try them on.

A little bell tinkled as she entered, a quaint nod to a more traditional past, and the shop girl, a skinny brunette in a striped minidress, pushed herself away from the counter. Music was playing. There was a record player behind her next to the till, beside it an album cover with a close-up of a man's crotch in blue jeans.

'Hey,' said the girl, glancing quickly at Florence's get-up. 'Do you need any help?'

Florence took a deep breath. 'Actually,' she began, 'I do. I'd like to update my look.'

'Cool,' said the girl, smiling. 'Cool.' She put her hands on her hips, smiled again and crossed her legs over each other. Neither of them spoke. She was waiting, Florence realised, for instructions.

'I really don't know what to get.'

'What did you have in mind? Hippy look? Stoner? Boho? Peasant?'

Florence opened her mouth to reply but she didn't know what any of those things were. She paused. 'I'm not sure. What do you think will suit me?'

'Do you want to look at jeans? We could start there?'

Behind the shop assistant the record came to an end and, without fuss, she wandered back to the counter and turned it over. A song called 'Brown Sugar' started to play. Florence looked towards a rack of jeans. She'd never owned a pair. In fact, she'd never considered trying a pair on. They seemed very unlike her. To hell with it. 'Yes,' she said, 'I'd like to look at the jeans.'

'Cool.' The girl nodded and slithered over towards them. She looked back at Florence, making a mental assessment, then pulled out a pair from the line. 'I think you should go for boot-cut,' she said.

Florence had no idea what she was talking about. 'All right.' She glanced towards the record player. The song was thumping and exciting. 'Who is that?' she asked.

'Rolling Stones. Mick Jagger's a dream, isn't he?'

Florence didn't know who Mick Jagger was. 'Yes, he is,' she lied.

'Here,' said the girl, handing her the pair of jeans. 'Try those on. I'll bring you some smock tops too, if you like? And some knee-highs. I think you'd look good in knee-highs.'

Florence took the trousers and felt denim for the first time. Truly, she thought, this was uncharted territory.

# 23

Agnes emptied the contents of her rucksack onto the floor. Nothing was inspiring her. These new days required something more than an acceptance of the usual. They needed to be dynamic, daring. They were Mr Adler's Go Getting Ladies now and they needed to look the part.

'Librarians out for a walk with an owl. I ask you,' said Bea, shaking her head. 'He can talk. He looked like someone had stuffed a Pez dispenser into a toilet roll. I mean, I know he's in charge but there's no need to be rude.'

'Do you know, Bea,' Agnes said, holding up a rather ancient-looking jumper, 'I think I packed a little too quickly. I don't think I've got the right clothes with me at all.' She leaned back on her heels. There was something soul-destroying about knowing you look dreary. She wasn't sure what to do about it. Agnes glanced over towards Bea who was sitting on the mattress, back against the wall, cross-legged. She was rereading *The Female Eunuch*.

'Do you think Germaine wants us all to stop shaving our legs?' Bea said, pondering the page in front of her. 'I'm all for embracing my libido and being vigorous but I'm not sure I want to do it with a pair of pubic shorts.'

'I don't think we're going to impress Mr Adler or lose our virginity if we look like the Forest of Dean from the knees down, no.'

Agnes dropped the jumper to the floor and picked up a floral blouse. Everything she pulled out was making her anxious. She lifted the blouse to her nose and sniffed. 'Smells like a wet box. Honestly, Bea, all my clothes are awful. What am I going to do?' Her voice sounded thin and stretched, the way it did when she was pleading.

'Are you feeling a bit stressed?' asked Bea, looking up at her.

'Yes, I am. I *hate* clothes.' Agnes crumpled the blouse between her fingers. She resented how much it mattered. 'They make me miserable.'

'Sasha's away,' said Bea, letting the book drift downwards. 'We could have a rummage in her wardrobe. We can't turn up for whatever job Mr Adler sends us to looking like *librarians out for a walk with an owl*.' She pulled a face. She was trying to lighten the mood.

'I can't take her clothes; that wouldn't be right.'

'No, you goose, to try things on. See what suits you.' Bea's voice was soft, encouraging. 'If you like something, we can go shopping. Find something like it.'

'Do you think she'd mind?'

'Of course not. Beside, nobody's here. Nobody will mind.'

Bea threw her book down and leapt up, grabbed Agnes by the hand and dragged her towards the door.

'But what if ...' Agnes began, pulling back.

'I bet she's got *incredible* clothes,' said Bea, dragging her out into the hallway. 'Come on.'

Sasha's room was at the other end of the corridor.

'Are you sure we should be doing this?' said Agnes as Bea pushed the door open.

'Yes. Absolutely. Oh wow,' said Bea, looking in. 'This is amazing.'

Sasha's room was an Aladdin's cave of hippy jumble: lamps draped with silk scarves, Moroccan tambourines on the walls, enormous poppies made from tulle, an amp, a discarded guitar, a poster of Jimi Hendrix, one wall painted purple with a large orange and yellow CND sign. There were beads, patterned Indian saris hung above the bed, cushions scattered across the floor.

'I've never seen so many cushions,' said Bea, picking one up. 'Where's the wardrobe?'

Agnes looked round. 'There doesn't seem to be one. It's like they can't *bear* furniture ...'

Bea pointed over to the corner of the room. 'Behind the screen. Look.'

Sasha's clothes were hanging from two rails, the sort you could wheel about through empty studios. There were yellow silk shirts, a multicoloured Acrilan-knit vest, gored printed skirts, doll-print blouses, green corduroy cuff pants, violet-aqua smocked camisoles, a long black sequinned evening gown, a Gucci jacquard wool skirt with a horse and bit trim, a patio dress with daisy-patterned cotton lace and bib, a Persian-style coat dress, a startling chevron-striped evening dress with choker neckline. It was all so beautiful.

'Look at these,' said Agnes. She gently fingered a pair of peach and mahogany parquet high-rise trousers. She'd never seen anything like them.

'Here,' said Bea, who was flicking through the rail behind her. 'Try this on.' She held up a magenta shirtdress with a gold chain belt.

Agnes looked at it and shook her head. 'I can't, Bea. I really can't.'

Her hand drifted down to her protruding stomach. She felt a flush of the usual self-consciousness. It wasn't so much that she minded looking foolish in front of Bea, it was more that she didn't want to be reminded of how little she thought of herself. Agnes was no waif, she knew that, but Sasha was thin, willowy, delicate. Agnes felt neither thin nor willowy nor delicate enough to wear a magenta shirtdress with a gold chain belt. Besides, it was tiny.

'I can't.'

'Yes,' insisted Bea, 'you can.'

She thrust the garment into Agnes's chest.

'Go on, try it.'

Agnes let her fingers run across the heavy links of the belt. It felt expensive.

'How much do you think this cost?' she said, her voice muted.

'More than a car, I imagine. I think that belt's real gold. Do it, Agnes,' Bea whispered. 'Put it on.'

Agnes looked up into Bea's eyes. 'But it's not going to …'

'Stop worrying. Look at it. It's so go-getting.' Bea clapped her hands together. 'Come on. Get it on. I'll lounge on the sea of cushions. Come out when you're ready and twirl about the room.'

Agnes hung the dress back onto the rail in front of her and slipped off her shoes. She was wearing a pair of dark blue polyester trousers and a long-sleeved cream T-shirt that had seen better days. She pulled her top over her head, dropped it to the floor and unhooked the fastening on her trousers. She stared at the dress and was filled with a grim sense of dread.

'I'm not sure this is going to work,' she said, fingering the straps over her shoulders.

'Stop worrying,' said Bea, from beyond the screen.

Agnes yanked at the zip. It snagged just above her hip. 'Oh no,' she mumbled. She twisted her head and gave another tug. 'Bea,' she called out, 'the zip's stuck.' She stepped from behind the screen. She felt panicked. 'I told you it wasn't going to …' She pulled again at the zip.

There was a ripping noise. Agnes covered her mouth.

'Oh dear,' said Bea, sitting up sharply.

'More than a car, you said,' Agnes cried out. 'I knew this would happen. I should never have put it on.'

'Wait,' said Bea, taking the bottom of the dress in her hand. 'Look. It's along a seam. I can fix that. I can fix that, Agnes Ledbury! We'll be fine! I have a sewing kit!' She patted Agnes on the upper arm.

It was all very well knowing the accident could be fixed but the usual sense of failure loomed large. There was no point pretending to be something you're not. Agnes was furious with herself.

# 24

Florence couldn't stop looking. The jeans were a perfect fit, the low-cut smock top showed off her cleavage to great advantage, but it was the black suede knee-high boots that changed everything.

She had never looked like this. She had never felt like this. She was sexy and younger and different.

William would be home shortly. A beef and ale pie was slowly heating in the oven. She'd made it yesterday and put it in the freezer. Eleanor was right. It had made things easier.

Look what she had done with her free time, she thought. She had reinvented herself.

She should introduce her new self gradually: start with the haircut, then the top. William might not like her in jeans and knee-highs.

He might not like it at all.

A small, nagging doubt blew through her and, turning away from the mirror, she quietly took everything off, down to her underwear. She folded the jeans and smock top into a paper bag and hid them, together with the boots. They would not be seen in the back of her wardrobe. They would be safe.

Glancing out the window, she could see William's car approaching the driveway.

She slipped back into her brown wool skirt, pulled on her chiffon blouse and slid her feet into her sensible beige shoes.

She didn't feel like putting a dress and heels on for him this evening. Tonight was about showing off her haircut.

She took a last glance at herself, touched the new fringe with her fingers, listened for the front door opening and made her way to the stairs.

William was already in the sitting room, pouring himself a Scotch. 'Oh,' he said, as if surprised to see her. 'I thought you were in the garden.'

'No,' she said, smiling. Her fingers were clenched together. She was waiting for him to notice.

He poured a little soda into his glass and looked towards her. 'What's for supper?'

'Steak and ale pie,' she replied.

He gave a short nod, walked towards his armchair and sat down. He picked up the unfinished crossword from the occasional table next to him.

'Peas and carrots?'

'Peas and carrots.'

'Jolly good,' he said, then, taking a pen, set about solving nine down.

Florence stood, her fingers unclenching. Crestfallen, she returned to her bedroom and quietly tied her hair up, back into her old style.

# WEDNESDAY

# 25

'Hello, Mr Adler. It's Beatrice Morgan. I'm with Agnes Ledbury.'

Agnes and Bea were squashed into a telephone box. Agnes was holding a notepad and pencil. A small pile of twopence pieces sat ready if needed. Bea was holding the receiver so Agnes could hear.

'Who?'

'We came in yesterday. You told us to call you.'

There was a long silence.

Bea curled her lip. 'The librarians. *With the owl.*' She rolled her eyes.

'Right. Right.' He gave a loud, throaty cough. There was the sound of spitting, the distant rustling of small pieces of paper and some indiscriminate mumbling.

'Get yourselves to Tottenham Court Road. Outside the tube station. Ten o'clock. You're doing promo for a woman called Gill. Got it?'

'Gill who?' asked Bea.

Another pause.

'Just Gill.'

'How will we know who she is? What does she look like?'

'She'll be waiting for you.'

'How does she know what we look like?'

'She'll have boxes. Look for a woman with boxes. It's promo.' Mr Adler was sounding a little rushed.

'What sort of promo?'

'She'll deal with that. I can't spare the time. My secretary's not here.'

Agnes shook her head and mouthed, 'Such a liar.'

'And to get paid, do we ... ?'

'Not now. Call me tomorrow.'

And with that, the line went dead. Agnes frowned. There was something about Mr Adler that made her feel uneasy.

'Did you get all that?' Bea replaced the receiver and pocketed the coins.

'Are you sure we should be doing this, Bea? I don't know, it's just ...' Agnes's voice trailed off. She didn't want to appear cowardly but what if she messed up?

'We'll be fine,' said Bea, brushing the moment off. She glanced at her watch. 'We better get going.'

She leaned back and opened the door with her shoulder. It was a rather lovely day. 'I do hope we're outdoors,' she said, staring up into the blue sky. 'That would be nice, wouldn't it?'

The sun was shining. Her friend was buoyant. There was purpose afoot. Agnes should have been feeling nothing but delighted. Instead, she was wondering how to squash the bubbling sense of dread. She was going to have to snap out of this.

# 26

Florence looked down into the palm of her hand. She still hadn't got the hang of decimalisation.

'Sorry,' she said to the baker, across the counter. 'My brain's still in old money.'

She mustered a frustrated smile.

'It's a crown,' he said, his hands flat on a floury chopping board. 'Five shillings. Twenty-five pence. Think of a hundred. That's a new pound. Then count back from that. Four crowns to a pound. Twenty shillings. A hundred pence. It's not as hard as you think once you get the hang of it.'

His index finger tapped it out.

Florence gave a small sigh. 'I don't know why we had to change at all,' she said. 'Everyone knew where they were.'

'That's the thing about time, Mrs Ledbury,' he said, with a sense of some regret. 'It keeps moving forward. And so must we.'

Florence picked out two tenpence coins and a five from her purse and placed them on the counter. 'There,' she said, 'I think that's it. Silly, isn't it? I just miss the old coins.'

'Nostalgia', the baker said, scooping the coins into his doughy hands, 'is for people with nothing new to offer.' He turned and put the money into a large grey till behind him. 'Right then,' he said, turning back, 'sure that's all you're wanting?'

'Thank you, yes,' said Florence, hooking her handbag over her wrist.

He picked up the brown paper bag with the buns she'd asked for, gave the ends a rather theatrical twirl and handed it over.

'I shall have lardy cake tomorrow,' he said, leaning forward and whispering. He shot her a furtive wink.

Florence knew this faux intimacy of old. A quiet nod, a hushed tip that made her feel special. He told everyone that came in.

'I'll keep one back for you,' he whispered, tapping his nose. He leaned back, looked at her properly, and smiled. 'Hang on. You've got a new hairdo!'

He seemed delighted.

Florence smiled softly. 'Yes,' she said, her hand flitting upwards to tuck a few strands behind her ear. She hadn't tied it up that morning. William was still yet to notice.

'You look lovely, Mrs Ledbury,' said the baker, slipping his hands behind the bib of his apron. 'Mr Ledbury is a very lucky man.' He gave a toothy grin.

Florence should have felt charmed by the compliment but she didn't. Instead, it made her feel sadder than she had in years.

# 27

'WOMEN NOW,' Bea said, staring at the stickers in the paper bag she'd been handed. 'Women now what?'

Gill was on her knees on the pavement, putting handfuls of stickers into two bags. 'Women now need to be treated like equals. That's what.'

It hadn't been difficult finding her. Gill was quite the character. She had long black hair, dead straight, a centre parting that would put the Red Sea to shame and was wearing a paisley kaftan with elasticated cuffs. Her toes, rather dirty, were peeping out from a pair of scuffed sandals. She had the faint odour of a bin.

Agnes wasn't quite sure about all this. Mr Adler was starting to strike her as the sort of man who skirts perilously close to the wrong side of right. He was a chancer, perhaps a charlatan, and here they were, working for him.

'Sorry, can you explain again what you want us to do with the stickers?' Agnes looked confused.

'We're going to stick them over every pair of tits on the Underground,' said Gill. 'Here,' she added, passing a stuffed paper bag up to Agnes. 'Every poster with tits.'

Agnes frowned. 'Are we allowed to do that? I thought we were doing promo. This is vandalism, isn't it?' Her voice was no more than a mumble.

She cast a side eye to Bea who was pressing stickers into her pockets.

'No. It's not vandalism,' said Gill, still stuffing stickers, 'it's promo. It's promo for activism.' She stood and shook her hair back. 'It's liberation.'

'Yes,' said Bea, trying to convince herself. 'It's liberation. Can I ask a question?'

'Yes, you can.'

'If we put these large round pink stickers on tits . . .' she fished one out of the bag and turned it over in her hand a few times '. . . won't they look like massive nipples?' She placed one on her own breast to emphasise the point. 'Are we worried about that?' She raised her eyebrows.

'No, we're not worried about that,' said Gill, looking a little irritated. 'We're supposed to draw attention to the tits.' She didn't sound entirely sure about that.

'We've got more to offer than tits, you know.' She squinted at them both, waiting for them to agree with her. 'That's the point.'

'Absolutely,' said Bea, nodding carefully.

'Right,' said Gill, swinging a hessian bag across her chest. 'Let's get started.'

She pressed off into the gloom of the tube station. 'We'll need to buy tickets. To get through the barriers.'

'Are we sure she's paying Mr Adler?' whispered Agnes.

'I think the best thing for the rest of the day', Bea muttered from the corner of her mouth, 'is to ask as few questions as possible. Liberation! Onwards.'

Agnes stood for a moment, anxiety fluttering through her. She had never done anything remotely illegal. Her mother would be appalled. Florence's pained face loomed into her mind: the wagging finger, the hurt expression, the furrowed brow that conveyed nothing but disappointment. She took a deep breath. Pulling herself away from the unfulfilling life forced upon her, she remembered, was never going to be easy. She must forge ahead.

'Come on, then,' said Agnes, and fished out her purse to buy herself a ticket.

# 28

Florence stood, staring at the display in the window of Blackwell's bookshop on the corner of Broad Street. It was propped up against a red velvet backdrop, the female torso hanging from a rod, the startling call to change.

She felt momentarily hypnotised by it, the way the naked breasts stood pert, the extension of the ribs on the left-hand side, the way the stomach drifted down towards the crotch, but the most startling thing about it, Florence thought, were the hard handles protruding from the hips.

Women were things. They were garments to be worn. They were objects. There was no face on the cover of *The Female Eunuch*. This is what women were. Nothing.

Florence felt herself breathe, suddenly, as if she had forgotten to do so for many years.

She glanced over her shoulder, as if she didn't want to be caught in this small, illicit act. Seeing no one paying her any attention, she walked in through the large black doors.

She had no intention of buying anything else.

## 29

'Oi!' A heavyset man was pounding towards them. He looked furious.

'Ignore him,' urged Gill, slapping another sticker onto a glistening breast in a bikini. 'Don't stop.'

'You can't do that,' the man said, his voice thick and angry. 'What do you think you're playing at?'

'We shall not stop,' said Gill, defiant. 'We shall only stop when this stops.'

She pointed up towards the poster of a woman, breasts thrust forward, mouth pouting, and promptly stuck two stickers on it. The man, incandescent he'd been ignored, lunged forward and snatched the bag from her hand but Gill, fearless, grabbed it back.

'Oh no, you don't,' she said, backing away from him. 'Equality for women, now!'

She thrust an arm up into the air.

Bea nudged up against Agnes. 'Put your bag behind your back,' she whispered.

Agnes had never been involved in an altercation with anyone in authority. These were the moments, she had to tell herself, that would push her forward. She did as she was told and pressed herself into the platform wall.

'Give me that,' the man shouted, his arm grabbing for Gill's bag of stickers. 'You're damaging private property. Do you want me to call the coppers?'

Gill thrust her jaw out. 'Yes,' she said, nodding. 'I do want you to call the coppers. Call away. I'm not stopping.' She pulled a sticker out from her bag and waved it in the man's direction.

'She's completely unhinged,' whispered Bea.

Agnes stared on, adrenalin surging through her. Clenching her fists, she closed her eyes then opened them again in an effort to reset herself. 'We should go back and see Mr Adler,' she said quietly, 'to sort out the money. How long have we been at this?'

Bea glanced at her watch. 'Two hours.'

'Are we supposed to get money off her? Because if she's going to be arrested, I don't know what to do.'

'We can't. We don't want to get arrested as well. Or *do* we?' Bea had a slight glint in her eye.

'No, Bea, we don't.'

They looked back towards the unfolding drama.

'I'm warning you,' the man was shouting, wagging a finger.

Gill peeled the back from a sticker with some theatricality and stood, holding it aloft.

'Don't you dare,' the man yelled.

Gill, with the speed of a dart, slapped it onto the man's forehead.

'Oh lord,' muttered Bea. 'This isn't going to end well.'

The man, incensed, grabbed Gill by the arm. Gill looked delighted. The bag in her hand fell to the floor and stickers tumbled onto the platform. The deep rumble of a train sounded from within the tunnel.

'You're nicked!' the man shouted as a hot wind pushed its way towards them.

'Pick up the stickers!' yelled Gill to Agnes. 'Pick them up!'

The stationmaster turned and stared at them. 'Are you two part of this?'

'No,' they both said, shaking their heads. The thought of being arrested tumbled through Agnes. It was inconceivable. Their parents would be alerted and that would be the end of that. It could not happen.

Stickers flew up into the air as the train pulled into the station; Gill was being dragged away along the platform, bemused passengers stopping to watch. Above them, the stickers fluttered, a strange modern blossom. The stationmaster had hold of both Gill's arms and was trying to bend them behind her back but she managed to twist herself away. As she did, she kicked out at him and her foot landed, with some force, in the depths of his groin. He gave a sharp groan and, letting go of her, staggered backwards.

'Oh no,' said Bea.

Agnes quietly threw her bag of stickers under a nearby bench.

'Run for it!' shouted Gill, to nobody in particular, and off she scarpered, like a mad Afghan hound.

'Are you all right?' Bea said, going towards the stationmaster who had turned a strange shade of puce.

He had one hand against the wall and was breathing heavily. 'Bloody feminists,' he mumbled.

Agnes watched Gill disappear. The stationmaster was bent over double, Bea was rubbing his back and, beyond them, a woman caught one of the stickers from the air, looked at it, and stuck it onto her chest.

Agnes could feel herself breathing. For the first time in longer than she could remember, she didn't feel worried about the past or anxious about the future. She was here, in the moment.

She had never felt more alive.

# 30

'We were there for over two hours.'

'Putting stickers on tits,' added Bea. 'And she was very irresponsible, Mr Adler. She almost got us arrested. I'm not sure what we were doing was entirely legal.'

Mr Adler leaned back into his chair and chewed his bottom lip.

Agnes glanced towards the walls. They were covered in framed headshots of gnarled variety types: fleshy men in bow ties, women draped in feather boas, bubblegum kids with their chins resting on the back of their hands. None of them struck her as archetypal Go Getting Ladies.

One of the phones rang. He picked up. 'Adler.' He glanced up towards them, cupped his mouth round the receiver and swivelled so they were facing the back of his chair. 'I can't talk about that now,' he mumbled. 'No. Can't be done.'

Agnes peered a little closer at one of the pictures on the wall. She nudged Bea and whispered, 'Is that Gill?' Bea followed Agnes's finger as she pointed towards a black and white photo of a woman with long straight hair. She was wearing a witch's hat, and had her hands up like something out of a *Hammer House of Horror*. 'What's going on?' mouthed Agnes.

Bea shook her head.

Agnes couldn't shake the sense that Mr Adler was not quite what he appeared to be but she was so used to the small nagging voice that held her back she was ready to dismiss it.

'Call me in fifteen minutes.'

Mr Adler put a hand on his desk and turned his chair back towards them. He clicked his tongue and rapped the top of his desk with his thumb.

'Two hours, you say?'

They nodded.

'She ran off,' explained Bea. 'We weren't sure if we were supposed to get money from her.'

'Is that her, over there?' Agnes pointed back towards the photo.

'Not at all,' said Mr Adler, rather too quickly.

'I thought you didn't know what Gill looked like?'

Mr Adler narrowed his eyes. 'Two hours. Two hours.'

He reached into his jacket pocket and pulled out a bunch of keys, stood and went over to a small safe on a chest behind him. Opening it, he fished out two one-pound notes.

'There you go,' he said, handing them over like an uncle at Christmas. 'Don't spend it all at once. Now listen, ladies. I might send you out on some ...' he shifted on his feet ' ... interesting gigs. You're not going to keep coming in moaning, are you?'

'No, Mr Adler,' said Bea, folding her pound note into her pocket. 'More interesting the better. We're all for it, aren't we, Agnes?'

Agnes nodded. She wasn't sure she believed it.

'Good. Good.' He stared down at them. 'Right then. You carry on calling in the mornings. Come see me Friday and we'll square up.'

'Secretary not in again?' asked Bea.

'No,' said Mr Adler, returning to his desk. 'Off sick. There's a lot of it about.' He sat down, picked up a small tape and stuck it into a dictation machine in front of him. 'That's it. We're concluded.' He waved his finger towards the door.

He clicked the machine on. 'Letter to Larry Watts. Re: the incident at Park Royal.' He waved again towards the door.

Agnes glanced back towards the wall, and then to this odd man she couldn't help but not trust. She never would have known of him or be standing here feeling bemused, interest piqued, ready for new things, if it wasn't for Bea. She needed to smother her doubts. This was not a time to be worried or regretful. Those were feelings she wanted to leave behind. Anything new would always be a challenge, what needed to shift was her attitude: she needed to feel grateful for the chance.

They stepped out into the corridor.

'He's like something out of a black and white film with James Cagney,' said Bea, walking towards the stairs. 'Don't you think? I rather suspect Mr Adler is a thorough rogue, and all I can say to that is: I'm all in.'

'Thank you, Bea,' said Agnes, putting a hand on her friend's shoulder. Her tone was sincere, heartfelt.

'What for?' Bea glanced back.

'For all of it. I'm all in too.'

# THURSDAY

# 31

'It really doesn't leak!' said Florence, forcing a smile, 'and to prove it, I've filled this one with soup.'

She held up a long flask-like container and gave it a shake.

'Now, who is going to put all their trust in Tupperware?'

She looked round the room at the women gathered on every surface: Madeleine, face like a hatchet, whose husband preferred the company of his homing pigeons; Teri, fleshy and robust, who poured gin into a mug every evening, pretending it was tea; Yvonne, mousey and insubstantial; Mary, chain-smoking, arms folded, eyes narrowed suspiciously.

Over all of them hung an air of resigned misery. How had it come to this?

'All right,' said Mary, stubbing her cigarette out in the ash-tray in front of her. 'I'll do it.'

'Are you sure the lid won't come off, Florence?' said Madeleine, her tone wary.

'Remember the Tupperware promise, ladies,' said Florence, walking towards Mary. 'Once it's sealed, nothing can spill. Ready?'

She put the tips of her fingers on Mary's shoulder. It always worked best when she was more theatrical.

Mary put her hands on her knees and closed her eyes. 'Ready as ever.'

Florence held the flask of soup above Mary's head. All eyes were on her. With a flourish, she turned it upside down. A flurry of small, impressed noises fluttered around the room. Mary opened her eyes and touched her fingers to the top of her head.

'Not a drop,' she said, towards the others. 'Not the slightest drop.'

'That's very impressive,' said Yvonne, in a thin simper.

'It means you can store food in your fridge on its side, upside down, it doesn't matter.' Florence put the soup container back down on the small display table. She felt pleased with herself: another successful demonstration. 'That's the beauty of Tupperware. Designed to make your day-to-day life a little bit easier.' She held out her hands the way she had been shown to do: open and obvious.

'Talking of a bit easier, did I hear you've got a washing machine and freezer?' Madeleine barked the words out.

They all stared at Florence, waiting.

'Yes,' she said, pressing her shoulders back. 'Presents from Eleanor. I'm very lucky.'

'Well, let's see them.' Madeleine pushed herself up and brushed down the front of her skirt.

'Yes, let's,' said Mary, also standing.

Florence could feel her control of the situation slipping away. There was only so much she could ever think to say about Tupperware. It kept things fresh. It didn't leak. It was stackable, almost impossible to break. Normally, she would have to eke that out for an hour but now, watching her guests all getting up and staring at her, she realised there was little point in continuing. She gestured feebly towards the arrangement of containers. 'Shall we finish this later?' she asked.

'Yes,' they all said as one.

'I'll show you the washing machine first,' she offered and all their eyes lit up with excitement. 'It's in the pantry.'

She turned and walked towards the door. The women behind her suddenly energised. Mary flew into action.

'Did you hear about Shirley Muller?' she said, her voice little more than a hushed whisper.

'No,' said Madeleine, tucking in.

'You know she's just had her fifth child?'

'Five!' said Florence. 'My goodness.'

'It's that dreadful husband of hers,' said Mary, her voice registering mild disgust. 'Never leaves her alone and won't let her take the pill. It's monstrous.'

The group all mumbled in agreement.

'So she was struggling. You can imagine.' Mary was enjoying taking the floor. 'And she went to the doctor's. Doctor prescribes some pills to keep her going. She takes them. Feels absolutely marvellous. Incredible! She's got energy! She's never tired. She feels fabulous.'

'I could do with a few of those,' muttered Yvonne.

'But they run out so off she trots back to the doctor and asks for some more. He won't give them to her.'

'Why ever not?' Madeleine sounded affronted. They all stopped and turned to wait for Mary's explanation.

'Because,' said Mary, folding her arms and pursing her lips, 'he said they were addictive.' She lowered her head and whispered. 'He'd given her *speed*.' She elongated the word for emphasis.

'No!' said Madeleine, mouth agape.

'The drug?' said Teri, looking confused.

'The drug,' said Mary, nodding. 'I mean, of course a doctor prescribes drugs, but naughty ones? I ask you.'

'Sounds fabulous,' said Madeleine, with a small snort. 'Perhaps we should all go to the doctor!'

They all laughed. Florence stood watching them. There was something about the moment that opened them out.

'Are you happy?' she asked them, suddenly.

'What do you mean?' asked Mary, wiping her eyes.

'Doing this. Being housewives. Are you happy?'

The laughing petered out and they all looked at her, not quite knowing what to say.

There was a silence, an air of awkwardness. They were furtive, as if a great and dark secret was about to be revealed.

Mary stepped forward. 'I don't know how to say it but I know I'm unimportant. I know I have to do whatever my husband asks. I know if I get pregnant again, I'll be forced to keep it. I know my life is ...' she struggled to find the word ' ... controlled. I have no freedom. Not really. I know that.'

Florence reached for her hand. 'I feel that too,' she said.

The floodgates were open.

## 32

Agnes and Bea had spent the morning as extras for a Public Information Film about purse snatching in supermarkets.

'Don't wear anything fancy,' Mr Adler had told them. 'They want normal as you like. Plain. You're perfect.'

It had been filmed in a store in Ealing. They'd arrived, excited beyond belief. The lead, the purse snatcher, was a middle-aged man with a dripping moustache. He was in a brown suit, with a rather ostentatious yellow shirt and tie. They didn't recognise him, which was a little disappointing but all the same. Apparently, he'd been in rep with an actor who'd been in a few episodes of *Coronation Street*.

They'd lucked out. All the other female extras were in their forties and fifties and, being the youngest by a considerable margin, they were told by a frantic woman with a clipboard to stand by a checkout and wait. They were going to be in shot, not just staring at tins in the background. It was too thrilling. They had stood side by side, chatting, as the purse snatcher leaned in and did his worst. A couple of takes and they were done and back on the bus they went.

It was heady, all this freedom.

Agnes, for the first time since arriving in London, felt giddy. It was a relief. She felt like saying yes to everything: in for a penny, in for a pound, just like Bea. When was the last time she'd felt like that? The dark curtain that hung across her future had slipped open and here she was, peering into the brightness.

They had arrived back at the house, full of chatter, fizzing with excitement. Agnes felt like light air, a balloon on a string. They bounced about, laughing, singing silly songs about pickpockets. Agnes felt unburdened and the leash was off. She felt up for anything.

'It'll be fun! You'll enjoy it!' Kiki was lying on the sofa in the communal room, her legs up, ankles resting on the arm. She was cradling a mug of coffee and was wearing very little other than a pair of violent-pink panties and a matching bra.

It was five o'clock in the afternoon. She'd only just got up. 'I can have a word with the girl on the door. Make sure you get in.' She took a delicate sip from her mug.

Agnes glanced towards Bea. This was an enticing prospect: a free trip to the infamous Playboy Club.

'That would be amazing. What do you think, Agnes?' Bea asked, grinning.

'Yes! Why not? I'm on board.' Agnes was sitting sprawled in an armchair by the window. 'I mean, we're film stars now so I imagine we'll have to be batting them off.' She smiled, not at their going out, but because she was filled with a sense of enormous optimism. Only days ago her first instinct would have been to say no, yet here she was, embracing whatever the days threw at her.

'We've joined a rather peculiar agency,' explained Bea. 'Mr Adler's Agency for Go Getting Ladies.'

Kiki laughed. 'What?'

'He's clearly a total wrong'un, which is absolutely tremendous,' Bea continued. 'We were extras today. Yesterday we almost got arrested.'

'Arrested? Camilla will be pleased,' said Kiki, leaning up. 'Camilla's always trying to get herself arrested. I think she managed it once. Sasha had to go and bail her out. You have to admire her, even if she is bonkers. Anyway. What were you almost arrested for?'

'Liberation,' said Agnes. 'We had to put stickers on every breast on every poster on the Underground. EQUALITY FOR WOMEN NOW!' She thrust her arm into the air and grinned at Bea.

'Ugh. Don't be sucked in, girls,' Kiki said. 'Men aren't as awful as they make out.'

'I don't think men are awful,' said Bea. 'We're still trying to lose our virginity.'

'They're a bit awful,' said Agnes. She stopped and looked away, briefly. It was the last remaining hurdle to her resurrection.

Kiki gave a small indulgent snort. 'You two are so sweet.' She tilted her head to look at them. 'Have you ever been drunk? Either of you?'

'I drank sherry once from my father's cabinet and ended up on my hands and knees trying to eat raw runner beans from the pantry,' Bea offered.

'What about drugs? Dope? LSD? Speed?'

Agnes screwed her nose up. 'We come from Brill. Not Chicago. A wild night in Brill is half an apple cider and a packet of salted crisps.'

'Seriously, though, how are you still virgins at twenty? Are you terribly religious?'

Agnes shook her head.

Bea glanced towards her. 'Agnes was rather put off, weren't you? She kissed a boy,' she added, 'and everything spiralled off.'

'What do you mean? He went too far?' Kiki sat up.

'No, nothing like that,' said Agnes. 'He was ill, mononucleosis. He gave me what he had.'

'Glandular fever,' Bea explained. 'Ag was ill for the best part of a year. She barely got out of bed for a month. And even when she got up she was like a ghost. Ruined everything. She was all set to go to Oxford.'

'Not quite. I was trying to get in.' Agnes's mood shifted.

'She would have got in,' Bea said, nodding towards Kiki.

'Oh well,' said Agnes, staring down at her fingers. 'All in the past.'

She hated revisiting the memories: the long days that melted into nothing, the endless exhaustion, the slipping away of everything she had worked for.

'And it's put her off,' explained Bea. 'Chaps. That stuff.'

Kiki put her mug down on the tatty carpet. 'Well, this needs to change. Say you'll come. Ignore the moaners. It's fab, really. It'll be an experience.'

'And it'll be rammed with fellas,' said Bea, wanting to raise Agnes's spirits. 'None of whom will be ill.'

'Absolutely bursting with them,' said Kiki, pushing herself off the sofa. 'Famous ones too. Tony Curtis was in last night.'

'*The* Tony Curtis?' Bea's eyes widened.

'Yes. *The* Tony Curtis. We get the lot. Footballers. Film stars. Everyone wants to hang out at the Playboy Club. You'll love it. Just don't tell Camilla. She can be quite the bore. Girls like me have to make a living somehow.'

Bea grinned. 'We won't tell Camilla ... come on, Ag, say yes.'

They both looked towards her. Agnes paused, then took a deep breath. She wasn't about to let her newfound optimism slip away. 'Blow Camilla,' she said, standing. 'Let her be furious. All right. Yes.' She gave a soft smile.

'I'm so pleased!' Kiki took Agnes by the hands and swung them apart so she could look at her better.

'Now then,' she said, sounding more serious, 'we can't have you going looking like convent girls. What are you going to wear? Have you got an evening gown?'

Agnes grimaced. Clothes. Again. 'I've got a nightgown. Evening gown? No.'

Kiki glanced over towards Bea who was standing, legs slightly apart, looking like a goalkeeper.

'What about you? Brought anything glam with you?'

'*Glam?*' Bea said the word as if it was ridiculous. 'Sorry. Have you met us?' She fingered the air between her and Agnes.

'Hmm,' said Kiki, letting Agnes's hands fall back down to her sides. 'Come with me. I've got some things you could try on.'

Agnes shot Bea an anxious look. 'No, it's fine. I've got an A-line skirt somewhere in my rucksack. That'll do.'

'I've got a tank top with a sequin daisy on it,' proffered Bea. 'It's quite sparkly under a decent light.'

'Lord above,' said Kiki, shaking her head. 'Are you two for real? Stop panicking and come with me. I have just the thing ...'

As she turned and sashayed away towards her bedroom, Bea punched Agnes on the upper arm. 'Come on, Agnes Ledbury,' she said, with a wink. 'We are on.' Then, with a hush, 'You've still got those pills, yes?'

'I have, Beatrice Morgan, I have.'

Bea wagged a finger, nodded and skipped off towards Kiki's room, humming a tune that sounded an awful lot like 'Ride of the Valkyries'. Agnes smiled. Her confidence was growing, the world was opening up, but best of all, she could feel her old self returning. It felt good to have her back.

# 33

William sat at the head of the table, a book between him and Florence.

She had served the lamb stew and dumplings, the soft carrots, the beans she had picked from the garden. She had positioned his plate and retired to her own chair, served herself and looked up to see the back of his book.

He had no interest in her whatsoever.

She prodded at her food. She didn't even like lamb stew and dumplings. Her fork slipped from her fingers onto the tablecloth and she sat back, looking at her husband and the book.

It was *In Cold Blood* by Truman Capote, the true story of a murder in small-town America.

A dark thought flittered across Florence's mind. Was she capable of killing someone? No, she knew she wasn't. Besides, she didn't want William dead. She just wanted things to be different.

She shoved back from the table and walked out towards the hallway. Bending down, she reached into her bag, pulled out her book and returned to the dining room. She sat, pushed her plate away and began to read.

William lowered his book. 'What's that you're reading?' he asked. He sounded surprised, almost affronted.

'*The Female Eunuch*,' she replied, not lowering it to look at him.

'What a peculiar cover,' he said. His tone was dismissive, derisory. 'Is it any good?'

'It's better than good,' she said, turning another page. 'It's wonderful.' She paused. 'I might get my hair cut,' she added, to test him.

He didn't reply. Of course he didn't.

# 34

Agnes and Bea stood side by side. Their preparation for an evening at the Playboy Club was going surprisingly well. Agnes was in a gypsy-style organza rumba dress with long sleeves. Bea was in a red-printed flannel smock dress with an oversized yoke. On Kiki, they looked billowing. On Agnes and Bea, they fitted.

'Do I look like a road sign?' said Bea, glancing down at her long, pale, white legs. The smock dress finished at Kiki's knee. On Bea, it was mid-thigh.

'I think you look lovely,' said Agnes, meaning it. She stood, staring at herself in the mirror. She barely recognised herself. 'I hate dressing up. I have no idea what I'm doing.' She pulled at the end of a sleeve. 'Do I look all right?'

'I think you look smashing,' said Bea. 'Needs must. For tonight, Agnes Ledbury, we shall become women!'

She closed her eyes and punched a finger upwards.

Agnes wasn't sure that was going to be true, certainly not in her case. She was still terrified of intimacy. It was irrational, she knew, but fears are never dispatched until you face them. She looked at herself again in the mirror. Bea was right. She *did* look smashing.

'Shall we have a pill, Beatrice Morgan?' Agnes asked, spinning round. 'A whole one. Each?'

Bea nodded. 'Whole hog, Agnes Ledbury. Yes. A whole one. Let's go mad.'

Agnes reached for the washbag in her rucksack. She had hidden the strip of pills in a box of plasters in case her mother had wanted to add throat lozenges or lip salve or an emergency emery board. She pulled them out and held them in her palm.

'There they are,' she said, her voice muted. She stared down at them. She was aware her hand was trembling.

Bea plucked them from her and peered at the writing. 'It says to start with the pills in the green section. There's days of the week. Do we have to have a Thursday? There isn't a green pill with a Thursday.'

'I'm not sure if the pills are aware of what day of the week it is,' said Agnes. She wanted to stop her hands shaking so she clenched her fists and dug her fingernails into her palms. 'Perhaps we should have a green pill each and not worry too much about the days?'

'Yes,' nodded Bea. 'Let's do that.'

Bea turned the strip over, pressed out two small pills and held them in her hand. A surge of something empowering filled the air. This little pill, Agnes understood, was the future.

'Here,' Bea said, holding her hand out towards Agnes. 'Take one.'

Taking the pills gently between their thumbs and forefingers, the young women stared each other in the eye. The world was opening out before them. It was a world in which women made choices, were in control, could be who they wanted to be. This little pill had changed everything. Now all Agnes and Bea had to do was catch up.

Bea tapped Agnes's pill with her own.

'Cheers,' she said, and threw it into her mouth and swallowed. 'And that's that,' she said, beaming.

'Bottoms up,' said Agnes, following suit. She'd never been any good at taking pills. It was difficult to swallow and left a bitter taste in her mouth. She hoped it wasn't prescient.

Agnes stared up at the black awning with the gold Roman trim. From the outside, the Playboy Club on Park Lane looked posh and impressive. Underneath the canopy stood a doorman in beige and russet livery. He wore white gloves and a top hat and, from a distance, looked like one of the lizards in *Alice in Wonderland*.

Kiki had assured them there would be no difficulty in getting in: she would square it with whoever was on reception. Their names would be on a list, she said. All the same, Agnes wasn't entirely sure it would work. She felt like a fraud. She longed to be the person who lit up the room, who could wander in, sit down and wait for people to gather round her. She wanted to be confident, to shine, to know who she was, just like Eleanor.

Behind them a dark blue MG pulled up, top down. A man, in black tie, hopped out and opened the passenger door for a woman in a cream catsuit. Holes trimmed in dark navy flanked her torso, tanned and toned. He took her hand and helped her from the car, shut the door and escorted her to the entrance. She glanced towards Agnes and Bea, wafting a beatific smile in their direction.

'Do you think we'll ever get out of a car like that?' mumbled Agnes.

'No,' said Bea, 'but then, I'd rather be driving the car.'

The doorman tipped his hat, opened the large doors and off they disappeared.

'This is silly,' said Bea, giving Agnes a nudge. 'We can't stand out here all night. Besides, we're starting to look suspicious. He won't let us in if we look weird.'

Bea was right. They'd been standing doing nothing for the best part of half an hour, side-stepping on the pavement, chewing their nails, eyes narrowed every time the doorman looked at them. Agnes had bottled it on seeing him. She couldn't help herself.

'Do you think we look weird?' asked Agnes, casting an eye down at herself.

'I think we look a bit weird, yes,' replied Bea, her patience running thin. 'But we always look a bit weird. And my glasses are filthy, which doesn't help.' She slid them off and cleaned them on the bottom of her dress. 'But, Agnes, we look weird in the best clothes we've ever worn in our life so let's not forget that.'

It was frustrating, the return of feeling gauche and unready. Agnes glanced back towards the doorman. 'He keeps watching us.'

'Are you trying to come in?' the doorman shouted over towards them.

Agnes froze. 'Oh no.'

'Are you waiting for someone?' He had an East End accent and looked like a tradesman from a Victorian novel who might end up dead in entirely avoidable circumstances.

'No, we're on a list,' said Bea. 'In there. One of the bunny girls, Kiki, she's our flatmate.' She shot him a smile. Agnes didn't dare look up.

'How old are you both?' He looked at them carefully.

'Twenty,' said Bea. She pulled at Agnes's arm to draw her in.

'What are your names? I'll check the list.'

'Beatrice Morgan and Agnes Ledbury.'

'Wait here.' He disappeared into the foyer.

Bea turned to Agnes, her hand gripping her friend at the wrist. 'Ag, come on, buck up. You look lovely. You smell lovely. We can do this.'

Agnes stared down at the pavement. It had rained, briefly. There was a small puddle in front of her and she looked into it, an odd version of herself reflected back, blurred and shifting.

'We can do this,' Bea said again. 'And then we work out how we have sexual intercourse with male members of the species. It's going to happen.'

She leaned forward to look into Agnes's eyes. She was buoyant, determined, positive. Agnes wasn't quite there yet; it was her last mountain to climb. She stared back but couldn't quite muster the same enthusiasm.

'It'll be all right, Ag,' Bea said softly, squeezing her hand. 'I promise.'

The door into the Playboy Club opened and the doorman waved them towards it.

'You're in, ladies,' he called out.

'Ready?' said Bea, releasing her grip.

Somewhere, Agnes thought, there was a braver version of herself. She had to dig deep and pull it out. She gave a nod, stepped towards the door and into the foyer.

## 35

Florence hadn't been able to put *The Female Eunuch* down. After clearing away supper she took herself and her book to the long sitting room that looked out over the garden.

It was a fine evening. There hadn't been many of them of late, and a warm, golden glow was illuminating the edges of the shrubs and trees. A blackbird was chattering away in a small silver birch and two collared doves were cooing from the terrace. Florence watched them as they bobbed together, side by side. They made her heart break.

William had taken himself off to the small sitting room, as he always did, no word of thanks for the supper she had made, instead a push back of his chair and off he went, thumb in his book.

He was a bachelor in a marriage, a man for whom anyone infringing on his time was treated with indifference if not contempt. Perhaps that was too harsh. They were two people who didn't know each other or how to be in a relationship. They were islands staring at each other across a cold strait.

Florence looked out at the ebbing sun. Her thoughts flitted to Agnes.

She'd be in France now, enjoying the long evenings, sitting on broad boulevards, laughing. Florence worried about her, she couldn't help it: the odd, awkward little girl who seemed to lack all sense of direction. She would be timid, dragged along by the others, anxious. Florence wondered if she'd be able to keep up. She felt consumed with sadness: she knew the illness had taken its toll but, more than that, she had instilled in her daughter nothing but caution and restrictions.

'My fault,' Florence murmured. 'It's my fault.'

She glanced back down towards her book. She had finished it, reading greedily as words struck her like darts. It was a passport to a different way of existing. It had made Florence feel alive.

'I wonder where you are, Agnes,' she whispered.

From the bottom of her heart, she wanted to apologise.

# 36

Agnes pressed her back into the leather booth. They were sitting in a round banquette in the corner of the casino. It was noisy: loud chatter, the odd raucous scream, all underpinned with anonymous piped music. Two weeks ago, being here would be unimaginable.

Agnes's palms were flat down either side of her as if she was steadying herself on a keeling boat. She was feeling anxious, again. Old habits die hard, but she was here and had found a place that felt safe: a dark hide in a very modern jungle.

Kiki had come over, all corset and ears. It was ridiculous.

'All about the tail, darlings,' she said, tray aloft. She gave a wiggle and a wink and put her other hand on her hip. 'Are you having fun?'

Bea nodded. 'Thanks for the drinks.'

Agnes picked up her own glass and sniffed. 'What is it?'

'Martini,' said Kiki, splaying one leg out to the side. 'Fella over there bought them.' She nodded towards a man leaning against the roulette table. He was dark, swarthy and looked like a knock-off Oliver Reed.

Bea's eyes widened. 'For us?'

'No,' said Kiki. 'For me, but we're not allowed to accept drinks when we're working. I asked him to buy them for you two instead.'

Bea smiled over in his direction. Agnes stared, flatly. He raised a glass back.

'He's got a yellow Rolls-Royce,' Kiki told them. 'East End gangster.'

'Really?' Bea sounded shocked. 'A proper one?'

'Apparently,' said Kiki. 'Let me know if you want anything. Have fun!' She twirled away, hips sashaying like a boat bobbing on the waves.

Agnes was still staring towards the gangster. He was leaning, cigar stub between his fingers. He was wearing a dark blue suit, jacket open, tailored waistcoat. He had a large gold signet ring on his left hand. In his other, he held a tumbler with a flash of something golden in it – whisky, probably. She wouldn't trust him further than she could throw him, but then she knew she would never be asked to. He had no interest in them. Of course he didn't. He was only watching Kiki. 'He looks a bit creepy,' she said.

'Oh well,' said Bea, 'bottoms up.'

There was a gloom to the place: the air was heavy with smoke, clouds of it swirling in the lamplight. Under it, the steady hum of conversation, the odd outburst of manly laughter. This was a masculine place, thought Agnes, a place that belonged to men. She scanned the room: black ties, power and money, status. It was cosmopolitan, smart but old-guard, shoring up the conventional. It was desirable and reprehensible. It was a place clinging to the past.

'There's an odd atmosphere in here, don't you think?' she said. 'Can't quite put my finger on it.'

'Posh. It feels posh.'

'No, it's not that. It feels like they all might know the game is up.'

'Have you tried it? The Martini?' Bea sniffed at her drink.

'No. Shall we do it together?' Agnes held out her cocktail glass.

'It smells very strong,' Bea bent down and sniffed more deeply, 'like something out of a Fifth Form Chemistry Fume Cupboard. Ooof. Schoolgirl error there,' she added, rubbing the end of her nose. 'I should have wafted it. Waft.' She scooped the air above the drink towards her nose. 'Waft it. Waft.'

Agnes laughed. She shifted forward and leaned onto the table. All she needed, right now, she told herself, was this. They spent their time together so naturally, it was easy to take their friendship for granted, but she had to remember to enjoy every last second. The days would drift too fast, the rest of their lives would take hold and they'd be back in Brill soon enough. All this had to be more than a temporary respite. It needed to be the beginning of another adventure.

Bea raised her glass. 'May our virginity be lost magnificently,' she said, smiling. 'To us!'

'To us,' said Agnes.

They clinked and drank.

Across the room, on a raised platform in front of a parquet dance floor, a band had appeared: four men, all stacked hair and sideburns, in outrageous two-tone trousers and tight jackets. The lead singer, a gap-toothed sexpot, cradled the microphone stand.

'All right?' he asked, to nobody in particular.

'Band,' said Bea, nudging her head towards them. 'Shall we go and have a dance?'

'Nobody else is on the dance floor.'

'Exactly,' said Bea, pushing herself up from the banquette. 'This is how we begin our assault, Agnes. Come on.' She stood, flattened down her dress, and began to weave her way through the crowd.

The dance floor, flanked by four pillars erupting with sprays of palm leaves, was like something out of the last days of Pompeii. Bea took up position, hands on hips, waiting. Agnes, having battled past a knot of small tables of men with their arms round younger, miserable-looking women, slid up behind her. She had mumbled apologies to everyone she passed.

'Do you think we should wait until it's got going a bit?' Agnes looked round the room. Absolutely nobody else was looking as if they were going to join in. She'd never been one for getting the party going. She felt self-conscious.

'No,' said Bea, sticking her chin out. 'This is definitely what we want to be doing.'

'Right then,' said the lead singer, nodding to the lead guitarist.

'Hooray!' shouted Bea, cupping her hands around her mouth.

'Are you drunk?'

'Not in the slightest.'

The guitarist began picking out an instantly recognisable intro: 'Bend It' by Dave Dee, Dozy, Beaky, Mick and Tich. It was a barely veiled anthem to having it off.

Bea, delighted, began dipping in time to the music, legs apart, as if she were trying to drop a dangling weight into a bottle. Agnes held her arms at right angles from her side and twisted herself back and forth. She wasn't really one for dancing. She stood, swaying her head and trying to smile. Casually, she glanced over her shoulder at the mass of people behind them. Nobody was paying them the blindest bit of attention. Not even the band was looking at them.

'Come on!' yelled Bea, who had moved from dipping to crouching.

Agnes looked back through the tangled maze of suits and ties, high heels, the smell of expensive aftershave, the personalised cufflinks, the polished leather, the manicured fingers, the lash extensions, the tiny waists, the broad shoulders, the wealth, the fame. She saw Kiki, tray in the air, dipping for a man in his forties, cigar clamped between his lips, beside him a winsome blonde.

Everywhere she looked, men were in control: gifting chips to wide-eyed girls at the roulette table, big hands resting on little backs. Here she was, on a dance floor, in a borrowed dress. It was exciting to be here, she couldn't deny it, but it was a wonderland in which nobody felt lucky. They felt chosen. They felt entitled.

Agnes felt none of these things but she had her friend and she had this moment. She would take it. She had to. Her life depended on it.

# FRIDAY

# 37

By the end of the evening, neither of them had managed to have sex.

Bea, after a fourth Martini, had fallen into one of the palm displays and thrown up behind the drum kit. It hadn't seemed funny at the time, but now, lying in their bed on the floor, they couldn't stop laughing.

'What a shambles.' Bea shook her head. 'I have no memory of getting home. None whatsoever.'

'Kiki put us in a cab after the vom incident.'

Bea gave a loud hoot. She threw herself back down onto her pillow. 'I mean, I don't feel terrible? Do you feel terrible?'

'No. I am ready for whatever Mr Adler and his Agency for Go Getting Ladies is readying for us to go get.'

Bea smiled and turned to stare up at the ceiling. 'Nobody chatted us up, though, Ag,' she said. 'Not one person.'

'Does it matter?' replied Agnes, 'We had fun, didn't we?'

'Yes, we did.'

Bea rolled onto her side to look at Agnes. 'Are we ugly?' She gazed into Agnes's eyes. 'Is that what it is? I mean, I don't think you're ugly at all. Is it just me? Me and my stupid wonky face? I'm holding you back.'

Agnes frowned and reached out to move Bea's fringe to one side. 'You're not remotely ugly. You have the most interesting face I know.'

Bea grimaced. 'That's total code for proper ugly, Agnes.'

'Don't be silly. We're … unique. We're not … homogenous. That's all.'

'House points for "homogenous", Agnes Ledbury.'

'Thank you, Beatrice Morgan.'

They both smiled and flipped onto their backs.

'All the same,' said Bea, 'I did think last night was going to be the night. I really did. I was ready for it, but sensible heads on. We can't compete with sticks with tits in evening gowns, Ag. We need to go hang round a farm and wait for a pair of muddy lads to jump down from tractors.'

'There are no tractors in London. Perhaps we could find a couple of mathematicians. A male version of us.' Agnes was humouring her.

'No,' said Bea, closing her eyes and shaking her head. 'Terrible idea. Double virgins are like magnets.' She put her index fingers together and mimed them pushing away from each other. 'We can't do it with chaps who have never done it. We may come away with entirely the wrong impression.'

The door into their room opened. It was Kiki. 'You're both still alive, then?' she asked, peering in.

'Sorry I vommed.' Bea craned her neck to look up at her.

'Did you have fun?'

'We did,' Bea said, sitting up. She looked towards Agnes. 'Didn't we?'

Agnes nodded. She was pleasantly surprised. Despite the gnawing doubts, she really had.

'Nobody chatted us up, though, Kiki,' Bea complained. 'We drew an absolute blank. Not one chap. We're never going to lose our virginity at this rate. We had the pill. Got togged up. Nothing doing.'

Agnes pushed herself from the mattress and pulled a jumper from the top of her rucksack. 'I mean, it's not like we're trying to fall in love,' she said, putting it on.

'Hell, no,' said Bea. 'Just sex, thanks. Do it, shake hands and on our way.'

Kiki leaned back. 'God. I remember my first time so vividly. I fell in love with a married man when I was sixteen. I was mad for him. Friend of my father's. Can you imagine? Had sex with him in the back seat of his car. That was my first time: one foot up on the ceiling and sitting on an A–Z. I thought I was so in love.' She shook her head. 'He was just a dirty old man having sex with his friend's daughter. And the saddest part is, I carried on doing it. Having sex with him in the back of that car.'

Agnes turned and looked at her. 'How long for?'

'Until I found out I was pregnant.'

'Have you got a …' The words drifted from Agnes. There was no evidence of a child in Kiki's life. Perhaps something had gone wrong.

'I was sent away. To one of those mother-and-daughter centres.' Kiki shifted on her feet. 'Driven there in the dead of night by my appalled mother and left there. We weren't allowed out. I was there for five months. I had a baby girl. Called her Emily.'

She stopped and stared down at her fingers.

'Where is she now?' Agnes leaned forward.

'Don't know.' Kiki's voice trailed off. She stood, her lips knitting themselves into a full stop.

Agnes looked towards Bea. She wasn't sure what to say. She was well aware of the shame of getting yourself into trouble. All the same, she'd never met someone who actually had.

Bea got up and went towards Kiki. 'My parents have a pair of friends who can't have children,' she said, taking her hand. 'Greatest sadness of their lives. And last year, they adopted a little boy and he's been their greatest happiness. You can hold onto that.'

Kiki gave a small nod but said nothing. Agnes watched her carefully. Whatever they did, they mustn't stop taking those pills.

# 38

Florence bent down and picked up the blue envelope lying on the doormat. She turned it over. It was addressed to her, French stamp. She was surprised how happy it had made her. She tucked it into the pocket of her apron, walked to the kitchen and put the kettle on.

Agnes had remembered her. She felt lifted up.

Having made herself a cup of tea, Florence walked to the long sitting room and settled into the large armchair that looked out over the garden. It was a little overcast that morning; the day had started with a light drizzle. Good for the tomatoes, Florence had thought, and she'd set about her morning chores, but now she had Agnes's letter and she wanted to read it.

*Dear Mother.*

The words made her want to cry.

*We've finally made it to Paris. You're probably wondering why it took us so long but we met a man on the ferry who specialises in rebinding very important and very old books and he told us he had a house in Normandy. He asked us if we would like to stay. His wife died in mysterious circumstances and he has been devastated by it, utterly.*

*So of course we took pity on him. Besides, the offer of a free hols could not be passed up. Well. Imagine our surprise when we arrived. It turned out he lived in a huge chateau! It was like something out of a fairy tale. I slept in a four-poster bed like* The Princess and the Pea *and had a butler called Pascal, who I discovered, was a war hero. He had a wooden leg.*

'Goodness.' Florence turned to the next page.

*'Pascal!' I would shout, every morning, 'breakfast please!' and up he would come with a silver tray and a silver pot of tea (English, of course), a croissant, some apricot jam and some strange toast that bore no resemblance to English toast in any way. I'm not even sure it was made of bread. I felt a little bad making a man with a wooden leg climb all those stairs every morning but he seemed to enjoy the exercise. The stay was delightful. We played tennis on a grass court in the grounds and swam in the pool while our host spent his days quietly rebinding a very important, very old book.*

Florence stopped and frowned. Agnes wasn't normally this effusive.

*But now we are in Paris, which is 233 miles upstream from the English Channel. What an attractive city! The gastronomy! The haute couture! The painting, literature. Truly it is 'La Ville-Lumière'! One can only imagine the excitement when the Frankish King Clovis took the city from the Gauls in 494 BC.*

'What is she going on about?'

*Today we're going to the Notre-Dame cathedral. It's the most famous of the Gothic cathedrals of the Middle Ages. Did you know the foundation stone was laid by Pope Alexander III? Napoleon crowned himself Emperor in it. I know we're not supposed to think much of him but he* did *save Notre-Dame from wrack and ruin so he can't have been all bad.*

'Honestly, Agnes,' said Florence, shaking her head, 'did you take Eleanor's encyclopedia with you?'

*I hope you are having a lovely summer. It is very hot here, of course, but Bea and I are sitting in the shade at all times. I know some people like a tan but we don't.*

'Really? Normally I can't get you out of the sun.'

*Bea is terribly well. Brenda is still alive. The day goes well! I will write again when we are in Italy. All love, Agnes. PS Love to Daddy.*

Florence gave a small smile and folded the letter gently.

She held onto it for a moment, wanting the connection to last.

Paris. She had never been. In fact, she'd never travelled anywhere. Summer holidays were always a caravan in Dorset. Two weeks of windbreaks and boiled eggs on the beach, Eleanor and Agnes trying to find fossils while William was off, who knows where, but not with them.

Florence looked out, beyond the garden to the distant horizon. There was no going to Dorset this year. They hadn't been away since Agnes was at school. Might she and William go away somewhere together? See out the rest of the summer under grape vines, or a glorious wisteria, the sound of cicadas the permanent backdrop to long, languid days?

Florence laughed out loud. The notion was ridiculous.

Her face fell. It was ridiculous, ridiculous, ridiculous. She felt a surge of anger, the need to right a wrong. Pushing herself up from the armchair, she tucked Agnes's letter back into her pocket. She needed to find her driving shoes.

Florence was going out.

# 39

Mr Adler's instructions were quite firm. They were to head to a house in Fulham. They were to provide tea, coffee, biscuits, sandwiches. They were to look after the client's every need.

'You know,' he said. 'Runners.'

'I'm very bad at running,' whispered Bea, ear close to the receiver.

'Bea is very bad at running, Mr Adler.'

'Horrific at it,' added Bea.

'No. Not that running.' Mr Adler sounded put out. 'Running around after other people. Being a dogsbody. That running. Get up there. Come and see me after. And you can get paid.' He grunted and, with that, he hung up.

'He never says goodbye,' said Agnes, putting the phone down. 'It's quite disconcerting. Did you write down the address?'

'Bettridge Road. We're to ask for Candy.'

Bea scooped up the loose coins that were always ready for use and pocketed them. 'Right then,' she said with some purpose. 'Let's get at it.'

A magazine was having a photo shoot in the kitchen of someone who had agreed to it weeks ago but was now clearly wishing she hadn't.

'Is there any chance everyone could take their shoes off?' she was asking, one arm folded across her chest, her other hand hovering over her mouth. She looked as if she wanted to scream and tell everyone to get out.

The location manager, the infamous Candy, took her by the elbow. 'Perhaps it might be better if you went out for a few hours. Shopping? Lunch? Gallery? There's some good films on ...' She steered the woman away. 'What about that *Willy Wonka* ... that looks good ... is that out yet?'

Agnes was standing holding a plate of biscuits. In front of her was a model, a hairdresser, a stylist, a make-up artist, a photographer's assistant, the photographer, three women from the magazine who looked furious and a man from an advertising agency whose idea this was. Bea was hunched over a row of mugs. Beside her a notebook where she had dutifully noted down everyone's requirements.

Agnes wasn't quite sure what to do other than try and look helpful. There was an air of slight frenzy. The stylist had turned up late, a flat tyre he'd said, and had brought a rack of clothes that were a size too large. The clothes, which were supposed to be figure-hugging, were hanging loose. This was not the image of clean lines the client wanted.

'I can peg it at the back,' he was saying, top lip sweating.

'Have you got pegs?'

'No.'

It was fun, all this. Agnes stood back, quietly drinking it all in. Enjoyment was starting to overtake worry. Despite her reservations about Mr Adler, he was facilitating a want: Agnes had been ripped from a safe, same-old existence and plunged into worlds she couldn't have imagined. There were other things to do, other people to be. This job was allowing her to peer into different ways of living She could stay for a while, see if she liked it, then leave.

'Would you like a biscuit?' She offered the plate to the man standing on her left.

The photographer's assistant was rake-thin, cream leather jacket and flared jeans. He wore a Jimi Hendrix T-shirt and his hair was a soft brown, long to the shoulder. He had gentle eyes and a lucky expression. He was called Sam.

'All right,' he said, picking a custard cream off the plate.

He was rather beautiful to look at. Agnes watched him catching crumbs on his bottom lip and wondered if he would ever be interested in her. Doubtful. The model was also rather beautiful to look at and he hadn't taken his eyes off her.

'Christ,' said Candy, walking back in. 'Thank God I've got her out the house. She was on the verge of a nervous breakdown.'

'Biscuit?'

'Yes please.' She picked two and crammed one, whole, into her mouth. She shouted across the room. 'Look, can we get this moving? We've got three hours tops.'

The shoot sparked into action. The model stood, staring off, as a dumpy woman all in black reached up on tiptoes to reapply her make-up. The hairdresser was endlessly touching the model's fringe with the end of his comb. The stylist was trying to work out how he was going to tighten her clothes. Could he use a grip from the lights? Could he stand behind her and be out of sight? The three women, sour faces all, discussed whether the set dressing was on trend. Would a woman like this have a teacup or a cafetière or a lobster?

Sam sloped off to put film in the camera, lights were set, the photographer stood ready.

'Music please,' he demanded, and shoved his sunglasses to the top of his head.

Agnes gravitated away to the corner of the room. A large beanbag was resting against the wall and she slumped into it, joining Bea who was already there.

'I'm feeling a little fragile,' said Bea. She held a hand to her forehead. 'The lights are very bright.'

'Do you want a biscuit?'

'No.'

They sat, quietly watching. The shoot was fast: the photographer had a manic energy to him, bouncing around, crouching, leaping up ladders. The model was his 'darling', his 'babe', his 'treacle'. What she didn't seem to have was a name.

'It's mad, isn't it?' said Bea. 'All this for one picture in a magazine.'

'The effort of perfection,' mumbled Agnes, her head leaning back against the wall.

Perfection. It was something she once aspired to, all those years ago, before the future she had taken for granted had crumbled away. She wondered where she might be now had it not gone wrong, what she might be doing: probably finishing her second year, an undergraduate in English literature. Her chest hurt with the thought of it.

She looked back towards the model. Her control over the room was palpable.

The photographer was taking the last shots and, as he did, she reached her hand out in Sam's direction. She didn't have to say a word. He came, like an obedient dog, placing his hand on the back of her neck. She leaned into him and he began to caress it.

It was so suddenly intimate, Agnes felt startled.

'Do they know each other?' Bea was lying on her side, cheek cradled into the palm of her hand.

Agnes didn't reply. She was wondering what it might feel like to have someone stroke the back of her neck.

'I think we've got it,' said the photographer, slipping his sunglasses back down.

A smattering of applause rippled round the room. The model wafted gentle smiles as she stepped away from set. She curled herself around Sam and kissed him.

'They must know each other.' Bea was frowning.

The hairdresser deftly undid some pins; the stylist helped the model out of a jacket; the make-up artist asked her if she needed cleaning up. The model waved them all off and took Sam's hand. She walked him towards a door into another room.

'Right, you two,' said Candy, gesturing towards Agnes and Bea. 'Let's get this cleaned up.' She swept her hand across the room. 'You've got half an hour. Then Hatchet Face is back.'

Agnes stared towards the door, quietly shut to close everyone out but them.

Candy noticed. 'She always does this. Shoots make her randy.' She picked up a pile of magazines and threw them into a box.

Bea paused. 'Are they going to have sex?'

Candy looked at her dismissively. 'Of course they're having sex.'

'They're going to have sex, Agnes,' Bea muttered, as she picked a packet of J-cloths out from a plastic bag on the floor.

'I know,' said Agnes.

'It's not even night-time.'

'I think people can have sex at most times of the day, Bea. I don't think there's a strict schedule.'

'She's only just met him.' Bea was still trying to whisper but not quite managing it.

'So it seems.'

'This is what we need to be doing, Agnes,' said Bea, picking the cooked lobster out from the sink. 'We need to do jobs that end up with us behind closed doors having sexual encounters.'

Agnes looked off towards the shut door. No, she thought, what they needed was a sense of purpose and achievement.

# 40

The travel agent was a young woman with lips that pursed together into a knot every time she had a serious thought. 'So romantic. Second honeymoon?' She pushed her chair back towards a rack of leaflets.

'Yes, something like that,' Florence lied.

'Any preference as to where? I have some wonderful city breaks. Rome. Milan. Or you might like a cultural tour. Tuscany is *excellent* for that.'

'Have you been?' Florence asked.

The travel agent hesitated. 'No, not yet.' She threw a thin smile towards her. 'But I will!' Her voice was high and tinkling. 'What about this?' She pressed a leaflet across the table towards Florence. 'Venice. Perfect for couples. When might you be wanting to go? It can get rather crowded. I wouldn't recommend August. You won't be able to move for French people wandering about.'

'I don't know yet.'

Florence fingered the leaflet and picked it up. She stared down at the photographs: a couple entwined in a gondola, a couple standing on a bridge at sunset looking over the Grand Canal, a couple in a restaurant laughing. Couples everywhere, in love, having the time of their lives.

'Have you got anything else?'

'Venice not for you?' The woman pursed her lips. 'It is rather expensive ...' She turned again and scoured the rack. 'If you can leave in the next few weeks, there's a very nice resort hotel on the Amalfi coast. Very exclusive. Look at the colour of that sea ...' She pushed another pamphlet towards Florence, her long red nails tapping at the image of water as clear as gin. 'Lovely beaches too,' she added. 'If you like that sort of thing.'

'Perhaps you could just give me some leaflets I can take home,' Florence said, looking past the woman to the rack behind her.

'To discuss with your husband, yes.' The agent nodded. 'Let him decide, then come in together and I can make the arrangements with him. I'll add some in for the South of France,' she muttered as she began to amass a pile into the crook of her right arm. 'Portugal? And there's always Spain. Flights there are becoming quite economical.'

Florence pushed her chair back and stood up. She looked round the small, rather cramped office. The wallpaper was a faded green flock, the carpet a dull beige. Trinkets from other people's holidays adorned the walls: a pair of castanets, a sombrero, a small straw donkey, a wine bottle that had been turned into a lamp, a poster of a bullfighter.

'There you go,' the woman said, handing Florence the pile of travel brochures. 'Have a look through with your husband. Then you can both pop back in.'

Florence gave an involuntary laugh. The thought of William sitting in this room was inconceivable.

'Sorry,' said the woman, registering a moment of confusion. 'Did I say something funny?'

'No,' said Florence, shaking her head. 'Not at all.' She turned and walked off towards the door.

'You will come back, won't you?' The agent's voice had a tinge of anxiety.

Florence didn't reply. She knew she'd never see the woman again.

# SATURDAY

# 41

'Five quid each. That's all right that.'

They were staring down at the wages given to them the afternoon before by Mr Adler.

There had been no sign of the elusive secretary despite him mentioning her again. Bea had enquired after her health. She was, according to him, 'on the cusp of recovery'. He'd handed them a small brown envelope and told them 'not to fight over it' before puffing himself back to his chair. His flies had been undone and his tie had egg on it. He'd looked an absolute state.

Agnes was enjoying herself. Despite everything, she was beginning to find Mr Adler amusing. It was a game to be played that cemented their sense of Them Against Him, Them Against their Parents, Them Against the World. They couldn't believe they were getting away with it. It felt wonderful.

'Something is surging through my veins,' said Bea. She was thumbing through her purse. 'Ambition. Can you feel it?'

'I can. I'm almost afraid of it.'

Bea picked out a fifty-pence piece and handed it over to the man on the fruit stall. 'That's the smallest coin I've got. Sorry.'

They were buying cherries. Big, fat, juicy ones.

'Afraid? Why?'

'Because it's given me hope. And unless something major happens, we're still crawling back to secretarial. Face it. We'll go back. Parents will be having none of it and off we'll trot to a grey life of letters and envelopes and forever doing what we're told.'

'Not a chance. Over my dead body. We have opened a different door, Agnes. Take a dictation? No thanks.'

The man on the stall shovelled a large handful of cherries onto an ancient set of scales, tipped the bowl into a brown paper bag, gave the ends a twist and held it out. 'There you go, darlin'.'

They wandered off down Hampstead High Street. The day was warm and there was no threat of rain. It was so lovely here. They could spend a day lazing on the heath or go for a swim in the ponds but Agnes had more on her mind. She had discovered a road to purpose but the end destination was not yet in sight. Agnes was starting to feel the pinching of her life – she may not know where she wanted this adventure to end but that wasn't the point. She wanted to try again.

The day was so delightful, they had decided to walk across the heath. They were on a wooded path. Above them, through sun-dappled trees, a blackbird was making itself heard. Ahead of them, a brown spaniel was leaping through the bracken, tail up, nose down. A woman was pushing a toddler in a buggy.

'Do you want children?' Bea spat a cherry stone into her hand and tossed it off into the ferns. She was looking at the little boy, strapped in, asleep, head lolling heavily to one side. His mother pushed him on. Her face was blank.

'Children? Of course,' said Agnes.

'I'm not sure I do,' said Bea, coming to a stop. 'Is that terrible?'

'No, but you might change your mind. If you fall in love.' Agnes twirled a finger in the air as if the idea was something magical, to be produced from a hat.

'Fall in love?' Bea sounded incredulous. 'Fall in love with who? Mr Adler?' She let out a guffaw.

They walked on, quietly sharing the last of the cherries. There was contentment to these moments. Agnes loved her friend so fiercely. It was hard to imagine anyone replacing her.

'What do you think we'll end up doing?' The thought felt urgent and important.

'I have absolutely no idea,' said Bea. 'But it won't be taking bloody letters.'

'No, it won't.' Agnes paused for a moment. 'I want to be happy. I want to get up every day and look forward to it. I want to be able to make choices. I don't want to be my mother, dreading every minute.'

Bea threw the cherry pips in her hand away into a bush. 'We will. I don't know how. But we will.'

Agnes slipped her hand into Bea's. 'Shall we go for a swim?' she said. 'I haven't got a costume. Do you think anyone will mind?'

'Matching pants and bra?'

'Always.'

'I haven't. Do you think I'll be arrested?'

'Oh, I hope so,' said Agnes and off they went.

A week ago, it wouldn't have occurred to her to even suggest it. Something in Agnes was shifting.

# 42

'I wasn't expecting you today,' said Eleanor, opening the front door. 'Was I?' She leaned forward and kissed her mother on the cheek.

'No,' said Florence, mustering a smile, 'you weren't. I was at a loose end. Thought I'd pop down to see you.'

'Loose end? You?' Eleanor pulled a look of incredulity. 'Has the earth shifted? Has there been a lunar eclipse?' She widened her eyes further. 'Wait. You've had a haircut!'

'I have.' Florence forced a smile.

Eleanor beamed. 'I love it. It really suits you. Big change! My goodness. Oh, I get it. You're just going round showing it off.' She gave her mother a playful poke.

'No. Your father's off watching cricket,' Florence told her. 'I was just rattling about the house so ...'

She stopped, aware there was something a little unconvincing about the lie she was telling.

'Daddy's gone to watch cricket?' Eleanor turned to walk towards the kitchen, her voice surprised. 'What's going on? Have you both had some ghastly row or something? Do you want tea?' She unplugged the kettle and carried it to the sink.

'I'm not interrupting your day, am I?' Florence ignored the questions and slipped off her jacket. She wasn't quite sure what to do with herself now she was here. They'd never had a sit-and-chat relationship. She felt awkward, a little like someone about to take a chair in a dentist's waiting room.

'No, not at all.' Eleanor turned the tap on and filled the kettle. She glanced over her shoulder at her mother. 'Are you all right? You seem a little ...'

There was a battered leather sofa at one end of the kitchen and Florence settled herself into it. 'I went to the travel agent yesterday.' She wanted to change the direction of the conversation. 'I got some brochures. Italy, France. They're in my bag if you want to take a look.'

Eleanor stopped what she was doing and stared in her mother's direction.

'Brochures for a foreign holiday? What *is* going on?' She returned the kettle to the wall and pressed the plug into the socket. 'Haircut. Cricket. Holiday abroad? And Dad's up for it, is he?' She flicked the kettle on, turned and leaned back against the counter.

Florence brushed at her skirt towards her knees. She wasn't sure how best to broach what she was thinking. She wasn't sure she should reveal the dark thoughts swirling within her, not yet.

'I don't know,' she replied, pushing herself into the back of the sofa. 'I haven't discussed it with him.' Her voice was a little flat, as if she were hoping for Eleanor to encourage her.

Eleanor folded her arms the way she did when she was giving things serious thought and went to speak but stopped herself. She was mulling how best to respond but nothing would come.

'What are you most surprised by?' Florence asked, her hands resting palm down on her thighs. 'The fact I went to a travel agent or the thought of your father on a beach in the Mediterranean?'

Eleanor let out an awkward laugh.

'I'm not sure. It's just … unexpected.' She gave a small shrug. 'I think it's fantastic, actually. I do. I'm wondering how you're going to persuade him. All our family holidays involved grey days and drizzle and wearing jumpers on the beach. He doesn't strike me as the sunlounger type. But who knows? People can change, can't they?'

Could William change? Florence was far from sure. She was setting up a trap for him and she knew it. So many thoughts burned inside her, thoughts that would change things forever, thoughts that meant no going back, but now was not the time to let them fly.

'Can I have a look?' Eleanor asked, pushing herself away from the counter. 'At the brochures? Charlie and I should go abroad. God, I'd *love* to go abroad.'

Florence gestured towards her bag on the floor. 'Help yourself.'

She sat back, aware of how still she was trying to hold herself, as if the slightest movement would betray her real intentions.

Eleanor peered into her mother's basket bag and pulled out a thick brochure with a gondola on the front. 'Venice!' she exclaimed. 'Terribly romantic, Mother,' she added, thumbing through. 'Will you be able to cope?'

The comment was throwaway, light as a feather. It landed with a punch.

'With the heat or the romance?'

Eleanor looked up briefly, said nothing, then cast her attention back to the brochure. She hadn't taken it seriously.

Florence wished she had the capacity to have her words carefully considered, but she was coming to realise, with every passing day, that her life was a mirage off in the distance, something somebody might notice in passing but pay no attention to.

'This looks lovely,' said Eleanor. 'Can I keep it? Might show it to Charlie.'

Florence cleared her throat. 'I haven't shown it to your father yet.'

'But he's not going to say yes, though, is he?' Eleanor's voice was matter of fact, as if the notion of her parents in a hot, Italian city was as likely as them going to the moon.

'No,' Florence said softly, 'he probably won't.'

'Great,' said Eleanor, giving the brochure a small triumphant shake. She threw it onto the table. 'Thanks, Mum. Ooh! Imagine if we end up going to Venice!' She skipped towards a cupboard and reached down two mugs.

'Earl Grey?' she asked and, just like that, the ground had shifted.

Florence looked at the tops of the remaining brochures sticking out from her bag. She got up from the sofa and walked towards them. She pulled the lot out with one hand and pushed them across the table towards her daughter. 'Have them all,' she said, her voice defeated.

Eleanor dropped a teabag into a mug and opened the cutlery drawer. 'Thanks. If you don't want them?' She wasn't even looking at her.

'What's the point?' said Florence. It was no more than a whisper.

'Sorry,' said Eleanor, not noticing, 'did you say you wanted Earl Grey or ...' She pointed towards a few jars of teabags pressed up against the wall. 'I've got English Breakfast. Assam ...'

Florence picked up her bag and hooked it over her shoulder. 'Actually, I won't stay,' she said. 'Sorry. I should have said I was coming.' She needed to leave, before everything exploded out of her. She forced herself from the kitchen and walked towards the front door.

'Mum?' Eleanor was calling from the kitchen. 'I didn't mean ... what's going on?'

But Florence was out of the front door and gone before Eleanor could put down the kettle.

# 43

'You'll like everyone there,' said Camilla, eating a banana. She was lying on the beanbag in the sitting room, one hand behind her head, her legs crossed lazily at the ankles, her feet bare. She was wearing a faded blue T-shirt and a pair of pink cotton hot pants. 'There'll be all sorts. You might find it . . . *interesting*.' She broke off another piece of banana.

Camilla was offering to take them to a party in a house in Notting Hill. It had been unexpected. 'Do you want to come, Kiki?' She glanced up as their housemate entered the room.

'To a party? Can't. I'm on tonight.' She draped herself into a chair and spread her legs out so that her toes were stretching down into the floor.

Agnes watched her, then looked back at Camilla. There was a difference between them and her. It was more than the maturity, the confidence, the street smarts. It was how they both enjoyed their own physicality. Agnes stared at Camilla. There was something quite magnetic about her.

'I don't think I've ever been to a house party,' said Bea, 'not a proper one. Sunday lunches at your relatives don't count, do they?'

'No,' said Camilla, finishing her banana, 'they don't.' She waggled the skin in Bea's direction. 'Save that for later …' She tossed it onto the top of the radiator behind her.

'Why are you saving it?' Bea asked. 'Want to trip me up?'

Camilla gave a laugh. 'Sort of,' she said, with a mischievous smile. 'You can try later if you like.'

Bea frowned. 'Try what?'

'You dry the skins out and smoke them,' explained Kiki. 'People say they make you high. I'm not sure it's true.'

Camilla stretched herself, like a cat. Agnes couldn't take her eyes off her.

'Not sure I want to get high on a banana,' Bea offered.

Camilla pushed herself up so that her elbows drifted over her knees. 'Look, do you want to come? Or not?' She sounded irritated.

'Yes,' said Agnes immediately, 'I want to come.'

'And you?' Camilla looked towards Bea. She tilted her head. She seemed provocative.

'Actually,' interjected Kiki, 'you should go. It'll be better than the Bunny Club. There'll be people more your age.'

There was something off with Bea, a hint of something reluctant. Agnes wasn't sure what was driving it. They'd been enjoying themselves, embracing new experiences, but Camilla, despite her charisma, was tricky and unpredictable. Agnes wasn't entirely convinced Bea liked her.

'Come on, Bea,' said Agnes, 'it'll be fun.'

'All right,' said Bea, eventually. She didn't sound enthusiastic.

'Good. That's sorted then,' said Camilla, getting up. 'We'll go in the Beetle. Stop at Portobello, pick up some booze. Wasn't so hard, was it?' She glanced down towards Bea with something of a smirk. 'Late developer,' she added, and tapped her on the top of her head.

Bea's mouth dropped open but she said nothing. Instead, she picked at the rim of the mug she was holding. Agnes watched her.

Kiki leaned forward. 'Ignore her,' she whispered. 'You're both doing great.'

Bea put her mug down on the floor and wandered off towards their bedroom.

'Is she OK?' Kiki asked, watching her go.

Agnes nodded. 'Just tired, I think. It's all been a bit over-whelming.' It was a sudden thought but it stopped her short. It was true: everything had happened so fast. She stood to follow Bea. 'We will enjoy it, won't we? Tonight, I mean. We'll be all right?'

'Yes,' Kiki replied. 'You'll be all right.'

# 44

Portobello was an explosion of colour and sound and smells: cabbage leaves and squashed oranges rolled in the gutter below Agnes's feet, and over the faint aroma of decay there were accents of patchouli oil. Stallholders were packing up for the day: a lady, face like crumpled tissue, wrapped glasses into old newspaper; a man with a Frank Zappa moustache heaved boxes of vinyl into the back of a van; butchers with strings of sausages, antique dealers with their trinkets. It was like the song in *Bedknobs and Broomsticks* – everything you could want was here.

The party was in a dilapidated town house off Lisson Grove, a squat for artists and musicians: mattresses strewn across the floors, people in capes, odd costumes, tall hats with feathers, the walls were orange, there was rush matting, everything was draped with scarves and the air was thick with the smell of cannabis.

'There's a naked woman on the table,' said Agnes, as they passed the doorway into the kitchen.

Bea peered in behind her. The outstretched woman had her arms above her head. She was having her breasts painted by two men.

'You don't get that at the Brill village hall,' offered Bea.

'Pepper!' shouted Camilla, waving over towards a woman on a large paisley cushion. She had a bonfire of flame-red hair and was sitting next to a rather intense-looking man. He was cross-legged and playing a shakuhachi.

'Oh super,' muttered Bea, 'a hippy with a flute.' Agnes nudged her to be quiet.

'They are hippies,' said Camilla, turning to look at Bea. 'But it's worse than that. She's into star signs and pyramids and the power of vibrations.' Camilla ran the end of her fingertip over Bea's chest. She winked.

'Thank God,' said Bea, holding Camilla's gaze. 'We'll have so much to talk about.'

Ahead of them a naked man wandered across the corridor.

'Bloody hell,' mumbled Bea. 'What are we doing here?'

Agnes gave Bea's hand a squeeze. She could feel a tension building and was keen to squash it. She wanted to enjoy herself. 'Don't leave me on my own, will you?' she whispered. The small physical touch was a familiar moment to tether Bea back in. For the first time, it wasn't Agnes who needed reassurance.

'No,' said Bea. 'I won't.' She looked grateful.

'Hey!'

Pepper's face was alive and open. She had piercing blue eyes and porcelain skin. She was small, shoeless and wearing a loose cotton kaftan, a swirl of purples and greens.

'So here they are. These are my *visitors*,' Camilla offered, thumbing back towards them. She said it as if this was a conversation they'd already had. 'This one's Agnes. That one's Bea.' She pointed at them as if presenting a pair of oddities found at the back of a jumble sale. Camilla had clearly been talking about them, laughing perhaps.

'Hey,' said Pepper, nodding.

'Behold, the virgins,' added Camilla, throwing her arm out to present them properly.

Pepper's eyes widened. 'I know, wow.'

Bea shot Camilla a despairing look. 'You don't need to tell people,' she said.

'Trust me, I do,' Camilla replied, sitting down. 'It's the only interesting thing about you.'

It was casual but unkind. Agnes burned with embarrassment.

'They're from a weird village, Pepper,' said Camilla, reaching up and taking a handful of peanuts from a bowl. 'A weird village where nobody seems to have heard of sex.'

Agnes and Bea exchanged a look. Camilla was making fun of them.

Pepper gave a small baffled laugh. 'You're so *rare*,' she said, leaning forward. 'Special little birds.' She made a whistle and rotated her fingers in the air.

Camilla leaned back and smiled up at Agnes. 'Special little bird,' she echoed.

Agnes didn't know how to respond. Camilla had a power over her, already. She was scared of her and yet she wanted her to like her.

'Shall we get this opened?' Bea asked, pointing towards the bottle of wine in Agnes's hand. 'Let's get this opened.' She pulled Agnes away.

'Camilla is such a cow,' she whispered. 'Awful mean streak. And everyone here is mad.'

Agnes felt disconcerted. Camilla was laughing behind their backs. It was hurtful.

They pressed their way towards the kitchen. Peacock men, hands on the wall, were pinned against women in low-cut dresses. She and Bea were not like any of these people: the painters in the kitchen, the hippies on the floor, Camilla. The thought hit her like a brick. 'We should have had a pill,' she said suddenly. 'Everyone seems ready to go.' The words fell out of her but Agnes was aware she didn't mean them. She wanted to fit in. She didn't want to be the weird one people talked about.

Perhaps changing meant pretending? Everyone was pretending, weren't they?

She looked down at herself. She was in a pair of navy corduroy bell-bottoms. Around her waist, a cream belt with a string of capital A's running round it. It had been a gift on her thirteenth birthday. Her T-shirt was a faded blue, the front emblazoned with the Banana Splits. It hadn't occurred to her that she might look like a kid tagging along to a party but she did. Her sense of fashion was stuck back then, before she was ill; everything about her was. Her mind cast itself back to Eleanor's exhibition, pressed into a corner, wanting to be ignored. She looked at the women around her in the corridor, backs to the wall, being kissed by long-haired men, their hands on their bodies. Agnes was an innocent. She wanted to leave her old self behind, become someone new. She wanted Camilla to like her.

She thought about the kiss that had ruined her, the boy whose face she could barely remember. Did he have brown eyes? What had he been wearing? Afterwards she had found herself ill in bed for months, all energy gone, unable to do anything other than sleep or attempt small mouthfuls of food, spoon-fed by her mother. The experience had stolen Agnes from herself, left her as someone she barely knew: fearful, anxious, weak. The life she had promised herself had faded away, and now, here she was at another party, in London, terrified that her life could unravel again.

'Ah,' said Bea, stopping at a sideboard. An abandoned corkscrew was lying in a bowl of crisps. She picked it up and shook it into the air.

Agnes looked into the room opposite. There was a group of people sitting round a woman. She was reading *The Hobbit*. Bea followed her eyeline. 'I feel as if we're being catapulted from one insane tableau to another,' she said, pulling off the top of the wine bottle. 'Nobody, and I mean *nobody*, will ever believe us.'

'Don't leave me, will you?' Agnes asked again, pressing her hand into Bea's.

Bea stood and looked into Agnes's eyes. 'I'll never leave you, Agnes. Promise.'

Agnes breathed in. It had felt so easy, earlier, agreeing to come here.

# SUNDAY

# 45

'Do you need a hand?' Charlie stood in the kitchen doorway.

Florence was standing at the sink, her hands immersed in soapy water.

'Don't be silly, Charlie,' she said, her voice a little flat. 'I can do this. You go and sit down, read the papers, put your feet up.'

'Lunch was delicious,' he said, smiling, 'as always. Thank you.'

Florence turned and looked at him. It was impossible not to feel charmed, a little jealous even. Eleanor didn't know what she had.

'You know, you're the only person who ever thanks me,' she said. 'Truly.'

'That can't be true.'

'But it is.'

There was a short silence.

'I've brought back your travel brochures, by the way,' said Charlie, easing himself into the room. 'Eleanor told me you'd seemed a little ... upset? Is that the right word?'

He leaned against the edge of the kitchen table and tilted his head. He was probing – sent by Eleanor to find out what was the matter, no doubt. Florence was more likely to open up to him. She knew what they were up to.

'I'm fine, Charlie,' she said, and turned her attention back to the small saucepan in her hands.

'Are you, Florence?' His voice deepened and he sounded serious, yet tender. 'I like your hair, by the way. It suits you.'

Florence stared down into the water below her. It was becoming murky, tinged with brown gravy and bits of cabbage. She could tell him everything, she thought, tell him every last feeling, every fear, every blind terror she'd been fending off for weeks. She could do it now, a great unburdening, but she knew unleashing the gate would release all the demons. There would be no going back once it was done and she wasn't quite ready for it. Not yet.

'Honestly,' she lied, 'you don't need to worry. I really don't need the brochures back. I'm sure we won't use them.'

'Have you asked him?' Charlie wasn't letting it go.

'William?' Florence hesitated. She reached down into the water and pulled at the plug. 'No. I haven't.'

'Why don't you? You never know. He might surprise you.'

'I don't think so, Charlie.'

Her voice was slipping away. She was in danger of being honest. She swirled at the water with her hand, catching bits of leftovers in her fingers before they clogged up the plughole. Behind her, she could hear Charlie shifting closer. He wanted to have a conversation she wasn't prepared for.

She turned, her hand cradling dripping matter for the dustbin. Charlie was closer than she thought. She shifted towards the waste bin. 'I just need to . . .'

Charlie put his hand on her arm. 'You can talk to me, you know,' he said.

His voice was low and soft and caring and there was something so gentle about him, Florence found herself disarmed.

'I know I can,' she said, meeting his gaze. 'Charlie, I . . .'

She stopped and continued towards the bin, lifted the lid and tipped the contents of her upturned palm into it. She stared down at her hand, now smeared with grease and small specks of anonymous matter. She'd forgotten to put her washing-up gloves on. How had she not noticed?

'Oh,' she muttered to herself. 'I've never done that before.'

She returned to the sink and ran her hand under the tap. Charlie picked a tea towel from the back of a chair and handed it to her.

'I hope I'm not speaking out of turn, Florence,' he said. 'It's just, you don't seem to have been yourself of late.'

She looked at him, her eyes betraying the deep confusion within her.

'Really? I'm not sure what "myself" is. I don't seem to know any more. If you mean someone who makes herself not matter then yes, I might agree with you.'

Charlie, if he was surprised, didn't betray it. 'Why would you think you don't matter?' His voice was steady, his attention complete.

Florence went to open her mouth but, instead of words, a broken sob pushed its way out of her. She clamped the tea towel to her face, trying to smother it back in, but it was pointless.

She felt Charlie's hands on her elbows.

'Florence,' he whispered, 'what's wrong?'

'Everything,' she said.

# 46

'Honestly,' said Kiki, holding the scissors, 'you've got nothing to worry about. I spent a summer working in a hairdresser.'

'But did you cut hair, Kiki?' Bea was staring at her, her back thrust against the wall in the sitting room.

'Sort of,' Kiki said, with a shrug. 'Yes. Let's say yes.'

'No, let's not say yes unless yes is what it was.'

'Just sit down.'

Kiki pointed towards the chair she'd planted in the middle of the room. 'I can just take a bit off the back and sort your fringe out. You'll love it.'

She snipped the scissors together into the air between them.

Agnes was lounging on the beanbag looking up. Bea was splattered against the wall as if she were trying to avoid being hit by a car on a narrow country lane. Kiki was standing, one hand on her hip, scissors aloft in the other, and looking like a woman who wasn't going to take no for an answer.

They had come back from the party late, their mood sombre. They hadn't enjoyed themselves, if truth be told. Camilla had disappeared, her interest in them confined to the grand entrance and nothing more. They had risen the next morning feeling flat and despondent, and Kiki was hell-bent on doing something about it.

Camilla's words were still ringing through Agnes. She didn't mind that she had catching up to do, she didn't mind that she was behind the times. What she minded was that she was perceived as dull, undervalued and underestimated. Agnes knew with all her heart that was not deserved. Or did she know? Perhaps it was more a hope. Bea was the most interesting person she knew. Interesting people don't choose to hang about with dullards, do they? All the same, something needed to shift. It wasn't about looking the part or changing who they were. It was about becoming more comfortable in their own skins.

So here they were, with Kiki and her pair of scissors.

'Go on, Bea,' she encouraged. 'You'll look great.'

'How do you know?' said Bea, her voice rising. 'When you require the work of an expert, go to an expert. Could I shear a sheep? No, I could not.'

'Am I missing something?' said Kiki, with a puzzled frown. 'I only want to tidy you up.'

'Why don't I go first?' said Agnes, pushing herself upwards. 'Would that help? Then you might stop being so hysterical.' She shot a teasing look to her friend.

'I'm not being hysterical, Agnes,' Bea protested, 'I have thin, lanky hair that is currently arranged with a minimum of fuss. I am naturally wary of any inappropriate styling that may require maintenance. Do you remember when Brenda had all her hair cut off? Remember that?'

Agnes winced. 'Oh, yes,' she said, her voice falling, 'I do.'

'Well, then. Lovely for one day. And then she had to look after it. And it stopped being lovely. It was like a backcombed doormat for weeks.'

Kiki looked at the pair of them. 'Do you want me to cut your hair or what?'

There was a pause.

'Yes,' they both said.

'Well then,' replied Kiki, shaking her head, 'get in the chair.'

# 47

Charlie had steered Florence away from the house and she stood, her back to the long sitting room, facing the tomatoes.

She couldn't stop crying and she wasn't sure what to do about it.

'No,' she had asked, as Charlie tried to comfort her. 'Don't. If anyone sees then I'll have to explain it.'

Charlie had stood back, hands in pockets. 'We can say you've been giving me advice on growing peas,' he had said and smiled. His mood was calm in order to soothe the crumbling woman before him.

His kindness helped. It left her without embarrassment. She was grateful for it. She had never cried in front of any of her family, not least her son-in-law, and his lack of awkwardness filled her with relief but the tears wouldn't stop coming and she needed to pull herself together.

She closed her eyes and took a deep breath, trying to calm the waves of sobs as you would hiccups. Gulping her sadness down, she breathed out and opened her eyes.

Charlie wasn't looking at her: another small moment of

kindness to spare her. To their right a magpie was sitting on top of the garden shed, chattering noisily.

'One for sorrow,' mumbled Florence, taking a tissue from her pocket and dabbing underneath her eyes. 'Goodness. I'm sorry, Charlie, I didn't expect that.'

Charlie pulled a pea pod from a plant to the left of the tomatoes and ran a thumb down its centre. 'Want one?' he offered.

Florence shook her head.

'They're so good fresh, aren't they?' he said, popping them into the palm of his hand. 'Can't resist them.' He threw the peas into his mouth.

Florence breathed out again and could feel herself settling. She wasn't used to displays of emotion and felt startled by the suddenness of it. All the same, the deluge had left her feeling a momentary release, the way the pain of a boil might be abated by lancing, but she also knew the tears had fixed nothing.

'Do you think Eleanor loves you?' Florence looked at him directly.

'Yes,' he said, with a nod, 'absolutely. And I love her very much.' He chucked the emptied pea shell into a shrub behind him.

'I don't know what that feels like.' Florence stood, her eyes confused.

'Eleanor loves you too,' said Charlie. 'Daughters might not always show it but she does.'

'No, I don't mean Eleanor or Agnes,' said Florence, shaking her head. 'I mean William. I have no idea what it feels like to be loved.'

Charlie paused for a moment. 'I'm not sure how to respond to that,' he said quietly. 'But you saying that makes me sad.'

'It makes me sad too. Agnes's going away has shone a spotlight on things. The world is changing, isn't it?'

'Yes, I suppose it is.'

'I thought I had a rather full life. The girls. The polite acquaintances. The stiff socials. But it's not enough. It's all for other people. I'm wasting my life.'

Charlie blinked. 'Do you really feel that?'

'And the brochures ...' she tried to grapple with her own thread of thought ' ... they're just glossy promises. They represent something I don't have. I have no fun, Charlie. I have no life. I have no love.' She stopped, worried that the tears might come again. 'I'm not saying this because I want you to feel sorry for me.'

'I know you're not.'

'I'm trying to work it out.'

There was a pause and they both stood, staring out at the horizon. They could see rolling fields and church spires and sunflowers and swallows dipping. It was a perfect English summer day.

'It's such a shame,' Florence began, 'I don't seem capable of changing my own story.'

'Is that what you want?' asked Charlie. 'For things to change?'

'Yes, I do. But I don't have the courage.'

'I think you do, Florence,' said Charlie, his voice gently encouraging. 'I'm glad I brought your brochures back. I think you should make full use of them. Perhaps it's exactly what you need? A holiday away.'

'William will never agree to it.' Her voice sounded deflated.

'Nothing ventured, nothing gained,' said Charlie. 'If you don't ask, you don't get. What have you got to lose?'

Florence didn't respond. She was too afraid of the answer.

# 48

Agnes and Bea peered at themselves in the mirror.

'What do you think?' said Kiki, just behind them, beaming. 'I've done a good job there. Even if I say so myself.'

'Is my fringe wonky?' Bea tilted her head back and forth.

'No,' said Kiki.

Bea flattened it down with the palm of her hand. 'It is,' she said, narrowing her eyes. 'Look at it. That bit is higher than that bit.'

'It's not.' Kiki was insistent. 'I can take more off if you want?'

'No, thank you,' said Bea. 'I've never had a fringe before. I need to wait until I feel less startled.'

'I think it suits you,' said Agnes. 'Very Cathy McGowan.'

She ran her fingers through her own hair. It was a little shorter, less straggly. It was, she thought, something of an improvement.

'Look at you both,' said Kiki, sweeping up the towel she'd lain on the floor to catch the hair. 'The chaps won't know what's hit them.'

'It's not about the chaps,' said Agnes, turning round. 'It's about us.'

She was startled by her own strength of feeling but she wasn't being entirely truthful. Her first thought, staring at her new do, was to wonder what Camilla might think of it.

Bea peered a little closer. 'I'm not sure that fringe is straight but to hell with it. I'm with Agnes.'

'Last night,' Agnes began, 'Camilla told someone that the only thing that made us stand out was the fact we were virgins. She said it was the only interesting thing about us.'

She couldn't let it go. It was still bothering her.

'I told you about Camilla,' said Kiki, tying a knot in the towel. 'She's got a dark soul. Don't listen to her. She loves to make people feel uncomfortable. Don't take it to heart. So what if you're virgins? You won't be forever.'

'I don't know about that,' said Bea, checking her front teeth in the mirror. 'We've been hopeless. Absolutely hopeless. Not sure I can even be bothered any more.'

Agnes felt fired up. 'We have not been hopeless,' she said. 'Bea, remember that day on Christ Church Meadow? We were giddy. We were going to change everything, embrace the modern world, join the sexual revolution, and it was going to be fabulous. And that was fun and sweet but what we were really saying was we were going to forge our own paths. Change our future. And that's precisely what we *have* been doing. To hell with not having had sex yet. It'll happen. It will be the least interesting thing that happens to us.'

'Besides,' said Kiki, picking the chair up and carrying it to the edge of the room, 'you've only been here a week. You haven't found your stride yet. You've got new haircuts, I've lent you some clobber. Sky's the limit.'

'But it's not about that.' Agnes became more passionate. 'It's about liking ourselves. It's about believing we can be the people we are meant to be.'

Bea turned away from the mirror. 'Amen.'

'I'm fed up being told we're dull,' continued Agnes. 'Everyone's interesting in their own way. Well, I'm finding out what my way is.'

'I feel like punching the air,' said Bea. 'Can I punch the air?'

'Punch away,' said Kiki, beaming. 'Agnes fights back. I love it.'

Agnes stood, her heart thumping. There was no surrender. It was time to stand up and be counted.

# WEEK THREE

# MONDAY

# 49

'How you fixed for the next few days?' Mr Adler was pointing a half-eaten sausage at them. 'You've done all right,' he added, chewing. 'I can trust you. So I've got something a bit special. But you'll need sleeping bags.'

Agnes and Bea exchanged a quick look.

'Have you had haircuts?' He narrowed his eyes.

'Yes,' said Bea. 'We have, actually.'

'Your fringe is off.' He bit another inch off his sausage.

'Knew it.' Bea ran a hand across her forehead.

'Where are you sending us?' Agnes asked.

He consulted a piece of paper to his right. 'Glastonbury Fayre,' he said. 'It's in Glastonbury.' He peered closer. 'Actually, no it isn't. It's near Glastonbury, in Somerset. But you don't have to worry about that. You're getting a lift.'

'We're going to work at a fairground?' Agnes tried not to sound perturbed.

'No, it's a fayre with a y. And you've got to pretend to be fans of a Daevid with an e.' He gestured over to the wall at a photo of a man with a mass of dark curls. He had a strong jawline, smothered in stubble, and was bare-chested. Around his neck hung a pendant of Celtic design. He looked very pleased with himself.

'Dav*ide*?' asked Agnes, emphasising the last syllable as if it might rhyme with seed.

'No,' said Mr Adler, finishing his sausage. 'Daevid. With an e. Don't get it wrong. It makes him furious.'

They had managed to work out that Mr Adler's Agency for Go Getting Ladies was an offshoot of the larger, more productive Mr Adler's Talent Emporium. He looked after all sorts – old variety acts, hypnotists, snake charmers, magicians, contortionists, burlesque ladies, the lot – but he also looked after a few proper up and comers: actors, directors, photographers and singers. He was the broadest of churches, but if you could make him a few bob he was interested.

'So you go there,' he said, tossing the greased paper into a bin, 'stand around talking about him. Big him up.' He waved his hands in the air and clutched his face. 'Ooh I love him.' He dropped his hands back to the desk. 'That sort of thing. Create a buzz. Then scream when he's on.'

'People get paid to do this?' Bea frowned.

Mr Adler looked incredulous. 'Yes. People get paid to do this. How else do you think stars get going?'

'*Really?*' Agnes asked. She didn't sound convinced.

'Yes. Really. Now off you go. Here's a couple of quid to keep you going.' He reached into his pocket. 'And don't let me down.' He held out the notes but, as Agnes was about to take them, he pulled them back. 'What's he called?' He jabbed his forefinger at her.

'David.'

'*With an e.*'

'With an e.'

He handed over the money. 'Now hop it.'

The pick-up point was at the junction of Frognal and the Finchley Road. Agnes and Bea had rushed back to pack and now they were standing, rucksacks on, idly watching the steady stream of traffic, waiting for the arrival of what they'd been told was the 'Love Mobile'.

Agnes was feeling pretty happy. The haircuts had given them a boost and they were getting away from the flat. Not seeing Camilla for a few days would do her good, help to clear her head.

'Do you want a bit?' Bea offered up half of the cheese sandwich she'd made for the journey.

'Already?' Agnes said, looking at it. 'We only left twenty minutes ago. What time is it?'

Bea checked at her wristwatch. 'Nine forty-three.'

'Well then,' added Agnes, 'it's nowhere near lunchtime.'

'I have a strange compulsion to eat any packed lunch within half an hour of making it. I can't think of a single occasion when I was at school where a packed lunch made it through to lunch. Same with school trips. Gone by the time the coach had left the premises. It's an illness, Agnes Ledbury. And there it is.'

Bea took a bite.

'All right,' said Agnes, eyeing her chewing. 'Give me a bit.'

'See,' said Bea, holding it out. 'It's an illness.'

Agnes took a bite and behind them, coming down the hill, was the thick parp of a car horn. She turned and saw a red camper van, a large purple CND sign painted across the front bonnet with flowers scattered around it. There was a huge orange love heart with the word PEACE written through it, enormous green and yellow daisies and the word LOVE, in white, emblazoned down its side.

'Thank goodness,' said Bea, swallowing, 'we're travelling in something that won't get us noticed.'

Agnes laughed. The van pulled to a stop. The driver leaned out from his window. Agnes recognised him from the photo on Mr Adler's wall. It was Daevid with an e. He stared at her. Behind him, a girl reached across.

'Hey!' said the girl. 'Are you from Mr Adler's?'

They nodded.

'Come in, come in!'

The side door behind Daevid opened and Agnes saw three men, some bongos, a guitar, a mess of sleeping bags and a large roll of plastic sheeting.

'Hey!' they all said, raising a hand in Agnes and Bea's direction.

'Hey,' said Agnes, raising a hand back at them.

Agnes turned to Bea. 'Three boys,' she mouthed.

'And all prettier than we are,' muttered Bea, glancing towards them. 'And off we go.' She bundled her rucksack in through the door. 'Hello!' she said, climbing up. 'Does anyone want a bit of cheese sandwich?'

Nobody answered.

Daevid looked over his shoulder at them. 'I'm Daevid. With an e,' he said.

'We know,' said Bea, sitting on her rucksack.

'You're the whipper-uppers, right?' The words curled out of his mouth.

Agnes nodded again. 'The fans. Yes.' He was sexier than his photo, she noted.

'OK then,' he said, banging the steering wheel with purpose. 'Then let's get going.'

He shoved at the gearstick and one of the boys behind them slammed the side door shut. The girl in the passenger seat pulled a small turquoise transistor radio out from a bag by her side. She turned and looked at them.

'I'm Penny,' she said, holding out her hand.

'Agnes,' Agnes replied, shaking. 'And this is Bea.' She gestured back towards her. Bea gave a small wave.

'Cool, cool.' Penny switched the radio on, pushed the volume up and stuck it on the dashboard. She leaned back into her seat. 'This is going to be fun, right?'

'Right,' said Daevid.

Agnes and Bea exchanged a small knowing glance. They were going to enjoy this.

The three boys were Jevon, Carter and Jeff: shoulder-length hair, chiselled cheekbones and skinny in the androgynous style that was so in vogue. The engine was noisy so chat was at a minimum and the boys slept for most of the journey, waking only to pee in hedgerows. Occasionally, Jevon would twang his guitar. The mood was relaxed. Agnes, like Bea, sat on her rucksack, window open, and closed her eyes into the warm sun. This was more like it, she thought: getting away, feeling free, with people who hadn't formed any sort of opinion of her. She felt light and unburdened. They hadn't seen Camilla to tell her they were going. She wondered if she'd noticed? Miss them? She dismissed the thought. Her mother would be missing her, of that she could be sure. Did she miss her mother? Not a bit.

'Have you been to a music festival before?' Penny looked over her shoulder towards Agnes.

Agnes's chin was resting on her forearm. 'No,' she said, 'I've been to a barn dance. Don't think that counts.' She smiled, aware of her own gaucheness, but here, somehow, it felt charming.

'No,' Penny said, laughing, 'it doesn't.'

'I've been to Glyndebourne,' said Bea, chipping in. 'That was mostly very posh people hunkering down on picnic hampers sent from Harrods.'

'Yeah,' said Penny, 'it's going to be a bit different from that.' Her face lit up. 'It's going to be amazing. AMAZING! I went last year. First time they had it. You're going to feel ALIVE.' She grabbed Agnes's hand and shook it as if it were a tambourine.

'It's going to be wiiiiild!' Daevid laughed. He handed Agnes a soft packet of cigarettes. 'Light me one up, will you, baby?'

'Sure,' Agnes replied, then hesitated. No man had ever asked her to light a cigarette, let alone called her 'baby'. She swallowed the moment then tapped one out and placed it on her bottom lip. Taking a box of matches, she lit the cigarette quickly, sucking clumsily, then passed it back towards Daevid.

'No, put it here.' He tapped his lips with his finger.

Something struck her. Penny was sitting next to him. He could have asked her to do this but he hadn't. It felt deliberate. She leaned forward and placed the cigarette into Daevid's mouth. As she did, she felt his lips brush her fingertips. It was the single most erotic moment of her life.

'Thanks,' he said, 'you're a babe.'

'No worries.'

She sat back against her rucksack and felt the wind blowing through her hair. For the first time since leaving Brill, she properly thought about having sex.

## 50

Florence stared down at the beef suet pudding in front of her.

This was not a life. It was a conveyor belt of expectation and duty and joylessness. She had to rid herself of this endless existence of mending buttons and ironing shirts and folding, folding, folding.

She looked around the kitchen. It was spotless, as ever. What would happen, she wondered, if just once, she didn't sweep the floor or scrub the surfaces or polish the taps? What horrors would unfold if the chairs were not tucked under the table precisely? Would the world end if fresh flowers weren't in the vase or the tablecloth was smudged or the tea towels weren't all hanging to the same length?

Everything about Florence's life was about order yet she felt nothing but chaos.

Somehow, from somewhere, she needed to muster some courage.

She had put the travel brochures in the back of a cupboard in the hallway. In six days it would be her birthday. Would anyone remember? She might get a phone call from Eleanor. Agnes was away. William always forgot. Each year she went through the charade of picking herself out something nice: a silk scarf, a silver pendant, the latest historical novel. She would wrap it up, place it on William's desk, an unsigned card on top. He would find it (one year he didn't), sign the card and gift it to her as if she'd had nothing to do with it whatsoever.

She tried to think of an occasion in which someone had gone out of their way to make her feel special. She couldn't think of a single one.

She went to the cupboard, pulled out the glossy brochures and stared at them. Charlie was right. If she didn't ask, she didn't get, and if she didn't get then it would be the catalyst for change.

All Florence had to do was ask for it.

# 51

Before them was a vast field of brown grass. Beyond it, a pyramid of unfinished scaffolding. Sheets of yellow plastic flapped lazily into the air and, as Agnes peered, she could see men in flares, shirts off, dotted amongst its skeleton. Strange birds in an even stranger tree. The field was strewn with bodies, a few tents scattered around the edge. It was warm, getting hotter. Agnes felt excited.

They were walking towards the Pyramid, rucksacks on backs. The boys behind were carrying sheets and bits of old tarpaulin. They were going to make a teepee, they said; at least, that was the plan. Daevid was carrying nothing. He was strutting, bare-chested, a large black Stetson holding down his curls, intentions hidden behind a pair of dark shades.

'Over there,' said Daevid, pointing towards an open patch. 'We'll pitch it there.'

A man, wearing nothing other than a Jesus thong and a mass of coloured beads and bangles, danced around them pinging a tiny tingsha between his fingers. Beyond him, a man in an orange waistcoat was banging a bass drum. Between them, two men on their knees writhed at each other like rearing snakes.

Behind them, the noise of a motorbike thrummed, thick and meaty. Agnes turned. It was being ridden by a naked man.

'This is nothing like Glyndebourne,' said Bea flatly. 'We must cling very, very close.'

Agnes didn't reply. For the first time, she was wondering if she wanted to. An even more startling thought wafted through her: she wanted to be here, she was rather glad it was so odd and wild. The energy was making her bold.

Penny, deciding she'd found their perfect spot, sat cross-legged on the grass. Jevon, Carter and Jeff set about trying to tie some poles together with rope. Daevid stood over them, patting his bare stomach with the flat of his palm. Taking his sunglasses off, he bent down and pulled a small axe out from a duffel bag. He tossed it into the air, caught it and winked at Agnes.

She dropped her rucksack to the ground. 'What are you going to do with that?'

'Chop down some branches from over there,' he said, pointing off to a line of trees at the edge of the field. He flipped the axe into the air a second time.

'Are you allowed?' asked Bea, heaving her rucksack from her shoulder. 'To chop down trees, I mean.'

Daevid threw his Stetson onto the grass and flicked his hair back. He had a raw sexuality, a presence that was unnerving. Agnes thought about his lips on her fingertips. She clenched her fingers into the palm of her hand.

'Of course I'm allowed,' he said to Bea. 'Everything is allowed.' He held his arms out as if to welcome in the world.

A low cheer rumbled up towards them from the stage. Cupping her hands over her eyes, Agnes could see a band walking out. 'Shall we go and watch?' she said to Bea. 'We can practise being fans.'

Daevid pointed the end of the axe towards them. 'You're here to be my fans, remember.' His tone was proprietary.

'Would you like us to come and scream while you chop branches?' Bea raised an eyebrow.

Daevid held the axe out and twisted it in his hand. His jaw stiffened, his look dark and disarming. She was making fun of him but he'd let it go. His arm fell.

'No, go watch the band.' He ran a hand across the top of his hair and walked away towards the edge of the field.

'I'm not sure you should be rude to him,' Agnes said. 'I don't think he likes it.'

'I wasn't being rude. I was pulling his leg.' Bea scuffed at the dried grass with the end of her shoe. 'It's all right to tease him, isn't it?'

Agnes gave a small shrug. 'It doesn't matter, come on, let's go.'

There was an air of tension, a palpable bristle of irritation.

'What's the matter?' Bea asked. 'Why are you bothered if I tease him? He's full of himself.'

Agnes batted away the question. 'What's the matter with you? You seem a bit off.'

'I'm fine,' Bea replied, a little tersely.

They both stood for a moment, not saying anything. A man in a floppy hat shambled past them. Off to their left, someone was throwing up into a plastic bag.

'Actually, I'm not,' Bea said. 'I dunno. It feels like something's going to go wrong.' She chewed at her bottom lip.

'We've only been here five minutes,' said Agnes. Bea didn't reply. Her face was crunched towards the stage. She didn't want to look at her friend. 'It'll be fine, Bea,' Agnes added. 'Chill out, it's going to be fun.' It had taken so long for her to reach this point it was difficult not to feel a sharp sting of frustration. 'Enjoy it. We'll stick together,' she continued, trying to be conciliatory. 'Like we always do.'

'Will we?' said Bea. She turned and looked at her. Her eyes were half-closed, peering into the sun behind Agnes.

'Of course we will,' Agnes replied.

But there was something in the air, Bea was right. Nothing felt certain. Agnes put her hand on Bea's arm but, as she did, Bea let it fall back down to her side.

'Let's just watch the band,' she muttered and, sticking her hands firmly into her pockets, walked off towards the stage.

Agnes wasn't sure if she had the desire to be accommodating. If Bea was going to be a misery, this was going to be a bore. All the same, she'd have to show willing: up to this point, Bea had put up with everything. Agnes was going to have to reciprocate. Problem was, she didn't want to. Agnes wanted to enjoy herself.

# 52

Daevid was standing back, cigarette hanging from his bottom lip and staring up. He looked fabulous and he knew it.

'Bit to the left, mate,' he yelled towards Jevon who was on the shoulders of Carter. Jeff passed up a flapping pink bed sheet.

Penny was lying on her back, arms outstretched, eyes closed towards the sun.

Agnes and Bea had come back, having watched the band in near-silence, sitting on the grass, not talking. Bea had sat scrunched into a ball, arms round her shins, chin on knees. There was something small and worried about her. It was something Agnes didn't know what to do with. Everyone around them seemed so at ease, so relaxed, they should be embracing the experience, but Bea's reluctance was putting the dampeners on. More worrying, it felt catching. Agnes wanted no part of it.

'Do you need a hand?' Agnes asked.

Daevid cast her a crooked smile. 'How was the band?' He didn't sound as if he particularly cared.

'Good, I think,' she said. She kicked off her shoes and pressed her feet down into the dry grass.

'Singer was rather dreamy,' added Bea. It was the first thing she'd said since getting back.

'Rather dreamy?' said Daevid, mimicking her voice. Now it was his turn to make fun of her.

'When are you on?' Agnes said, moving the moment on.

Daevid's easy smile drifted away. He shook his hair back. 'Tomorrow.' He turned back to the teepee. 'Tie that bit up there.' His finger pointed towards a loose piece of tarpaulin. 'Seriously, Jev, you've missed that bit. Come back this way, tie it in.'

'Here,' said Penny, from the ground. She was holding out a rolled-up cigarette. 'Just for you,' she smiled.

'I don't smoke,' said Agnes.

'It's not that sort of cigarette. Take it,' encouraged Penny, waving it in her direction. 'It's a gift.'

Bea bent down and took it instead. 'Thanks,' she said, tucking it into her pocket.

Agnes glanced at her friend. Perhaps she'd decided to pull herself together, get with it. She hoped so. It would lighten the mood.

'You're welcome,' said Penny, throwing her arms above her head.

Agnes looked back at her. She looked like a snake, basking in the sun. Her top, a tie-dye cotton vest, had ridden up over her belly and Agnes could just see the bottom of her left breast. She wasn't wearing a bra and her nipples were standing proud, asking to be noticed. Was she Daevid's girlfriend? Was she in the band? Who was she?

'Do you like my body?' Penny ran a grass-covered hand over her torso. She was staring at Agnes, her look curious, her voice expectant.

Agnes was startled by the question. There was something creepy about it. She wasn't sure she wanted to respond.

'Have I made you feel awkward?' Penny's thumb circled her belly button.

'A little,' said Agnes, shifting her feet. Beside her, Bea said nothing.

'Hmm.' Penny closed her eyes again and tilted her face upwards to the sky. 'It's so warm,' she murmured. 'It's so lovely.' She made a noise like someone licking cream from a spoon.

'We should find some food,' said Bea, changing the subject. 'I haven't eaten since this morning. Are you hungry?'

Agnes shook her head. 'Not especially.'

She cast a look towards Daevid and the others. He had one foot up on a wooden pole and was tying in a branch with a length of blue twine. His torso was glistening with sweat. The muscles in his arms were taut and veined. A thin line of dark hair snaked its way from his trousers to his belly button, his chest hairless and smooth. He was beautiful but she had a bad feeling about him. He reminded her of Camilla: charismatic but controlling.

She looked back towards Bea. 'Perhaps we should get food for everyone?'

Bea nodded and shouted up. 'We're going to get food. Do you want some?'

Daevid shook his hair back from his face. 'Sure thing,' he said with a lopsided grin. He jumped down and lifted Penny's hand. 'What do you want, baby?' He pulled her from the grass and leaned down to her upturned face. In front of them, he kissed her. Penny's arms drifted around his neck and one leg curled itself into him. His hands dug into her lower back, his thumbs gripping her skin. They kissed again, this time more passionately.

It made Agnes uncomfortable. She blinked and looked away. Bea was wearing an expression of thinly veiled bemusement.

Penny stopped and ran the back of her hand across her mouth. 'I don't mind,' she said.

Jevon jumped onto the grass and slid his hand down Penny's arm. She turned her face towards his, cupped his cheek with her hand and kissed him.

'What is going on?' said Bea, shaking her head. 'Come on, Agnes, let's leave them to it.'

Agnes stood for a moment. This strange tableau left her jealous: jealous of the ease with which Penny gave herself to enjoyment, jealous of the attention she freely received, jealous of the energy, jealous that Daevid wasn't kissing her.

She turned and followed Bea. Her heart was pounding.

# 53

William was sitting in the garden finishing the crossword: *The Times*, cryptic. The lid of his fountain pen was resting against the cleft in his chin. It was what he did just before committing to writing in an answer, a reflective pause to check he had it right. Florence watched him from the window of the long sitting room. It was a fine day, warmer than it had been of late, and the evening air was delightful.

She had finished the washing-up, dried the dishes and put everything back in the places they belonged. Normally, she would now be folded into the corner of the two-seater in the front room, sewing basket on the cushion next to her, old treacle tin of buttons to her right, but that was not where she wanted to be at this precise moment.

*If you don't ask, you don't get.* Charlie's words rang through her. He was right.

She pushed open the large French doors into the garden and stepped out onto the terrace. The red tiles were baked from a day of sun and Florence was enveloped with a thick, woozy heat. She walked down towards the garden steps, treading carefully through the daisies. It was an old habit; as a child, she'd been told each daisy was a dream: crush it and a wish dies. Today, she would tiptoe through them, as delicate as a gazelle.

In her hand she clutched one brochure, a touring holiday of Tuscany that meant ten days away and took in Siena, San Gimignano and the city she was named for.

In a few days it would be her birthday. She was not intending to buy herself his present this year. This year, she was going to ask for it.

'William.' Her voice was low but steady. 'Can I have a word?'

The pen was resting against his chin. 'Incapable of being fully understood ...' He mumbled the words softly.

'Sorry?'

He tapped the end of the pen once against his chin and then gently lowered it to the page. 'Unfathomable. Yes. Unfathomable.'

Florence watched as he inked in his answer. He was slow and methodical. It came first. She could wait.

'William,' she said again.

'A. B. L. E.'

He looked up, the evening sun catching his eyes. Raising one hand to his forehead, he seemed not surprised or puzzled but inconvenienced. 'Yes?' he said. 'What's the matter?'

'Nothing's the matter,' said Florence, shifting so she was between him and the sun. She didn't want him squinting at her. She wanted him to see her in full. She wanted to see his eyes. 'I've got something for you to look at.'

'I'm doing the crossword, can it wait?' He glanced back down at the paper and tapped gently at it twice with his pen. His voice had the low hum of a bumblebee or a distant lawnmower.

'Not really, no,' said Florence, persisting. 'It's my birthday on Saturday and I'm not buying myself a present from you this year.'

She stopped, momentarily, to read his face, but he was staring up, immutable, unblinking. They didn't have conversations that began like this. There might be a reaction, however small, to tuck away and remember, but looking at him, waiting for something to hold on to, there was nothing.

'I had my hair cut last week. Did you notice?'

William shifted in his deckchair, then frowned a little. 'Has something happened?' He looked past her to the house as if half-expecting to see it in flames.

'Yes, in a way,' she said, her voice softening, 'it has. It's my birthday in five days and I want you to look at this, William.' She held out the brochure. 'I would like us to go here.'

He sat back, leaning into the striped canvas as if he'd been shoved hard and pinned down. His eyes glanced over the cover of the travel brochure in front of him.

'Tuscany?' he mumbled. 'That's in Europe.'

'Yes, it is in Europe,' said Florence. 'Yes, it is.' She didn't move her arm. She wanted to force him to take it. 'Will you look at it, please? I'd like you to.'

William hesitated. She could see that he was trying to work her out. He opened his mouth as if to speak but stopped and instead turned his attention to his fountain pen. He put the lid back on, methodically, and tucked it into the top of his newspaper.

'Will you read it?' This time she was more insistent.

Without speaking, William took the brochure from her. She could hear her heart beating in her ears and she stood, clenching her hands into fists to stop them from shaking. She stared down at him waiting for a moment, however small, of something pleasurable registering in his expression. Tuscany, for goodness' sake! Her mind was screaming. Look at it! This wasn't a week on a beach in the drizzle trying to peel eggs. It was old towns and history and skies as blue as cornflowers. It was an *experience*.

He flicked through, quickly, not lingering on any given page, his attitude idle and cursory.

'Where did you get this from? Eleanor? Is this her idea?' His tone was flat, as if he might be asking about a broken tap.

'I went to the travel agent's in Oxford. So no.' A thought drifted through her. If it had been Eleanor's idea, might he take it seriously? 'I showed them to her. A few days ago. She was rather impressed.'

He glanced up at her, his expression entirely puzzled, then turned his attention back to the brochure. 'Are these the prices?' he said, almost talking to himself. He cleared his throat. 'I'm not sure now would be the best time to ...' He held the brochure back up towards her. 'Imagine the heat.'

She took it into her left hand and let it drift down to her side. 'I would very much like to go, William,' she said, her voice calm but insistent. She was not pleading with him, she reasoned; she was making it very clear what she wanted.

'Wrong time. Sorry.' He unhooked his pen from the top of the newspaper.

Florence paused. Normally, that would be the end of the matter but she felt emboldened. 'When is the right time?' She wasn't going to stand down.

'Sorry?' He glanced back up towards her. Blinded by the setting sun, he raised a hand to his forehead.

'I'd like to know when you think the right time to go might be?' She could feel the pages of the brochure blowing against her leg. 'September? October? November? Christmas in Italy? That would be charming. Or perhaps in the New Year? February? Spring? When, William, do you think is the right time to go? Because it's my birthday in five days. And I would like to make arrangements.'

There was a long silence. She had never challenged him like this, not once, in all the years they had been married. It felt terrifying.

'I'm not sure I've made myself clear,' he said, looking back down towards his crossword. 'We won't be going to Tuscany.'

As his pen drifted up to rest in the cleft of his chin, Florence, without speaking, looked down towards her feet.

She was standing on the daisies, all hope crushed.

# TUESDAY

# 54

They had not slept well.

The teepee build had been abandoned after Jevon and the others downed tools for a few 'well-earned' joints. The late afternoon had drifted into a long evening and Bea, who'd decided that they weren't being paid by Mr Adler to become drug addicts, had quietly scooped up their sleeping bags and found a corner of the field where they could get away from the jaw-grinding nonsense.

Despite the brief sigh of relief, they had been unable to enjoy anything other than an insubstantial sleep. The partying all around them hadn't stopped: impromptu breakouts of jamming with varying degrees of success, revellers shouting at the moon, small scuffles, stoned loners asking them for food; it had gone on and on. Tonight, they decided, they would have to brave the teepee. At least in there they wouldn't be constantly woken up.

Agnes sat up and looked across the field. It was like a scene from a war film except everyone had been decimated by drugs and alcohol rather than bullets.

Somewhere over to her right, a thin line of smoke was wisping upwards from a fire trying to take hold. A man wrapped in a blanket stood over it, staring down, willing it to get going. In his hand was an electric kettle. Agnes gave an incredulous laugh. She wanted to point him out to Bea but, lying beside her, she was finally sleeping.

It had taken so long for them to drift off, she didn't want to wake her.

There was a small tor beyond the field and, with the dawn rising, people were making their way to the summit. Agnes felt an urge to join them. There was a new boldness to her and she wanted to embrace it. Wriggling herself out from her sleeping bag, she pressed her feet into a pair of battered deck shoes and pulled a large jumper over her head. It was a little damp, the morning dew having done its worst, and, with a short look back towards the still-sleeping Bea, Agnes began to pick a route through the battlefield of festival goers.

The dawn sky was beautiful: slashes of deep pink and orange splayed against the dusky blue of a cloudless night. As Agnes mounted the tor, she marvelled at it. The sky seemed so vast she could feel her own insignificance. Life passed so quickly. A blink in time, really, and that's it, you're done. The days were passing faster than she wanted. Soon enough she would have to return to the unchanged reality she had left behind. Agnes had two choices. She could remain as she had been: timid, compliant, ignored. Or she could embrace a different version of herself: bolder, adventurous, unafraid of failure.

It was better, Agnes was learning, to try and fail than never try at all. She had failed once and never tried again. Well, not any longer. No more blaming a moment in a village hall, no more blaming the boy whose name she couldn't remember, no more blaming the illness that struck her down. No more excuses. It was time for Agnes to try.

A handful of people were gathered: some sitting, some standing, all gazing out towards the dawn. One man, semi-naked, was in a yoga pose, legs folded, his arms lifted up towards the sky. He had long, golden curls tied back with a wreath made from the hedgerows. He looked like a child's idea of a Greek god.

Agnes sat down on a mossy stone and pulled her knees into her chest. There was an energy in the air, magical almost, and she stayed there for a while, watching the people around her. Some had been up all night; others, like her, just waking. A few were wide-eyed, high on something or other, dancing to music only they could hear. There was sadness and there was hope: a yearning for something to end, something to start. All chapters need a breaking point, a cliffhanger from which all new things push forward.

She kicked down at the ground with the end of her shoe. She could feel her own sadness, her own hope. She thought about her parents: her stiff, unloving father, her immovable mother. She thought about her exam results, the noose about her neck. She needed escape routes, her own breaking dawn. Nothing was inevitable. Inevitable is only what you're prepared to accept.

She thought about Daevid with an e. He was intoxicating: the way his hair curled across his shoulders, the way his lips pouted when he smoked a cigarette, the glint in his eye, the ease with which he existed. He stirred in her the precise feelings she had journeyed to find, but he was also brittle, thin-skinned, imperious. There was no lightness to him, no sense of fun.

She cast her mind back to those heady moments in Christ Church Meadow, the declaration that they would embark on an odyssey to lose their virginity. She let out a small, involuntary laugh. It felt so gauche, so ridiculously innocent. She glanced back up towards the early-morning sky. The sun had risen. Fires were stirring to life in the field below. The Pyramid was golden in the dawn sun. It was time for Agnes to stop apologising. It was time for Agnes to stop giving up.

Pushing herself up from the rock, she dusted down the back of her shorts. She raised her face towards the sun and pulled off her jumper, wrapping the arms around her waist. She would walk back down and find Bea.

Today, she thought, would be a good day to finally have sex.

# 55

Florence hadn't slept a wink. She turned over and glanced at her bedside clock. It was just before six.

Beside her, William was gently snoring, sleeping like a baby. It was a source of quiet resentment, how easily he was always able to fall asleep. She hadn't really been aware of how many nights she lay awake, staring at the ceiling. Now she was painfully so.

She slipped silently from under the eiderdown and walked barefoot across the carpet towards the door. Slithering out, she stood very still and tried to collect her thoughts. A rage burned within her, a fire that had no outlet. It was threatening to destroy her. She felt ill with it, as if her skin itched or she had a physical tic she could do nothing about. She had lost all sense of who she was, blinded by an injustice she could no more understand than control. She felt aggrieved, hard done by, bitter. It was poisoning her and she needed to walk out from the man lying asleep in their bed and get as far away from him as possible.

She held her hands to her throat and closed her eyes tight shut. She wanted to choke the pain out from her, an exorcism of a grief she couldn't yet let go. It was her birthday in four days and she wanted to go to Europe.

Her hands drifted down to her side. She would have an hour, hour and a half tops, before he came downstairs, oblivious to anything she might think or feel.

She walked to the bathroom at the far end of the landing, opened the door and stood, her feet cool on the cold tiles, staring at herself in the cabinet mirror. She barely recognised herself. She was like a woman awake, the blinders off. She was seeing herself, properly, for the first time. He noticed nothing. He cared nothing. Would he even notice if she were gone? she wondered.

She looked down at her hands as if somewhere, in them, she might find answers. She thought of Marjory, of the life her friend had been brave enough to seize. Did she want a divorce? She didn't know. Did she love William? She didn't know. What did she want?

Above everything, in this moment, she wanted to get away.

She looked up again at herself in the mirror. She was tired, washed out, drawn. She needed to escape, but on her own terms. William had made his feelings clear.

Somehow, she had to do the same.

# 56

There was a young woman up on stage. She was sitting, cradling a guitar that seemed vastly bigger than she was, her voice low and sensual, her delivery earnest. There was something vulnerable and lonely about her and the crowd, rather than dancing, sat quietly to listen. The mood was reflective.

Agnes was lying on her back watching the clouds. Bea was next to her, on her side, her face cupped into her hand. It felt like a rare moment of calm; there was an ease between them again.

Agnes looked at her watch. 'We'll have to leap up and start shouting "Daevid. With an e!" soon.' She gave a short sigh. They were rather dreading it.

'It's funny, isn't it?' Bea said. 'We did all this to try and have sex. And I haven't felt remotely sexy. Not once. I'm not sure I even want to do it any more.'

Agnes glanced sideways. 'Nobody has to do anything,' she said, locking her fingers together across her chest. 'Neither of us. Not if we don't want to. From now on, we only do what we want.'

'Do you want to start screaming at Daevid with an e?'

Agnes paused. She was perfectly happy staring at him and wondering what it might be like to lie with him naked, but screaming at him?

'No. Not remotely.'

They both laughed.

Off to their right, two naked men and a naked woman were rolling in some mud. Bea sat up and leaned back on her elbows to watch them.

'How do they do that? Where do they find the ... what's the word I'm looking for? The ... *desire* to do it, the *inclination*. I'm sitting here thinking about where I might find a cheese sandwich. Or how I'm ever going to be clean again. Or why I seem to have developed the musk of a dead cat. The absolute last thing I am thinking about is sexual contact of any sort. I'm not even sure I want to shake hands with anyone. That's how bad it is. But look at them – sorry ...' She stopped and peered towards them a little harder. 'Is that man making a mud pie on the other man's you-know-what?'

Agnes looked over. 'Yes. He is.'

Bea shook her head. 'I mean, I'm not a religious person – far from it. But you start to wonder whether hell is an actual thing.' She threw herself onto her back and stared upwards. 'Ugh,' she exclaimed, 'I was almost feeling relaxed. Not any more. I don't think I've ever felt more tense in my life.'

'Perhaps we should smoke that thing?' said Agnes idly. 'The joint Penny gave you. Have you still got it?'

'Yes, I think I have.' Bea reached into her pocket. It was squashed flat and half of it had fallen out. 'It's not inspiring me, Ag,' said Bea, turning it over with the end of her finger. 'Is it you?'

'No. Not really.' Agnes rolled onto her elbow. 'Still, everyone seems to be doing it.'

'Yes,' agreed Bea, 'they smoke it and then they take their clothes off and make mud pies on their genitals.' She looked at

Agnes and squinted, her glasses a little off. 'It's funny, isn't it? I thought I was up for it. Turns out I'm not.'

Agnes pursed her lips. 'I've got a terrible confession to make,' she mumbled. She screwed her face up. 'I think I fancy Daevid with an e.'

'Oh no, Agnes.' Bea sat upright. 'You can't mean it?'

Agnes shook her head. 'I'm afraid I do. I've thought about having sex with him more than once.'

'*Really?*'

'I mean, I think he'd have sex with a log.' Agnes paused, then looked thoughtful. 'I think I just want it out of the way, Bea.'

There was a silence and Agnes could see Bea trying to squash down her obvious disappointment.

'You'll tell me, won't you, if you're going to try,' Bea said, her voice resigned. 'I'm not sure I want to watch that.'

'Bea!' said Agnes, aghast. 'I'd never make you watch me have sex!'

'Please don't,' Bea entreated. She turned over so that her back was towards Agnes. There was something small and wounded about her but, before Agnes could reply, a smattering of applause rippled around them. The singer was done. Next up was Daevid with an e.

'Come on,' Agnes said, touching Bea's shoulder. 'The time for screaming has arrived. Let's get this over with.'

There was a sadness to Bea that Agnes would have to deal with, but not now. She pulled her friend up by the hand. They would stand near the front. That way they wouldn't have to watch the people grimacing behind them.

# 57

'I want to go to Italy.' Florence was standing by the cooker, her hands gripped. She meant what she said and she was going to be heard.

William looked up at her, in front of him the perfectly cooked egg and bacon that Florence had just put down.

'I'm sure you do,' he said, flicking a napkin onto his lap, 'but I'm afraid I don't. Is there some softer butter?' He peered into the butter dish. 'This won't spread well.'

Florence licked the top of her teeth inside her lip. She was not going to lose her temper but she was not going to budge.

'No,' she replied. 'I forgot to take it out of the fridge last night. You'll have to manage.'

William picked up his knife. 'Is something not right with you, Florence?' He scraped at the top of the butter. 'You seem very out of sorts.' He wasn't looking at her.

'I'm perfectly well,' she replied. 'I'd like to go away to Europe. I've thought about it a lot and that is what I'd like to do. And I'd like you to reconsider.'

William tried to smear the cold butter across his toast but it snagged and refused to move. He gave a small tut and put it to one side to warm on the toast. Letting his knife hang in the air, he picked up his fork and turned his attention to the egg. 'I haven't made arrangements to have time off, Florence,' he said, piercing the skin of the yolk.

'Then you can ask today.' Florence felt the blood pumping through her chest.

She did not feel anxious or unsure or worried in the least. She was driven with the righteous certainty that she was making a stand. This, she had decided, was the hill she was prepared to die on.

William sliced his knife across the middle of the egg and scooped a mouthful onto the back of his fork. She wondered if he felt shocked or surprised or angry. His face betrayed nothing. He paused for a moment, then took a bite and glanced down towards the rough mound of butter stuck on his toast. He tapped at it with the end of his knife.

'Still hard,' he murmured.

'William,' said Florence, persisting, 'did you hear what I said?'

'Yes,' he replied, his voice a little baffled, 'I did.'

'Well, then,' said Florence, 'will you ask? At work? Today? You're sufficiently senior for it not to be a problem.'

He sat back in his chair and wiped at the corner of his mouth with his napkin, then folded it methodically and placed it to the left of his plate. He was being neat and precise and controlling the moment. He placed his fingers on the edge of the table and spread them out, his index finger tapping softly against the tablecloth as he thought.

'Florence,' he began, 'I'm not sure if this is because Agnes is away and you've developed a burning desire to join her. Is it?'

He looked at her as a teacher might look at someone carpeted for a misdemeanour.

Florence shook her head. 'No, William,' she said, 'it has nothing to do with Agnes. I'd like to go abroad for two weeks. It's really not too much to ask. It's a holiday. You might enjoy it.'

She stopped, a sharp thrill coursing through her veins.

'I think this can wait until this evening,' said William, picking his knife back up. 'I think you need to calm down.'

He prodded his knife into the lump of butter still sitting at the edge of his toast. It moved a little. William cleared his throat. He wasn't interested in the conversation she was trying to have. He was shutting this moment down.

Something burned deep within her. Florence shifted on her feet. She unclenched her hands. 'Good,' she said, with a nod, 'I'll leave you to it. I've got a lot to do.'

She walked past him and out of the kitchen. She wasn't lying. There was a lot to be done.

# 58

To be fair, Daevid with an e hadn't been entirely awful.

'If existential prog rock sung slightly out of tune was my bag,' said Bea, as she and Agnes wandered back to the teepee, 'then I might have thought that not half bad. I'm being magnanimous here. Can you tell?'

'My arms hurt,' said Agnes, rubbing the top of her shoulder. 'I'm glad we don't have to do that again.'

'I very much enjoyed the bit where you pushed all your hair over your face and swayed like something found in the attic in a Victorian novel.'

'Thank you.'

'He can have no complaints.'

'No.'

'We did precisely as asked.'

'We did.'

Despite their reticence, they had found themselves having fun. It had been refreshing, leaping about and screaming. It had vented something, released the pressure. Bea stopped for a moment, as if she was trying to work something out, to let something go. The moment hung. Bea looked as if she wanted to make an effort.

'I feel as if we should smoke that joint?' Bea reached into her pocket and fingered it out. It was even more squashed. 'There's only about half of it left. I can't imagine that amount will be cataclysmic.'

They both stared down at it. It was mangled, half-bent and looked a little forlorn. They'd never done drugs before but everyone around them was and they all seemed perfectly happy. This was a momentous occasion.

'In for a penny and all that,' said Agnes.

'To hell with it. Let's do it, Agnes. What's the worst that can happen?'

'All right,' said Agnes, smiling. 'Let's do it.'

It was exciting this, both of them back on the same page. They borrowed a small box of matches from a man whose bell-bottom trousers were tied up with a bit of green rope. His breath smelled of pears. They sat facing each other, cross-legged, and lit it.

'Suck it,' said Agnes, flicking the match dead.

Bea drew a large breath in, paused, shook her head, blew her cheeks out and coughed. She handed it to Agnes. 'I need to get better at that,' she said, coughing again.

'How do you feel?'

'I don't feel any different. At all.'

Agnes sucked. There was a sticky, distant sweetness, nicer than tobacco. She'd tried the usual fag round the back of the bike sheds at school but hadn't liked it. It had given her a coughing fit and the taste had been bitter and unpleasant. The deep breath in made her feel heady. She handed it back.

'Not sure I can do another puff,' said Bea, still coughing. 'Actually I do feel a bit different. I think.' She looked around her and narrowed her eyes. 'I'm not really sure.' She grabbed Agnes by the forearm. 'You won't leave me, will you?'

Agnes took another sip from the end of the joint and shook her head.

'Promise me, Agnes.'

'I promise.'

The joint, reduced as it was, was quickly dispatched. They sat for a moment, waiting for the effects to settle in. Agnes looked around the field. A man in a grey tank top, naked from the waist down, was screaming at the sky. A boy with a crow on his shoulder stared off while it pecked delicately at his mouth. Behind them on the stage, a man, eyes sunken into dark diamonds, was whipping the audience into a frenzy. The sound of penny whistles and bongos was omnipresent. Agnes sat, wondering if she felt more mellow or more in tune with this weird world, but all she was aware of, in that moment, was an overwhelming desire to change into a lighter top.

'I'm a little hot,' she said, fluffing at her cardigan. 'Let's go to the teepee.'

They headed off.

Whoops and loud laughs were coming from inside. The others had returned and, by the sounds of it, celebrations were in swing.

'We should join in,' said Bea. 'I think it would be good for us.' She looked utterly serious. She clasped her hands behind her back. 'Perhaps not good,' she added. '*Essential*.' She said the word carefully.

Agnes looked at her and was consumed with a sudden and desperate sadness: the clasped hands, the dirt on the bottom of her flares, the conviction that this was the right thing to do. Bea was the person she probably loved most in the world and she was doing this for Agnes.

Agnes stepped forward and clasped her friend to her. 'I love you, Beatrice Morgan.'

'Remember your promise,' Bea whispered, then pulled herself away.

Agnes could hear muffled voices beyond the heavy tarpaulin door: soft laughter, the quiet twang of a guitar. Pushing it to one side, Bea stepped within. Agnes followed. The atmosphere was warm and intense; clothes hung above their heads, dripping down from the branches chopped from the hedgerows.

Daevid was undressing. Getting changed from his stage gear, Agnes noted. She liked watching and felt painfully aware of it.

'Hey,' she said, raising a hand. 'You were great.'

'Very competent,' added Bea.

Carter was on the floor to Agnes's left. He was wearing nothing except a pair of bright blue underpants. He was splayed, like a starfish, a half-smoked cigarette hanging from his bottom lip. Jeff was to her right, curled into a ball, and Jevon was towards the back, wide-eyed, topless, shoeless, still playing his guitar. He seemed a little wired. In front of him was Penny, undressed to her bra and pants, lying like Cleopatra, propped up on a mound of pillows, eyes closed and smiling.

Daevid got down next to her. He had ignored the pair of them. Sitting cross-legged, he pulled an old cake tin out from a bag.

'We thought you did really well,' Agnes said, trying again.

He was cutting something from inside the tin. 'Have some of this. You'll like it.' He handed Bea what looked like a small piece of chocolate cake.

She took it from him and sniffed it.

'Want some?' he said to Agnes.

She glanced towards Bea. She was taking a bite.

'Yes, all right,' she said.

'Cool,' said Daevid and passed her up a piece.

It was no bigger than a lump of Turkish delight, moist, and as she squeezed it, something viscous dripped onto her finger.

'Don't lose that,' said Daevid, watching. 'Nicest bit.'

He lay back and gazed up at her. 'Go on. Try it.'

Agnes licked at the liquid running down towards her thumb. It had a slightly odd, acrid taste and, to rid herself of it, she popped the cake into her mouth and swallowed. It was thick and chocolatey.

'Nice,' she offered. 'What is it?'

'Welcome to Wonderland, little Agnes,' he said, looking at her, then laughed.

Penny, curling herself into Daevid's armpit, began to laugh too, followed by Jevon and Carter behind her. Jeff rolled onto his back, a strange wild look in his eye. Agnes glanced over to Bea. She had gone down onto her haunches and was holding her head.

Agnes, not fully understanding why they were laughing, tried to join in but something odd was happening. The world was slowing and she had a sudden sense that she could not only feel but see the air. She slumped down and put her arms out to touch it. Beside her Bea was moaning.

Penny, pushing herself onto her knees, crawled towards her. Across her forehead, Agnes now saw, was the word LOVE written in red lipstick.

'Can you feel it?' Penny whispered, sitting opposite her.

'What's happening?' Agnes said, looking for Bea. 'I don't understand.'

'It's beautiful,' Penny replied, cupping Agnes's cheek and pulling her face back towards hers. 'It's so beautiful.'

She rolled onto her back and, taking Agnes's hand, placed it onto her stomach. Agnes felt Penny's skin with her fingertips, soft and silky and firm. She looked towards Daevid who was leaning back, smiling. She wanted to go to him, to curl herself into him like Penny had done, but she didn't seem able to move. She looked back towards Bea whose legs were folded under herself. She was rocking.

Agnes pushed herself across the floor. She had to concentrate on her breathing. Beside her, Carter was crawling towards Bea. In front of her, a ladybird was between near-dead blades of grass. Agnes stopped and stared at it. She could hear its legs moving.

She looked back to Penny. Daevid was kissing her. Carter was removing Bea's top. What was happening?

Jeff was ahead of her. He looked pale, his eyes rolling back into his head. His breath smelled of something dank and unpleasant. She reached forward to touch him. He recoiled, as if her finger had electrocuted him.

Agnes could feel her chest pounding. Behind her, the guitar playing had stopped and she could hear small moans of pleasure coming from the scatter cushions. Above her, the clothes, hanging from the branches, swayed.

'I'm going to have sex,' she muttered to herself. The moment had finally come and she was going to do it with the most beautiful man on the planet.

She let her head fall to her right. Penny was now naked. Daevid was kissing her on the lips. Bea seemed to be trying to get away from Carter. He had hold of her ankle. Agnes didn't know what to do. She had a cardigan on. Should she try and take it off? She looked back towards Jeff.

'Can you help me?' she mumbled, but he was staring open-mouthed at the ceiling, not moving.

She tried to push herself onto her knees. She was going to have sex but she had a cardigan on and she hadn't had one of her sister's pills. Consumed with the need to find one, Agnes pulled herself across the floor, digging into the earth with her fingers. Where was her rucksack? She wasn't even sure if she could remember what it looked like.

She crawled across a mound of dirty clothes, discarded shoes and a sleeping bag that smelled of a damp cellar. Over in the corner, stacked one on top of the other, she could see two rucksacks. Behind her, Penny was moaning.

Bea had pushed herself against the edge of the tent. Carter pulled her back.

Agnes really needed to take this cardigan off. She tried to get one arm out but it didn't seem to want to come off. She lay by the rucksacks, breathing heavily. Where were they? Where had she put them? She glanced over her shoulder. Daevid was taking his trousers off. Oh God. She was going to have sex.

Using the rucksacks, she clambered onto her feet and, still trying to remove her cardigan, staggered towards the mass of writhing bodies in the centre of the teepee. She got one arm out. Progress. Perhaps one of the others would pull the rest off for her.

'Daevid,' she said, looking down at him.

He looked up at her.

'Shut the flap of the teepee on your way out, yeah, babe?' he said, sticking his hand into Penny's groin.

Agnes stood and blinked. Two men were having sex with one woman and Bea seemed to have disappeared under Carter. Nobody was trying to have sex with her. She turned, stumbled to the tarpaulin and fought herself out.

Agnes couldn't understand what she had done wrong but she was not having sex.

# 59

Florence packed the last of the Tupperware into the freezer: two weeks' worth of stews and pies and sliced vegetables. She had labelled everything: what it was, day of the week, how hot to make the oven and how long to keep it in.

From the moment William had left to go to work, she had made herself busy: she had taken herself to the shops, bought lamb, beef, chicken, leeks, flour, suet, carrots, cabbage. She had prepared batches of dishes she knew would be easy for him to cope with. She knew what she was going to do and she wanted to be prepared and organised and clear.

She undid the apron around her waist and folded it into a neat square. Putting it down, she walked through to the pantry where the washing she had done earlier was waiting to be arranged. She stood, methodically sorting through the things she wanted, then took the small pile she had chosen upstairs to a suitcase that lay open on the top of their bed.

She packed sparingly and light. She only wanted to take the bare essentials. She didn't want to feel burdened or inconvenienced. She pressed a small washbag into the side of the suitcase and clicked the top shut. She glanced up towards her bedside clock.

Quarter past five.

She changed, quickly, into the jeans and top she had retrieved from the back of her wardrobe. She pulled on the knee-length boots she hadn't had the confidence to wear. She ran a hand through her hair and reapplied some lipstick. She looked at herself in the mirror.

Turning, she picked up the suitcase, carried it to the front door and dropped it gently to the floor beneath the coat hooks. Outside, she heard the crunch of tyres on gravel. She walked back down the hallway and into the little sitting room.

She poured herself a small Scotch and waited.

An air of calm had descended, as if she found herself in the moments after a storm. She had drawn her red lines, she had built her barricades; now was the time for her to finish what she had started.

William walked in and stopped, surprised to see her. His eyes scanned her from top to bottom. This was new. He looked disarmed.

'Are you feeling any better?' he said, reaching past her onto the drinks cabinet.

'I am,' she said, lifting her glass. 'Much better. I'm leaving you, William.'

His hand paused over the tumbler he was about to pick up. He looked at her.

'What are you talking about?'

He picked up the glass and dropped an ice cube into it.

'I've filled the freezer with meals. You've got enough to get you through the next two weeks – more if you're careful. The oven is simple enough. I think you can manage to work out how to put it on.'

She took a sip from her glass.

Without looking at her, William poured the Scotch, returned the bottle to the cabinet and turned.

'This is happening why, exactly? Because I don't want to go to Italy? You can't be serious, Florence.'

'I am serious, William.'

He let out a small laugh and turned away to settle into his armchair. He shook his head and, placing his glass next to him on the side table, picked up the newspaper he had left there that morning.

'Don't be ridiculous,' he mumbled and reached for the fountain pen in his jacket pocket.

Florence watched him, the way he turned his attention to the crossword, to the pen in his hand, to the way he crossed his legs as if nothing untoward was happening. He didn't believe her. She drained her glass and placed it down in front of the ice bucket.

'Goodbye,' she said. 'I'm sure you'll manage.'

He glanced up at her as she walked out of the room but said nothing. He thinks I'm being melodramatic, thought Florence, as she walked down the hallway. She was surprised she wasn't sobbing. She was surprised she didn't feel hysterical. She was neither of these things. Instead, she was deeply enjoying the sound of her knee-high boots as they click-clacked across the hall tiles.

Florence picked up her suitcase and left.

# WEDNESDAY

WEDNESDAY

# 60

Florence looked at her watch. It was just after two in the morning.

She was lying in the back of her Morris Minor waiting for the first ferry to France. She still had hours to go and she couldn't sleep.

She sat up and rubbed at her eyes with her fingers. A few street lamps flickered in the distance and she could just make out the back of a commercial ferry sitting beyond her in the dock.

She thought about William, what he might be feeling or thinking. Would he be sleeping like a baby tonight? she wondered.

She felt her chest heave with relief.

She had traveller's cheques in her purse, some French francs she'd bought from a bureau de change; she had her passport, clothes, a small bag of fruit.

She felt unencumbered, weightless.

She felt like someone else entirely and it was wonderful.

For the first time in her life, she was free.

# 61

Agnes opened her eyes and sat up. Where was she? She ran a hand across her face, brushing away some mud dried to her cheek. Beside her a large metal pole reared upwards. She was on the ground next to the Pyramid. A piece of plastic flapped just above her head.

Agnes felt startled. How had she even got here? She looked down at herself. A cardigan was hanging off one arm. She pushed herself up. She was cold. She pulled the cardigan on and did up the buttons. Gripping herself around the middle, she looked up. There was no moon. In the distance a few fires were burning.

Where was Bea? She needed to find her.

The patch of field in front of the Pyramid was bare apart from the odd couple for whom passion didn't want to wait. Agnes's mind flashed back to the teepee. Awful. Awful.

She stumbled her way towards the edge of tents and sleeping bags, the strange shoreline that represented, not hope, but help. She paused for a moment and peered into the darkness. She couldn't quite get her bearings. She span round to try and find the tor but, with no moon, it was hard to make anything of the landscape.

She veered sideways between a break in the hedge, onto a long dirt track. Patches of cowslips and corncockles peered up from the edges. There was a smell of something chemical and agricultural from the field to her left.

She stopped. Could she hear something? A Japanese flute? What was that?

She pressed her chin down into her chest and cocked her ear towards the darkness. There was something, ahead of her and to the right.

She was so cold. She had no idea what Daevid had given her but it had left her shivery and thirsty and with a gnawing hunger. A headache was pumping across her forehead and her tongue felt dry and swollen.

The track was thinning, becoming less definable, and as Agnes stumbled, she was surprised to find she was in grass up to her knees. She swept her fingertips across it: coarse, soft, a smell of something almost comforting, the chemical smell replaced with something sweeter, more natural. She was in a meadow. She stopped, aware of a stillness that was almost eerie, and listened.

The noise wasn't a flute. It was someone crying.

It was coming from behind her.

She turned back, but as she did, her foot collapsed into something deep and narrow. She let out a yelp. Her ankle twisted and a sharp pain pierced up towards her knee. She put her hand out to try and soften the fall but she went down awkwardly, landing hard.

The crying, just ahead of her, stopped.

Agnes gasped for breath. She could hear someone coming through the grass. She rolled onto her back and tried to glance down at her ankle. It was agony. Pushing herself onto her knees, she felt down and then tried hopping upwards onto her good leg. The pain was unbearable and, after a few steps, she fell again, this time letting out a howl.

As she tried to push herself up again, she felt hands on her shoulders. She looked up. Bea was standing over her.

'Oh, thank God,' said Agnes. 'I've twisted my ankle.'

Bea stood staring down. Her face was tear-stained and confused.

'You promised you wouldn't leave me,' she whispered.

Agnes stared into her friend's eyes. Something was very, very wrong. Bea was looking at her in a way she never had before: betrayal, disappointment, horror. Freedom and all that it had to offer, it turned out, wasn't everything it was cracked up to be.

'Bea, I ...'

'I don't think I want to be here any more.'

'Shall we get out of here?' Agnes said, without hesitation.

Bea nodded. Agnes didn't need telling twice.

# 62

Florence looked out across the square. She was in Calais and had found a small café with tables and chairs on the pavement. It was delightful.

In front of her was a warm croissant, a small pot of strawberry compote and a coffee, the size of a bowl of soup. It was called a cappuccino and she'd never had one before. She'd never had any of it.

She dug her knife into the compote – whole strawberries, no less – and smeared a large, sticky lump onto the end of her croissant. The pastry was flaky and crisp, the taste exquisite. Memories of flaccid bacon, barely heated beans and tinned mushrooms flooded back: miserable B&B owners; William poking at a greasy egg; the girls, elbows on tables, complaining of warm milk on cornflakes.

Not this summer, thank you.

Florence licked her fingers and reached down into her bag. She'd bought a small map on the ferry and she pulled it out.

Opening it up, names leaped out at her: Paris, Reims, Cannes, the Alps, Lausanne, Milan, Florence. She could barely believe it. She would go wherever she wanted, spend as much time as she liked, sit when she wanted to sit, eat when she wanted to eat. She would find ivy-clad *pensions* and small boutique hotels and tiny, family-run restaurants and she would walk through fields of sunflowers and drink wine in the sun and listen to the cicadas singing under canopies of grapes.

This is what she would do and nobody was going to stop her.

She sat back, a smile flickering across her lips.

She'd done it. She'd actually done it.

# 63

William looked into the long sitting room. She wasn't there.

There was no sign of her car in the driveway.

He glanced at his wristwatch. Ten past nine. He was already going to be late for work and wasn't sure he could leave it any longer. She must have gone to Eleanor's, he reasoned. Yes. That's what she had done. She would return later today.

She'd be back later this morning. Or perhaps after lunch, if she decided to go to a gallery. Yes, that's what would happen.

He would not mention it when he came home tonight. There was little point and it might risk reigniting the disagreement.

She'd already made him late for work.

How ridiculous of her, how embarrassing. All this, simply because he didn't want to go to Italy.

Perhaps he should send her to the doctor? See if there was anything wrong with her. Last child gone, that's what this was about. He recalled a chap in the office talking about when their youngest headed off to university.

'The wife doesn't know what to do with herself. She's gone quite mad.'

Yes. It would be that.

Perhaps she should be on pills until the worst of it passed?

He would tread carefully, William decided. She didn't mean what she had said.

Florence, he was quite sure, was simply unwell.

# 64

'Egg sandwich?' Sister Annunziata turned round and held out a small Tupperware box. 'Help yourself. We made plenty.'

Bea and Agnes had been picked up by a pair of nuns heading to London. Sister Susan was driving because she had distance glasses and Sister Annunziata did not. She'd 'lost them somewhere in a vegetable patch', she'd told them. 'I'll probably find them when we dig up the potatoes.' It was a relief, to be with people who had all their clothes on. The egg sandwiches were perfect.

Sister Annunziata was quite young, early thirties, though it was hard to tell through the wimple. She had deep brown eyes and long lashes, her lips a rose-red bow. Her skin was clear and bright. She looked enormously happy. Sister Susan was considerably older, perhaps late fifties, but her face was impish, sparkling. They exuded calm. It was precisely what was needed.

Bea was next to Agnes in the back, squashed against the door, pushed as far away from Agnes as she could. It had not gone unnoticed. They had barely spoken since they'd found each other. It was frightening. Bea didn't know what had happened. She had no memory beyond eating the cake. Agnes had a vague recollection of Carter taking Bea's top off but that was it. Bea had woken semi-naked, cold and confused. Feeling embarrassed and ashamed, she had grabbed her things and run from the teepee, disorientated and disturbed, and ended up in the meadow where she had sat, not knowing what to do.

Agnes leaned into the window, her forehead pressed against a rolled-up jumper. She was racked with guilt. She had made a promise and not kept it. She would never forgive herself.

'What were you doing?' asked Sister Susan, glancing over her shoulder. 'You seemed a little rattled when we picked you up ...'

Agnes cast a glance in Bea's direction. Bea looked away, pointedly.

'It was a festival. We thought it was going to be fun but ...' Agnes's words trailed off. How do you tell people? Besides, it was for Bea to tell people, if she wanted, not her.

'It wasn't.' Bea's voice was flat, lifeless. 'I'm so tired.' She put a hand over her eyes.

Agnes wasn't sure if Bea was trying to sleep or hiding that she was crying. She felt useless. She simply didn't know what to do or say.

'All you have to do now is rest,' said Sister Susan, looking at them in the rear-view mirror. 'You sleep and we'll practise our madrigals.'

Sister Annunziata nodded.

'We'll wake you when we get to London. Don't worry. You're safe now.' She looked in Bea's direction then back to Agnes.

Agnes looked away. She couldn't bear it. Whatever happened last night had broken everything. She closed her eyes as the nuns sang 'Jesu, Meine Freude'. For the first time in weeks, Agnes wanted her mother.

# 65

William stared down at the note on the kitchen table.

He had missed it before but now he stood, his overcoat still on, and read it.

*William*, it began, *I have prepared enough suppers to get you through the first two weeks. After that you'll have to ask for help. I have left instructions. All you have to do is turn the oven on and follow them. If you are struggling, Mrs Benson next door will be able to show you what to do. Florence.*

He frowned and turned it over but there was nothing further. He wasn't sure how he felt about this. What was she playing at? A second night at Eleanor's to teach him a lesson?

*First two weeks?*

The inconvenience rattled through him. Mumbling small profanities, he looked at the note again. What had she said to him the last time he'd seen her? He couldn't quite remember but then he never really listened to her. He paid her no attention at all.

Anger flushed through him and, screwing the note into a ball, he threw it across the kitchen table. Where were these suppers?

He walked to the fridge and opened it to stare at one brown box of eggs and a half-full bottle of milk. Below them there was a small butter dish and a Tupperware box with a few beans from the garden.

'This is intolerable,' he muttered.

He slammed the fridge door shut. He had half a mind to phone Eleanor and demand Florence come back home.

No, he wouldn't give her the satisfaction.

If she wanted to make a fool of herself, so be it. He would drive to Boarstall and get himself some fish and chips. Yes, he'd do that, he thought. He'd enjoy it. He walked back towards the front door. He could manage just fine without her, thank you very much.

Florence could go to hell.

# THURSDAY

# 66

They were back in Hampstead. Bea had rallied, a little. They had arrived home to an empty house and she had collapsed into bed and fallen into an immediate and deep sleep. The shutting down had done her good. Agnes, on the other hand, had been wide awake and fretful, scrabbling for what to do. What can you say beyond sorry? How do you make something better when you don't know what to fix? Agnes had been drugged too. God knows what Daevid had given them but there was a chance, however slim, that nothing much had actually happened. Carter, from what Agnes could remember, was in the same state as they'd been. He couldn't have been capable of anything.

But Daevid was a different matter.

Bea was sorting through clothes. Her manner was brisk. She wanted to clean everything she had, and quickly. Agnes, to show willing, was going through her own rucksack and, as she pulled out her wash bag, the strip of contraceptive pills fell to the floor. They both stopped what they were doing and stared at them.

Agnes picked them up. She wanted to get rid of them, forget she'd ever tried to grow up.

'Do you think we'll ever have another one of these?' she said, looking to Bea.

'I don't know, Agnes,' Bea replied, her voice weary. 'I'm a bit off the whole escapade, if I'm being honest.'

Agnes immediately regretted asking. What was she thinking? What a thing to even bring up. What was the matter with her? She threw them and they skittered into the corner of the room.

'Are we giving up?' said Agnes. 'On this? Maybe we should?'

'I'm not sure I care,' Bea said, bundling some clothes into a plastic bag. 'Do you know what I think? We're with people who are nothing like us. We've tried to be like them but we're not. And we did something we shouldn't have done. And here we are, not liking ourselves.'

'I like you,' Agnes offered. It was meant emphatically.

'Do you? Really? I didn't feel as if you did when we were at Glastonbury Fayre.' She turned and stared at her.

Bea's words cut Agnes to her core. She deserved it. She had been irritated with her, carried away with her own wants. Something happened in the teepee and Agnes should have stopped it.

'Bea,' Agnes began, 'I was drugged too. I couldn't ...'

'The thing is,' Bea said, interrupting her, 'I was happy with myself before we came away. I liked myself a lot, in fact. I may not have been popular at school. I may not have been popular at the Sec. But I didn't care because I liked who I was. And I had you. But now, here, I don't like myself at all, and as for you ...'

'Bea, I ...'

'I can't remember what I did. I woke up with no top on and my knickers round my ankles. I got myself into that mess because of pretending to be something I'm not. But it's not just what happened or didn't happen. It's about you and me. It's about playing parts. And the truth is, I don't want to play any more.'

'What do you want to do?' Agnes could feel her hands trembling.

Bea looked up at her. 'Honestly? I want to go home but you're not ready to do that, are you?'

Agnes thought for a moment and turned to look out of the open window. There was a warm breeze. She could see silver birches and rooftops, the sky mottled with thin clouds. Songbirds were in full voice. It made her think of Brill: of the beautiful garden; of her father, stiff and distant; and her mother who always looked after her. She thought of her sister and the independence she had carved for herself.

If Agnes went back now, she would return to being the little sister dispatched to fetch tomatoes and peas who would start a job tapping out letters at summer's end. She had tasted freedom and she wasn't ready to give it up.

'I can't. I'm sorry, Bea,' she said, turning. 'I don't think I'm ready.' She sounded as apologetic as she felt.

'Well, then,' said Bea, returning to her clothes. There was a heavy pause. 'If I did have sex,' she added, her voice no more than a whisper, 'I might be pregnant.'

'No, Bea,' said Agnes, 'that can't—'

'Of course it can,' Bea snapped. She ran the back of her hand across her eyes. 'And what then? This isn't who I am, Agnes.' She pulled at the front of her T-shirt, and picked up her bags of dirty clothes.

This wasn't who either of them was. But Agnes knew if she gave up again, she was done for. This wasn't just about a moment that had turned everything sour; this was survival.

## 67

*My goodness, it's warm.*

Florence stood, map spread out across the bonnet of the Morris Minor. It was held down by a bag of peaches she'd bought from a tiny woman dressed in black who had spoken no English.

She leaned back, her hands just above her hips, and looked up into the sky. There wasn't a cloud in sight. She wasn't sure where she was. She'd stayed in Calais the previous night. She'd been tired – the night in the back of the car had rather done for her – so she wanted to keep things leisurely. For the first time in her life, she was in no rush. She would move when she felt like it, and last night she hadn't.

She'd stopped in a lay-by on a long, straight road that seemed wedged between endless sunflower fields with tall cypress trees standing to salute on either side. There was a noise too, drifting on the tinder-dry air, that was unfamiliar and now she had stopped, she was almost deafened with it: the steady singing of the cicadas, rhythmic and soporific.

She thought she might have been lonely or afraid but she'd surprised herself with how utterly at ease she felt. The ground beneath her boots was dry, the tips covered in a pale dust. It was far too hot for them but she was almost reluctant to take them off. They were her battle boots, the footwear she would forever associate with her moment of victory. All the same, she'd stop at the next town and buy herself something inexpensive. Some flip-flops, perhaps, or a pair of those rather lovely canvas shoes she'd seen a lot of the natives wearing: espadrilles, she thought they were called.

She reached into the bag of peaches and pulled one out.

It filled her fist, the aroma intense and heady. Peaches came in tins in Brill. This was a rare treat. The slight fuzz of the skin brushed the bottom of her nose and, as she bit into it, she almost gasped. It was so delicious, so sweet. Juice ran down her chin. She curved her body away from it. The peach was dripping.

Behind her, a dark blue Citroën truck rattled past. There was a man in the open-top back, blond hair, tanned, one arm drifting over the side, and as she looked up he raised a hand in her direction and smiled. Before she could react, he was gone. She bit back into the peach, cupping her hand underneath it. She wanted to give it her full attention. She wanted to remember this peach for the rest of her life.

As she sucked at the last of the stone, she turned and leaned back against the car. There was the slightest of breezes. She was convinced she could smell lavender. Tossing the peach stone into the scorched grass, she held a hand to her forehead and stared out across the fields ahead of her.

Swallows were flitting and high up, almost too far away to see, she could just make out the slow-circling silhouettes of a pair of very large birds. Were they buzzards? Eagles? She should have brought binoculars.

Her forearms were turning a little pink, she noticed. When she stopped to get shoes, she'd get sun cream and perhaps a pair of sunglasses? She'd never owned a pair. Another first.

This was all wonderful. She'd done the right thing.

# 68

It was so hard not to feel despondent. Agnes, arms folded, waited for the kettle to boil. Bea was yet to return. A small part of her worried if she even would. There was nothing to stop her. Bea could just get on a train and never come back. Agnes, on the other hand, had to stay. She couldn't give up again.

Agnes thought about who she had been: the girl outside the pub in Brill in her school tracksuit; lying on the lawn, spread-eagled amongst the daisies; scuffing back from the baker's with a bag of iced buns; sitting in the tiny room filled with typewriters; watching the back of her father's books; putting away the dishes; feeling stupid at parties for her sister. That was who she was and, if she went home now, it was who she would return to.

Agnes's story had shifted: she was no longer the girl racked by illness, she was the young woman who had tried to grow up in a faraway field in Somerset. She hadn't fared too well at that, she had let down her friend, but this time, despite the urge to run, she had to find the courage to stay.

Get up, try again.

'Making tea?' said Kiki, behind her. She'd rolled in from a party, a little worse for wear. There had been booze and drugs and the usual casual sex and it was all water off a duck's back.

'Do you want one?'

'Love one.' Kiki slid in and leaned against the counter. 'Aren't you supposed to still be at that festival? Why'd you come back early?'

Agnes gestured down towards her ankle, which was black and swollen. 'Couldn't stay with this,' she said. It was obvious she was lying.

'Does it hurt?'

'Not really. It looks worse than it is. I don't think I could run on it.'

'No,' said Kiki. She stretched her arms over her head and yawned. 'God, I must go to bed.'

Agnes glanced at the clock on the wall. It was twenty past eleven.

'Where's Bea?'

In front of them, the kettle began to whistle.

'Laundrette,' Agnes said flatly. 'I'm not sure she's going to stay much longer. Here, I mean.' She reached up for another mug and dropped a teabag into it.

'Why? What happened?' Kiki folded her arms.

'Umm …' Agnes wasn't sure how much to tell her. 'We got ourselves into a bit of a mess.'

'What sort of mess?'

Agnes paused. It felt hard, wrestling with whether to be honest. She wouldn't be standing here doing this with Camilla, but Kiki was different. Kiki had told her secrets so perhaps it was all right to tell her theirs. She took a deep breath. 'I made a bit of a fool of myself.' She poured water over the teabag and looked for a teaspoon. 'And I let Bea down.' Her voice was full of regret.

Kiki tilted her head. 'What do you mean? Do you want to tell me?'

Agnes stirred the tea slowly. She couldn't look up. 'We got into a situation.'

'With blokes?'

Agnes, head down, nodded quickly.

'What happened, Agnes?' Kiki's voice was firm but kind. She reached a hand out to Agnes's shoulder.

'I'm not sure I really understand.' Agnes shook her head and took another breath. 'We were up – you know, in a good mood – and then this bloke gave us some cake. It had something in it. We didn't know. I just thought it was cake.'

'Ah,' said Kiki, moving closer.

'And everything took over. I was out of it. And I left her. I left her in a situation and she doesn't know what happened and now I don't know what to do.' Agnes spilled it all out, quickly and sparingly. It was a relief to tell someone.

'So you were both drugged and Bea thinks a bloke had a go on her but neither of you are quite sure?'

Agnes nodded, her chin on her chest.

'Well, that's shit.'

'It's my fault.'

Kiki's hand gripped her a little tighter.

'No, Agnes, it isn't. Some bloke did a shitty thing. It's not your fault. It's not Bea's fault. And don't let anyone tell you it was. Did you have sex? Did that happen?'

'No, I didn't,' Agnes faltered. 'Bea doesn't know.' She started to cry. 'I don't know how to help her.' She held a hand to her mouth.

Kiki took her in her arms.

'It's not your fault, Agnes,' she whispered.

'But I think it is,' Agnes mumbled into Kiki's shoulder. 'I feel so ... stupid, and ugly ...'

'Stop it,' said Kiki, leaning back and cupping Agnes's cheeks in her hands. 'Look at you. Beautiful eyes. Noble nose. Wonderful smile.' Kiki widened her eyes to encourage her. 'And as for stupid. Please. You're as bright as a button. Men are very predictable. Really. Some men are shits. Not all of them deserve us. Remember that. I'll talk to Bea when she gets back. When did this happen?'

'Yesterday.'

'All right,' Kiki said with purpose, 'then we can do something about it. Leave this with me. It's going to be all right, Agnes. I promise.'

Agnes mustered a small nod. It was a relief to unburden but this wasn't just about understanding what had happened, it was about acknowledging what it had done to them.

For all her longing for success, desire and popularity, Agnes knew that her greatest demon was the voice inside her own head that told her she was worthless and unlovable. Everything that had happened in the teepee had brought it crashing back.

Somehow, she had to persuade herself she was wrong. Somehow, she needed to make it up to Bea.

# 69

Florence pointed her toes away from herself and tilted her head. They looked good, these bright red espadrilles, cheap too. Yes, she'd take them. She nodded up towards the young woman behind the stall.

She had driven to Amiens where she had found a bustling market in the town square. Stalls were heaving with olives, saucisson, small glazed pastries, sun hats, nougat, fruit, herbs, rotisserie chickens. People with weathered faces and honest hands surrounded her. There was a liveliness to it, an energy that was attractive.

She sat on a small wicker stool and waited for the woman to put her espadrilles into a brown paper bag. She touched the tag on a pair by her side. Twenty francs. It was nothing really. Reaching into her bag for her purse, she thumbed through the unfamiliar notes and pulled out two tens.

'*Merci, madame,*' said the woman, smiling.

Florence stood and took the bag. She'd wear them now, straight away, she thought: remove her hot boots and slip her feet into new shoes. Her car was parked just beyond the market square and she strolled back towards it, stopping to look at some enormous strawberries. She thought about William in this setting: the ambling, the browsing, the idle interest. He'd have hated it, seen it as pointless, would have stared at his watch and wondered what time they were leaving in order to get to wherever it was they were supposed to be going.

Florence didn't have anywhere to go to. She was simply being, in the moment, taking the day as it found her. She loved it.

She threw her boots into the back of the Morris and turned to look up towards Amiens Cathedral. It was on a ridge, just beyond the River Somme. She had an urge to go to it: feel the cool air within, breathe in the incense, to sit, to think, to light a candle. She had been born and raised a Catholic and, despite losing her faith years ago, there was something about a church that always felt like home.

She checked the Morris was locked, bought a small cheese and salami baguette to take with her and headed off.

The interior was stunning: the vast nave, the Gothic choir stalls, the statue of the weeping angel at the high altar, the baroque pulpit held up by Faith, Hope and Charity – all of it filled Florence with a sense of the divine. But she wasn't really here for the architecture and the statues. She wanted forgiveness. Not for what had passed but for what she knew was to come.

She slid, silently, onto a long wooden pew and sat for a moment. The drop in temperature was a blessing. The midday sun outside had been relentless. The coolness made her calm. She stared off towards an adjacent aisle A few tourists were meandering slowly. A priest was chatting to a man in a red sun hat. Off to her left, two nuns were looking up at the altar, gift-shop bags in hand.

Did she want a divorce? The thought fell suddenly. It startled her. Divorce was so final, so absolute. Marriage was all she had known for more than twenty years. Was it a space she still wanted to inhabit? Too soon for decisions. She had room to breathe, to think, to be. She had time on her hands: languid mornings, lazy afternoons, long evenings in a warm sun. She had espadrilles and peaches. The answer would come to her. Don't rush.

A man was sitting two pews down, his hand draped across the back of the thick rim. He was staring up at the ceiling, his blond hair thick and tussled. Florence narrowed her eyes. She'd seen him before somewhere. Wait ... he was the man in the back of the Citroën truck.

He was wearing a cream linen shirt, crumpled, his arms so brown she could make out the fair hairs running to the end of his wrist; his hand was broad and she watched as his fingers slowly caressed the dark wood beneath them. He was beautiful.

Florence stared at him. He was about Eleanor's age, she thought. What did he do? she wondered. Writer? Insurance salesman on his holidays?

He turned and caught her staring and, rather than look away, she held his gaze. He smiled and Florence smiled back. Running a hand through his hair, he pushed himself up and draped a hessian bag across his chest. Florence watched him as he drifted off towards the transept then she looked back towards the small chapel to her right.

She reached into her pocket to find a franc coin. She would light a candle for her mother and father and think about who she wanted to be next. That decision was still to be made.

## 70

Agnes pressed herself into the wall next to Kiki's bedroom. Behind the closed door she could hear Kiki talking, her voice low and muted. Under it, the sound of Bea, softly crying.

She leaned her forehead against the wallpaper, her fingers splayed behind her. She was trying to listen. Bea hadn't wanted her in the room. Perhaps it was for the best. Kiki knew what she was talking about.

There was a pause in the hum of conversation, footsteps. The door opened. 'Come on,' said Kiki, stepping out. 'We'll do it now.'

Bea followed her into the hallway. She was still crying, her shoulders down.

'I'm taking her to see a nurse I know. Check her over. We won't be long,' said Kiki, picking up her bag.

'A proper nurse?' Agnes suddenly felt panicked that something dark was in the offing, something she had heard rumours about, something that desperate women had to resort to.

'We're just getting her looked at,' replied Kiki, helping Bea into her coat. 'That's all. Don't worry. I'll look after her.'

Agnes glanced at her friend. She seemed so small, so vulnerable, so beaten down. 'Do you want me to come with you, Bea?' she mumbled, reaching out to her.

'No.' Bea didn't look at her. Instead she followed Kiki out through the front door.

The latch clicked shut and Agnes, still pressed against the wall, felt as if the sun had gone in forever.

# FRIDAY

# 71

'I've sprained my ankle, Mr Adler.'

Agnes stared down at the floor of the telephone box. The corners were filled with fag ends and scraps of paper covered in hastily scribbled numbers.

He gave a low grunt. 'How long is that going to take to get better?' He coughed loudly.

'I think if I keep it up today, I should be fine. Sorry.'

'What about the other one? Wonky fringe?'

Agnes hesitated. She'd rather assumed that if she couldn't work then neither would Bea. Besides, she wasn't sure Bea wanted to go anywhere other than home.

'Has she got a leg hanging off as well?'

'No,' said Agnes, reluctantly, 'she's ...' She wanted to say 'fine' but it wasn't true. Bea was far from fine. 'Her leg is working perfectly well.'

'Good. Tell her to get to Foyles. Charing Cross Road. Setting up for a book launch. Three o'clock. Got that?'

'Yes, but—'

'Then tell her to come and get your wages.' He hung up.

'Ugh,' Agnes muttered.

She pushed open the door with her shoulder and hobbled out. Bea was sitting on a bench next to the telephone box, her face blank and distant. Agnes sat, heavily, beside her.

'He wants you to go to Foyles.'

'The bookshop?'

'Yes. Help organise some sort of do. He said to go see him after. For the money.' Agnes paused. 'You don't have to go if you don't want to. He didn't say that, but you don't.'

Bea nodded and looked off again.

They sat, for a moment, in silence, watching the buses and the cabs and the men on bicycles. Bea had kept herself to herself since coming back last night, taken herself off to bed and slept, again. Kiki had assured Agnes that everything was fine. The nurse hadn't seen any signs of bruising or injury. Now all that had to happen was for Bea's period to start.

'Are you all right, Bea?'

Bea pushed her bottom lip out. 'No, I don't think I am. I think I will go,' she said, quietly, 'to Foyles. It'll be good to think about something else.'

Agnes twined her fingers together in her lap. Their friendship was stuttering. She wanted to ask whether Bea was really going to get away from her too but she couldn't bring herself to. She didn't want to know the answer.

'I'll help you back up the steps.' Bea pushed herself up and held out her hand.

They moved slowly.

'I'm sorry, Bea,' said Agnes. 'For everything.' She wanted to make things right.

'I know you are.'

It should have lifted Agnes up, but Bea's voice was resigned and inevitable. It made Agnes more anxious than ever. She seemed unable to say the right thing. Bea was slipping away from her and there was nothing Agnes could do about it.

## 72

William was at his wit's end. The note had said there were meals. He'd used up all the eggs and wasn't far off finishing all the beans from the garden. He was feeling rather forced into a corner and he resented it.

He picked up the telephone and dialled.

'Hello?'

'Eleanor,' he said, clearing his throat. 'It's me, your father.'

'Yes,' she said, unable to hide her surprise. 'I know. Has something terrible happened?'

William paused. Yes. Something terrible had happened but he was damned if he was going to admit to it.

'No,' he said, 'I just have a question for your mother.'

There was a short silence.

'Right?' said Eleanor, her voice puzzled, waiting for more.

'So can you put her on?'

The moment hung in the air. 'Are you all right, Dad?'

'Yes, I'm perfectly fine.'

'Mum's not here.'

William felt a wave of relief. 'So she's on her way back?'

'No, Dad, she hasn't been here. What's going on?'

William faltered. 'Sorry, I thought she'd … she must be out with … Marjory … or …' He couldn't immediately think of any other of his wife's friends.

'Dad,' said Eleanor, sounding more worried. 'What's up? Are you sure you're all right?'

'Of course I am.' William tapped his fingers on the telephone table. Damn. This hadn't been the plan. He tried to think. 'Sorry. What I meant to say, she's out tonight seeing Marjory and I thought she was visiting you today. I think she'd mentioned something. Must have got the day wrong. But she's left me a meal and I can't seem to find it.' He stopped. He closed his eyes briefly. He felt ridiculous.

'Oh, right,' said Eleanor, sounding more relaxed. 'Have you looked in the freezer?'

'Freezer?'

'You know I got Mum a freezer?' She waited for an answer that didn't come. 'It's at the back of the garage. Big white thing. Go and look in that. It'll be in there if it's not in the fridge.'

'Right,' he said, relieved that his story had been believed. 'I'll do that. Thank you, Eleanor.'

'You had me frightened for a minute. I don't think you've ever called me before.' She gave a small laugh.

'No, no,' William began, but his voice petered out. He wanted to tell her, suddenly. He wanted to tell his daughter that her mother had left him and he didn't know where she was but the words stuck in his throat and wouldn't come out. 'I'll go and find the freezer,' he said.

'Call me again if you need help heating it up,' said Eleanor, now entirely breezy. 'You don't need me to come over, do you? I can always send Charlie.'

'No,' said William, lying. 'I'll be fine. Thank you.'

'OK. Tell Mum I'll call her at the weekend.'

William put the phone down and stared at it. He had never wanted to see his daughter more in his life.

# 73

Florence was still in Amiens.

She had found a small, charming hotel run by a woman with white hair tied up with impeccable precision. The Madame had thin, tissue-like skin and, as she handed Florence the large key to her room, Florence could see the bones in her fingers. There was something of the fairy tale about her. It all felt rather perfect.

The bed was much larger than she was used to and she had gladly lost herself in the luxury of it. It was all space and deep pillows and no snoring William, no grimly hoping he didn't wake up and need to have sex.

There was a bathroom down the corridor and she had come back in the late afternoon to enjoy a rather luxurious soak in an old ceramic slipper bath that stood on iron feet shaped like goose heads. She lay back and marvelled at the odd yellow colour to the water and the size of the room. It was enormous and the slow, methodic drip of the hot tap echoed between the floor and ceiling. The bathtub faced a long tall window that looked out over the town: a bath with a view. It was quite something.

She wasn't sure anyone else was staying at the hotel and had been in no rush to vacate. She stood for a while, wrapped in a large white towel laid out for her by the madame, and stared towards the street, one hand against the window frame.

She opened the window a little to let out the steam and a wave of dry, hot air blew through her hair. There was a smell of fresh bread wafting up from the boulangerie below and Florence had a sense of – what was it exactly? Renewal? Maybe that was too optimistic. She wasn't there yet. Renovation? She had laid herself bare; now she was ready to be remade.

She closed her eyes momentarily, took a deep breath and exhaled, long and slow, as if she was pushing out all the last bits of the old Florence, the person she didn't like, the person she wanted to shed.

She opened her eyes again. The sky was blue, there were swallows in the air, and there was fresh bread and cheeses she'd never tried and glistening fruit tarts and orange juice in funny-shaped bottles that fizzed on her tongue. All these things were waiting for her.

'Build yourself up, Florence,' she murmured. It was time to dress, pack and journey on.

## 74

William stared down into the freezer. He couldn't believe he hadn't noticed it.

How long had this been here?

He put his hand on the lid and paused. The first moment of self-doubt was beginning to take seed. Had Florence been right? Should she have left him? Had he given her reason to do so? Was he a bad husband? A hopeless father? A useless man?

He shook the thought away. Of course he was none of these things. He'd provided for his family more than adequately. That was all that was required, wasn't it?

He opened the freezer and peered in. Row upon row of frosted Tupperware stared up at him. He pulled one out and ran a hand across its top.

'Cottage pie,' it read. 'Gas mark 6, 40 minutes.'

Looking down, he noticed how many there were. They all had instructions. Florence, it would seem, had not simply disappeared for a few days.

Closing the lid of the freezer, William walked back through the house towards the kitchen. It was unnaturally quiet. The radio, which murmured away as Florence prepared breakfast or supper, was noticeably absent. The soft noises of her chopping, plumping cushions, the gentle clink of a teaspoon in a china cup: the tiny sounds of an uncomplicated domestic life were gone.

Where was she?

William placed the frozen cottage pie on the kitchen table and stared at it. Should it be kept in the fridge until he cooked it? he wondered.

Where could she have gone? Where was she hiding? He had no idea.

Thoughts turned to anger. How dare she? She was out of her mind. He'd been a good husband. He'd played his part. He didn't deserve this. Anger turned to fury and, with a yowl, he picked up the frozen container and threw it against the wall. It ricocheted off a corner and rattled into the sink.

The ferocity shook him and he stood for a moment, breathing heavily, trying to compose himself. How dare she reduce him to this humiliation? He gripped the back of a chair, his knuckles white. He would pull himself together and when she returned, he told himself, he would make it quite clear her behaviour was entirely intolerable.

She would be punished for this, he thought. Yes. She would be punished.

He stared down at his hands gripping the chair and released them. How embarrassing. This wasn't who he was. His breathing steadied, his anger replaced with a sense of terrible loss.

It wasn't Florence who would be punished. It would be him.

# 75

'You left Glastonbury Fayre?' Camilla was cutting an apple into quarters. 'What on earth for? I thought you wanted to lose your virginity? Or have you done it?' She narrowed her eyes.

She had returned.

'No, I didn't,' said Agnes, folding her arms. She didn't want to tell Camilla a thing. 'There was a weird vibe.' Her voice trailed off. She was painfully aware she was being economical with the truth but she didn't want Camilla to have any ammunition.

Camilla raised an eyebrow. 'Want a bit?' She offered up a slice of apple.

'No thank you,' said Agnes.

'So you're still a virgin?' Camilla asked pointedly.

'Yes, I'm still a virgin.' Agnes spread her fingers out on the counter and looked down at them.

Camilla bit into her piece of apple. 'Where's your chum? I thought you two were joined at the hip.'

'She's at work. I can't go today.' Agnes pointed down to her ankle.

'Looks painful.' Camilla didn't sound remotely concerned.

'It is.'

Camilla swallowed and picked up another slice. She leaned back. 'You two not getting on?'

'No, we're fine,' Agnes replied, too quickly. 'I just can't go to work today.'

'Really?' Camilla didn't believe her. Not one bit.

'Yes, we're fine.' Camilla made her feel hot and awkward and young and everything she no longer wanted to feel.

Camilla was staring at her, watching her carefully. 'You'd rather be doing this on your own, wouldn't you?' She spoke it quietly and slowly.

Agnes wasn't sure how to respond. Camilla was always poised, waiting for something to happen, for the air to change, but to what purpose? Her own amusement? She was a trouble-maker, divisive, mischievous.

Camilla slipped another slice of apple into her mouth. 'Well?'

'No. I don't know,' said Agnes. She sounded irritated. She was annoyed she couldn't hide it.

They both stood listening to the soft noises from the street: the birds, the muffled radio coming from an open window beyond. Camilla picked up her plate and walked towards the sink.

'It's all right to be yourself, *Agnes Ledbury*.' She mimicked Bea. 'You know that, don't you?'

Agnes didn't want to reply. The mocking of Bea made her angry but, more than that, Camilla was mocking them, their friendship. She pushed herself away from her. Somewhere out there, Bea would be on her own, feeling low and alone.

'Did I touch a nerve?' said Camilla, drifting to the doorway. 'Everything ends eventually, doesn't it?'

Agnes watched her disappear. She didn't want her to be right.

# 76

Florence threw her bag into the boot and slipped down the sunglasses from the top of her head. She had thought about driving to Paris but wondered if she might save that for the way back. Instead, she would head south-east, towards the Alps and Italy. She had waited until the heat of the day was past its peak. Even with all the windows down, the leather seats of the Morris didn't make for comfortable driving in blazing-hot weather but now, with a soothing early-evening breeze, she was ready to begin again.

She had done very little with her day other than visit the Jules Verne house and the Musée de Picardie, gently strolling through exhibits of other people's lives. She wondered, if there was a museum of her own life, what would be in it: a few letters from her daughters, a photo album from when she was a child, a small hat knitted for her by Agnes for a school project. Would any of it tell people who she really was?

It was a gorgeous evening.

Old men in blue caps stood on dusty rectangles, silver pétanque balls cradled in their hands. The smell of Gitanes cigarettes hung in the air. Lovers, arms draped around shoulders, loped together, fingers entwined. Little boys stood in line at a rotisserie truck waiting to take home herb-roasted chickens; waiters, in white shirts and black waistcoats, served small coffees from trays to people lounging at café tables.

Florence had driven no more than a few hundred yards beyond the town limit when she saw him: the same man who had waved to her from the truck, the beautiful chap from the cathedral. He was sitting on a pile of crates in a lay-by, a haversack between his legs, his thumb out. It was the third time she had seen him but, even so, she drove past.

She looked back in her rear-view mirror. He was watching her. She slowed down.

'Why not?' she mumbled and shifted the gearstick into reverse.

Seeing her drive back towards him, he stood up. Carrying his bag in one hand, he came to the lay-by's edge. The passenger-seat window was already wound down and, as she came to a halt, he rested a hand on the ledge and peered in.

'Hey,' he said, smiling. He had an accent she couldn't quite place.

'Hello,' she said, returning the smile. 'Would you like a lift?' She spoke slowly, not sure whether he understood.

'Thank you,' he said, holding up his bag, 'where do you want this? In the back or the boot?' His English was perfect.

'Boot, please,' said Florence. She sat, her hands gripping the steering wheel, as he opened the back and threw his bag in. She could feel her heart thumping. She'd never picked up a hitch-hiker before and was vaguely aware that it wasn't necessarily something that was sensible for women on their own to do.

'To hell with sensible,' she muttered, then leaned over and opened the door for him.

He got in. He was wearing black cotton shorts and a faded white T-shirt with a red star at its centre. He had blue flip-flops on his feet and two leather bracelets on his wrist.

'I'm Bram,' he said, holding out his hand.

'Florence,' she said, shaking it. His hand, to her surprise, was noticeably soft. This was not a man who laid bricks.

Florence put the car into first gear and started to drive. 'Where are you headed?' she asked.

'Nowhere in particular,' he said. 'Where are you going?'

'I'm heading to Italy.'

'That's fine.'

Florence blinked.

'Not that I mean I'll come with you the whole way. I'm not crazy.' He gave a laugh.

'I hope you're not,' Florence replied, laughing back. 'Sorry,' she added, 'your accent. I can't quite place it.'

'I'm from the Netherlands,' he said, smiling. 'From Amsterdam, actually.'

'Very flat, isn't it?'

'Very flat,' he agreed, nodding.

Bram rested his elbow on the open window edge, stretched his legs down into the footwell and leaned his face towards the breeze. 'So lovely to be moving,' he said. 'The air was so still.'

'Do you enjoy travelling?' Florence asked. 'You're very brown.'

He glanced down towards his legs. 'Yes and yes. How about you?' He looked at her.

Florence wasn't sure how much to tell him. She could tell him anything, anything at all. She could be a bored heiress, a diplomat dispatched to deal with a crisis, a courier of rare antiquities, a specialist bookbinder on a mission to save a manuscript. She could be whoever she wanted to be.

'I've left my husband. I'm sort of on the run.'

His smile spread to a wide grin. 'Are you really?'

She nodded, her eyes sparkling. 'Really.'

He let out a laugh. 'How exciting. I'm being driven by a fugitive.'

Florence gestured over her shoulder. 'There are peaches in the back. Help yourself.'

He leaned back and reached for the paper bag and, just like that, they settled.

# SATURDAY

# 77

William picked up the Tupperware container he'd thrown into the sink the night before and opened the lid.

The cottage pie had defrosted but he was unsure as to what to do with it. Could he keep it? Should he throw it away? Might it go back into the freezer?

He lifted it to his nose and sniffed. It smelled fine. He looked back at the lid and the instructions. Perhaps he should have it for lunch?

He walked to the oven and stared at it. Gas mark 6. What did that mean? He bent down and peered at the knobs.

He opened the oven and placed the Tupperware container on the baking tray inside. He stood back puzzled, by the knobs. Choosing one, he turned it to the right.

Was that it? Did that make it work?

He glanced up at the clock on the wall behind him. 'Forty minutes,' he muttered and trudged off, back to his armchair and the crossword, boiling with resentment.

She would be back today, he reasoned. Perhaps he wouldn't speak to her? He didn't want to give her the satisfaction of a blazing row.

He would barely acknowledge her return, give her a little silent treatment, and she would know that her ridiculous gesture had been pointless.

Yes, he thought. That is what he would do.

# 78

Florence pressed her hand against the window of the gondola as it creaked away from the station.

They had driven for eight hours, taking it in turns, and, on a whim, had headed up to the resort of Courchevel in the French Alps. Bram had skied there a few times but out of season, he'd told her, it was just as pleasant. They could walk the mountains, he said, have lunch with a view of Mont Blanc. There were glaciers they could climb and the air would be crisp and clean and wonderful.

She hadn't taken much persuading.

They'd arrived in the early hours of the morning. Bram had a friend who owned a chalet. He had found the key and let them both in.

She had slept in a large double bedroom with pine walls and enormous windows. A wooden chair sat in the corner of the room and there was a cupboard with an empty vase on it. The owner, Bram told her, ran an advertising agency in Amsterdam. Bram, it turned out, was a graphic designer. That would explain the soft hands, Florence thought.

He was twenty-five, the same age as Eleanor, and, in an incredible twist, had met her, once, at a gallery in London. It had eased them into a comfortable companionship. He had met her daughter. This was fine; it made him seem entirely safe.

Florence had woken early, a combination of a bright dawn shining in through shutters she had forgotten to close and a sense of excitement at this new stage of her adventure. She had liked the days on her own but having someone to travel with, chat to, eat with, was a welcome change.

Bram had brought her a large bowl of coffee in bed, a small gesture that left her a little embarrassed. No man other than William had ever seen her in bed. What's more, she had slept in nothing but her knickers and, as he'd come in, she'd had to pull the white cotton sheet up over her breasts. It had been a long time since she'd felt compelled to preserve her modesty. There was something rather electric about it.

He had waited for her to bathe and dress and told her he wanted to take her up to the top of the mountain. He had found passes for the lifts and now here they were, sitting thigh to thigh in a pod, her hand against the window.

'It's so beautiful,' Florence murmured, looking down.

'I love it up here in spring,' said Bram, leaning across her to look at the slope below, 'I never understand why people wait for the snow. Do you ski?'

'No, never have.' Florence shook her head and turned back towards him. He was very close and she could just feel his breath. 'Holidays were never a top priority in our house. Very much bundle the children into the back of the car and head for the nearest beach whatever the weather. Camping, mostly.'

Bram smiled. 'I'm not sure I can imagine you camping.'

'Neither can I,' Florence laughed. 'It's national service for children, honestly. No getting out of it, I'm afraid. But the girls enjoy it. At least I think they do.' She paused. 'Why can't you imagine me camping?' She frowned a little as if to suggest she hadn't understood what he meant.

'Because you're so ladylike,' said Bram. 'Refined. I'm not sure I can see you slumming it in the damp.'

Florence gave a soft smile and looked away. It wouldn't do to show him quite how much she enjoyed the compliment.

'What do you think your husband thinks of you running away?' Bram asked, leaning back into his seat. 'Do you think he might imagine you're sitting in a gondola in the French Alps with a man you only met yesterday?'

Florence gave a loud laugh. 'No, he wouldn't be able to imagine that for a single second.'

Her thoughts tripped back to Brill. Saturday lunchtime. She knew exactly what he would be doing. He'd be sitting in the small sitting room, television on, crossword on lap, waiting for the wrestling. They would have sausages and onions in thick white bread, eaten in silence at the kitchen table, and Florence would spend the rest of her day talking to nobody but the vegetables and the flowers and, if she was lucky, the occasional passer by.

It was very hard, she thought, to feel sorry for William. He had made her life an empty vessel. She looked back towards Bram and smiled.

'I'd much rather be here. I'm very glad I stopped and picked you up.' She tapped his knee.

'So am I,' said Bram. 'You've saved me, Florence.'

Florence was sure he was simply being polite but she felt warm and liked and appreciated and she wasn't sure what to do with that.

# 79

There was a terrible smell coming from the kitchen. William frowned and pushed himself up from his chair. As he walked into the hallway, the letter box rattled and something small and blue fell onto the doormat. He cast a look at his wristwatch and gave a tut. Their postman took his time on Saturdays. It really wasn't acceptable.

He went to it and picked the letter up.

Postmark Milan.

'Agnes,' he murmured.

It was addressed to Florence but he held it for a moment wondering whether he should open it. No, he reasoned, he would leave it with the pile of other letters he was amassing for her return. The larger the pile, the guiltier she would feel.

He tossed it onto the sideboard and walked back towards the kitchen. The smell, acrid and synthetic, was coming from the oven and, as he opened the door, a thick cloud of dark smoke plumed upwards. Grabbing a tea towel, he pulled out the baking tray to reveal a congealed mess of plastic and mince and potato. The lid had collapsed in on itself, the meal beyond saving.

'I mean ...' William began, his voice tired and exasperated, 'what am I supposed to do with this?'

He glanced over to the bin in the corner of the room. He'd need a knife or a spoon or something. Still holding the tray, he went to the cutlery drawer and tried to pull it open with one hand but the drawer caught and, as he pulled at it, the tea towel in his other hand shifted, exposing his thumb to the full heat of the metal.

William let out a sharp yelp and the tray clattered to the floor, sending a sludge of ruined cottage pie across the linoleum.

'God damn it!' William yelled.

He kicked out at a chair with his foot and stood, breathing heavily. He took himself to the sink and stuck his burning thumb under the cold tap. He had never known resentment like it.

## 80

Sasha, their glamorous host, was back from another shoot and having a blazing row with her boyfriend. The furious couple were in her bedroom, door tightly shut.

It seemed he'd slept with someone else. Two people, actually, one of whom was Sasha's friend. *She* was crying and furious. *He* was incredulous at being held to account. Possession was a thing of the past, jealousy so old-school. Men could do what they wanted, right? Everyone could! A week ago he was madly in love with her? Now this?

'This is awful,' said Bea, trying to read. 'I think I'll go out. Do you want to come? Is your ankle up to it?'

She folded her paper onto the table and leaned forward, her hands hanging between her knees. She was looking at Agnes, not with a sense of camaraderie, but of duty. Bea, Agnes knew, did not really want to go anywhere with her.

'I'm not sure.' If she was honest, Agnes wasn't sure whether she preferred to be on her own too. It all felt a little cowardly.

'Kiki said something about going for afternoon tea with

Camilla,' said Agnes. 'Is that something you might … ?' She knew what the answer would be.

Their enjoyment of each other had ground to a halt. There was a wariness to them that, had they been lying on a beach or next to a pool, might have gone unnoticed, but here it felt painfully acute.

'No,' said Bea, staring at her hands. 'I'm not sure I fancy that.'

'Has your—' Agnes proffered, lightly.

'No.' Bea shut it down.

Agnes wondered what a day together now might be like? What might they talk about? That night, again? What Bea would do if her period never came?

'I should probably rest, anyway,' said Agnes.

'Yes,' said Bea, nodding. 'Probably for the best.'

Bea stood but stopped before leaving the room. She looked back. 'Remember when we were at the Sec? And people ignored us and paid us no attention and didn't like us for no reason? And we stuck together.'

Agnes looked up towards Bea. She wasn't entirely sure where this was going.

'It would be nice,' Bea continued, 'if you remembered that.'

She didn't wait to hear an answer. She hadn't sounded angry or put upon. It was worse than that. It was disappointment.

What had she meant by that? Why hadn't she given her a chance to respond? Agnes wasn't sure if she could bear it. 'Bea!' she called. She tried to push herself up. They'd have this out. 'Bea!'

The front door slammed.

Agnes hopped to the corridor, grabbed at the latch and looked into the road but Bea was gone. A hot rage surged between her ears.

What was Bea accusing her of, precisely? Ignoring her? Not

paying her enough attention? Not going home because she wanted to? Not caring enough?

Well, she did care. She cared a lot. But the lines of their friendship were shifting, and Agnes did not yet know where the change would take them.

But that didn't matter right now. It was impossible not to feel furious. Agnes's blood was up.

# 81

Florence stared out across the view. It was stunning.

They were sitting on the wide wooden terrace of a restaurant that sat on a ridge just beyond the lifts. They were side by side, backs of their chairs against the stone wall of the restaurant, enjoying the warm afternoon sun.

In front of them, on a table covered in a red-checked cloth, were the remnants of a rather decadent lunch. They'd had a meat fondue and a raclette: an enormous half-wheel of cheese slid under a grill; scooping out just-melted cheese, Florence discovered, was her new favourite thing. There were baked potatoes, a green salad. Everything had been delicious.

'I'm ruined,' she said, letting her hands rest over her stomach. 'I will never be able to enjoy Cheddar from this moment forward. Never had cheese like it. What's it called again?'

'Raclette.'

'Raclette,' said Florence, with some regret. 'As if I'll ever be able to find that in Brill.'

'More wine?' said Bram, reaching for the bottle of Chablis to his left.

'Should I?' she asked, fingering the stem of her glass. 'Do I need to drive anywhere today?'

'Not if you don't mind staying?' said Bram. 'I've spoken to my friend. He's not here until September.'

'I'm not sure I can stay here till September,' said Florence sleepily, 'although it is tempting just for the cheese ... All right,' she added, pushing her glass towards him. 'I'll have a little more.'

Bram poured and then tipped the dregs into his own glass.

'*Sante*,' he said, tipping his glass in Florence's direction.

'What's cheers in Dutch?' Florence asked, taking her glass in her hand.

'*Proost*,' he replied, smiling.

'*Proost*,' said Florence and drank.

They sat, quietly looking out over the mountains beyond. A few hikers were dotted across the peaks and a large dog, a rather skinny-looking Labrador, was bounding across the grass below them.

Florence lifted her sunglasses and peered up into the sky, her hand across her forehead. 'Is that an eagle?' she asked, pointing. 'I saw some big birds when I was coming into Amiens. Not as big as that, I don't think.'

Bram followed her finger. 'Yes. Eagle.'

'I've never seen one before,' said Florence, shaking her head. 'What a treat. You're spoiling me, Bram.' She reached across the table and squeezed his hand but, suddenly aware of the intimate gesture, she quickly withdrew it.

'Of course, I arranged for this eagle to be here, at this precise moment.' Bram looked at his watch and tapped it. 'Actually,' he added, with a frown, 'he's a little late. I shall have to complain.'

'You're teasing me,' she said, taking a sip from her glass. 'I'm not sure that's entirely kind.'

'You can only tease people you like,' said Bram, putting his hands behind his head. 'Don't you think?'

Florence paused. She was aware she might be flirting. 'Yes,' she said, 'I suppose that's true.' She thought for a moment. 'My husband never teases me.'

'Well, he should, and often.'

'Thank you.'

'What for?'

'For liking me,' said Florence.

Bram turned his head towards her. 'You're a mystery, Florence. Here you are, having done the bravest thing. You're accomplished, capable, attractive. You don't need to thank me for *liking* you.'

His voice was calm and measured. Florence felt entirely startled by it.

'I'm not used to it, that's all. I'm used to not being noticed.' She chose the words carefully. 'I'm invisible in my own house. I don't feel particularly liked.'

'You need to put your foot down! Tell people how to treat you,' Bram said. 'If you feel sad, say it. If you feel angry, explain why. If you feel forgotten, shout it out. Tell people. Some people have to be told to change.'

'I'm not sure my husband can change.'

'Why not? You have.'

Florence looked off, back up to the mountains. She didn't have an answer to that.

# SUNDAY

# 82

Kiki was going to church.

'I just fancy it,' she said, tying her hair up into a respectable bun. 'Once a Catholic and all that ...'

'You haven't got a religious bone in your body,' said Camilla, cradling a mug of tea. They were all in the kitchen. 'What have you done? You must have done something. Lapsed Catholics only go to church when they've done something terrible. So which sin is it? Sloth? Gluttony? Adultery ...?'

She let the word hang.

'None of your business,' replied Kiki, pulling on her coat. 'Besides, I'd have to be out of my box to confess anything to you. That's the thing about you, Camilla, you're terribly judgemental.' She was wearing a knee-length skirt and flats and had managed to make her normally kittenish look demure. 'That to one side,' she added, 'do either of you want to come with me?' She looked rather pointedly at Bea.

Agnes was sitting, struggling through a rather unpalatable Weetabix. They'd forgotten to get milk and were on measly rations. She pushed at her half-dry biscuit with her spoon. 'I'm not Catholic.'

'Doesn't matter,' said Kiki, peeling a banana. 'You just can't take Communion.'

'I'll come,' said Bea, pushing up from the table. 'Not sure I want this,' she added, gesturing to her half-finished breakfast. 'It's like trying to eat tonsillitis.' She went to scrape it into the bin.

'Can I have your milk?' Agnes asked. 'If you're not having it.' It was the first thing she'd said to her since yesterday. Bea had slept on the sofa, having pretended to fall asleep reading a book.

Bea put her bowl back down on the table. 'Have whatever you want,' she said flatly.

'What terrible thing have *you* done, Bea?' Camilla asked as Bea brushed past her to get changed. Her tone was taunting and dark. Agnes's eyes darted to her. She wondered if she knew, if Kiki had told her.

'Shut up, Camilla,' she mumbled.

Kiki watched Bea go. 'You shouldn't pick on her, Cam.'

'I'm not.' Camilla spread herself across the kitchen worktop, elbows down, legs splayed out behind her. She was wearing a tight yellow T-shirt and a pair of blue pants.

'You know you are. Not everyone can take it, you know.'

'People need to toughen up,' Camilla said, with a shrug. She let her fingers slide across the formica surface.

'Don't be a bully,' said Kiki, tapping her on the shoulder as she left the kitchen. 'Kindness costs you nothing.'

Kiki went out into the hall.

'I'll see you outside, Bea,' she shouted. She checked in her bag for her front-door key.

Agnes tipped the milk from Bea's bowl into her own and squashed her biscuit down into it with the back of her spoon. She looked up to see Camilla idly watching her.

'Do you think I'm a bully?' Camilla asked, tilting her head.

Agnes pressed down so that the little milk there was seeped into the dry husk.

'No,' she said quietly, not wanting to be picked on. 'You're …
forthright. That's a bit different.'

'Forthright,' said Camilla, pushing herself up. 'Yes. I like
that. I am forth. And I am *right* …'

She emphasised the word, imbuing it with a different meaning that Agnes understood all too well. It made her feel
uncomfortable but that was clearly Camilla's intention.

# 83

Florence was watching Bram sleeping. He was bare-chested, one arm above his head. He was wearing a pair of red swimming trunks and she could see the contours of his penis.

She couldn't help staring at it. Thank goodness she was wearing sunglasses.

They were lying on long plastic loungers by a pool that belonged to the hotel next door. Bram had snuck them in via a side door and placed down towels he'd swiped from a tub only the attendants were allowed to use. The attendants swapped over at midday. They could pretend they'd been there all morning. They could even, he suggested, with a wicked grin, order drinks and put them on their fictitious room number. Florence was having none of that, thank you. It was one thing to break the rules and pretend you're a guest, quite another to steal.

'I am old enough to be his mother.'

She mouthed the words to herself like a mantra, a warning, a reminder that the thoughts beginning to swirl were not only ludicrous but unseemly.

She flicked open the French magazine she had bought the day before and tried to think of something else. She stared down at pictures of willowy French models, outrageous fashions, impeccable interiors, but her mind kept drifting back to the contents of Bram's trunks and it was making her feel uncomfortable.

She threw the magazine down and lay for a moment, legs stretched out, ankles crossed, toes, freshly painted red, pointing away. She felt – what was the word for it these days? Horny? When was the last time she'd felt like that? Too long ago to even remember.

She so dreaded sex with William. It was so perfunctory, so wrapped in duty, so joyless she had forgotten what wanting to have sex felt like. Did she ever want sex with William? She must have, at some point, surely? He had been her first, her only.

She cast her mind back to their wedding night, the slow closing of the door of their hotel room, the methodical removal of all but their underwear. She had a vague memory he'd kept his socks on. Surely not?

She remembered the self-conscious attempts to kiss him differently now they were married. She remembered pressing her tongue into his mouth because a friend of hers had taken her to a dirty movie in Soho to 'get her ready' and, of all the things she'd seen that day, that was the only one she felt capable of. He hadn't responded and so, as soon as she'd darted it in, she pulled it back out.

He hadn't wanted to kiss. He had just lain on top of her, his head facing away to one side, done what he needed to do and that was that. She didn't know what a man expected her to do. Her mother had never told her. She had no idea that sex was enjoyable or that women could be pleasured in the same way as men. She had spent all her married life lying back, letting him fumble up the bottom of her nightgown as she pulled down her knickers and he edged his penis out from his striped pyjamas and shoved it into her, thrusting just enough and then rolling off with a polite 'thank you' as if he were slightly ashamed.

That was their problem, Florence thought. They had spent their entire marriage feeling slightly embarrassed.

Now here she was, staring at a young man's erection as he dozed on a warm day, and all she wanted to do was to pull his trunks down and sit on it.

Oh Florence.

She shook her head and removed her sunglasses. She'd have a swim. That would cool her down.

# 84

Sasha had put a record on. Agnes picked up the cover and stared down at it, the androgynous boy in a dress draped casually on a chaise longue, cards scattered before him. His voice was jagged and Gothic. She liked it. 'Who is this?' she asked.

'David Bowie,' Sasha said, as if that were obvious. 'You must know him?'

Agnes shook her head. 'I'm rather behind on music,' she said. 'It's all choral and classical in our house.'

'Oh my God,' said Sasha, clutching her chest. 'I need to remember this moment forever. I've introduced you to Ziggy Stardust.'

Agnes frowned. 'Ziggy?'

'His alter ego. He's fabulous.'

Agnes looked down into the strange, odd-coloured eyes that stared back at her. Perhaps that was something she needed – an alter ego to consume her, to allow her to be a different person?

Sasha was sitting, cross-legged on a chair, applying lipstick. She was staring into a compact. She was going out again, taking her boyfriend to her parents' for Sunday lunch. They had made up, clearly.

'I wonder if I'll ever take a boy home for Sunday lunch?' Agnes said, putting the record cover down.

'Of course you will,' said Sasha, reaching into a small bag for a stubby black kohl pencil. She licked the end of it and held down her eyelid.

'I can't imagine it. Somewhere, out there,' Agnes wafted a hand into the air, 'is someone I don't know who is going to come with me to my parents' house and sit in our dining room and eat roast beef and potatoes while my mother stares at him.'

'Will she?' asked Sasha, patting at her eye with her fingertip. 'Stare at him?'

'Like a spy,' said Agnes, throwing herself onto the beanbag. 'Worse than a spy. I wouldn't be surprised if she sat there with binoculars.'

'Then she must love you very much,' said Sasha, dropping the pencil back into her bag. She gave a small pout and turned her face back and forth in her compact.

Agnes gave a snort of disbelief. 'I don't think so.'

'That'll do.' Sasha snapped her compact shut and dropped it into her bag. She unfolded her legs and stood up. 'That's the thing about mothers,' she added. 'They all secretly love you fiercely.'

She lifted a coat from the back of a chair and pulled it on. 'I don't know if I'll be back later. Will you be all right here on your own with Camilla?'

'Why wouldn't she be?' said Camilla, wandering in with a book. 'Honestly, it's like you all think I'm a monster.'

'Well,' said Sasha, gripping Camilla's chin in her hand, 'you are a bit.'

She leaned up and kissed her quickly on the lips. Agnes blinked. The moment made her uncomfortable.

'Bye-bye,' Sasha said, moving off towards the corridor. 'Be good. If you can't be good, be wicked.'

Camilla glanced towards Agnes and threw her book down onto the table. 'Shall we?'

'Shall we what?'

'Be wicked?'

Agnes tried to think of a reply, but couldn't. Instead, her cheeks were flushing. She lifted her hands to her face to hide it.

'Are they still not back?' Camilla tapped her fingernails on the tabletop. 'What are they doing? Confessing to murders?' She stared at Agnes, waiting for a response. She was digging. She knew something was up.

There was something about Camilla that truly unnerved Agnes. She didn't even like her and yet there was something so powerful about her, so unapologetic, it was impossible to dismiss. She felt every atom in the room pressing down on her chest.

'I don't know.' She struggled the words out.

'Bet you do,' Camilla said, one hand drifting up to her hip. Agnes could see Camilla's belly button peeping through the gap between her T-shirt and her shorts. She was reminded of that moment in the field with Penny. She looked away.

'I'm making coffee. Do you want one?'

Agnes didn't want to think about Penny or that field or that teepee. She pushed her mind to something safe, back to Brill, to her mother, to what Sasha had said. She'd love to believe Florence loved her fiercely. But she didn't. Only one person loved her fiercely and that was Bea. Or did she? Agnes's face was burning.

'Did you hear me?' said Camilla. 'Do you want a coffee?'

Agnes nodded.

'Are you blushing?' Camilla peered at her.

'No.' The word muttered itself out.

'Anyone would think I make you nervous,' said Camilla. She sounded delighted.

'You don't. I just need to ...' Agnes stopped. She pushed the window open. 'I was just a bit hot.'

'Just a bit hot,' Camilla mimicked. She flicked on the kettle. She was making fun of her, again.

This was torture. Agnes had been ready to change into some-one worthwhile. She had convinced herself she had the confidence to do it and here she was, friendship with Bea in tatters, clinging to a window ledge, unable to leave a room and praying for the front door to open.

There was clearly work to be done.

# WEEK FOUR

# MONDAY

## 85

William stood in Eleanor's kitchen. He was unshaven and the shirt he was wearing had an egg stain smudged over an upper button. Charlie watched him, not saying anything, and Eleanor, hands on hips, was frowning.

William cleared his throat. 'I'll ask again,' he said. 'Is your mother here?'

Eleanor cast a puzzled look towards Charlie then back to her father. 'No, Dad, I've told you, she's not. I haven't seen her and I haven't heard from her.' She stopped for a moment, then said softly, 'What's going on?'

William's mouth felt dry and he reached for the back of a chair to his left. He cast his eyes downward. He wasn't sure he wanted to see his daughter's face. There was something desperately lonely about what he was about to tell her, exposing, vulnerable. It was like laying bare a self-inflicted wound.

'I think your mother has left me,' he said, sitting slowly into the chair. His voice was barely a whisper.

'Sorry?' said Eleanor, sounding incredulous. 'She's what?'

'I thought she might be here.' William let his hand drift onto the kitchen table.

There was a thick, dark whorl in the wood and, as he spoke, his index finger gently ran round its circumference. 'I really don't know where she's gone. I thought she might have come here for a few days to put the frighteners on ...' His voice disappeared to nothing.

Eleanor and Charlie stood, waiting, the silence leaden.

'I thought she'd be back for supper ...' He lifted his hand to cover his eyes, his palm facing out towards Eleanor and Charlie. He hadn't cried in front of anyone since he was a boy but now there seemed nothing he could do to prevent it.

'Oh, Dad,' said Eleanor, going towards him.

She knelt down in front of him and placed a hand on his knee. 'What's caused this? Something must have happened? Did you have an argument?'

William turned his face away, his hand still covering his eyes, and shook his head. 'I don't know,' he mumbled. 'She wanted to go on holiday.' He reached down into his trouser pocket and pulled out a neatly folded handkerchief.

'She did talk to me about that,' said Charlie, resting his hands down on the tabletop. 'I thought she was just venting ...'

'You knew something about this?' Eleanor turned and frowned at her husband. 'Why didn't you tell me?'

'I ...' began Charlie, his voice serious, 'well, she asked me not to. I didn't actually think she would ... Sorry. Perhaps I should have said something.'

Eleanor let out an exasperated sigh and William, unfolding the handkerchief, wiped his eyes.

'I apologise,' he said, clearing his throat. 'I didn't mean to ... I'm a little embarrassed.' He looked up towards Eleanor and mustered a smile.

'Did she tell you where she was going?' Eleanor was pressing Charlie.

He looked up towards the ceiling, his mouth just open, like a baby starling waiting for something to be dropped in. He was casting his mind back to that moment amongst the peas.

'No,' he said, closing his eyes briefly, 'she didn't. She was upset about the brochures, thinking she wouldn't go abroad. She was crying. She was very upset.'

'About not going to Italy?' Eleanor asked.

'No,' said Charlie, treading carefully, 'she was crying because she ... I'm not sure if I should say. It doesn't feel quite right.'

'Just spit it out, Charlie.' Eleanor was trying not to sound irritated.

'William, do you really want me to ...' He let the sentence hang.

William wiped at his eyes again.

'She didn't feel loved,' Charlie said, his voice quiet and thoughtful. 'By you, William. She wasn't sure you loved her. I think it all felt a bit ... much.'

'But she didn't say she was leaving?'

'No, not at all.' Charlie shook his head. 'I think she was going to ask you if you'd go to Italy. That was it. She certainly didn't say anything about running off.'

Eleanor turned back to William. 'Did she ask you to go to Italy?'

He nodded and rested his forehead into the palm of his hand.

'And you said you didn't want to go?'

He nodded again and closed his eyes.

Eleanor heaved out an exasperated sigh. 'I mean, I can't believe she's upped and left because you didn't want to go on holiday. She knows you hate heat.'

'I don't think it was just about—' began Charlie.

'Be quiet, Charlie.' Eleanor put her arm round her father's shoulder. 'Stay here. With us. Until we can work out what's going on.'

He nodded once more. The tears were slow and thick and dripping from him. He kept his eyes closed tight.

'I think it's best. Is the spare room made up?' She looked up towards her husband.

'Yes, I'll open the window, give it an air.' Charlie stopped as he got to William and put a hand on his shoulder.

'No hard day lasts forever, William. Remember that. We'll help you through.'

'You know, she might just have gone to Italy,' added Eleanor. 'She might just have done that.'

'Yes,' said William, wiping at his eyes, 'she might just have done that.'

# 86

Florence stared up at the open window. She had washed a light cotton smock, stuck one cuff behind the top of the shutters to dry. She lay on the bed, watching it flutter.

She was naked, one hand behind her head, her breasts glistening with a light sweat, and she wasn't sure if she had ever felt more relaxed. She'd lost count of how many orgasms she'd had. Beside her, Bram was sleeping, again.

Yesterday's swim, it turned out, had not cooled her down at all and, one steak frites and a bottle of wine later, Bram had pressed her against a wall and kissed her. She kissed him back and let her hand wander down to his groin where she finally got to feel the contours of the magnificent penis she'd been staring at all afternoon. He had unzipped his shorts and she had taken it in her hand and guided it towards the top of her legs where she couldn't get it inside her fast enough. They had fucked, quickly, to get the intensity out of the way, but had then headed to the bedroom where Florence had spent most of the night with her legs wrapped round him.

She was feeling quite startled.

It wasn't that she had no idea her sexual appetite was quite this voracious, it had been the orgasms: box-fresh, the flock of birds inside her waiting to escape. She had stared, wide-eyed and open-mouthed, at the ceiling, her fingers gripped into Bram's golden curls, astonished there was this much beauty inside her.

She wanted to verbalise it, the way she felt, but, lacking the words, all she could come up with was 'My vagina has had the most incredible spring-clean' which, even she had to confess, was a sentence that should probably never be spoken out loud.

If Marjory could see her now . . .

Next to her, Bram stirred. She ran her hands through his hair. 'Hey,' he said sleepily and reached his hand out to her stomach, the tips of his fingers brushing the top of her pubic hair.

She felt wildly alive, like air rushing. She looked down at his hand, brown as a nut against her milk-white skin. Why not? she thought. She pushed it deeper between her legs.

After all, there was nothing else she needed to be doing . . .

# 87

Bea was having a bath – a long one, Agnes hoped.

Agnes was feeling in limbo, all the progress she had made whittled to nothing. It would be so easy to give up, as she had done before, but this time she understood the consequences. Giving up had left her with a suspended life. It was time to toughen up.

Waiting for the sound of surface water breaking and the tinkle of the hand-held showerhead, Agnes took her chance. Tiptoeing past the bathroom, she padded her way to the end of the corridor and quietly pressed open the door into Camilla's bedroom.

She didn't like Camilla at all, not even a bit, and yet there was something darkly fascinating, something so forthright and bold that Agnes was drawn towards her. She was unflinching, strong and charismatic, intoxicating. Agnes wanted to immerse herself in Camilla's space, breathe her air, touch her things. Agnes wanted to kick-start her stalled self, to borrow a different energy.

It was tidier than she'd expected: the bed was made, a deep-red coverlet neatly turned down, the pillow plumped. Beside it was a wooden chair, a pile of folded T-shirts stacked on top. There was very little furniture – no bedside cabinet, no wardrobe, no chest of drawers. The only thing of note was a table, a Formica fold-down, pressed against the wall underneath the window. A stool was tucked beneath it.

She turned her head back towards the corridor and listened for the gentle noises still emanating from the bathroom. Reassured, she walked slowly into the room and stood, very still. There was a scent, slightly floral. What was that? She looked round. Some bright freesias were sitting in an old baked-bean tin on the windowsill. Something about it surprised her, an act of sweetness that seemed at odds with Camilla's tough exterior. She liked small, fragrant flowers, Agnes noted. How unexpected.

There was a stack of papers on the table: a few smudged printouts of demos, sit-ins, meetings; a handful of political badges; a battered copy of *A Vindication of the Rights of Woman* by Mary Wollstonecraft; a typewriter, spare spool to the side; and, next to it, a notebook. Agnes picked it up.

It had a glued-on home-made front of marbled yellow ink. She ran her hand across and opened it. It was a diary. Words blurred up at her, but, consumed with disquiet, Agnes quickly closed it and put it back down. She wanted to know Camilla better but she didn't want to invade her privacy.

She stopped, thinking she had heard something, and stood still, like a heron on a riverbank. She felt a small flush of adrenalin. What was she in here for, exactly? To try and better understand the woman with dirty-blonde hair and a reckless regard for norms? What was she looking for? Signs of weakness? Signs of strength? What she liked? How to get her to like her?

She heard the shower again and relaxed a little. A piece of paper caught her eye. It was on top of a book, dropped idly, unimportant. A series of doodles: intricate swirls, squares, odd-shaped flowers and then ... Agnes stopped breathing. *A is beautiful*. She stared down at it, terrified. The words crashed into her.

She clamped a hand to her mouth to stop herself from shouting out. It felt dangerous, this sudden knowledge. Nothing Camilla had said or done had led Agnes to believe she held her in the slightest regard. She was sniping, cruel, hard, impenetrable, and yet here, in this room, Agnes saw delicate flowers and gentle smells and everything she thought she knew was wrong.

It was too much. Agnes wasn't brave enough to hold on to it.

*A is beautiful.*

Catching sight of the yellow T-shirt Camilla wore in bed, Agnes grabbed it and held it to her face. She breathed in, the sweet-sour smell of perfume and sweat filling her nostrils.

'What are you doing?'

Agnes, startled, span round. Bea was standing, her hair wet, wrapped in a towel.

Agnes dropped the T-shirt back onto the bed.

'I was going to go to the launderette,' she lied. 'I thought I'd see if anyone had any dirty stuff ...' She felt hot and awkward.

'Really?' said Bea, her expression a mixture of disgust and disbelief. 'It looks like you're just being a bit ... creepy.'

'Well, I'm not,' said Agnes, rooted to the spot. 'Besides, Camilla told me to try a few of her tops on.' Her voice petered off.

She knew she sounded ridiculous.

'This isn't real, you know,' said Bea, staring straight at her. 'All this.' She wafted her hand into the air. 'When we leave here, this isn't coming with us. And neither is Camilla. Or Kiki. Or Sasha. What do you think you're doing?'

'I'm not doing anything.' Agnes tried not to snap.

'Really?' said Bea, standing firm. 'You're in someone else's bedroom sniffing their clothes. What's happened to you, Agnes?'

'Nothing.' Agnes sounded defensive.

Bea stared at her, her face a vision of mild revulsion. 'You're embarrassing yourself,' she muttered then walked off, leaving small wet footprints behind her.

Agnes felt the twinge of Bea's words. Their friendship was in a state of disrepair and yet it felt very hard, in that moment, to feel truly embarrassed: the inconvenience of discovery and Bea's disapproval was not, to her surprise, outweighing the moment of elation.

Agnes's world had just shifted. She wasn't as poorly regarded as she had led herself to believe. Someone else thought her beautiful. It was time for Agnes to start believing it too.

# TUESDAY

# 88

On a whim, they had packed their bags and driven to Siena.

Courchevel was lovely but bad weather was forecast for the rest of the week and, rather than sit staring out at the rain, Bram had rung another friend and asked if they might crash at his villa.

He was so charming, Florence thought, so well connected, so liked.

It was impossible not to be overwhelmed by him: his constant capacity for adventure, the calm manner in which he was able to be spontaneous. It was hard not to compare him to William: William did not have a work colleague with a chalet in the Alps or a friend with a Tuscan villa he could call at a moment's notice. William would not be able to conceive of a day without a rigid structure, let alone a holiday where you upped sticks and drove into another country to find some sun. William would have sat, rain dripping down the window, arms folded, saying nothing, willing the whole thing over.

Did she miss him? She wondered whether he was managing with his frozen suppers, whether he'd worked his way through the clean shirts she'd ironed for him, what sort of state the house might be in. She wondered what he was thinking, feeling, if he missed her. She wondered if he was annoyed, shocked, perplexed. She wasn't sure she cared.

She didn't miss him at all.

The villa was set in the outskirts of the city amidst rolling olive groves and cyprus trees, honey-stone walls, a faded red-tile roof, windows small and shuttered and the floors throughout all clean white marble, a cool relief from the relentless dry heat.

They'd been welcomed by a young woman called Laila, a winsome brunette with large brown eyes and golden skin. She was wearing a polka-dot bikini, tied at the hip with a bow. One yank and she would be entirely undone, Florence noted, as they followed her lethargic sashay to the guest rooms towards the back. She was a singer, Bram had told her. It made sense. She had the aura of someone who thought herself important.

'You in one room?' she asked, her Italian accent drawling the words.

Bram had looked towards Florence. 'You want to share?' He smiled and opened the door to reveal an enormous bed.

'I'll take the room next door,' said Florence, feeling a sudden burst of propriety.

She didn't fully understand why. She felt annoyed with herself. Perhaps it was the young woman and her tilted head and her folded arms, staring at her. She could still have sex with Bram, of course, but she wasn't sure she wanted it being quite so obvious.

'There's a door between,' said Laila, making a little walking gesture with her fingers. 'You can just open.' She smiled and Bram touched her lightly on the elbow.

'Thanks. We'll sort ourselves out.'

'There are drinks and fruit by the pool,' she said, as she pushed herself away from the doorframe and wandered off back down the long corridor. 'No rush.'

Florence watched her go, the gentle sway of the hips, the soft pad of her feet on the marble. Bram was watching her too.

'She's very attractive,' said Florence, her voice a little wary.

She regretted it instantly. It made her sound jealous, worried, as if she needed reassurance. She looked towards Bram. He was still watching Laila.

'Yes, she is,' he said. 'Do you want me to put your bag in your room for you?' He pointed at it, sitting on the floor by her feet.

'No,' she said, picking it up. 'I can manage. I'll get changed.'

'Me too.' Bram disappeared into the room and threw his bag onto the bed.

Florence tried to dismiss her tendency to overthink small moments. There was nothing wrong with Bram thinking Laila was attractive. She was. Besides, it wasn't as if she was in a relationship with him, was it?

Her room was large and airy and she put her suitcase on the black-and-white tiled floor and walked to the shutters, pushing them out to let in the light. This part of the house was in shade and there was a soft, rather delightful breeze.

Below the window was a purple chaise longue that had seen better days. Next to it a long low cabinet with a ceramic jug filled with dried lavender. She bent down to smell it. The odour was surprisingly fresh. The bed behind her was vast and opulent. She sat down on one edge and gave the mattress a quick bounce. It felt deep and comfortable.

The door from Bram's room opened.

'How is it?' he said, walking in and looking around. He'd taken his shorts and shirt off and had an erection, she noted. Was that from Laila or circumstance? She dismissed the idea.

'Lovely,' said Florence. She lay back, her arms splayed above her head, the light from the window landing across the white cotton sheets.

Bram lay on top of her. 'Italian air suits you,' he said, leaning down to kiss her neck.

She could feel his penis against her thigh and, as he edged the buttons of her shorts open with his thumb, she turned her head to kiss him properly. She pulled at the side of his trunks and reached down to take him in her hand. He only had to touch her and she wanted him inside her. It was maddening really, she thought, as he yanked her shorts down towards her ankles and pushed himself into her. Thank goodness this didn't happen in Brill. She'd never get anything done.

# 89

Eleanor stared at her father. He was sitting at the end of the kitchen table looking like a man in the cold waiting for a bus.

'How long have you been here?' she asked, passing him to get to the kettle.

He seemed surprised that someone else was in the room.

'I'm not sure,' he said. 'What time is it?'

'Have you had anything to eat today, Dad?' Eleanor flicked on the kettle.

He paused, as if trying to remember. 'No.' His voice was little more than a mumble.

'Do you want something?' Eleanor glanced up at the clock on the wall. It was almost three o'clock. 'I could make you a sandwich?'

William nodded, his hands clenched between his knees.

Eleanor reached for the bread bin to her left and lifted out the nub end of an almost-finished loaf. 'Not sure I've got quite enough for a full sandwich,' she said, examining it. 'I could do you one of those open Danish things. Sandwich with no top on. Very on trend.' She was trying to be upbeat.

'It's fine,' he said, 'I'm not that hungry.'

Eleanor's smile slipped. 'You should eat something. Supper won't be till seven. I'll grate some cheese. Do you some cheese on toast. How's that?'

William wasn't sure what to say or do. This wasn't his house. He didn't know where the newsagent's was or where he might find a pen. He didn't know what books he might take from any given shelf. He wasn't sure which chairs in the sitting room belonged to who or where he might sit. He didn't know what to look at, or do. He didn't know where Florence was.

'Do you think she's all right?' he asked. 'Your mother? You don't think anything terrible has happened?'

Eleanor took down a large silver grater from a shelf to her right and walked to the fridge. 'I think if anything really bad had happened, we'd have heard,' she said, opening the door and pulling out a small plate with a lump of Cheddar on it. 'The police would have knocked on the door. Or we'd have had a phone call. Try not to worry, Dad. She used to be a Guide Leader. She can do knots and all sorts.' She turned on the grill and began to grate.

William watched her. He wished he could shift the terrible sense of unease but here he was, wondering if his wife was dead because that might be easier to believe than what had actually happened.

She had left him, pure and simple. His wife had walked out and he didn't know what to do about it.

# 90

Agnes leaned against the frame of the kitchen doorway. She'd brushed her hair and applied a little mascara. She was wearing a red T-shirt and a pair of blue shorts. She'd been out and bought them on her own the previous day. It was not her usual look and she liked it.

Bea had gone off again to Foyles. The manager had asked her if she'd like to do a few more days: one of their employees was off sick. Kiki had encouraged her to go for it and Agnes knew she was putting off going home until she felt a little stronger, until she knew what was what. Her period still hadn't come. She wouldn't want her family to know what had happened.

'Hello, Agnes,' said Camilla, noticing her. She was poking at something roasting in the oven. It was giving off a deep, peaty smell. She shut the oven door and threw the fork down on the work surface. 'Few more minutes.'

Agnes stood, her heart racing.

Camilla tilted her head and looked at her, taking in the outfit, then looked at her own. 'Are you copying me?' she said. 'We look like twins.'

'No,' said Agnes, a little defensively.

'Hmm.' Camilla narrowed her eyes. 'You've been here for weeks and I know virtually nothing about you. What's your surname again?'

Agnes knew full well Camilla knew what her surname was. She'd taunted her with it.

'Yes, you do,' said Agnes, frowning. 'Agnes Ledbury.'

'Oh yes. Agnes *Ledbury*.' Camilla repeated the name as if she might be remembering someone notorious, someone important. 'Where's your little pal?'

'At work. The bookshop asked her back. I think she might stay there. My ankle's almost better so tomorrow I'll ring Mr Adler and—'

'I didn't mean I was actually interested.' Camilla leaned back and folded her arms.

Agnes burned. Camilla was cruel and manipulative, she was perfectly aware of it. She wanted Agnes to feel uncomfortable, to be on the back foot. Well, she wasn't going to. She had powerful information. Camilla didn't think quite so little of Agnes as she liked to make out.

'What are you cooking?' Agnes stood firm.

'Beetroot. Do you want some?'

'I'm not sure I like it.'

'You'll like this.'

'Will I?'

'You won't know until you try.' Camilla stretched her arms above her head and clasped her hands together, pushing the palms up towards the ceiling. Her T-shirt rode up, exposing her belly. It was flat and toned. Camilla did this a lot, Agnes noted.

'There are lots of things I probably need to try.'

Camilla let her arms fall back to her side. 'Have you ever been to a demo?'

'No.'

'Do you want to come on one? Tomorrow?'

'Are you going?'

'Of course I'm going.'

'Then yes.' Agnes stared at her. Camilla blinked. She hadn't expected Agnes to agree.

'Don't you want to know what it's for?' Camilla looked puzzled.

'All right, then.'

'We're going to a protest at the Bunny Club.' She smirked.

Agnes opened her mouth but paused before replying. She shifted away from the doorframe, her bare feet spreading across the linoleum. She plunged her hands into the pockets of her shorts. There were no answers there. 'What about Kiki?'

'What about her?' Camilla turned and picked her fork up.

Agnes frowned. 'She'll be upset, won't she?'

'Any woman willingly participating in sexual objectification is a collaborator in the patriarchy.' She rattled it off. She opened the oven door and peered in. 'They're ready. Pass me that tea towel.'

Agnes picked up the tea towel lying on the counter to her left. It had a faded picture of the Queen on it. 'But you're going to tell her, aren't you?'

'No,' said Camilla, taking it from her. 'Why should I?' She folded the tea towel over twice, to thicken it, then reached into the oven, pulled out a small roasting tray and placed it on the top of the stove. 'Pass me a plate.'

Agnes opened the cupboard above her head and pulled a plate down. She felt uneasy. She liked Kiki but not as much as she was fascinated by Camilla. All the same ... 'I think you should tell her. It's only fair.'

'Do you think it's fair that men have all the power and women can only do what they let us?' She pronged the beetroot onto the plate.

'No, but—'

'I thought you came to London to become a modern woman? Equality is worth fighting for, Agnes *Ledbury.*' Camilla ground some pepper and pinched a little salt over the plate, then opened a drawer and took out a knife. 'Come here,' she added, cutting a slice and forking it. She lifted it up and waited for Agnes to do as she was told.

Agnes stepped towards her. She could smell the beetroot, the peppery earthiness, and, behind it, the sweet floral notes of the soap Camilla had washed in. She stared into Camilla's eyes and bit. Juice ran down her chin.

'You've got some on your T-shirt,' said Camilla, glancing towards Agnes's chest. 'I'll clean it off. Before it sets in.'

Picking up a clean dishcloth, Camilla ran it under the tap. Agnes stood, very still, and Camilla, taking the bottom of Agnes's T-shirt in one hand, pulled the fabric and held it taut. Agnes watched Camilla as she dabbed at the stain. She looked at the freckles speckled across her nose and cheeks. She looked at her eyelashes. She looked at the small mole just below her right eye. She looked at her lips and how she pursed them at one corner when she was concentrating. Agnes wanted to concentrate too, on every moment of this encounter: the way Camilla's fingernails were bitten down, the ink smudge at the end of her forefinger, the way her hair fell against her neck and shoulders.

'There,' said Camilla, tossing the cloth into the sink. 'That should do it.' She looked up at Agnes. She reached towards her and wiped just below Agnes's bottom lip with her thumb then put it into her mouth and licked it off.

Agnes steadied herself on the counter. It was frightening, how much power one person could have over you. This was not a meeting of equals. Bea would not approve. Not one bit.

# WEDNESDAY

# 91

It was hot.

Florence sat, facing out towards the pool. She was in a bikini, a light-blue wrap tied about her waist. She had borrowed a straw hat with a wide brim from Laila, but even that was not enough to cool her down. She had retreated to the verandah, overhung with a spent wisteria and a long oak table with benches on either side. She had a book in her hands, a just-about-decent potboiler she was trying or pretending to read, but her mind couldn't settle.

Bram was in the pool with Laila.

They had dragged an inflatable airbed from a side shed and Laila, having found a foot-pump, had idly watched, as Bram stood, hands on hips, pressing down on it. Laila was lying back, leaning up on her elbows, one knee bent up, her tanned body splayed on the white pool's edge. The pair chatted easily but Florence couldn't hear what they were saying. It was annoying.

Florence watched Bram's face, the way he stared down at her, the slight tilt to his head, that smile. He was flirting, she could tell.

Having pumped the airbed, he picked it up, clasped it to his chest and leapt into the centre of the pool. He looked very pleased with himself. He was showing off. Laila slid sideways into the water to join him, like a snake slipping into a river. She pushed herself onto the airbed, belly down. Bram drifted her slowly around the pool, his face close to hers. The soft sound of her laughter carried towards the verandah.

Florence didn't like it. All the same, she couldn't go and join them. That would look desperate.

Laila, it turned out, was far more dangerous than Florence originally thought. Bram was right. She was a singer, from Sicily originally, hell-bent on breaking into the opera scene. The man who owned the villa – away in Rome until Friday – was, by all accounts, the greatest singing teacher in Italy.

It was a treat, of sorts. Laila practised twice a day: once in the morning, like a very posh cockerel, then again in the evening when the heat of the day had passed its peak. Bram would insist on no speaking when she sang. She was quite the siren. Florence was unnerved.

It was impossible to know how to compete. Laila had enormous talent. Florence could make decent chicken-and-ham pies and iron a shirt perfectly. She could mend buttons and knock up A-line skirts with a reasonable waistband on her sewing machine. She could attach sleeves. She could weed a bed. She knew how to properly prune a rose. These were skills, she supposed, but they weren't talents. Talent was something else. Talent set you apart. Laila was young and beautiful and her talent filled the air with the shortcomings of all around her. Laila was a threat.

He liked her. She knew it. He had barely spoken to Florence at supper last night. Instead he had sat, his shoulders hunched to attention as Laila held forth, laying out her own legend so that nobody was in any doubt that she was very important indeed. He had lapped it up. He had offered to top up her glass, hold her chair out, pass her the bread. There was something bewitching about Laila. She didn't have to try.

Florence's mind floated away to her own talented daughter, the impossible Eleanor who also managed to be very important indeed. What must that feel like? She knew, precisely. She knew what it felt like. It felt like Bram, on top of her, her fingers dug into his back. That's what made Florence so terrified. She didn't love Bram. It was worse than that. He had made her feel important.

Bram swam to the edge of the pool and pushed himself up onto the side. He flicked his hair and an arc of water showered back across the white paving stones. Pulling at his trunks, he said something back towards Laila and walked towards the verandah, his wet footprints vanishing in the heat.

Florence picked her book up and pretended to read. He padded past, the faint smell of chlorine wafting towards her.

'Enjoying your book?' he asked, stopping in the doorway.

'Yes, thank you,' she said. Her voice was nonchalant, lazy, the way you might mumble the number of a bus you took every day. She didn't want him to know she was bothered.

'Great,' he said and wandered off into the cool of the house.

But she was bothered. What was he doing? Where was he going? Was he showering after being in the pool? Changing out of his trunks? Getting his own book so he could sit with Florence, reading side by side in the shade like an old married couple?

She glanced over towards the pool. Laila was pulling herself slowly from the water, walking out via the steps in the shallow end. She was methodical, careful. She stood, her back to Florence, the hazy morning heat complementing her shapely silhouette. If Florence squinted, Laila disappeared.

Ice in a glass sounded from within and Bram reappeared, holding two glasses: orange juice, it looked like, with red striped straws bobbing upwards. For a moment, Florence thought one might be for her but he didn't stop. Instead, he padded off towards Laila. She was scooping her dark brown curls into a ponytail. She made him wait, standing like a lapdog ready to serve her, then took the glass. She pointed off, sucked delicately on the straw, and Bram, putting his own glass down, dutifully dragged two sunloungers to the edge of the pool.

He had no interest in the shade, thought Florence, as she watched them sit cheek by jowl. The heat, it would seem, was what he was after.

## 92

'You can't protest against Kiki,' said Bea, pulling a jumper over her head. 'It's not right.'

'It's not protesting against her,' said Agnes, 'it's protesting the institution, the Bunny Club. It's outdated. I thought you wanted to be a second-wave feminist? We hated it when we went. You know we did.'

'No, we didn't.' Bea stopped and threw Agnes a baffled look. 'We had fun.' She shook her head. 'And it's got nothing to do with second-wave feminism. It's about being decent to people who have been kind. God, Agnes. Are you doing this to impress Camilla? Is that it?'

'I've got no interest in impressing Camilla.'

'Yeah, right.' Bea threw her jumper onto the back of her ruck-sack and tossed herself onto the bed. She picked a book out from a plastic bag she'd brought home with her, a copy of *One Flew Over the Cuckoo's Nest*. She'd been given it by the manager at Foyles.

'What's that about?' Agnes asked.

'Mad people,' said Bea, not looking at her.

There was a short silence but Agnes was still bruised from being challenged. 'It's no different from anything Mr Adler sent us to do. You were perfectly happy putting stickers on the Underground.'

'Agnes,' Bea began, her voice tired and irritated, 'we weren't friends with the posters. This is entirely different. Kiki is our friend.'

'Is she?' Agnes sounded defiant. 'You were saying she'd be long gone when we left. I'd be on my own, you said.'

Bea shot her a dark look. 'Have you forgotten what she did for me the other day? Helping me, when I needed it. Or does that not matter now? What a thing to say. You can't wave a placard in her face; it would be appalling of you. Is this another one of Camilla's *schemes*?' Bea sneered the word.

'No, she just told me about it.' Agnes began furiously folding a pile of washing.

'And she's going, is she?'

'Yes.'

Bea gave a snort. 'Well, that explains it.'

Agnes bristled. 'What does that mean?'

Bea stared down at her book. 'You have a pash on her, Agnes. A great big schoolgirly pash. It would be embarrassing if it wasn't so tragic. First sniffing her clothes, now this.'

'I wasn't sniffing her clothes. Don't be disgusting.' Agnes turned away, back to the folding. 'And it's not a pash. We're friends. Camilla likes me.'

It was alarming, how far their friendship had gone astray, but she wanted to find the words – not to explain, but to declare her intentions. She had to claw back who she was trying to become, the person she had peeked at before that night in the teepee. It wasn't enough to come to London and lark about on odd jaunts. You had to make your mark, stir things up, be noticed. Camilla seemed to manage effortlessly. Agnes had to shake herself up, get back on track.

'What on earth makes you think Camilla likes you?' Bea spat the words out for the nonsense they were. 'She doesn't like you in the least. She's mean, cruel, entirely self-motivated. You're a toy to play with. If you think that's friendship, well, good luck with that.' She flipped the page of her book.

Agnes said nothing. Her mind was whirring.

*A is beautiful.*

She wanted to turn and scream the words into Bea's face. She knew exactly what Camilla thought of her because she had seen it with her own eyes.

'You're just jealous,' mumbled Agnes, pairing some clean socks.

'Sorry?'

She turned round. 'You're just jealous, Bea.'

Bea stared at her. She looked winded.

Agnes went in for the kill. 'You can't bear that I find someone more interesting than you. Not just more interesting. More fun. She's more fun. In fact, you're no fun at all. You're plain and dull and all you've ever done is hold me back.'

She stopped. She knew she had gone too far but her heart was pounding and she was angry and she wanted to hurt her.

Bea opened her mouth and shut it again. She didn't look cross or outraged. She looked broken. Her shoulders fell and she stared off, down to the floor, as if she might find a trapdoor she could slip through and slide away, away, away

Agnes immediately knew she was being unkind. 'Sorry, I ...' she began but Bea pushed herself up from the floor, picked up her bag and left the room.

Agnes listened to her footsteps and the click of the front door and felt a dull ache of sadness. She could run out to her if she wanted, stop her, apologise properly, tell her she didn't know what she was thinking, hug her, spend the day with her and get back to normal.

But normal was no longer what she craved. They had needed to have a row, but not like this. She felt neither justified nor triumphant nor relieved but she had made a choice and now, come what may, she had to stick to it.

# 93

William stood at the bottom of the garden, hands in pockets, staring out at the river. Two swans were gliding, side by side, paired for life. He felt empty, that was the worst of it. He felt the cavernous void where Florence had once been.

Everything he thought about himself – strong, decisive, in control – simply wasn't true. He was dependent, weak, in need of help, and he didn't know what to do. There was no clear path, no signs to consult, no map. He was standing in the middle of a field with no horizon. He was lost.

'William.' Charlie was walking down the garden.

William turned.

'I'm going to the shops. Is there anything you need?'

He almost laughed out loud. Yes please. My wife.

Charlie was smiling, the same open, honest man he always was. William had rather underestimated him, listened to the small voice in the back of his head which found it peculiar that a man might bake a cake or do the hoovering or fill the fridge, but now, looking at him, he didn't see a pansy or a man who had given in: he saw a man comfortable in his own skin who knew his own strengths and weaknesses and was able to quietly exist, happily. He saw a man who understood how to be in a relationship.

'Anything you fancy? I'm getting sausages from the butcher. He does fantastic pork and sage ones. Fried onions? Do you like those?'

He was rattling it all off as if he might be talking about football scores or whether England might win the Ashes. William had never really been consulted about what he might like. He was presented with things and if he liked them he didn't have to say a word. William, he was slowly realising, never had to make a decision.

'Sounds lovely,' he said. 'Thank you.'

He stopped. Here he was, standing in a garden thanking someone for offering to feed him. When was the last time he thanked his own wife? His face crumpled at the thought. All the things she did, the small turnings of the wheels that made his life completely uncomplicated. All of it gone and, like a large, rusting machine, he had ground to a halt.

'I should have thanked Florence,' he said. 'For everything she did.'

Charlie reached out and placed his hand on William's shoulder. 'I'm sure you'll get the chance to,' he said, 'don't despair. Right then,' he added, patting William twice, 'I mustn't hang about. The best ones go in minutes. I won't be long. Eleanor's here, if you need anything.' He gestured towards the studio shed. 'She won't mind the interruption.' He smiled and turned away to bound back up the garden.

He was like a content dog, William thought: unconditional love and duty that came with no preconditions. He was a good man.

'I am not a good man,' William whispered. He looked back towards the swans and was engulfed with sadness.

# 94

'Laila wants to go and eat ice cream.' Bram was buttoning a thin cream linen shirt. 'Do you want to come with us?'

Florence had wandered back to the bedroom. She had finished her book and was looking for a new one. She had noticed the open door into Bram's room and drifted in. She was in the grip of a dark suspicion and she didn't like it.

'Where?' She tried to sound nonchalant.

'Main square. Siena. There's a very good ice-cream parlour. So she says.' He reached for a pair of white cotton trousers on the bed.

Florence wasn't sure what to do. She was in her bikini, her hair dirty from the heat. All the same, she felt anxious about letting Bram out of her sight. She didn't trust him, of course, and there was nothing to be done about it. He was inviting her – freely, it seemed. Perhaps she should let him go, not appear possessive.

She pulled off the wide-brimmed hat and ran a hand through her hair. 'When are you going?' she asked. 'I need a bath.'

Bram pulled on his trousers and glanced at her. 'You look fine. Just throw some clothes on. It's only ice cream.'

He smiled and buttoned his trousers. He hadn't put any underwear on, she noted. How provocative. He came towards her and kissed her lightly on the lips.

'Come,' he said, moving off towards the corridor. 'I love proper ice cream. Don't you?'

And with that he was gone. Florence let the brim of her hat slide sideways through her fingers. Somewhere off in the depths of the house she could hear Laila doing scales: not the formal singing practice she was used to, but the casual singing of someone whose mind is elsewhere.

Florence knew precisely where Laila's mind was. She walked towards the adjoining door. She could be ready in five minutes.

Nannini, the pasticceria of some note, was on the main thoroughfare leading to the Piazza del Campo. The city was gearing up for the Palio, the famous race where horses with bareback riders tore round the ancient square. There was a sense of something feverish and buildings all through the city were decked with flags, the colours of the seventeen *contrade*.

'It's more important than life,' said Laila, as they stood peering at the pastries on offer. 'Seriously. It's crazy. Men cry. Riders, if they lose, get beaten up. Madness. We should take some of these back,' she added, pointing down at the rows of glazed strawberry tarts and slices of tiramisu, 'don't you think?'

Florence glanced around the shop. The interior was incredible: beautiful russet and cream marbled floor, a grand bar with a walnut façade, the air filled with the aroma of fresh coffee and sweet tones from the pastries. Oh! The cakes! Forget the odd cream bun and slice of Victoria sponge, this was art: pistachio cannoli, sfogliatelle, madeleines, profiteroles, zeppole. It was wonderful. Everything looked too good to eat.

Outside, the sound of drums and singing rumbled between the narrow lanes. Laila put her hand on Florence's arm. 'You should see this,' she said, nodding towards the doorway. 'They like to practise.'

She gestured for Florence to follow and stood, just beyond the doorway, one leg extended to her right as if in pose. Florence glanced over to Bram. He was in a queue waiting to place their ice-cream orders. Nannini, it would seem, was immensely popular.

Walking out to the street, Florence leaned back against the grey stone wall of the pasticceria. She could feel the drums and the women's voices resonating up through her feet and chest. Men, dressed in medieval costumes, waved huge flags. Behind them, the drummers; beyond them, the women: arms linked, the colours of their *contrada* tied about their neck.

'Onda,' said Laila, pointing towards the blue and white flags. 'The Wave. The colour of heaven, the force of the sea. They hate the Torre, the Tower. It's all very ... *passionate.*' She smiled as she elongated the word. 'Do you have such things in England?' She peered at Florence over the top of her sunglasses.

'No, I don't think we do.'

'No,' said Laila, slipping her glasses back up her nose. 'The English don't care for *passion*. It embarrasses them. Don't you think?'

Florence said nothing.

'Here,' said Bram, appearing behind them. 'Strawberry for you.' He handed a small pot to Laila. 'Vanilla for you.'

Florence took the pot and picked out the small plastic spoon from the peak. Laila was testing her, making fun of her, she was sure, but she wasn't going to rise to it.

'Wow,' said Bram, watching the standard-bearers toss their flags high into the sky. 'This is so cool. When's the race?'

'Friday,' said Laila, licking a small spoonful of ice cream. 'We should go.'

'Yes, we must.'

'Everyone should see the Palio once,' said Laila. 'Emotions run very high. Would you like it, Florence? Or will it shake you?' She sipped at the top of her ice cream.

'Why would it shake me, Laila?' Florence kept her voice clear and steady.

Laila gave a small shrug. 'Sometimes these things can be … too much. Do you like your vanilla ice cream?' A smile flitted across her lips.

'It's very nice,' Florence said, her voice clipped.

As the procession of the Onda passed them, the beating drums, the singing girls, Florence looked at Bram: the broad grin, the way he held the tiny spoon in his large hand. Despite his size, he looked like a little boy. Laila shifted towards him and turned her face to his to say something. The drums were deafening. Bram bent down and she went up onto her tiptoes to whisper. He pulled back and looked at her then she pulled him back in, her hand on the front of his chest, her lips pressed tight into his ear. What was she saying?

Laila rested back and dug her spoon into her ice cream. Bram looked at her, glanced to Florence, then turned back to watch the singing girls. 'Come on,' said Laila, sliding past Florence. 'I think we have seen enough.'

Florence watched as she slithered off towards the piazza. She reminded Florence of a fuse line stretching to a hidden stick of dynamite. She was alight and at some point she would explode. Bram wolfed down the last of his ice cream and tossed his pot into a bin.

'You coming?' he said, walking past her to chase after the flame that was zigzagging through the crowds. He couldn't get after her quick enough.

Perhaps Laila was right. Perhaps Florence didn't care for passion at all. It was just so exhausting. Laila was wrong about one thing, though: Florence didn't find passion embarrassing. Turns out it made her furious.

# 95

There was an energy to the protest, visceral and febrile. The sexual status quo needed to be smashed and made again. They were the new suffragettes, convinced they were on the right side of history. They were empowered, righteous and angry. Nobody changed anything without upsetting people: that was as true as the tides. They were here to stay and they were trouble.

Despite her argument with Bea, Agnes had still gone. She needed to feel its worth, to convince herself she was trying to make a difference. She believed she was, of course – she was all for equality and the sexual revolution – but that wasn't really why she was there. She was trying to prove herself, again.

She was standing holding a placard handed to her by a waif of a girl called Sandra, jet-black hair down to her waist and a face that looked red and sore. She had jumped out from the back of a blue van, her arms full of cardboard.

Sandra was yelling at a man in black tie dress. He was strolling, casually, taking the time to finish his cigarette. He didn't look threatened or chastened. He simply looked bemused. This was their problem, Agnes realised. Nobody took them seriously. Women were not to be taken seriously. It was a horribly familiar feeling.

Camilla was leaning against the building opposite, one leg bent up behind her, foot flat against the wall. She was with a woman called Bella who had been introduced quickly before Camilla had dragged her off to discuss something Agnes wasn't meant to hear. The woman was quite an imposing figure: taller than Camilla, she had bright red hair. It was tied up and, against the early-evening sun, looked like a flaming torch.

'Who is that?' Agnes nodded over. Camilla and Bella were deep in conversation. There was intensity to them.

Sandra was back from screaming. She was panting slightly, a bit like a dog that's chased a ball. 'Bella. Didn't you just meet?'

'Yes, but who is she?'

'Runs a magazine. Camilla's desperate to work for her. She's very ... impressive. Head screwed on. Super clever. Went to Oxford. That sort.'

'Oxford?' Agnes turned to look at her again. 'Which college?' She felt the usual pang.

'I dunno. It's all one college, isn't it? Oi!' Sandra span and thrust her finger into the air. 'We see you! Down with the objectification of women!'

Two men in suits were getting out of a cab. They glanced over briefly, laughed, and drifted into the club.

'Bloody bastards.' Sandra reached into her pocket and, pulling out a crumpled tissue, sniffed and wiped at her nose. 'Have you been on one of these before?'

Agnes shook her head.

'They're quite good fun, normally. I quite like shouting at strangers.' She stuffed the tissue back into her jeans pocket. 'You got a fella?'

'No,' said Agnes. 'Have you?'

Sandra nodded. 'Yeah. Almost engaged.' Her face broke into a smile. 'I say almost but we are really. We just haven't made it official. Don't tell the others, will you? They get a bit funny about it.'

'What does he think about you doing this?'

'He helped make the placards,' she said, lifting one up. 'FREE THE BUNNIES! He came up with that. Quite good, right? MALE OPPRESSORS!' Sandra suddenly yelled at a man with silver hair.

'One of my flatmates is a bunny girl,' said Agnes. 'She doesn't know I'm here.'

Sandra turned, wide-eyed. 'You live with one?'

Agnes nodded. 'She's really nice.' Her words disappeared away from her.

'How can you bear it?' Sandra was staring at her. 'She's helping the enemy.'

'You've got a boyfriend. You don't hate men.'

'I bloody do. I just don't hate him.'

Agnes shrugged. She wished she hadn't started this conversation. 'Well then,' she mumbled. 'I don't hate her either.'

'Can I have a pic, ladies?' A bloke came towards them, smiling. He had a small camera up to his eye. Beside him, a thin man in a trench coat, holding a notebook and a pencil.

'*Evening Standard*,' said the bloke in the coat. 'What's all this then? DOWN WITH MEN, is it?'

The others began squeezing in, holding their placards up, shouting for the camera. Agnes felt a flush of panic. She couldn't have her picture taken. She'd be found out. She went to move but Sandra grabbed her by the arm and pulled her in. 'No,' shouted Agnes, yanking herself away. The camera flashed. 'I can't.'

She walked, arms folded against the crisp breeze, towards Camilla. Her heart was racing, not from excitement but fear. Had the photographer taken her picture? She wasn't sure. If her mother saw it she was done for.

'I can't do that,' she heard Bella saying. 'It's not possible.'

Agnes came to a stop in front of them. She was nervous, the way you are when you want to impress and you're not sure how to do it. Camilla looked up but Agnes, having made her move, was standing, mouth open, with nothing coming out of it.

'What's the matter with you?' Camilla asked. She sounded irritated.

'Nothing,' said Agnes, clearing her throat. She thumbed back to the melee in front of the photographer. '*Evening Standard* are here. Are you all right?'

'Of course I'm all right. I'm having a private conversation,' Camilla replied, pointedly.

'I just ...' Agnes could feel her cheeks flushing.

'Go away.' Camilla turned back to Bella.

The old feelings of being unimportant washed over her. Agnes wanted to stay, to join in, to feel equal, not just with the men in their black ties; Agnes wanted to be an equal among her peers.

She turned and walked away. The humiliation made her burn. She couldn't go back and risk being photographed. With nobody watching, she let her placard slip gently to the ground. Nobody would notice her leaving. Nobody ever noticed her. It would be fine.

# THURSDAY

# 96

There had been something of a tense impasse, the atmosphere tight and brittle. They hadn't talked since Agnes's outburst the previous day. Neither of them were shouters, both natural avoiders of conflict, and instead of properly having it out, they were stuck in a thick fog of brooding and unspoken resentment.

Agnes knew this couldn't go on. Bea was in the bedroom, sorting through her rucksack. Agnes was in the kitchen. She stood, hands in pockets, idly waiting for the kettle to boil. In front of her was one mug. She reached up into the cupboard and pulled another one down. Perhaps now was a good time to have a chat.

She made the coffees and walked back towards their bedroom. Pushing open the door with her elbow, she held the mugs out. 'I made coffee. Do you want one?'

Bea glanced up. She was sitting cross-legged on the floor.

'I don't want to be here any more.' Her voice was flat, without edge.

'Right.' Agnes placed the cups of coffee next to her on a ledge.

'I can hold off till Saturday. But that's when I'm going home. I have to wait till then not to give the game away.'

'Has your ... ?'

'No.' Bea shook her head.

Agnes felt conflicted. Part of her was relieved, there was no denying it, but the greater part of her felt the sadness of a friendship that had been so light and easy, dragged down and disrupted. Bea's predicament hung heavy; the weight of it had taken its toll.

'What about Mr Adler?' Agnes was trying to be practical.

'What about him? I'll do today and tomorrow and that will be it.' Bea bent forward and carried on going through her bag, tossing out things she didn't need: old bus tickets, shop receipts, pens that no longer worked. 'What's the time?' she added.

'Almost nine,' said Agnes, her voice deadened, neutral. 'We should call him.'

Bea didn't look angry. She looked tired and hurt and fed up and done. The joy had been sapped out of her. It wasn't right that Agnes let this moment drift. She needed to be braver, more magnanimous.

Agnes slid down the wall and sat. 'I'm sorry,' she said. 'I should never have said those things. It was unkind.'

'But you meant them, Agnes. I'm not sure you can take them back.'

Agnes put her hands on the top of her knees. She needed to speak carefully, but it was difficult when her thoughts were in such turmoil. She pulled at a hangnail on her thumb.

'But I didn't mean them, at all. Not one word. I don't think you're plain or boring or—'

Bea put her hand over Agnes's. 'You don't have to explain. I know why you said it.'

Agnes looked sideways. Bea had her forehead in her other hand. She looked exhausted.

'Do you?' Agnes asked. It was all very well thinking she knew what she wanted but everything was so confusing. She was drawn towards Camilla, but why? Last night, she'd been roundly ignored, brought along just to carry things and stand about. To top it off, Camilla had disappeared, leaving Agnes with Sandra and a few stragglers posing for the *Evening Standard*. Bea would never have treated Agnes so casually. With Bea, there was the respect she craved.

*A is beautiful.*

Agnes had been unable to shake that moment away. If she'd thought more of herself to begin with, perhaps it wouldn't have had such a profound effect on her.

'We didn't get this right, did we?' Bea broke the silence.

Agnes shook her head.

'How was last night?' Bea rested her chin on her own knees. Her voice was low.

'No fun at all,' said Agnes, honestly. 'We stood about not doing anything really. Some of the girls shouted at men in suits and that was it.'

'What about Camilla?' Bea turned her face sideways to look at Agnes.

Agnes chewed at her lip. She gave a shrug. 'I don't know. She went off. Not sure where.'

'She didn't come back here?'

'I don't think so.' Agnes looked away. She could feel tears pricking at her eyes. The intensity of it all was startling. How had they got to this point? Bea had been her everything for so long.

'Agnes,' Bea began, 'sometimes it's all right to accept that there are people who simply don't like us.'

Agnes pressed her forehead down onto the backs of her hands. Camilla did like her, she'd seen it in that note, but everything felt wrong: this, Bea going home, hanging round for someone who was intense and complicated, and for what?

'I think you've met someone who's turned your head a bit, made you giddy. You look up to her and you don't know what to do with it.'

'I know ...' Agnes was crying now. 'I wish I didn't. It's like I'm in love with her or something. Except I can't be. I think she's horrible. Why am I trying so hard?'

'Because she's a bully. This is what they do. You're not in love with her. You're scared of her. You don't want her to turn on you.'

They sat for a few moments, the silence heavy. Agnes felt weighed down, her eyes closed, the dampness of her tears seeping between her fingers. She felt vulnerable and embarrassed that she was receiving kindness from someone to whom she should have shown more.

'We've never properly talked about that night,' she said. She gulped at the words and pressed her eyes shut. This was a conversation she should have had long before now.

'I know.'

'Do you want to?'

'I'm not sure I can.' Bea twisted her hands together. 'I still don't know what happened. No memories have come back. I doubt I'll ever know what really went on. Well, I will if it turns out I'm pregnant.' She sounded so tired.

'When's your period due?'

'Two days ago.'

'That might be normal.'

'I know.' Bea pushed herself up from the floor. 'I should never have tried to be something I'm not. I took the drugs. I got myself into that situation. And there it is.'

Agnes stared up at her. 'It wasn't your fault, Bea. They took advantage of us. We didn't know what we were doing.'

'Except we did,' said Bea. 'We wanted to lose our virginity. It was my idea. Well. Not like this.' She heaved a sigh. 'Come on,' she said. 'We need to call Mr Adler. Let's get it done.'

Agnes pressed herself up and they stood for a moment, neither of them quite sure what to say or do. A touch of a hand, a smile, a kindness meant – anything that might have been the rope to haul their friendship to safety – but they were both frozen.

# 97

Laila was chopping tomatoes: big, juicy, aromatic things that filled the room with the smell of summer. There was a dish next to her and, on a chopping board, a pile of green leaves. Florence picked one up. 'What is this?' she asked, smelling it. It had a certain pungency she wasn't familiar with. 'Is it edible?'

Laila nodded. '*Basilico*,' she said. 'Basil. Try it,' she added, pursing her lips. 'The English only seem to have one herb: parsley. You put it on plates and then don't eat it. Most peculiar.'

Florence noticed the small dig.

'We do eat it,' she said, picking at the basil. 'And besides, we have plenty of herbs: sage, rosemary ...' Her voice petered out. What was the point? 'I'm not sure I like that,' she added. 'It's rather strong. Bit soapy.'

Laila took the handful of leaves and ripped them into the chopped tomatoes. 'You can always pick it out.'

She gave a soft, rather insincere smile and padded towards a wooden dresser behind her, where she reached down a dark green bottle. 'I expect you don't know what this is either?' she said, giving it a little shake. 'Olive oil. First press. The best.' She pulled out the cork and poured a thick, yellow-green oil over the tomatoes. She ran her finger under the top of the bottle and licked it. *'Bellissima.'*

If she didn't know better, Florence thought, she'd think Laila was flirting with her, but of course she wasn't. It was far more insidious. She was trying to get Florence to like her. Florence wasn't interested.

'How long are you here for?' Laila drained a round egg-shaped cheese from a tub of water and tore into it with her fingers.

'I'm not sure,' said Florence.

'Bram said he thought you were leaving soon,' Laila added, idly scattering the torn mozzarella across the tomatoes. 'I hope you'll at least stay for the Palio.'

Florence frowned. The race was tomorrow. 'You must have misunderstood,' she said, keeping her voice light. 'Bram is looking forward to the Palio.'

'I know, but he's not leaving. You are.'

The words hung in the air.

Florence composed herself. 'No, I think we're planning on being here till—' She stopped. Actually, she had no idea.

She realised, quite suddenly, that she was there because of Bram. She had not been invited. She was nobody's guest. If Bram wanted her to leave, then she would have to go. Her hand instinctively went up to the small necklace of pearls she always wore. It had been a gift from William on their wedding day, a promise she would always be looked after.

She cleared her throat. 'I'd like to see the Palio. Like you said, everyone should experience it once.'

'Oh, there are lots of things everyone should experience once.' Laila stared up at her. 'Like *basil*,' she said with emphasis, then twirled off towards the verandah, taking the salad with her.

Florence watched as Laila skipped towards Bram. He was lying, arms raised above his head, Laila above him. She put the plate down and trailed a fingernail slowly up the inside of his arm. Bram didn't jump or flinch, Florence noted, and in that moment, she knew.

From that one, small act of physical intimacy she knew, somehow, they had already had sex.

# 98

William tapped lightly on the studio door. He had found some sweet peas that needed cutting in the garden and had put them in a jam jar.

'Hello?'

'Hello,' he said, peering in. 'I thought you might like these.'

Eleanor turned and looked at him. He'd never brought her flowers and, despite him coming to stay, it was unlike him to seek her out.

'How kind. You did that for me?' she said, smiling.

'Well,' said William, a little embarrassed. 'They were going to seed. I hope you weren't saving the jar for jam.'

'Jam? Can you imagine me making jam?' Eleanor wiped her hands on the bottom of her smock.

'Do you not?' William put the jar down on a table covered in half-squeezed tubes of oil paints, a few sketch pads and a tin filled with brushes.

Eleanor frowned. 'I'm nothing like Mummy. Haven't you noticed? I don't make biscuits or cake or jam or steamed sponges or custard from scratch. If you want any of that, you'll have to ask Charlie, I'm afraid. You don't know how lucky you are.' She faltered, realising what she'd said. Not wanting the moment to hang, she picked up the jam jar and breathed in. 'So lovely,' she said, closing her eyes. 'Almost my favourite smell. Almost.'

'What is your favourite smell?'

'Do you really want me to tell you?' Eleanor put the jar back down and tilted her head. She slipped her hands into the pocket of her smock.

'Yes, if you want to.'

'My favourite smell is your shoe polish.'

William shifted. He hadn't expected that. 'Really?'

She nodded. 'It always makes me think of being home, you sitting in the kitchen, me at the other end, elbows on the table, *very forbidden*.' She cupped a hand round her mouth as she whispered the last words. 'And you would polish your shoes and not notice me at all.'

William felt himself wilt. 'Of course I noticed you.'

Eleanor reached out and tapped him reassuringly on the upper arm. 'You didn't. But it doesn't matter. I just liked the smell. And I liked watching you polish your shoes.' She smiled and turned back to her painting.

It was a portrait of someone William vaguely recognised.

'Who is that?'

'Actress from that big costume drama that's been on.' Eleanor looked over her shoulder.

'Yes. Yes.' Sometimes it was easy to forget his daughter moved in high circles.

'She spent most of the sitting crying. Hence the rather melancholy expression.'

'Why was she crying?'

'She'd just found her husband in bed with two women.' Eleanor gave an involuntary hoot. 'I shouldn't laugh. Can you imagine, though. Found them in bed, then had to pick up her bag, turn round and come for a sitting. What a trooper. The show must go on and all that.'

William wasn't quite sure how to react. He was shocked, of course, but his thoughts tumbled, as they always did these days, to Florence. Was she on her own? It hadn't occurred to him that she might have left him for another man but now the thought gripped him. 'Do you think Florence has gone off with someone else?'

'Don't be ridiculous. Of course not.'

They stared at each other, shocked by the idea.

Eleanor picked up her brush and dabbed it into a small blob of white paint on her palette. 'No,' she added, to draw a line under it, 'not a chance. Absolutely not. Anyway, what's *your* favourite smell? Just-cut grass? Bread fresh from the oven?'

'It's your mother,' said William, without having to think for even a moment.

He paused, then, 'I did notice you, Eleanor,' he said. 'I want you to know that.'

He let himself out and walked down the garden to the water's edge. After all, he didn't need her to see him crying again.

# 99

'Would you like to explain this?'

Mr Adler had asked them to come in. He was holding up a copy of the *Evening Standard* and was pointing at a picture of Agnes. He pulled a magnifying glass out from a drawer and theatrically peered a little closer.

'Well, well. Ankle looks fine.'

He tossed the magnifying glass down and leaned back into his chair. He ran his tongue across his top teeth.

Agnes shifted. She felt nervous. 'It started to feel a lot better yesterday afternoon.'

'I bet it did.'

He looked towards Bea. 'And where have you been for the last few days?'

Bea went to answer but he held his hand out to stop her.

'Don't bother. I know where you've been. Backhanding under-the-counter cash in hand at the bookshop.' He pointed a finger at her.

'But,' Bea began, her voice hesitating, 'they asked me to ... I'm not sure it's any of your—'

He cut her off. 'You two might think you've pulled the wool over my eyes.' He stabbed a finger at them. 'But nothing gets past me. DAEVID!' he shouted past them. 'COME IN.'

'What?' mumbled Agnes, panicked. 'Oh no.' She shot an alarmed look towards Bea, her fists were tight and she was trembling.

Behind them, the door opened and in he came: black leather jacket, white flares and the stupid hat. Agnes couldn't bear to look at him. Beside her, she could hear Bea breathing heavily.

'Perhaps you'd like to share again where these two hopped off to?' Mr Adler's voice was aggressive, triumphant. He had set this up to humiliate them.

'I dunno,' said Daevid. 'Woke up, they'd scarpered. Penny spent hours looking for them.'

Mr Adler shook his head in disgust. 'And what about when you were on?' He was drumming his fingers on his desk.

'Nothing special. Lacklustre at best.'

Agnes was consumed with fury. 'Perhaps you might like to tell Mr Adler what else you got up to.' She could feel herself shaking with rage.

Bea's eyes were dark, hard and furious.

'What you talking about?' Daevid gave a shrug and dug his hands into his pockets.

'You know full well.' Agnes was bristling, her lips tightening. She looked towards Mr Adler. 'He drugged us. God knows what with. Bea woke up with half her clothes off.'

Daevid gave a scoffing laugh. 'Darling,' he said, his voice incredulous, 'I'd never be that desperate.'

Mr Adler joined in. 'Bloody mad,' he added, 'the pair of them.'

This is how they did it. This was how men kept women down. In that moment, the crushing reality of the world Agnes and Bea found themselves in became crystal clear. *The Female Eunuch* had warned them of everything: men hate women and they always would. More fool them for not paying enough attention.

'I've heard it all now,' said Mr Adler, sneering at them. 'Off you go, the pair of you. You're done.' He gestured towards the door.

'You're a liar.' Bea whispered it out. Agnes glanced towards her. She was staring at Daevid.

'You what?' Daevid cupped his ear, mockingly, and laughed again.

'You're a liar,' Bea said again, louder. Agnes instinctively reached for her hand.

'Liar, am I?' he snorted. 'Bloody birds, right. They're all funny up here.' He tapped the side of his head.

'Go on!' said Mr Adler, flapping his hand. 'Get out.' He was standing now, his mood threatening.

Agnes pulled at Bea's arm. 'Come on, let's get out of here.'

Bea stood rooted, blind hatred in her eyes. Agnes pulled again. Daevid was laughing at her, Mr Adler yelling. There was no point in staying. They were being treated with derision and, worst of all, the two men were enjoying it.

Agnes dragged Bea towards the door. Behind them, she could hear raucous laughter. It nauseated her. The pair of them stumbled down the stairs; Agnes pushed open the door into Poland Street and gasped up towards the sky. She could barely breathe. She turned to Bea. 'Are you all right?'

Bea's face was like stone: dead and empty. 'This is it,' she said flatly. 'This is what we have to get used to.'

Above them, it had started to rain. Bea looked up into the dark clouds, her anorak unzipped. She was beaten.

# FRIDAY

# 100

The Maestro, the owner of the villa, was larger than life. He had arrived in an open-top sports car, popping out like a ball squeezed from a tube. He was jolly and smiling and seemed to enjoy walking about with his arms in the air, as if constantly expecting ovations.

'My darlings!'

Laila had leapt from her sunlounger, run to him, curtsied (a gesture he very much enjoyed) and thrown herself into his arms. She hung about his neck like a silk scarf.

Florence watched, dead-eyed, behind her sunglasses.

They chattered for a while in Italian, expressive and sing-song, showing off to the gallery. He was holding Laila's hands, the way you might before spinning a child, indulged and adored. She leaned in and whispered something. As she did, his eyes darted towards Florence and his expression changed slightly.

What was it? Shock? Disgust? Embarrassment?

Bram was walking from the house, cold drink in his hand. He was in his trunks, flip-flops on his feet, and his hair was combed back, wet from the shower. They had not slept together last night. He had found some fine wines, opened a few bottles, and Florence, unable to keep up, had drifted off, thinking he might follow. He hadn't.

'Mr Bram!' The Maestro stood, arms apart. 'So glad you could come! Have you been having fun? Laila tells me you have been having fun.' He wagged his finger at him and let out a thick, chesty laugh before pointing towards Florence. 'Fun! Yes?' He laughed again.

Bram laughed back and gave a faux shrug that Florence found distasteful. Look at the three of them. Standing there, laughing. It's all so funny. Laughing at them. Laughing at her. She bristled.

'And who is this?' the Maestro said, shimmying towards the verandah and Florence. 'Who are you? You must tell me *everything*.' He bent towards her and pursed his lips as if waiting for a tantalising piece of gossip.

Should she get up? She was reclining, her legs crossed at the knees. He was staring down at her and it was unnerving. She stood and held her hand out. 'Florence Ledbury,' she said.

The Maestro looked at her outstretched hand and let out another loud guffaw. Grabbing it, he pulled her to him and kissed the air lightly on either side of her cheeks.

'So formal!' he shouted, laughing again and pushing her away to look at her. 'Is it *true*?' He leaned in and put the back of his hand to his mouth as if conveying a secret message. 'That you have left your husband and *run away*?' He cast a look towards Laila who was standing, arms folded, in the sun.

'Yes,' said Florence. 'It is.'

He clasped his chest with his hands. 'My God! So romantic and fabulous and *desperate*!' His eyes widened. He turned and thumped Bram in the arm. 'You old dog! You dog!' He was finding the situation quite the riot. He turned back to Florence and grabbed her by the elbow. 'Of course you know he is not to be trusted?' He winked back towards Bram. 'You are running with the *wolf*, my darling.'

Florence glanced towards Bram who was sipping his drink. His face betrayed nothing.

The Maestro clapped his hands together. 'Well!' he announced, spinning round. 'We must get ourselves ready! Palio! Palio! Palio! *Drama!*'

He threw his arms up in the air and shook his head. He had thick, black hair that danced on his shoulders and a close-shaved beard that hid the hint of a double chin. He turned and plucked Laila's hand like a flower.

'*Bambina*,' he purred, lifting her hand to his lips. 'We leave in an hour, yes?'

Laila squirmed with delight. 'I shall look beautiful!' she sang, span round on the ball of one foot and skipped off towards the house. As she passed Bram, she ran a hand down his arm. 'Wear those trousers,' she ordered. 'The ones I like.'

It was an act of violent intimacy.

Florence was glad she had sunglasses on. Her stare might have burned Laila to death.

# 101

'Hang on,' said Charlie, staring at his copy of the *Evening Standard*. He peered closer. 'It can't be. Eleanor,' he said, looking up. 'Agnes is in the paper.'

'What are you talking about?' Eleanor was stretching a canvas, a long tack in one corner of her mouth.

'I'm telling you,' said Charlie, standing from the armchair in Eleanor's studio. 'Agnes is in the paper. Look.'

Eleanor removed the tack and leaned to see. Charlie folded the paper over and held it out. He tapped at the photograph in question. 'There. It's her.'

Eleanor put down the small hammer in her hand and took the paper. 'Where?'

'Far right, holding the SAVE THE BUNNIES placard. Looks furious.'

Eleanor peered.

'Oh my God.' Her face lit up. 'She's not in Europe. Hang on. Let me read it ...

'*A group calling themselves Liberation for Women held a demonstration outside the Playboy Club in Park Lane ...*

'WHAT? Charlie! She's run off to London to burn her bra ...

' ... *protesting against what they call the club's "gross objectification of women". "It's 1971, for heaven's sakes," said a spokesperson. "Women don't have to dress up as rabbits for men's pleasure."*

'I BET that was Ag.' Eleanor let out a hoot. 'Mum will blow a GASKET if she sees this.'

'Should we tell William?'

Eleanor paused. 'I don't know. What do you think?'

'Probably should. She's instantly recognisable. Someone will tell him.'

Eleanor stared down at the picture. 'I can't believe it. *Agnes Ledbury.* Who knew you had it in you?' She gave the paper a small punch. 'Good for her.' A thought stopped her. 'Dad said Mum had had letters, though. From France and Italy. I have no idea what is going on.'

'Do you think you should try and contact her? Tell her about Florence?'

Eleanor looked up. 'I don't know.' She paused to think. 'No. Let her enjoy a state of ignorant bliss. She'll know soon enough. Wow. I wonder if she *is* coming back?'

She looked back down at the photograph: the new haircut, the clothes that were clearly not her own. She appeared older and hopeful. Eleanor shook her head, a wide smile unable to stop itself from spreading. 'Little Agnes,' she said. 'Little Agnes has grown up.'

# 102

Agnes was filled with despair: the humiliation of the encounter with Adler and Daevid, the crumbling of her friendship with Bea, and now this.

The *Evening Standard* was splayed open at the relevant page.

'I'm supposed to be in Europe. What if someone sees it and phones my mother?' She sounded panicked.

'So what?' said Camilla, eating an apple. She was sitting on the kitchen counter, one arm drifted across herself, her legs idly dangling. 'Why do you care?'

'I don't know ...' Agnes mumbled. 'Because I'm lying. This is a nightmare.'

Camilla gave a shrug and bit into her apple. She was back, from who knows where, giving off the aura of someone who had been doing nothing but having sex.

'Where have you been?' Agnes asked. She felt anxious to her guts.

'You jealous?'

'No.'

'Liar.' She bit again into her apple.

Kiki wafted in. 'Can I get to the kettle,' she said testily. 'Or would either of you like to yell at me? Wave a placard?' She folded her arms and stared at them.

Agnes felt a flush of embarrassment and turned the paper over to hide the picture.

'Don't bother,' Kiki said, glaring at her, 'I've already seen it. Nice way to thank me. I thought we got on?'

Agnes's blood ran cold. 'Kiki, I—'

'I don't want to know.' Kiki held a hand up. She pulled a mug down from the cupboard and stood with her back to the pair of them. Agnes looked towards Camilla. She was smirking.

Behind her, Bea appeared. She was in a pair of burgundy polyester trousers and a purple T shirt.

Camilla glanced at her. 'You look like a giant plum.' She bit again into her apple.

Bea ignored her and walked to the fridge, opened the door and took out a plate of cheese and a small loaf of bread. She began to make a sandwich and said nothing.

Agnes eyes flitted between them. The atmosphere was awful, the air bristling with resentment. Bea looked deadened, Kiki furious, and above it all, like a crow waiting for road-kill, sat Camilla smirking down. There was something about her so awful, so unforgiving, so relentless. Camilla wasn't someone to look up to or admire. She was simply exerting the awful power plays of men. That wasn't liberation. It was copying of the worst sort.

'Everyone seems in a frightful mood,' said Camilla, tossing her apple core into the sink. She pushed herself off the counter. 'I should have stayed out.' She looked Agnes up and down. 'At least you're not pretending to be me today,' she said and left the room.

Agnes hated herself for seeking her approval.

# 103

The Piazza del Campo was a riot.

The centre of the square was filled to capacity, bodies crammed shoulder to shoulder. The Maestro had reserved seats in the bleachers, next to the start. He had arrived to be cheered by the locals and had stood, like something out of a medieval tableau, a rotund emperor greeting his people. He was wearing the white and blue flag of the Onda, tied lightly about his neck, and held a blue handkerchief in his hand. Despite the heat, he wore a cream linen suit and a panama hat with a dark navy trim. He was luxurious, resplendent, at home.

Laila was in a white lace dress, another flag of the Onda *contrada* tied up into her hair. She was not from Siena, of course, but it wasn't the done thing to carry the colours of a rival, not today. She was perched, her hand on the Maestro's shoulder, and as the crowds waved and cheered him, she seemed to feed off their adulation. One day, Florence could see her thinking, all this would be hers.

Bram was sitting between them. He was wearing thin blue cotton bell-bottoms that hugged his crotch. No wonder Laila had asked for them. He had picked up a slice of pizza, dripping with mozzarella, from a stall and was eating it pinched between a napkin.

The noise was deafening. Competing *contrade* were singing their lungs up, chests out, faces defiant: the men of the Torre gesticulating towards the Onda, wishing humiliation, cuckoldry and death upon their rivals. Drums were beating. Men in medieval outfits, the standard-bearers, tossed huge flags aloft. Ripples from centuries past, there was something timeless about it.

'This is a bit different from the Brill village fete,' Florence offered, touching Bram on the wrist.

'What?' He turned and bent his ear towards her. The sound of the singing was blocking everything else out.

'Bit different from a village fete in Brill. Harvest Festival. May Day. That sort of thing.' Florence was shouting.

He leaned back and shook his head and gestured around him to tell her he had no idea what she was saying. No. Neither did she. He finished his slice of pizza. A small piece of melted cheese dripped onto his chin. Laila, noticing, took the scrunched napkin from Bram's hand and wiped it away. She tossed it down between a gap in the stands.

Florence watched every move from behind her sunglasses: the way Laila pressed her thigh into his, the light familiar touch of her hand on his arm. She was aware of every tiny power play. Laila had got what she wanted, now all that remained was the complete victory.

Off to the left, the sounds of horns rang around the square. A great roar went up, so intense it made Florence feel on edge. Everyone leapt to their feet, arms aloft, waving their colours. The energy was urgent and tense. It felt dangerous.

The horses of the *contrade* paraded in: some proud, some twitchy and unpredictable. Florence found herself clapping. It felt as if trouble could break out at a moment's notice.

The start was a rope pulled taut across a sawdust track. The riders, all bareback, were pulling hard on reins: wide-eyed stallions, snorting, pounding at the ground. Florence glanced sideways towards Bram. He had his fingers in his mouth, whistling. The Maestro, arm aloft, was swirling his hat in circles as if scaring crows. Laila stood expressionless, aloof to it all. This wasn't about her, that was the problem.

Below them, a cannon went off.

The horses bolted. At the first bend, three riders were tossed sideways, one going under the hooves of a horse coming from behind. Florence's hand went to her mouth. Two men ran on and dragged the rider sharply by the arms into shadows. The primary objective was to clear the track. The riders had to go round three times. The race, it would appear, was more important than life or death.

The horses raced on towards the sharpest bend, a corner so dangerous it was covered in mattresses. A dark horse clattered into it, causing a violent pile-up behind: it was all legs and wild, terrified eyes and riders rolling, rolling, rolling.

A lone horse, a beautiful black mare with a single white foot, wearing the colours of the Panther *contrada*, emerged from the melee and off it ran. As the rider pressed forward, hunched low, his hat disappeared in the wind. If he could just hang on ...

He did and, as he crossed the finishing line, the square was filled with triumph and despair. The winner was pulled from the horse and lifted onto shoulders like a religious relic. The losing *contrade* were already down on the track exacting revenge. Some riders were being beaten up, others running for their lives. Men were crying, women were screaming. It was like a storm from an ancient legend played out year on year. Florence couldn't grasp the passion of it.

'And that is that,' said the Maestro, wiping his face with his handkerchief. 'Come, come,' he said, gesturing towards the gangway, 'we must leave before the *killing* starts.' He threw his head back and a thick, deep laugh roared out of him.

Laila reached back for Bram's hand. He let her take it. 'Help me, please,' she said, tiptoeing on her high heels.

Florence stared down at her espadrilles. They were already fading in the sun. She knew how they felt.

# SATURDAY

# 104

It would be their last night out, Agnes had said, an evening to see Bea off. Agnes hadn't worked out what she was going to do when Bea left. That, like everything else, was a problem to think about tomorrow. Bea had needed persuading.

Neither of their hearts were in it. They had applied the minimum of make-up in silence, pulled on clothes that were clean and plain. Bea stood in the living room, arms by her side, bag slung across her chest. Everything about her seemed already halfway home.

The Gateways Club was on the corner of Bramerton Street in Chelsea, a dark green door set into a windowless wall with a sign above it that betrayed nothing.

In contrast to her two companions, Camilla was in sparkling mood. She was buoyant, in charge, dressed in a figure-hugging white roll-neck tucked into a pair of cotton navy bell-bottoms and braces. It had come as a surprise that she had invited them out but there was still a voice deep inside Agnes that told her it was all right. Camilla liked her really. She was just prickly, awkward. The aggressive front was the brittle façade to someone deeper, friendlier, magnanimous. After all, she liked small flowers, didn't she?

Bea had barely spoken on the bus. She had taken the seat in front, her shoulders hunched, her head resting against the window. Agnes knew Bea didn't want to be there. And yet it felt important to go through the motions of saying goodbye even if, in reality, that had happened long ago.

'I can guarantee,' said Camilla, as they arrived, 'that you will never have been anywhere quite like this.' Her thumbs were tucked behind the silver buckles of her braces.

Bea said nothing. She looked haunted and undone. This adventure had quite ruined her. Agnes thought back again to that moment on Christ Church Meadow: the optimism, the expectation, the plan hatched in the pub. Now look at them.

Camilla knocked on the green door and a woman appeared, cigarette hanging from her lip. She was wearing a dark suit with a long black tie, her hair slicked back. Opposite her in the hallway was an identically dressed woman, her hair cut short and boyish. 'All right,' she said, her accent thick East End. 'How many?'

'Three,' said Camilla and in she sauntered.

The tiny entrance was no more than the top of some stairs. Behind the woman to the right was a ledge with a book of tickets and a bucket for money. The other woman leaned back against a bright orange wall. She had a toothpick and was using it to clean the dirt from a forefinger.

Agnes looked at her and the woman winked.

'I'll get these,' said Camilla, reaching for her purse. 'Goodbye treat for Bea.' She flashed a small insincere pout.

Bea rolled her eyes. This had been going on for days. Since Bea had announced she was going home, Camilla had focused in on her, not all cruel, but unrelenting and unkind. It was astonishing Bea had managed this long. Agnes knew full well she was putting herself through misery so that Agnes would be all right. It was another moment for shame and regret. Bea still, after everything, was putting Agnes first. Bea did not deserve this but they were here now and would have to make the best of it.

A pulsing noise was coming up the stairwell and the smell of smoke and beer hung heavy. Camilla skipped lightly down the stairs then turned, rather dramatically. 'Welcome to heaven,' she said, placing one hand high on the frame of the doorway. 'Or hell. You can choose.'

Bea shot Agnes a despairing look. Beyond her there was a dance floor, a mass of bodies and pounding music. Agnes rested her hand on Bea's shoulder. This might be the last evening they had together for who knows how long. Bea's hand went up to Agnes's and, for a moment, they both remembered: they'd been in this together, through thick and thin. It had all begun with such hope, such joy. Now here they were in a club they didn't want to be in, in a city they'd stopped enjoying. Neither of them wanted to be there.

Camilla was pressing her way towards a bar at the far end of the room. The walls were covered in coloured murals: large faces and garish swirls. A band, four girls in shift dresses, was playing on a platform jutting out from an alcove. Agnes, trying to keep sight of Camilla, began to push through the swollen crowd. She reached back for Bea's hand and pulled her with her.

'There are no men here,' Agnes said, looking around.

'What?'

She had to shout 'No men. Anywhere.'

There were women in short skirts, patterned dresses, hair bobbed and backcombed, and then there were other women, dressed in suits. The butches and the femmes, dancing together, heads on shoulders, hands on waists, content and safe. Not a single man. They were in a gay club.

'Of course she's brought us here,' said Bea, pulling her hand out from Agnes's. 'Let's get to the bar.' She was on edge.

The cold dampener of yet another mistake trickled through Agnes. She hadn't known where Camilla was taking them but it was another provocation, one that would make Bea's last evening awkward. Despite everything, Agnes had hoped tonight might be a return to the old days: a few drinks and the easy larks, the endless quips would return and they would remember the joy of a friendship that mattered. The likelihood of that happening now appeared slim.

'I didn't know we were coming here,' she offered but Bea wasn't looking at her.

Camilla was leaning against the bar, one foot up on the rail that ran around it. A woman in a short-sleeved T-shirt with a white rim was pulling pints, her hair cropped short. She wore no make-up and might, from a distance, be mistaken for a lad.

Camilla tapped out a cigarette from a packet pulled from her trouser pocket. 'Want one?' she shouted.

Agnes shook her head.

Camilla reached past her. A woman in a checkered waist-coat, her hair whipped up teddy-boy style, was holding up a lighter. She whispered something to Camilla who said nothing but shook her head. The woman moved off. Agnes felt rattled. She didn't know what she thought about lesbians other than they were incredibly dangerous and, if you were one, your life was ruined. She looked at Camilla. 'Are you a lesbian?'

'No,' said Camilla, blowing out a plume of smoke.

'Two ciders and whatever she wants,' shouted Bea to the bar-maid, who was leaning across the bar, one palm down, to catch the order. She nudged her head in Camilla's direction.

'One of those,' said Camilla, pointing towards the large green bottle of Gordon's hanging in the optics. 'And a slice of lemon.' She put a hand on Bea's wrist, and whispered something. Bea frowned and mouthed something back. She looked annoyed.

Agnes felt a rush of indignation. Camilla had manipulated them both and what for? Her own amusement? A fury that she had fallen for it overwhelmed her. 'Leave her alone,' she said, grabbing Camilla by the forearm.

Camilla stared down at Agnes's hand, looked up and cocked an eyebrow. 'I'm not doing anything.' She gave a small shrug, narrowed her eyes and took another drag on her cigarette.

'Leave it,' said Bea, handing Agnes her bottle of cider. 'It's not worth it.' She took a sip from her own. She looked dismayed.

'Shall we find somewhere to sit?' Agnes shouted into her ear. Bea nodded.

'Come on,' said Agnes, and pulled her towards the far wall. Camilla watched them go. Agnes looked back. She was laughing.

The band was playing something upbeat and pounding and the dance floor was full. The atmosphere was raucous and cele-bratory. Agnes was so used to lesbians being thought of as disgusting it was something of a shock to see so many of them looking entirely normal. It looked like any pub or club in any town. It looked like a Saturday night anywhere. The only thing that was different was that there were no men. Bea was picking at the label on her bottle. Agnes glanced back again towards Camilla. Her arm was raised, waving at someone. Agnes fol-lowed her eyeline to see Bella, the flame-haired woman from the demo.

'Are you going to be all right?' Bea was shouting at Agnes.

'Sorry?' Agnes turned and squinted. It was so loud.

'When I leave. Will you be OK?' Bea looked over Agnes's shoulder towards the bar.

Agnes nodded. 'Don't tell anyone I'm here, will you?'

Bea shook her head.

'If anyone asks about the picture, just say it wasn't me. Some-one who looks like me or something.'

Agnes looked back towards Camilla. Bella was pressing her way towards her. The tempo of the music changed: slow, melodic and romantic. The women on the dance floor paired up.

'Do you feel weird?' Agnes turned to Bea and asked. 'Being here, I mean.'

'I'm probably feeling precisely what Camilla wanted me to feel.' Bea sounded scornful, pissed off.

Another woman approached. 'Fancy a dance?' She was skinny, square jaw, blue suit, hair slicked down to one side. She looked as if she might work in a government ministry.

'No, thank you,' said Bea.

'You two together?' The woman floated a finger between them.

'No,' they both said.

'I might have to get thunderously drunk,' Bea said gloomily, as the woman drifted away, one hand in her pocket. Her face, despite the moment of bravado, was filled with regret. Agnes glanced back again towards the bar. Camilla was laughing, head back, cigarette balanced between two fingers. She was spreading herself out, offering herself up. Bella was running her hand around Camilla's waist. She leaned in and kissed her passionately and, as they did, Agnes's world ground to a halt.

Bea watched her carefully. 'Do you know who that is?'

Agnes looked away. 'She was at the demo. Bella or something.'

'Arabella.'

Agnes stared at Bea's mouth, her own open slightly in horror. 'Arabella?'

'Bella. Short for Arabella. I heard Camilla talking about her.'

She thought back to the note in Camilla's bedroom. *A is beautiful.*

It hadn't been Agnes at all. She had let herself be strung along. And it had all been for nothing.

# 105

Things were not going well for Florence. She stood at her bedroom window and looked down over the courtyard. She had dressed for supper: a light, airy, floral frock that swayed like summer and just, but only just, matched her fading espadrilles.

She was reminded of all the evenings she would scurry up the stairs to freshen up for William. It felt a lifetime ago yet here she was, mustering herself to impress the man who was currently standing below her kissing another woman against a wall. Laila's hands were dug deep into Bram's hair, one leg wrapped high around his thigh.

Florence had watched as they walked through the olive grove beyond the house, Laila twirling every now and again, performing for his delight. She was coquettish, ethereal, in control. As they had reached the courtyard, she had slowed to a halt and leaned back against the golden sandy walls, her arms splayed, her head tilted. It was no coincidence, Florence thought, Laila had managed to arrange this tableau quite precisely opposite her bedroom window.

It would be foolish to underestimate Laila. She wanted Florence gone.

Bram had shifted towards her, one broad hand on her tiny thigh, and she had pulled him in and now here they were, going at it like two people who hadn't eaten in a month. Bram reached down to his fly and Laila shifted, lifting herself up and on to him. Florence stood, part-horrified, part-fascinated. He didn't last long and, as his back tensed and his face went skywards, Florence could have sworn Laila looked straight at her.

She turned away from the window.

Her heart was pounding. Somehow she had to navigate herself out from this situation with her dignity intact. There was no point in making a scene. Laila would delight in it. As for Bram, well ... he was Eleanor's age and single and he had probably felt sorry for her and she could have no complaints. Finally, it had come to this.

There was a temptation to pack her bag, here and now, slip into her car and drive far away. What was stopping her? Manners, that's what. An ingrained sense of politeness. Her Englishness. She didn't have it in her to have people she barely knew think her rude.

*What a ridiculous situation.*

She took a deep breath and turned to look at herself in the mirror. She'd lost a little weight, she thought, not much but enough for people at home to pass comment. Perhaps it was the tan? Whatever, she looked different. She hadn't thought of home, not much. She had catapulted herself away but now she was going to have to think about how to get back.

What would she do when she returned to England? Where might she go? She could head to Eleanor's first. That would be best. She wondered if William had told her. She doubted it. He'd be far too embarrassed to tell anyone. He would never allow himself to be that vulnerable. She would have to be the one to do it. She'd need to prepare for that, work out how to say it. As for Agnes ... well. Eleanor could tell her.

She wondered if William had managed with the frozen meals.

Suddenly, she felt a weight of sadness: a marriage done; two people, thrown together all those years ago, who had never bothered to get to know each other. What a terrible waste.

She picked up a loose scarf from the bed and gathered it around her neck, something to set off the outfit. She looked nice enough. She had felt free these past few weeks but now here she was, standing in a room, feeling pointless because of a man. Again.

Possession was done, the clarion call had gone out: women, enjoy yourselves. Take control, be promiscuous, reject your slavery, be free. Florence had tried freedom to the full and yet here she was, trapped

Music sounded from within the villa. A record was playing. Florence left her room and trod slowly towards it. The Maestro was standing on the verandah, a cocktail in hand, eyes closed, humming along. Florence recognised the piece but couldn't place it: a soaring aria from an opera. There was no sign of the others.

'You're the first down,' he said, seeing her. 'I've made Aperol Spritz. Would you like one?'

Florence nodded.

'Another beautiful evening,' he said, wafting a hand towards the pink sky 'We are so spoiled here. I don't know how you can bear to spend so much time under such a grey sky.' He picked a glass from a silver tray and dropped some ice cubes into it.

'England has its charms.'

'Does it?' He poured a vibrant orange liquid into the glass. 'Rose gardens and green fields and broad oaks and country pubs and roast beef and what are those things called?' He paused. His voice was sing-song and mellifluous.

'Yorkshire puddings.'

'*Yorkshire puddings!*' He pronounced every consonant. 'And gravy. You are so mad for gravy. And custard. It's all you do. Constantly want to hide things. Quick! Pour on the gravy! Pour on the custard! Don't look at what's underneath!' He let out a loud laugh. 'Honestly! It's like you're embarrassed of what you're eating. Of course, you must not think me rude,' he said, picking up a soda fountain and squirting a cloud of bubbles into the drink. 'It is how I see things. I like to observe. To watch.' He smiled and handed her the cocktail. '*Salute!*' He lifted his glass.

Florence sipped. It had a certain bitterness. She wasn't entirely sure she liked it.

'I have been watching you, Florence.' The Maestro shut one eye and wagged a finger in her direction. 'What do you think I see?' He leaned back on his heels, waiting.

'I don't know.' She paused. 'You'll have to tell me.'

'I see a woman who is far away. Here but not here. It's time to fly home, Florence. Fly away home.' He made little butterfly gestures with one hand. 'Of course, Laila now has Bram.' He stopped and took a delicate sip of his cocktail. 'This is to be expected. You cannot be surprised?'

Florence wondered if she should feign shock at his candour. She straightened her shoulders. 'No surprise. I rather think Laila is used to getting what she wants.'

The Maestro let out a boom of a laugh. 'But of course! She must be denied nothing. But Bram is ...' He reached for the word he needed. 'An opportunist. He is a boy. He cannot help himself.' He waved his fingers through the air. 'I hope', he said, taking her hand, 'you do not take these things personally.' He looked at her kindly. 'We are all brief visitors. Some people are lucky, able to stick to the rocks. Others are forever carried on the tides.' He bent and kissed the ends of her fingers. 'I like you, Florence! I do!' He laughed again, his great barrel of a chest heaving. 'But perhaps,' he lowered his voice to a conspiratorial whisper, 'it is time for you to let go of the rock.'

He leaned back and watched her. She understood full well what he was saying.

She looked out at the blushing sky. The sound of cicadas filled the air. The tide had come in. Time to let go.

# SUNDAY

# 106

'I think that's everything.' Bea stood and blew out. There was something about her that looked familiar. Something Agnes had forgotten. She looked happy.

'Well. I suppose this is it.'

Bea turned and smiled. The smile, Agnes noted, was not for her. The smile was entirely for Bea's own benefit. It was neither sad nor regretful. It was the smile of something awful being over. It was the smile of release.

Agnes felt desolate. There was no hiding it. She had tried to be a better version of herself but instead had lost her way. She had failed to have sex, failed to stay true to herself, failed to be a good friend. She had finally broken away from the chains of her illness but, in doing so, had given up her bond with Bea. In this moment, it didn't feel worth it. What on earth did she want to stay here for?

'Can I come back with you?'

Bea paused. 'Back to Brill?'

Agnes nodded. She looked pleadingly, hoping to see a glimmer of the old fondness that had once bound them together, but instead she watched a broad smile wither to nothing.

'I don't know if that's a good idea.' Bea's voice was quiet and sure.

Agnes felt blindsided. She was losing the person who meant the most to her in the world. 'I'm not sure if I can stay here,' she said. 'If you're going home, I should go too. So it doesn't look strange.' She was aware of how desperate she sounded.

'I'm not bothered about it being strange.' Bea was looking at her directly, seriously.

'Bea, I'm sorry I ...' Her words petered out. She felt sorry for all of it. This stupid idea. The catalogue of disasters.

'Agnes.' Bea took her hand. 'You can't come with me. It's not fair.'

Agnes frowned. 'Not fair on who?'

'Both of us.' Bea let go of Agnes's hand and walked towards her rucksack. She picked it up off the floor and leaned it against the wall. 'You don't know what I'm talking about, do you?'

Agnes shook her head.

'It's very difficult,' Bea began, 'when one person is the only source of your happiness. I've become too reliant on you. It scares me, actually, how much I depend on you.' A small, kind smile returned. 'And that's rather embarrassing. We can't go through life clinging to each other. We can't stay forever in the goldfish bowl we made for ourselves. If I have you to fill in all my gaps, I'll never move on. I have to make my own mistakes. And I have to take responsibility for fixing them. It's time for me to stand on my own two feet. We're too old for all this, don't you think?'

She pulled a face to cover the awkwardness.

'Don't worry. I'm not going to go weird. I'm all right about it. I've worked out why I was unhappy. And working it out has made me happy. If that makes sense?'

Agnes stood very still.

Bea paused. 'I've loved being your friend.'

Agnes blinked. 'What do you mean? You're still my friend.' She shook her head. She couldn't quite comprehend what was happening. Bea going home early was one thing; telling her their friendship had to end for good was entirely another.

Bea hesitated, thinking how best to say it. 'I will be again one day,' she said carefully. 'But I need to not do this for a while.' She waved a finger between them.

Agnes could feel tears pricking at her eyes. She shook her head. 'What are you talking about? You're my best friend. I don't know what to do without you.' Her mind tumbled. Everything she had learned about herself – the confidence, however temporary, the sense of purpose – all of it was because of Bea. Bea had given her the strength to get there. She owed her everything.

Bea picked up the rucksack and slung it onto her back. 'Do you know what?' she said. 'You're going to be all right and I'm going to be all right.' She gave a fulsome nod.

'How do you know?'

'That we'll be all right?'

'No,' said Agnes, rubbing at her eyes, 'that you're …' she retrieved the words ' … too *reliant* on me. How do you know? What does it even mean? We've just had the weirdest time. That's all.'

Bea stood, her tall shoulders a little hunched, her top rucked up under the straps, her arms hanging down like socks on a line. She took a deep breath.

'When we started out on this, we were together. We were like one person. And then …' she paused to get it right ' … it started to become about you. About what you wanted. And I went along with it. And then there was the night in the tent. And what happened happened and you didn't step up or give anything up. I felt lost. And what that taught me is – I have to learn to make myself happy. Nobody else is going to do it.' She waited, then, 'I'm not cross about it but I have to move on. It's time.'

Agnes lifted her hand to her mouth. Her throat was tight, her chest heavy. 'I'm not sure what to say.' She could barely get the words out.

'You don't have to say anything,' said Bea. 'This is on me. I'm the only person who can fix it.'

Agnes looked at Bea's wonky nose and her big teeth and her kind eyes. She thought about Bea running towards her across Christ Church Meadow; she thought about how they always shared each other's sandwiches; she thought about the endless laughter, the nuns, the ridiculous and awful Mr Adler. She thought about the kindness, the good, good heart. Agnes couldn't bear it.

'Can't we just …'

'No, we can't. I need to – and please take this with the greatest respect – get as far away from you as possible.' Bea let out a laugh. 'Can you even believe I said that out loud?'

'No!' said Agnes, shaking her head. 'It's awful. I feel awful. I can't believe this is happening.'

'Well, it is,' said Bea, exhaling. 'Good luck with everything. I don't know about you but I'm really looking forward to the grilling I'm going to get about our trip to Europe. How was Milan? Yeah. It was super. What do you mean you took no photographs? Lost the camera. In the Seine. Etcetera.' She was trying to lighten the moment but it was no use. She stopped and looked again at Agnes. Her jaw tightened and her eyes began to water.

'Bea …' Agnes thought back to what they had been, the years they had spent in each other's pockets. It couldn't end like this. She went towards her but Bea raised her hands up and backed away.

'No goodbyes,' she said. 'No goodbyes. I love you, Agnes Ledbury. See you when I see you.' She gave a short salute and left.

Agnes held herself tight. She was trembling, her heart aching. She heard the front door slam. No, she couldn't leave it like this. She ran to the front door and threw it open. Bea was already halfway up the street.

'Beatrice Morgan!' Agnes called out.

Bea stopped and looked back.

'I love you too!'

Bea raised a hand, held it high for a moment, then turned.

Agnes stood and watched her go. She crumpled downwards. She had never known a sadness like it.

# 107

Florence lay in her bed staring up at the large wooden fan in the ceiling.

She was being forced to listen to Laila noisily riding Bram in the room next door. She turned her face towards the open window. It was another beautiful, deep-blue day. The sun was endless here. It bleached everything.

She thought about the conversation she'd had with the Maestro. She thought of her garden in Brill. She wondered if the beans were all picked, whether the roses had been watered. She wondered about the lawn and the little bird table she liked to leave bacon scraps on. She wondered about the tomato plants and the lavender and whether the bees had sucked them dry.

It was almost time to cut them back, ready for another year.

She wondered about her home. She wondered who might have cleaned it in her absence, whether it had been at all. She wondered about her freezer and her washing machine and she wondered about the endless piles of Tupperware.

She wondered about the clothes in her wardrobe, the neat line of shoes. She wondered about her bed and what a sterile, joyless experience sex with William was. She wondered about her husband. She wondered if he'd missed her. Had she missed him?

She pushed herself onto her elbows. Next door, Laila was putting on quite the show. She didn't need to listen to this. She dropped her feet to the floor and slipped them into her dusty espadrilles.

It was time to go home.

# 108

Agnes wiped at her face. The stone steps underneath her were cold and uncomfortable.

She got up, stepped back into the hallway and closed the door behind her. Everything felt wrong. She looked down the corridor towards the open door of their room. She didn't want to be here. She could slip away and never have to see Camilla again. She wouldn't even say goodbye to her. She would send a card to Kiki, apologise.

What was the point of staying here a second longer? She would pack her bag and go.

# 109

'Leaving without saying goodbye?'

Laila was draped against the corner pillar of a pergola, above her a clutch of grapes. She was wearing a thin white cotton shift, her hair wet. The sun was behind her. She was naked underneath.

Florence closed the boot of her car. 'Yes,' she said. 'Everyone was rather busy. Thought I'd leave you to it.'

She turned and removed her sunglasses. She wanted to look at her properly, honestly. She wanted Laila to know she was leaving of her own accord.

'Bram is taking a bath.' Laila thumbed back into the house. 'Do you want to say goodbye to him?'

'You can say goodbye for me.'

It was strange, watching her now. Laila had, by any stretch of the imagination, got what she wanted but Florence could see the disinterest already settling in.

'Where are you going?' Laila tossed her wet hair. Florence felt tiny specks of water tickle at her face.

'Home. To England. I think I can do it in two days.'

'Are you planning to stop?'

'Not really.'

'You must be keen to get back.'

'I suppose I am.'

Laila pouted a little and stretched one arm up to pick at the grapes above her. 'Do you think these are ready?'

'I wouldn't know. You'll have to taste one.'

What was the point of this? Was Laila still trying to get Florence to like her before she left? The sheer audacity of it struck Florence as comical.

Laila bit delicately into the small green grape pinched between her fingers. She winced a little. Sharp. 'Not quite,' she said, tossing the rest to one side.

'I should get going.' Florence turned towards the car.

'Florence,' Laila said, slithering towards her. 'I hope you don't mind what happened.' She looked up, through her eyelashes.

Ah. That was it. She wanted forgiveness.

Florence looked at her. Laila was standing before her, bare feet, her toes dusty from the tiles. Her hands clasped in front of her. All in white. Ready for Communion. Good as gold.

'You do what you need to do, Laila,' Florence said, slipping her sunglasses back on. She got into the car.

Laila leaned down and rested her fingers on the open window. 'It wasn't personal,' she said, cocking her head to the left.

'Laila,' Florence began, 'one day you will need people to be kind to you. Remember that.'

She turned the ignition key. Laila stood, staring at Florence with an expression of dark confusion. Florence pulled away. She wouldn't bother looking back.

# 110

'Hello?' Agnes called out and dumped her rucksack onto the hall floor. She had taken the train, worked out what she would tell her mother about being home a week early, geared herself up for a grilling, but nobody seemed to be in.

The familiar smells of home were a little off. There was no baking, no faint tinge of something clean and sharp. She paused at the sideboard in the hallway. There was a pile of letters addressed to her mother. She picked them up. Three were from her. They were unopened. What was going on?

'Hello?'

She walked to the kitchen. There was a mess on the floor, a smear of something unknown. A plate was discarded on the side. A mug with some tea in it, a thin film of mould beginning to form, sat on the table.

Agnes' stood very still.

Something was badly wrong. She went to the fridge and opened it, nothing in it other than a half-full bottle of milk giving off a thick, wretched stench. Grimacing, she emptied it into the sink. She turned round and walked through the house to the small sitting room. Nobody was here.

She went to the telephone, picked it up and dialled. 'Eleanor?'

'Agnes! Where are you?'

'I'm in Brill. There's no one here. What's happened?'

There was a short silence.

'I saw your picture in the paper.'

Agnes felt the tight grip of having been caught out.

'Did Mum see it?' She cupped the telephone to her mouth.

'No, Mum's not here.'

'Where is she?'

'We don't know. Dad's here. I'd send Charlie to get you but he's in Edinburgh interviewing someone or other.'

'Why's Dad with you? Where's Mum? What do you mean, you don't know where she is?'

'I need to tell you in person. Get the train. Come here.'

Agnes paused. She was so tired. All she wanted to do was trudge to her room, lie on her bed and ground herself. 'Do you mind if I stay here tonight? I can come tomorrow.'

'All right, but you must come.'

'Can't you just tell me what's happened?'

'I'm not going to tell you on the phone. And don't worry. Nobody's died. By the way,' Eleanor changed her tone, 'did you steal my contraceptives?'

'Yes.'

'What have you been up to?'

'Nothing.'

'Have you been having loads of sex?'

Agnes hesitated. 'Yes. Loads.' Her hand was shaking.

'You sly dog.'

'Eleanor, what's going on?'

'Everyone's gone a bit mad.'

Agnes stared at the receiver in her hand. Yes. They all had.

# WEEK FIVE

# MONDAY

## 111

William was sitting in a deckchair at the bottom of the garden, staring out over the water.

'He's been like that for days,' said Eleanor, draping her arm around Agnes's shoulder. 'You look terrible, by the way. Like you've got an obscure Victorian illness or something.'

'Thanks.'

'You're welcome.'

They both stood, quiet for a moment, gathering themselves. It had been quite a shock, discovering her mother had run off.

'Is this my fault?' Agnes frowned.

'How can it be your fault?'

'Because I told her to read *The Female Eunuch*. We kept banging on about it. And now look.'

'Don't be ridiculous. A book can't make you leave your husband. In any event, no. It's their fault. They're the only people who can fix this. *If* it's fixable.'

Agnes, beyond the initial look of surprise, wasn't sure how to react. She'd just spent the last three weeks trying to change her horizons, she could hardly be cross with her mother for trying too. All the same, it left her with a worried, deadened feeling.

'Who were you having loads of sex with?' Eleanor side-eyed her.

Agnes gave a deep sigh. 'Nobody. I'm still a virgin. I thought very, very briefly about being a lesbian.'

'How did that work out?'

'Really badly.' She folded her arms and stared upwards. Clouds were skittering: a high wind making the sky look like a sea of mackerel. 'I told you, I'm not dangerous enough. I've mucked everything up, Eleanor. Turns out I'm useless.'

Agnes chewed at the corner of her mouth. It was a humiliation, to return like this.

'No, you're not. Don't be ridiculous. Shoulders back. Feeling sorry for yourself gets you nowhere. You went, you tried something different, doesn't matter that it didn't work out. I was rather proud of you, you know, when I saw that picture.'

Agnes squinted at her sister. 'Really?'

'Really.' Eleanor tapped Agnes's shoulder. 'Go and talk to Dad, will you? He's really looking forward to seeing you.'

Agnes frowned. 'Is he?'

'Yes. He's quite changed. Brace yourself. He's started *hugging*. Go on.'

Eleanor gave her a squeeze and released her arm.

'Go chat to him. I'll put the kettle on.'

Agnes walked carefully down the garden. The lavender was still in bloom, the gentle hum of bees softening the air. The lawn had been mown and the sweet aroma of just-cut grass was something of a comfort. She came to a stop and put her hand on the back of the deckchair. 'Hello, Dad.'

He was wearing a white straw hat, not quite a panama but almost. He looked gaunt. 'Agnes,' he said and, pushing himself up, took her into his arms.

Agnes, caught unawares, stood with her arms by her side. She was unable to recall ever being this physically close to her father. Her cheek was pressed into his chest. He smelled of something woody and substantial. She liked it very much.

'Has Eleanor told you what's happened?' His voice was soft, reluctant.

Agnes nodded and pulled back. She looked up into her father's face. His eyes, a watery blue, looked haunted. Every inch of him was filled with regret.

'Did she really not tell you where she was going?'

He shook his head. 'Charlie thinks she might have gone on holiday.'

'To Dorset'

'Italy. She wanted me to go to Italy. And I was rather stupid. Stupid and stubborn.'

'Dad, I didn't go to Europe.'

He paused, then gave a small nod. 'Eleanor warned me.'

'I went to London to try and lose my virginity. That was the plan. I didn't manage it. Actually, everything went a bit wrong.' She stared into his eyes.

He looked down at her. 'Are you happy, Agnes?'

'No, I don't think I am.'

'Neither am I.'

'What are we going to do about Mum?'

'I don't know,' he said, taking his hat off. 'I have to work out how to make things up to her. If she'll let me.'

That was it, thought Agnes, the crux of the matter. When you've made a terrible mistake, it's not about being sorry, it's about whether the person you've let down is prepared to open the door and allow you back in.

'I've ruined things with Bea,' said Agnes softly. 'I'm not sure if I can ever forgive myself for that.'

William put a hand on her shoulder. 'Do you want to tell me all about it?'

'Yes,' Agnes said, squinting into the sun. 'I think I do.'

They both sat: William in his deckchair, Agnes on the grass, knees to her chest.

It was a start.

# TUESDAY

**112**

They had decided to go home, back to Brill. Florence, they thought, would have to return at some point. She had only taken a small suitcase. Her flight, it seemed, was not permanent.

Agnes had slipped seamlessly back into her old routine: get up, wash, brush her hair out, dress, wander off to the baker's to get whatever her mother needed, except there was no mother to ask. The house was empty without her. It was shocking, how much they felt her absence.

'This is what it'll be like,' Eleanor had whispered, 'when she dies.'

'Don't say that.'

They had stood, in the hallway, huddled by the front door.

'But it's true. Look at the mess we're in. We need to put this right, Agnes. Here,' Eleanor had said, handing her sister a pound note, 'get some bread and buns.'

The morning had something reluctant to it: the sky was pale and milky as if the sun couldn't quite get going. It was lovely to be home and yet it wasn't. Somewhere, on the other side of the village, Bea would be in her own home. The urge to go and see her was overwhelming but Agnes had decided the only right thing to do was honour her friend's wishes. She wondered if Bea's problem had resolved itself. It was inconceivable she didn't know the answer but Bea didn't want to see her and she had to respect that.

Agnes pushed open the door into the bakery and the usual warm smell of bread and pastries washed over her. The familiarity of it made her want to cry.

'All right?' Thomas, the boy from the pub, was picking up the bread for lunchtime opening. He was holding a wooden pallet packed with loaves.

'All right,' Agnes replied.

'You back from Europe then?'

'Sort of. Yes. No. Actually, I ended up not really going.' Agnes made a small grimace. 'I went to London instead.'

'That's still in the continent of Europe, though, innit?' He blew his fringe up from his eyes.

Agnes paused. 'Yeah. I suppose it is.'

'Well, then.' He moved towards the door. 'Here, give that a shove for us.'

Agnes held the door open for him. He stopped and looked at her. 'It's my birthday, Saturday. Want to come? Lock-in. We'll probably have peanuts on tap.'

'Yeah. All right.'

'All right. See ya.'

He sloped off.

'Haven't seen your mum in here for a while,' said the baker, one hand up on the counter, the other on his hip. 'She all right?'

Agnes shut the door and looked at him. It wouldn't do to gossip. It wouldn't do to give this man information that would shock or titillate or seep out in any way.

'She's away. And having a fabulous time,' said Agnes, mustering a smile. 'Cottage loaf and four finger buns, please.'

# 113

Florence cupped her hands across her forehead and peered out. The sea was sparkling, the horizon bleeding away to a faraway haze. On a clear day, they said, you could see Dover. But not quite today.

She was shattered. Two days of hard driving in searing heat. She could have veered off to Paris at one point but the wander-lust, for now, was spent. She needed to go home.

Returning filled her with unease: the sort of prickly, uncomfortable disquiet of a task undone. She had no choice really but as to what she would do when she got there was another matter. Should she ask William to leave? Did she pack up all her things and move to Eleanor's? Find herself an apartment? Oxford? London? The Outer Hebrides?

She was not the same woman who had left. They would have to accept that, all of them: William, Eleanor, Charlie, Agnes.

She was a woman to be reckoned with, a woman who had come to understand herself. She was sexual, curious, intelligent. She was not to be ignored, dismissed or underestimated. She had found strength. She had learned lessons and now she was going home and she wanted respect.

Respect has to be earned, they always say. Well, she had earned it in herself. She had earned it the moment she walked out, she had earned it the moment she took herself to France. She had earned it when she took a lover. She had earned it when she watched him with a younger woman. She had earned it when she realised she didn't care. It was the moment she understood she had strength.

She was happy with who she was. She was responsible for her own happiness. She had earned it.

Above her, gulls were floating. They were free. And so was she. She wasn't in retreat. She wasn't going back with her tail between her legs. She was going back to claim what was hers.

# 114

'Why don't you go and see Bea?' said Eleanor, thumbing through a copy of *Cosmopolitan*.

'I can't.' Agnes leaned back and looked at her toes. She'd taken some nail polish from her mother's dressing table for something to do.

'Why not?'

'It's complicated.' Agnes was aching for her but Bea was right: space was what they needed.

Eleanor took her sunglasses off and looked at her sister. 'What happened? You haven't really told me.'

'I'm not going to tell you.' Agnes leaned forward, her chin on her knee, and began to paint the toenails on her left foot.

'Did you have a row? Tell me.'

'No. Sort of. I don't know.'

Eleanor pushed at Agnes's shoulder with the end of her foot. 'Tell me.'

'Stop it. I'm doing my nails.'

'You must have done something horrific.' Eleanor put her sunglasses back on. 'Something utterly *shameful*.'

Eleanor was poking at her, trying to provoke her to respond, but Agnes wasn't taking the bait.

'It's nothing,' said Agnes. 'We've spent every minute of every day of the past however many weeks together. I expect she's enjoying not having me around.'

It felt like she was asking for a compliment. Agnes waited for a response, but none came. She peered upwards. 'Do you like me being your sister?'

'Course I do.' Eleanor turned the page of her magazine. 'Do you like me being *your* sister?'

'Yes. No. Sometimes.'

Eleanor let the magazine drift down to her lap. 'When don't you like me being your sister?'

'When you're being adored.'

'By Charlie? That's a bit mean. And weird.'

'No. By people you don't know. It turns you into something different, something you're not.'

Eleanor tilted her head and thought. 'But they're not adoring me. Not really. They're adoring the idea of me. They're adoring the fact they might know my name or recognise me from a paper. Imagine how silly that is. And as for it changing me, I'm afraid I'm going to thoroughly disagree.'

'No,' said Agnes, screwing the top back onto the nail polish. 'They're adoring what you're capable of. And it does change you, a bit. You go all lah-di-dah.' So much of Agnes had stemmed from being sidelined as a younger sibling. With Bea she had always felt an equal. No matter now, she'd blown it.

'Lah-di-dah?' Eleanor laughed out loud, then stopped. 'Does it make you jealous?' Eleanor said the words carefully. She was not trying to be unkind.

Agnes put the polish down to one side and leaned back into the grass. 'It's not easy being your sister.' She let the moment hang. 'I think it must be easy to be you.'

'Huh.' Eleanor looked off down the garden. She drummed her fingers on the sides of the deckchair, slowly. 'I don't think it's easy to be at all,' she began. 'People don't like *me*. They like what I can give them. Kudos. A sense of superiority. Smugness. People like you, Agnes, because you are kind and gentle and funny. They like you for who you actually are. You are so witty. Do you remember all those hilarious letters you used to send me when I was at art school?'

Agnes nodded.

'They used to make me howl. You're honestly the most interesting person I know.'

'That can't be true.'

'It is. You're a singular individual. I don't know anyone else like you.'

Agnes trilled her fingertips through the ends of the cut grass. She didn't know what to do with this. If she'd had the slightest sense of it, at any point, she might have saved herself years of self-doubt.

Eleanor reached down to take Agnes's hand. 'I know what being ill did to you, Ag. I know how it stopped everything.'

Agnes looked up into her sister's eyes. It had felt like a surrender, to be back in Brill, the little sister returned, but she wasn't the person who had left. She wasn't there yet but she had a better understanding of who she was meant to be and, more importantly, who she didn't want to be.

'Bea doesn't want to see me because she thinks she's too reliant on me.' Her voice was low and considered. 'I don't know what to do about it.'

Eleanor paused then leaned forward, resting her elbows on her knees. 'Oh. That's hard.'

'Yes. It is.'

They sat, not saying anything. On the road beyond the garden, a man cycled slowly past. The air felt still and heavy.

'Do you think Mum will be back soon?' Agnes asked.

'I hope so,' said Eleanor.

There was another pause. Agnes was so desperate for comfort but, more than that, she felt an urge to know that Bea was all right, that their friendship might recover.

'She made me feel like I mattered.'

'Mum did?'

'No. Bea. I might write her a note. Do you think that would be all right?'

'I think that would be a useful thing to do, yes.'

Agnes gave a soft nod. It was important, suddenly, that Bea knew how much she mattered to her.

# WEDNESDAY

# 115

Dearest Bea,

Here's the thing about friendships – you don't appreciate the importance of them until they're gone. I know that you need to go away and breathe and shore yourself up. I know that I can't quite be the person you would like me to be. But I know you have given me joy, strength, laughter, surprise, a sense of perspective, self-belief, the motivation to be the best person I can be. We went away and got lost and I'm sorry for that, especially my part in it. I hope everything is all right. But you made me feel noticed. You made me matter and I want to thank you but most of all to tell you how much you mattered to me.

    Yours,
    *Agnes*

Agnes slipped the envelope through the letter box. It was still early; curtains were drawn and cobwebs in the borders and hedgerows were glistening in the morning sun. As she walked away, down towards the Brill windmill, she felt relieved. Whatever happened now, she had said what she needed to say.

Today she would get her results and would be asked to think about jobs and taking letters and being the vessel for other people's ambitions. She sat down on a bench by the Pheasant. She needed to work out how to say no to it.

'All right?' Behind her, Thomas was coming out from the back of the pub. He had a cup of coffee in his hand and was smoking a fag.

'All right.'

He sat down next to her. He was in his pyjama bottoms, his feet and chest bare.

Agnes looked at him. 'How long have we known each other?'

He gave a shrug. 'Dunno. Since we were three or something.'

Agnes sat for a moment. She and Bea had run away to lose their virginity and it had blinded her to what was really important: sex was not the thing that would define her, her choices would be. The time had come to be rid of it.

Agnes turned towards him. 'Thomas, would you have sex with me?'

He raised an eyebrow, squinted at her and sucked on the end of his cigarette. He inhaled, swallowed, then blew a thin line of smoke out from the corner of his mouth. 'Yeah, all right.'

'I'm not in love with you or anything.'

'No. Course not.' He sucked again on the end of his fag.

'I just want to get the whole virginity thing out the way. I'm done with it. It's more trouble than it's worth.'

He nodded slowly and stretched his toes out across the grass.

'We can do it now if you like,' he said. 'When I've finished my coffee. And my fag.'

'Yes. Finish your coffee and your fag. There's no rush.'

The pair of them sat, perfectly at ease, as if they might have been arranging a lift to a station.

Agnes thought about Bea. She hoped she'd read the letter.

# 116

Florence turned the key off in the ignition and sat very still. Her mind trickled back to that moment all those weeks ago when she had sat here, gripping the wheel, and looked up to see Eleanor standing at the door. She barely recognised the woman she'd been then. She was a fading memory, a thin, insubstantial version of herself that might blow away in the slightest breeze. She looked up towards the house. Cars in the driveway told her everyone was here. Probably for the best. She could get this done in one go.

Charlie appeared at a window, looking down. She could see him shouting something off behind him. Eleanor's face appeared briefly and then disappeared. They were clearly in a blind panic.

'Oh well,' she muttered to herself. 'Let's get this over with.' Florence exhaled and pushed herself up out of the car, went to the boot and pulled out her suitcase. She wondered how she was going to feel when she saw her husband. Not in the least embarrassed, that's what.

'Mum,' Eleanor appeared in front of her. 'We've been worried sick. Where have you been?'

'On holiday,' Florence said, matter-of-factly. She dropped her suitcase to the gravel.

Charlie came up behind her. 'Hello, Florence,' he said.

'Hello.'

She was amazed how still and calm she was, how composed. She felt nothing other than absolute certainty. They, on the other hand, were rattled, as if she might be an unpredictable dog. There was something liberating about it.

She walked towards the house. 'Where's William?' she said, climbing the steps to the front door.

'Shaving. I've told him you're here.' Charlie was watching her carefully, as if he might jump on her and stop her from running off again.

'Seriously, Mum,' said Eleanor, as she followed her into the hallway. 'Where have you been?'

'France first, then Italy.'

She looked around. There was dust on the sideboard. The rug in the hallway was specked with mud. The house smelled musty. She picked up the pile of letters with her name on and rifled through. None of it bothered her. Her mood was idle and relaxed.

Upstairs, a door opened and William appeared on the landing. She looked up. He was thinner, but then so was she. There was something in his eyes she wasn't able to replicate. He was pleased to see her.

'Come on, Charlie,' said Eleanor, placing a hand on his arm. 'Let's leave them to it.'

They slipped away, burrowing themselves into a far corner of the house.

'Shall we go into the garden?' said Florence, putting aside the post in her hand. 'It's a rather nice morning.'

William stared down at her. He was ready to do whatever she wanted.

## 117

Thomas's room reeked. It smelled of grease and beer and fags and there were small piles of clothes on the floor that looked like dirty molehills. The bed was single and Agnes, staring down at the rather unsavoury sheets, wondered whether she should rethink this.

'Sorry about the mess,' said Thomas, with a sniff. 'I'll pull the curtains.'

'Have you done it before?' Agnes turned and looked at him.

'Yeah,' he said, dropping his pyjama bottoms to the floor.

It was the first time Agnes had seen an erection intended for her. She stood very still.

'Shall I get undressed?'

'That would help, yeah.'

He turned and picked a small transistor radio out from behind a stack of football magazines. Agnes undid her trousers, slipped them down and hung them over the end of the iron bedstead. She pulled her T-shirt over her head, folded it similarly and stood in her pants and bra. She didn't feel remotely nervous.

Thomas tuned into a pirate radio station. 'For All We Know' by the Carpenters filled the void between them and he placed the radio gently down and turned back towards her.

'You need to take them off,' he said, pointing down to her knickers. 'Thought I'd put some music on. Like a gentleman.'

'I haven't taken a pill,' said Agnes, kicking her pants off.

She went to the bed and lay down on it, hands splayed to the sides.

'I haven't got any johnnies,' he said. 'But don't worry. I'll pull out.'

'Can you give me an orgasm, please?'

He got on top of her and nudged her knees apart with his own. 'Yeah, all right.'

Agnes stared up at him. 'Should we kiss first?' she said.

'Yeah, we can do that.'

She could feel the wet tip of his penis against her thigh. He reached down and she put her arms around his neck. She'd kissed boys before, of course, but not naked ones, and even though she wasn't remotely romantically interested in Thomas, there was something tender about the way he kissed her that was incredibly endearing.

His hand reached down into her groin.

Oh. OK, now she got what the fuss was about. That was rather nice. She pushed herself into his fingers.

'You ready?' he asked.

She nodded.

'First bit might hurt. Sorry. I'll go slow.'

She braced herself and there was a short, sharp, elastic ping of pain and then he was inside her. She gripped onto him and, as he thrust, she experienced an odd, building tension.

'Oh blimey,' he said, pulling out of her. A thick blob of something wet landed on her stomach. 'Sorry,' he said. 'That was a bit quick. Did you have one?'

'I don't know.'

'Right-io.'

He slid down and pressed his face into her.

'Oh my God,' said Agnes, staring wide-eyed at the ceiling. It didn't take long.

'Well, there it is,' said Thomas, running the back of his hand across his mouth. 'You're not a virgin.'

He pushed himself off the bed and wiped at the end of his cock with a T-shirt from the floor. Tossing it off into another pile, he pulled on a pair of blue pants.

Agnes stared at him. She wasn't sure she could move yet, startled by what she had discovered her body was capable of. 'Thank you, Thomas,' she said, trying to blink.

'No bother.'

He grabbed a cream shirt with birds on it from the back of a chair and slipped it on. He glanced at his watch.

'I've got to go clean the taps. You all right if I leave you to it?'

Agnes nodded.

'All right then. See ya.'

He drifted off and she heard him bounce down the stairs, whistling. She looked down at her body, almost amazed that it hadn't bent into an entirely different shape.

Well. That was it then. She'd done it

## 118

'I slept with another man.' Florence looked William straight in the eye. 'Several times.'

She watched him carefully. He took the news standing up. His jaw tightened and behind his eyes she could tell it was causing him pain.

'Are you in love with him?'

Florence let out a laugh. 'No, not remotely.'

'Did you enjoy it?'

'Yes. Very much.'

Her honesty cut into him and he winced. He turned away from her and dug his hands into his pockets. They were standing by the tomatoes, of course. 'Are you leaving me, Florence?' His voice was low. 'Properly, I mean?' He looked pathetic, small.

'For the time being, yes.' She had wondered if she'd flinch at saying the words but she didn't.

William's head went down into his chest. 'I can't blame you. I'm not sure I've done anything to make you happy at all.'

'You gave me two wonderful daughters. And I need to do right by them. Especially Agnes.'

'What can I do?' He looked to her. 'I'll do anything. Please, Florence.'

'Things need to be different. *You* need to be different. I'm not convinced you're capable of that.'

He turned towards her. 'Nobody can ever change if they're not given a second chance.'

'No.' She paused. 'That's true. But for now, we do this.'

William straightened. 'I'd like the chance to try. I've missed you very much, Florence.'

She looked at him. His eyes were sincere, his lack of anger impressive. He was chastened, she could see that, and yet she couldn't step back into her old shoes as if nothing had happened.

'What do you want to do?' He looked at her, waiting.

'Right now? Time to think, here, now I'm back. I think I'd like a job. But what, I'm not sure. And Agnes needs to go to university. I need to speak to her when she gets back.'

'She's back already,' said William. 'She didn't go to Europe.'

Florence frowned. 'Really?'

'She went to London. Had a rather hellish time. She'll be glad to see you.'

Florence looked off to the house. 'Is she ...'

'Not sure. She tends to wander off in the mornings.'

Florence breathed in, deep. She had left home to come back again. She was still a mother. She was still this man's wife. She still had a family.

'I think you should do whatever you want to do,' said William. 'And then let's see where we are, shall we?'

'Yes,' said Florence. 'We'll see where we are.'

She looked down across the garden towards the road. Agnes was walking up it.

Florence was so pleased. 'Agnes!' she called out and waved her arm.

Agnes, seeing her, broke into a run.

'I need to live, William.' Florence placed a hand on his forearm. 'I can't go backwards.'

She turned and walked across the garden towards the gate. Agnes burst through it and threw herself into her mother's arms.

'Oh Agnes,' Florence said, holding her. 'I've so missed you.'

Agnes pulled back and looked at her. 'I've missed you too.'

# THURSDAY

# 119

Agnes's letter had arrived. She'd passed all her exams. Flying colours too, but it felt empty and pointless. She wondered how Bea had got on. It was so sad they weren't sharing this moment together, however much they had hated it.

'Over my dead body are you going to go and work in a stuffy office taking letters.'

Florence had changed her tune. She had decamped to the Randolph Hotel in Oxford and was organising her clothes into a chest of drawers. Agnes sat on the end of her bed.

'Are you sure you want to stay here?' Her hand ran across a plush eiderdown.

'For now, yes. And don't change the subject.'

Florence pressed a pile of light blouses down and shut the drawer.

'What do you want to do next, Agnes?' She turned and looked at her.

Agnes could feel the weight in the air, the chance she was being offered, yet she seemed stalled, snagged on a hook of her own making. She was a million miles from the girl who couldn't lift her head to finish an exam paper. London, for all its faults, had changed her. All the same, uncertainty stretched ahead.

'I'm almost too afraid to say.' Her voice was no more than a murmur.

Florence sat next to her and took her hand. 'I won't tell you everything I've been up to over the past two weeks,' she began, 'but I've learned this: that I can do things differently. I can dress differently, wear my hair differently, I can travel, have new experiences, I can be somebody new.' She squeezed Agnes's hand. 'It's never too late to become the person we're meant to be.'

Agnes stared down into her lap. She wasn't used to this.

'I owe you an apology.' Florence took a deep breath. 'I sucked away your ambition, surrounded you with barriers. I was wrong. I want you to forget everything, think big; I want you to try when I didn't. Now tell me what you want to do and I'll make damn sure I help you get there.' Her voice was quiet and determined.

Agnes was being offered a chance. She took it. 'I don't want to be a secretary, Mum. I'd hate it.'

'I know you would.'

'I don't blame you,' added Agnes. 'I thought I did. But I don't. You wanted to look after me, I get it. But everything's different now. I want the best bits of the girl I was, before it all went wrong. I want her determination, her sense of purpose. I want to go to university,' she said. 'It's what I've always wanted. I want to read English and be a writer or a journalist. I want to tell stories. Everyone says they like my letters ...'

'Your letters are wonderful.'

'So I think I want to do that.' Agnes could hear her voice trembling, so powerful was the desire to finally put in motion a hope that had long felt impossible. 'I want to stop giving up. I want to try again.'

'Good,' said Florence, tapping Agnes on the knee. 'Then we shall look into it. I'll ask Marjory. She knows people.' She paused, a small frown gathering. 'I haven't seen Bea. Where is she? Still in London?'

Agnes shook her head. 'She doesn't want to see me.' She stopped herself. She didn't want to cry again.

Florence gave Agnes a penetrating stare. 'What did you do?'

Agnes had rather underestimated her mother. She had spent her life thinking Florencedidn't know her at all and yet here, with one look, she understood her mother knew everything about her. 'I let her down. I'm heartbroken about it, actually.' She stared down at her fingers. She felt ashamed.

Florence stood and walked towards the window. 'It's stuffy in here,' she murmured. 'Let's let the air in.' She shoved up the sash window and the noises from the street drifted into the room.

'You know, Agnes, we can't be perfect all the time.' She turned and looked at her. 'Life is messy. Sometimes it's good to let it be. We can all do better, don't you think?'

'Are you going to divorce Daddy?'

'I might,' Florence said. 'But I've given myself a second chance and you're getting a second chance and we can't stand here and say he doesn't deserve one too. So let's see what he does. It's difficult, Agnes, when you finally recognise what you're capable of. I can't go back to the person I was. He needs to understand that.'

It was terrifying, all this honesty, blinding almost. Whether they could all rise to the challenge would be another matter.

'Now then,' Florence said, coming back to the bed. 'Tell me what's happened with Bea.'

Agnes slipped her hand into her mother's. She was stronger for it.

# 120

William was pretending to pick peas. The small blue Tupperware pot hung loosely in his hand. He was looking towards the horizon, wondering if he could just make out the spires of Oxford. Sometimes, he used to convince himself, he could.

Somewhere out there was Florence and he wanted to see her, to know what she was doing, to make amends.

It's a terrible thing, he thought, to realise how much you love someone. He didn't know what to do with himself, these intense feelings. What do you do, when you are immobilised with fear, when everything you've taken for granted is ripped away? He wasn't a nervous man, not at all, and here he was, his hand trembling.

He had underestimated her, thought her incapable of anything other than cooking and cleaning and writing shopping lists in which he had no interest. Without her, everything ground to a halt. Without her, William realised, he was entirely empty.

'You're not going to feed an army with that.' Eleanor had appeared behind him. She pointed towards the empty pot in his hand.

William glanced down towards it and felt a small flush of embarrassment. 'Sorry, I ...' he began, before scanning the plants for anything to pick.

'There's none there, Dad,' said Eleanor, reaching to take the bowl from him. 'They're all done.'

William cast a look over the wilting pea plants. They looked like he felt. 'Have you heard from your mother?'

'Yes, actually. Just now. She rang. Wants me to go for supper with her and Agnes this evening.'

William's heart leapt. He glanced at his watch. 'What time are we leaving?'

Eleanor paused. 'Just Ag and me, Dad.'

He nodded, silently.

'Don't worry. I'm leaving Charlie here. He'll do your supper.'

William felt another flush of embarrassment. It felt so weak, this constant need to be looked after. Had he always been like this? The boy looked after by his mother, the husband looked after by his wife? Handed on, woman to woman, the man who couldn't be trusted to look after himself. It had to stop.

'Everyone is changing,' he said.

'Yes, I think there is a bit of that going on.'

'I think I should too.'

'Do you think you can?'

'I don't know. Perhaps I should try.'

Eleanor turned the bowl in her hands and smiled. 'Come on, Dad,' she said, taking his arm. 'Charlie's made a cake.'

They drifted off up the garden, Eleanor pointing out small wild flowers that had taken hold in the lawn. He'd never noticed them before. They were beautiful.

## 121

'Marjory was quite hopeful. Says it happens all the time. People don't get the A levels they need. Slots everywhere, she said. Results won't be out till August, though. You should go round some campuses, see where you fancy.'

Behind them, a man in a black frock coat was playing a piano; around them, the idle chatter of diners. It was all very pleasant.

Florence was in generous mood. They had enjoyed prawn cocktail starters, a rare treat, followed by fillet steaks. Agnes barely had room for dessert but, when Black Forest gateau was on offer, it was hard to say no. She had waited for the usual disapproving look from her mother but none came.

'What about here? Oxford.' Eleanor was pushing a cherry onto her spoon with the end of her finger. 'You were supposed to do very well in your A levels, weren't you?'

Agnes nodded. 'Two As and a B.'

Eleanor sat back on her chair, astonished. 'You were that clever and you were packed off to secretarial? What were you thinking, Mother?'

Florence shook her head. 'She'd been so poorly but still. I don't think I'll ever stop wanting to make amends. Well. We're here now. And we can change all that, can't we?' She reached over and touched Agnes lightly on the hand.

'It's not Mummy's fault,' Agnes spoke softly. 'It was mine. I was the one who gave up. Besides, it's not going to happen. There's no way I'd get in here. Not now.'

'I thought you were done giving up? Nothing ventured, nothing gained.' Eleanor looked at her, pointedly.

'Honestly, I agree with your sister,' said Florence. 'Give it a go. You've got nothing to lose. What did I say? It's better to try and fail than not try at all.'

'Actually ...' Agnes cut into her cake with a fork. 'It's not that I don't think I could get in, it's more that I like the idea of a completely new start. I'm not sure coming back here will be good for me. I thought I wanted to study here. Turns out I don't. This place is all about my past. I want my future to be somewhere new.'

Eleanor reached forward and squeezed her forearm. 'Good for you,' she said gently.

'How's your father?' Florence threw the question out idly, as if she were enquiring about a distant cousin.

Eleanor dipped the end of her finger into a small mound of cream on the edge of her plate and licked it. 'Terrible,' she said. She wiped her hands on her napkin. 'I don't think I can eat another thing. I'm stuffed.' She blew her cheeks out and laid her hands on her stomach. 'I look pregnant,' she said, laughing. 'Absolute balloon.'

Florence eyed her. Two weeks ago she would have launched into the usual 'When are you having a baby' conversation but she let the moment drift. 'He did look thin, I must say.' She looked over Agnes's shoulder and waved towards a waiter. 'Do either of you want coffee?'

They both shook their heads.

'I made him a fortnight's worth of meals. Charlie told me they're virtually untouched.'

'He had an accident on day one,' Eleanor said, rubbing her belly. 'Put the whole tub in. Entire thing melted.'

'Oh lord,' said Florence. 'I didn't think he'd be that stupid.'

The waiter had arrived at the table.

'One coffee, please,' Florence asked. 'You don't do cappuccino, by any chance?'

'No, madam.'

Florence pulled a small face of disappointment. 'Just black then, please.'

The waiter walked briskly away.

'Honestly,' she added, 'if someone over here opened a shop that just sold delicious coffees they'd make a fortune.'

'Why don't you?' Eleanor leaned forward.

'Me?'

'Yes, why not? You love cooking. You could have a coffee and cake shop.'

'Yes, Mum,' said Agnes, chipping in. 'You should.'

The sisters shared a smile.

Florence continued. 'I can't. I haven't got the equipment. The coffee machines, the beans, the ... no, it's too—'

She stopped. Look at her, instantly coming up with all the reasons not to do something. It was the old Florence rearing up. Pushing her to one side, she thought properly. It wasn't that bad an idea. She could see it: perhaps one of the units in the covered market? She could see if there were any available. A bright red awning, perhaps. *Florence's*. She reached her hand up to her neck.

'I'd have to go back to Italy, to get it all.'

'Take Dad with you,' said Eleanor. 'I think he'd go if you asked again.'

'Do you?' Florence's face softened.

'One hundred per cent,' said Eleanor, looking at the pair of them. 'Exciting times.'

Agnes scraped the back of her fork across her plate and licked the last of the cherry jam. 'The Ledbury ladies are on the move.'

Yes. They really were.

# FRIDAY

## 122

Agnes had stayed with her mother at the Randolph.

They'd had a leisurely breakfast: two poached eggs for Florence, a bowl of porridge for Agnes. They were quiet, relaxed, happy to casually flick through the morning papers. They were at ease.

'Do you mind if I go for a walk?' Agnes wiped at her mouth with a napkin.

'Not at all.' Florence glanced up over her paper. 'You should have a proper think about universities. About where you might like. We could go and visit some campuses.'

Agnes smiled.

'There'll be admissions tutors and forms and small tests and interviews. You should be prepared.'

'What sort of tests?'

'For English? Poetry comprehension, that sort of thing. You can manage that, though, can't you?'

Agnes nodded. 'Yes, I can manage that.'

There was something so fundamentally different about them, the way they communicated, the mutual respect.

'I know you can do it, Agnes.' Florence put her paper down.

'I know you can open a coffee and cake shop.'

Florence raised her eyebrows. 'We'll see. That requires imagination and money. Imagination I have; the money, not so much.'

It was quite something, this feeling coursing through the pair of them: they were starting, finally, to believe in themselves.

'Shall I see you later?' said Agnes, pushing herself up from the table. 'Meet for lunch at the Eagle and Child? They do very good cheese sandwiches.'

'Yes. See you there. One?'

'Perfect.'

'Have fun.'

Agnes walked through the restaurant, past tables of families staring sullenly at their eggs, buttering toast in silence. We can all do better than this, she thought. She glanced back at her mother who was still watching her across the room.

Agnes stopped and raised her hand. 'I love you,' she mouthed.

Florence clasped a hand to her chest and smiled. 'I love you too,' she mouthed back.

Yes, thought Agnes, we can all do better.

## 123

Florence was thinking about Bram. She lay on the bed, around her a few discarded papers. She'd had a mid-morning tray of tea brought to her room. There were shortbread biscuits, not quite as good as the ones she made, but still. It felt luxurious.

She wondered what they were doing: Laila, the Maestro and him. Still in bed, probably. They were late risers. Perhaps Bram was having some light mid-morning sex? Perhaps Laila, the cat, had finished playing with him?

Florence let out a relaxed sigh and leaned her head back against the pillows stacked behind her. What was she going to do about William?

She thought about their sex life and laughed out loud. It wasn't a life. It was crawling, half-dead. From now on, anything that required a sense of duty was out the window. There would be no more lying back and thinking of England. Florence wanted to lie back and think about herself.

He can't enjoy it, she reasoned. The perfunctory thrusts and business here is concluded. It was so cold, so distant, so dull. Sex, she had discovered, was pleasurable. It was *fun*.

'Do I still love you, William?'

The question hung in the air. If she owed him anything, it was to get it right. If she was leaving him it would be because the fire was burned to the ground, no chance of recovery.

Somewhere, amongst the dust, there might be a green shoot of new growth. A burned common always comes back, not quite the same, but nature is a resilient beast. Her love for her husband was waiting to be remembered: romance and excitement were all well and good, but there had to be room for that, the different love that fills all the gaps.

She pushed herself up from the bed and slipped her feet into her espadrilles. She stared down at them. They were starting to look a little worn. They'd served their purpose.

Perhaps, before she met Agnes, she might get herself a new pair of shoes. It was impossible not to feel positive.

# 124

'Charlie,' said William, walking into the dining room, 'can I have a word?'

Charlie was sitting, sleeves rolled up, tapping away on his typewriter. He paused, fingers hovering, and looked up.

'Of course.'

'I'm not interrupting, am I?'

'Not at all,' Charlie lied. 'It's fine. I need a break anyway.' He pushed back his chair and stood. 'Shall we have a cup of tea?'

'Yes,' said William. He paused. 'But let me make it, will you?'

Charlie came towards him, smiling. He clapped his hand on William's shoulder.

'I would like that, yes.'

They walked together through the house.

'I'm not sure I know what you're writing,' said William, leading the way. 'Is it another book?'

'Yes. Political potboiler. Up-and-coming politician. Having an affair. Knocked off his bike and can remember everything except the last three months. Can't remember the affair. It's about whether you can fall in love with the same person twice.'

'And does he?'

'You'll have to read it when it's done.'

Turning into the kitchen, William put the kettle on and looked around for a teapot. Charlie noticed. 'It's in the cupboard to your right. Teabags in the caddy on the counter.' He leaned back against the sink. 'How are you feeling?'

William paused. Nobody had ever asked him. Not quite. Eleanor had skirted around it but always managed to veer away at the last minute. Had Florence ever asked him? He couldn't recall.

'I don't know,' he said quietly. 'Terrified, I suppose. Terrified of losing my wife. Terrified of not being able to adapt. Terrified I'll muck it up.' He looked over towards Charlie. 'Thank you for asking.'

'I think it's going to be all right, you know. I have a good feeling about things.'

William frowned and shook his head. 'How do you do it, Charlie? Tell me, please. You and Eleanor, you love each other but you're friends. You enjoy each other's company. You share things, you don't mind at all being—' He stopped. He wasn't sure he wasn't being offensive.

'Less important?' Charlie offered.

'Yes,' said William, but then, thinking on his feet, 'no, it's not quite that. You're happy to let Eleanor be. You know how to be married well. You're content.'

'Yes, I am.'

'How? How do you do that?'

Charlie paused for a moment, thinking. 'I don't do it,' he replied. 'We do it. Eleanor and I. Together. We're a team. That's how you do it. No man is an island and all that. Look at you – and forgive me, William, I'm going to be blunt. Married for years and you're still a single man. Going through the motions for food and sex. That's not a marriage. That's sharing space for convenience sake.'

The words resonated. 'Charlie,' said William, dropping two teabags into the pot, 'there's something I want to do. Will you help me?'

'Anything. What is it?'

William poured the water over the bags and slipped the lid on. He turned. 'First things first. How do you take your tea?' He smiled for what felt like the first time in weeks. He had a plan.

# SATURDAY

# 125

Agnes had got up early. She wanted to see him, say hello, check if things were normal.

She was surprised by how many times her thoughts had flitted back to him since Wednesday afternoon. It was odd. She'd known him all her life, passed him thousands of times, waved casually in his direction, chatted about nothing important, ever. He was just Thomas from the village but now he was a more significant character in her story. He was the young man who had shared with her an experience she would never be able to have with anyone else.

The bakery was open but Thomas had not yet arrived. She knew that because she had been in the phone box by the Pheasant pretending she was making a call. She'd been standing, receiver to her ear, for half an hour. Every time she'd seen someone she talked into it.

It was silly really. There was nothing stopping her from popping into the Pheasant and asking for him but it was something they had never done. Neither of them had ever intentionally sought the other. It was all chance meetings, nothing planned.

So here she was, leaning her cheek against an empty receiver with just the dialling tone for company.

There was another reason she was there, of course, even if she didn't quite want to admit it. She was waiting to see Bea. She had no idea whether she was still at home, no idea if she'd read her letter or what her situation was. It had been a week since she'd seen her, an unimaginable gap. She'd felt every minute of it.

She longed to see her. She wanted to hear her laugh, to watch her hold forth. She wanted to be in the company of her energy, her easy wit. She wanted to tell her she was hoping to go to university. She wanted to tell her she'd had sex. That she was finally on her way. But most of all, she just wanted to know that Bea was all right.

Thomas appeared from the side of the pub. He didn't see her. He was wearing a pair of red football shorts and a yellow T-shirt with Top Cat on it. He had an empty blue plastic crate in one hand and he was whistling.

Agnes put down the telephone and shoved the door open. She jumped out and it snapped behind her. 'Bloody hell,' she mumbled. It never got better.

Hearing the door, Thomas looked over his shoulder, saw her and stopped. 'All right,' he said.

'All right.' She wandered towards him.

'Bit early for phone calls, isn't it?' he said, blowing his fringe upwards. 'Who you calling? The milkman?' He grinned.

It was normal.

'Wasn't calling anyone,' she answered. That was another thing: she couldn't be bothered to pretend with Thomas. 'I was waiting for you.' She gave a shrug.

'You remembered, then,' he said, as they began to walk. Agnes frowned. 'My birthday,' he said. 'It's my birthday.'

'Yes, I know,' she said. 'That's why I'm here. I'm going to get you a cake in the bakery. For your birthday.'

He threw her a sideways glance. 'You're making that up, right?'

'Yes. I'm making it up.'

He nodded.

'Happy birthday.'

'Thanks.'

'Have you seen Bea?' They all knew each other.

'Yeah, yesterday. She was on a bike.'

'Bea was on a bike?'

'That's why I noticed. It was too small for her. Her knees were up by her chin.' He shook his head.

Agnes laughed and felt immediately sad. She wished she'd seen it. 'I've sort of fallen out with her,' she told him. 'I wish I hadn't.'

'Shall I ask her to my party? Tonight? I mean, it's not really a party. It's a lock-in. Same thing, though. There'll be peanuts.'

'You're mad for peanuts, Thomas.'

'I am Agnes, that I am.'

They had reached the bakery. While he went in she stood outside and picked at a long grass from the verge. Sitting on a low wall, she placed it between her thumbs. She had always wanted to be able to whistle with a blade of grass. She'd never managed it. Bea had showed her how to do it once, to no avail. The grass was lined up exactly as it should be. She lifted her thumbs to her mouth and blew. Nope.

Behind her, Thomas reappeared. He put his crate on the wall next to her.

'There's a knack to that. Hold the end of the blade here ...' He held his hands in front of her. They were small for a lad, the nails all bitten down, but they looked quick and lively. He pinched the bottom of the grass down against the lower part of his thumb with his third finger, then pulled the rest up tight against his thumb.

'Curve your hand a bit,' he said, cupping his other hand in. 'Purse your lips. Have it.' He blew and a thin reedy noise filled the air. He winked and handed her the grass. 'Your turn. Pretend you're blowing into one of those posh instruments. Clarinet. That sort of thing. No use just blow-ing like billy-o.'

She took it and, doing as he'd shown her, blew. To her aston-ishment, it worked.

'Yes!' he said and punched the air.

'That's the first time I've ever managed that. Ever.'

'Better get on.' He picked up his crate, now filled with bread. 'You going to come later, yeah?'

She looked up at him. His arms were full and he had a soft stubble round the edge of his chin. There was a scab on his left knee. He had blond hairs on his legs. His ankles were much finer than her own.

'Yeah, all right.'

'See ya then,' he said, turning to walk away. 'Go see Bea,' he added. 'No point falling out.'

She watched him go and found herself wondering if she might have sex with him again. 'Well,' she said to herself, real-ising she might. 'I didn't see that coming.'

## 126

She hadn't expected flowers. William had come to the Randolph. He called up to her room from reception and she had trotted down to find him in one of his better suits, hair slicked, shoes polished, holding a bunch of white roses. She had nowhere to put them, of course, but the gesture didn't go unnoticed.

'Shall we? I've brought a picnic.' He gestured to a small wicker basket on the floor. 'Thought we could take a punt. It's such a lovely day. Would you like to?'

Florence stared up at this stranger who had come to take her out. 'I'd love to,' she said.

His chest visibly rose and he gave a soft nod. 'I'm quite nervous,' he said, bending down to pick up the hamper. 'I hope you don't mind me telling you that.'

'Don't worry,' she said, following him towards the entrance 'So am I.'

He held the door open for her and she stepped out onto Beaumont Street, looking towards St Giles'. They took the scenic route to the punting launch at Magdalen Bridge, down Broad Street, past Blackwell's where she had bought *The Female*

*Eunuch* all those weeks ago. It felt like a lifetime. Tourists were gathered around the Bodleian, enjoying a normal day out. This was anything but.

At first, they walked in silence, William steering Florence down New College Lane. She stared up at the replica of the Bridge of Sighs. One day, she thought to herself, she would see the real one.

'What have we got for our picnic?' She wanted to make a start.

'Boiled eggs. Some rather nice ham. I got a couple of iced buns from the baker.'

'You went to the baker?' She stopped and looked at him.

'Yes,' he said, nodding. 'I brought wine too, in case you fancied it. I'm sorry it's not grander but I wanted to make it all myself.'

The moment landed and Florence thought about how to respond. She shouldn't fawn over him, make him out to be a god because he'd managed to boil a couple of eggs and walk into a shop. All the same, he was making an effort.

'We don't need grand,' she said. 'Eggs and ham are fine.'

There was quite a queue for the punts and they stood in line waiting for the usual steady stream of tourists to come back in.

'Have you thought more about a job?' William was being polite.

'Sort of,' Florence told him. 'I'm not quite ready to decide. I'm encouraging Agnes to apply to university, did she tell you?'

'No, she didn't.' William was unable to hide his disappointment.

'Talk to her, will you?' Florence asked. 'She needs you.'

'Does she?' He sounded unsure.

'Eleanor does her best but you know how her mind flits. I think if Agnes knew we were all behind her she'd be unstoppable.' She looked up towards him. He was clean-shaven, his jaw as square as ever. He had looked tired but today, she noted, he looked rather handsome. She had forgotten quite how handsome he was. 'You're going to have to take your blazer off,' she said, 'when we get going. You know how wet you get.'

She wanted to take it from him and fold it over her arm. She wanted to hook her arm into his. She glanced down at her left hand. She'd never taken her wedding ring off, she noticed. It hadn't even occurred to her.

They hired the punt for an hour and William, rolling his sleeves up, pushed them through the still, black waters. At the halfway point he tied their boat under a weeping willow. The sun was intense. He'd never enjoyed it. They sat on the bank of the river. Florence peeled the eggs and William uncorked the bottle and they ate and drank and chatted idly about birds they could hear in the trees around them.

'Florence,' William began. 'I have something to ask you.'

They had avoided anything serious. They were tiptoeing back towards each other, getting to know each other for the first time.

'Would you like to come for Sunday lunch tomorrow? We never did anything for your birthday.'

'At Brill?'

'Yes. The girls will be there. And Charlie. I wondered if you might like it.'

'Is Charlie cooking lunch?'

'No,' he said, rather nervously. 'I am.'

Florence shot him a disbelieving look.

'Charlie will oversee. Like a referee, I imagine. But I'm going to make it.'

'From scratch?'

'From scratch.'

Florence looked at him. He was looking at her in a way that seemed quite vulnerable. He was opening himself out to her in a way he had never done before.

'All right, William. I'll come to lunch.'

'Good,' he said, and reached for one of the iced buns.

She watched him intently. That was another thing she had forgotten. How beautiful his hands were. 'William,' she said slowly, 'I think when we leave here we should go back to the hotel and have sex.'

He stopped what he was doing.

'I think we need to start enjoying it.'

He paused for a moment. She was being quite serious. 'Is that what you ...' He was treading carefully.

'What I want? Yes.' Florence dusted bits of eggshell from her skirt. 'Good,' she added. 'Pass me a bun.'

## 127

Thomas was standing by the jukebox dancing on his own to 'Chirpy Chirpy Cheep Cheep'. He was holding a half-finished pint in one hand and a bag of peanuts in the other. He was in his element.

Agnes watched him. He was so happy, not a care in the world. She had no idea what that felt like. She wondered if she minded that she didn't know. Bea had not turned up. It was late, well after closing time, and despite the hour, Agnes had toyed with going to get her. But she hadn't. Truth was, she didn't have the guts to do it.

There were not many people there. The usual village locals, glued to the bar on their stools; a few lads Thomas played football with on Wednesday nights; the landlord, deep in conversation with a bald-headed man in a tight shirt – but that was it. It wasn't much of a birthday party, in fact it wasn't one at all, and yet Thomas didn't seem to care one bit. He was perfectly content. He'd finished his shift and he had some beer, some nuts and a singalong and sometimes, Agnes thought, that's all you need.

She'd made him a card. She was yet to give it to him. She felt a bit soft about having done it but there was nothing weird about giving someone a card on their birthday so she'd sat and cut some paper and drawn a picture of a pheasant on it because she realised she didn't really know that much about him. It wasn't a very good picture. Still, it's the thought that counts, isn't it?

The song ended and Thomas twirled back to the table, grinning. 'All right,' he said, sitting down. He reached for a packet of fags in his top pocket.

Agnes pulled the card out from her bag. 'Here,' she said, handing it to him. 'Happy birthday.'

He took it and looked at his name written rather ostentatiously on the front of the envelope. 'Thomas,' he said, with a wink. 'That's me.' He ran his thumb under the seal and ripped it open.

Agnes watched him. He was looking at her and smiling. She smiled back. He pulled out the card.

'What's all this then?' He looked down at it. 'A snake riding a rugby ball?'

'It's a pheasant.'

'Are you sure?'

'I'm not very good at drawing.'

'I'm not going to disagree with you, Agnes. I love it. Thank you.' He leaned across the table and kissed her on the cheek.

One of his pals, one of the football lads, was standing over by the jukebox. The opening bars of the Supremes' 'River Deep – Mountain High' rang out. He turned, with a flourish, and thrust his arms into the air. 'Come on, Tommo!'

Thomas, seeing him, let out a cheer and leapt up. Arms around each other's necks, they sang lustily, eyes shut for the high bits, pulling apart to dance to the instrumental breaks. This is what joy looks like, thought Agnes. Uncomplicated joy. She wished Bea was here.

Agnes pushed herself up and made her way to the toilet. Passing the Ladies, she went through a side door and stood outside. It was a clear night and the stars were in full bloom. If she walked towards the windmill she'd be able to see Bea's house. Her bedroom was at the front, top right. Agnes had lost count of the times she'd crept there in the dark, thrown stones up and they'd lain on the grass and chatted for hours. They had always been able to chat for hours.

She'd changed entirely in just one week: her life felt full of possibilities, her family undergoing an incredible metamorphosis, everything was on the up, and yet without Bea, none of it quite mattered.

She carried on away from the pub and past the windmill and stood where she could best see. The light was on. Bea was there and still awake. Agnes had had no reply to her letter but the curtains were open and she felt an urge to throw small stones, to get Bea's attention, to talk and laugh and be comforted.

Behind her, in the pub, she could hear the boys singing to the Beatles, 'The Long and Winding Road'. It had been a song that had always made her cry: the gentle longing, the sense of regret, the quiet stoicism. It was a song about finding your way home. As they sang the lyrics, she felt tears pricking. Brill wasn't her home, Bea was.

'Beatrice Morgan,' she whispered.

And like that, the light went out.

It felt startling, like the slamming of a door, and Agnes, despite everything, felt a lump catch in her throat. It is a great shame that we take the people we like the most for granted. You have to love your family, but liking someone is a choice. She thought about the last time she'd seen her, how Bea had told her they'd be all right.

'I will never like anyone as much as I like you,' she said, staring at the blackened window. She wiped at her eyes.

'There you are.'

She looked behind her. Thomas had come for her. She didn't love him, she was well aware of that, but they had an uncomplicated friendship which, in that moment, she was grateful for.

'All right,' he said, with a nod.

'All right.'

He took a last drag on his cigarette. 'Bloody hell, look at them stars. It's like someone's had a right go.'

'Thomas,' she said, turning to him. 'Would you like to come to lunch tomorrow? At my house?'

'Sunday roast?'

'Probably.'

'Not half. Yeah, I will.'

'All right, then.'

They stood for a moment, both staring up at the sky. Thomas flicked his cigarette and ground it into the dirt with his foot. 'Fancy a kiss?' he asked her, smiling.

'Yeah, all right,' said Agnes.

He took her into his arms and, as he did, Agnes looked over his shoulder towards Bea's blackened window.

'Ready?' asked Thomas, pulling back to check.

Agnes smiled. 'Yes, I'm ready.'

Bea, she had to remember, always had a knack of being correct. They'd be all right.

# SUNDAY

## 128

The kitchen was in chaos.

'Just don't go in there, Mum,' said Agnes, holding her hands up. 'The least you know about it the better.'

'Has he turned the chicken?' Florence went to the door of the long sitting room and shouted out along the hall. 'WILLIAM! HAVE YOU TURNED THE CHICKEN?'

'NOT YET.'

She shook her head and looked back towards Agnes and Eleanor. 'I mean, I could just go and do it. It would be easier.'

'No,' they both said together.

'He wants to do it,' said Eleanor, cradling a cup of tea in her hands. 'And you should let him.'

'Besides, you're not allowed to slip back,' said Agnes. 'You're done with all that, remember.'

'I'm still allowed to clean the house once a week, though,' said Florence, sitting back into the armchair. 'Let's not go completely mad.'

'But only once a week. Unless there's been an emergency.'

Agnes nodded in agreement. 'By the way, I asked Thomas for lunch. We've got room, haven't we?'

Florence and Eleanor stared at her.

'Thomas from the Pheasant?' Eleanor sounded astonished.

'I've had sex with him twice,' said Agnes. 'No. Wait.' She counted on her fingers. 'Four times.' She beamed.

Eleanor laughed out loud.

'Is he your boyfriend?' Florence asked, her voice curious.

'Absolutely not,' said Agnes, smiling.

Beyond them, the front doorbell rang.

'That'll be him.' She catapulted herself from off the sofa and ran out into the hallway. As she passed the kitchen, she could hear William cursing, Charlie offering encouragement. She yanked the front door open. Thomas was wearing a suit.

'My goodness,' she said. 'You look smart.'

'All right?' He had his hand behind his back. 'I got your mum something.' He pulled out a box of Milk Tray. 'And all because ...' he started.

Agnes smiled at him. 'She'll love you for that. Come in.' She held the door open and he walked through into the hall. 'My dad's cooking lunch. Go and see. It's hilarious.' She pointed towards the kitchen.

'I won't get asked to do anything, will I?'

'Doubt it. Unless it's put out some peanuts.'

He nodded and stepped gingerly down the hallway. Agnes turned to close the door but as she did she saw the glasses, the wonky fringe. It was Bea, on the bike that was far too small for her.

She called out to her, suddenly. 'BEATRICE MORGAN!' She couldn't help herself. She put her hand up into the air.

Bea stopped and looked up. It felt so wonderful to Agnes to be seen by the person who had shaped her, given her hope, been by her side through good times and bad. Bea had given Agnes the space to be herself.

Bea raised her hand back. Agnes stepped out from the house and walked down towards the road. 'What on earth are you riding?' She would keep it light, how it used to be.

'The finest steed known to all second wave feminists,' replied Bea, patting the handlebars.

Agnes smiled. It was so lovely to see her. 'I've missed you, Bea,' she said.

Bea gave a soft nod. 'I've missed you too.'

'I've got lots to tell you.'

'Did you pass all your exams?'

'Of course I did. Did you?'

'Failed the lot. Every last one of them. I am extremely proud of myself.'

Agnes frowned. 'But you're joking, Bea?'

Bea shook her head. 'No. I deliberately did appallingly in every one. I didn't tell you. I'd rather planned it as a great surprise but well' She stopped and looked up towards the sky. 'To hell with secretarial, Agnes Ledbury,' she said quietly.

'To hell with it.'

There was a short pause.

'Are you all right?' Agnes's voice was gentle. 'You're not ...'

'Pregnant? No.' Bea folded her arms and pushed out her bottom lip. 'It was tough, wasn't it?' She turned to look at Agnes.

Agnes nodded. 'Yes, it was.'

'But we needed something to happen to us. You know?' Bea narrowed her eyes. 'Mistakes are opportunities and all that. And I'm pleased for you, Agnes. I want you to be everything you want to be.'

'I want that for you, too.'

Bea shoved her glasses up her nose. 'I might go back to London. I quite liked it at the bookshop.'

There was an impasse, an unspoken moment that felt familiar. Agnes took a deep breath. 'Bea, would you like to come to lunch?'

Bea turned to look at her. 'Is there pudding?'

'I have no idea, my father is cooking.' Agnes shook her head. 'Mr L? Cooking? Sorry? What?'

'It's all kicking off, Beatrice Morgan. Everyone's gone entirely mad.'

'This sounds like something I shouldn't miss, Agnes Ledbury.' Bea smiled.

Agnes smiled back. 'I don't think you should miss it either.'

Bea dismounted her bike and pushed it towards the house. 'I better come then.'

They walked side by side to the front door. Agnes was beaming.

There was so much to look forward to.

# Epilogue

Florence stared out across the canal. She had returned to Italy, this time to Venice. She was hunting for coffee machines.

She had taken the lease of a small unit inside the covered market in Oxford. She would make cappuccinos and espressos using real ground beans. She would froth milk and she would bake croissants and cakes and wear the smart apron Agnes had made her and stand under the red awning Eleanor had painted.

She felt excited, hopeful, brimful with purpose. Agnes had inspired her, there was no doubt about that, and with a little encouragement from Eleanor, Charlie and William, her new path was set. Determination, it turned out, was catching.

Agnes had decided to apply to Durham. It had been a wonderful moment. She had knuckled down, done all the work herself, taken herself off for interviews and three weeks later had received a thick envelope that changed her life forever. Florence didn't know it was possible to feel such pride. No, it was more than pride: it was admiration. Agnes was an inspiration.

They had moved her into halls of residence a week previously. They had all cried, of course, and Florence had quietly left a hamper with a chocolate cake and some teabags while William had pressed a five-pound note into Agnes's hand and told her he was proud of her. Florence had had to hold his hand all the way back to the car. If someone had told her her husband would be happy to walk crying through the streets, she'd have never believed them but here they were: all changed for the better.

William, Florence was pleased to report, was doing rather well. He had come with her to Italy, at last, and was off, haggling with a gondolier. He was looking rather handsome. She'd bought him a white panama hat and got him into a pair of shorts. She had forgotten how lovely his legs were.

She pressed her face upwards into the sun. It was unimaginable, all this, a few months ago but here they were.

'I've got him down by a hundred lira,' William said, coming back to her. 'I said yes. Shall I try and get him down a bit further?' He looked to her for confirmation.

'I think a hundred less is fine.'

He took her hand in his. 'Jolly good. I'll tell him.'

He leaned in and kissed her on the lips.

She looked up at him. 'We'll see the Bridge of Sighs, yes?'

William nodded.

'We'll see everything.'

# Author's Notes

You might be interested to learn that I shared Agnes's predicament. It was 1985 and I was all set to go to Oxford: I'd had a conditional offer, against all the odds, and all I had to do was get two As and a B and that would be it, my dream accomplished. But, like Agnes, I went to a village disco in Kimpton, Hertfordshire and snogged a boy I'd never seen before and never saw again. He was like a Death Eater before Death Eaters had even been invented. He gave me glandular fever and I was the sickest I've ever been. It was almost two months before I could get out of bed and a full year before I was properly better. I fell asleep during a history paper, didn't get the grades and, instead of going to another university, I got a job in a hotel washing up dishes. I gave up.

You'll be glad to know I sorted myself out, picked myself up and tried again and, in the autumn of 1986, I went up to Oxford to read English. I had a lovely time.

*The Female Eunuch*, written by the wonderful Germaine Greer, was first published in 1970. It was a sensation and quickly became an international bestseller. I remember my mother shaking it at my father, while he was sewing a button onto a shirt, telling him she was done with the patriarchy. She never cooked me a meal, not once, in the fabulous forty-seven years I had her. She was a determined second-wave feminist and she bloody loved that book.

The Sherbet Fountain was a sweet made by Barratt. It was a small tube of sherbet that came with a stick of liquorice. There was another tube of sherbert called a Dip Dab. That came with a lolly. I spent most of my youth with sherbet down my front. Sherbet, you might like to know, is also slang for a beer.

Christ Church Meadow in Oxford, where Bea and Agnes first meet, is a flood-meadow behind Christ Church. It's lovely to walk in or picnic. I thoroughly recommend it.

The Eagle and Child pub where Bea and Agnes go for their celebratory cheese sandwich is on St Giles' Street in Oxford. Its local nickname is the Bird and Baby, hence Bea's referring to it as 'the Bird'.

*The Housewife's Pocket Book*, edited by Carlton Wallace, is a slim red volume that was a rigid set of instructions on how to be a perfect wife. It really does give advice as to what a woman should do at any given moment on any given day. It's quite something.

*World of Sport* was a Saturday television show that ran from 1965 to 1985. My father was rarely allowed to watch it, mostly because my mother had read *The Female Eunuch*. In 1971, the host was Dickie Davies, a mustachioed gentleman with fulsome hair. Wrestling invariably was on from 4 p.m. and could be enjoyed each week for around forty-five minutes.

'Brown Sugar', the song that is playing in the shop when Florence buys her new clothes, is from the Rolling Stones album *Sticky Fingers*. It was released in April 1971. The track was written by Mick Jagger and Marsha Hunt, his secret girlfriend. The lyrics, if you pay attention, are quite scandalous and touch on sadomasochism, cunnilingus, lost virginity, heroin, interracial sex, rape and slavery.

In 1942, Earl Tupper invented his first container and Tupperware was born. Tupperware parties were all the rage from the 1950s onwards. Tupperware hostesses weren't paid. Instead, they were rewarded with free products.

The purse-snatcher Public Information Film that Agnes and Bea appear in actually exists. You can google it and watch it. There are two girls standing at the checkout. I rather liked wondering if they might be Agnes and Bea.

The Playboy Club at 45 Park Lane first opened in 1966. In 1981, the casino there was the most profitable in the world. The Playboy Bunnies were a source of great controversy following the push for sexual equality and in 1971 there was a protest against the club. The Women's Liberation movement was vehemently opposed to Hugh Heffner's enterprise and saw the bunny uniforms as demeaning. On the other side of the coin, being a bunny was seen as a real privilege, a chance for girls who didn't have much else going for them other than their looks to make a good living. The club still runs to this day (complete with bunny outfits) but it's moved to 14 Old Park Lane.

'Bend It' was a massive hit for the British pop group Dave Dee, Dozy, Beaky, Mick and Tich in 1966. It was inspired by the film *Zorba the Greek* but was banned by many US radio stations for being an anthem to barely concealed filth. They had a point.

*Willy Wonka and the Chocolate Factory* was released in August 1971. It starred Gene Wilder and one of its more obscure delights is that, as well as the Oompa Loompas and naughty squirrels and near-fatal chewing gum, the film introduced the song 'Candy Man' which went on to become one of Sammy Davis Jr's biggest hits. The original in the film was sung by Aubrey Woods.

Glastonbury Fayre was the second year the festival had run. A documentary film was made: you can watch it on YouTube and you'll see pretty much everything as described in the book, including the penis mud pies. The seventies were weird.

The madrigal sung by the nuns is 'Jesu, Meine Freude' by Bach. The story goes that it was written for the funeral of the wife of the Leipzig postmaster. It's beautiful. Go have a listen.

The Palio is a horse race held twice a year on 2 July and 16 August in Siena. I've been twice. It's amazing and terrifying and very, very noisy. If you've never been, you should. Laila is correct: everyone should see it once.

Foyles bookshop, where Bea goes to work, is at 107 Charing Cross Road. It used to be in the *Guinness Book of Records* as the world's largest bookshop in terms of shelf length. It also used to have a payment system so crazy, people went there just to experience it: you had to get an invoice for the book, then pay the invoice, then you got the book. So you had to queue three times. Not only that, but books were categorised by publisher rather than author or subject. Thankfully, they've now allowed staff to handle cash.

The Gateways Club, where Camilla takes Agnes and Bea, was located at 239 King's Road. It was a members' club for lesbians from 1936 until it closed in 1985. It was one of the very few places lesbians could openly get together. It's featured in the film *The Killing of Sister George* and I took much of the detail of the interior from that.

'Chirpy Chirpy Cheep Cheep' by Middle of the Road was a big hit in 1971 but I've mostly included it because it's the first pop song I can remember singing along to in the car.

'River Deep – Mountain High' here is the Supremes and the Four Tops version which was released in 1970. The original was by Ike and Tina Turner. Whichever one you choose, it's a banging tune and no mistake.

'The Long and Winding Road' by the Beatles is one of my favourite songs. If you've read my book *The Tent, the Bucket and Me*, you'll recognise it from the chapter where dear old Bessy is finally sent to the scrapheap. It always makes me cry and I thoroughly recommend you put it on while reading the bit where Agnes stares at Bea's window. Sob.

I did a mass of research for the book and I am indebted to the following: *How Was It For You? Women, Sex, Love and Power in the 1960s* by Virginia Nicholson; *Perfect Wives in Perfect Homes* by Virginia Nicholson; *1970s Britain* by Janet Shepherd and John Shepherd; *Germaine: The Life of Germaine Greer* by Elizabeth Kleinhenz; *The Female Eunuch* by Germaine Greer (natch); *A Nice Girl Like Me: A Story of the Seventies* by Rosie Boycott; *When the Lights Went Out: What Really Happened to Britain in the Seventies* by Andy Beckett.

If you enjoyed this book and want to read another book featuring the same family, then you might like *The Things We Left Unsaid*, which is all about Eleanor and her daughter Rachel. Agnes is a young girl and older woman in the book and we see Florence very fleetingly.

I'd like to thank my amazing editor Emily Griffin, who isn't remotely terrifying (She is. She isn't.); my wonderful agent Sheila Crowley, who should be in charge of everything; and my wife Georgie, who is a far better person than I will ever be and who I look up to every day (she's 5 ft 11).

Thank you for reading! I hope you enjoyed it. You can contact me on Twitter. I'm @emmakennedy over there.

# ARE YOU FOLLOWING
# EMMA KENNEDY'S BOOKSHELF?

If you want to stay up to date with Emma Kennedy
and all the latest news on her books and more,
be sure to follow Emma Kennedy's Bookshelf.

Each month Emma hosts a different author
for a live Q&A about their book. You can also expect
behind-the-scenes information on Emma's next
books and surprise giveaways.

f @EKBookshelf

🐦 @EKBookshelf

www.facebook.com/EKBookshelf